DEATH WIND

DEATH WIND

ELVEN ALLIANCE BOOK THREE

TARA GRAYCE

Published by Sword & Cross Publishing

Grand Rapids, MI

Sword & Cross Publishing and the Sword & Cross Publishing logo are trademarks. Absence of ™ in connection with Sword & Cross Publishing does not indicate an absence of trademark protection of those marks.

Cover Illustration by Sara Morello

www.deviantart.com/samo-art

Typography by Deranged Doctor Designs

Derangeddoctordesign.com

Map by Savannah Jezowski of Dragonpen Designs

Dragonpenpress.com

To God, my King and Father. Soli Deo Gloria

LCCN: 2020909784

ISBN: 978-1-943442-12-6

E ssie would force her brother, King Averett of Escarland, and her elf brother-in-law, King Weylind of Tarenhiel, to cooperate even if she had to knock their overly hard heads together. She was in no mood to listen to them posturing...which sounded a lot like sibling bickering, to be honest.

"I am not going to step foot in your kingdom, simply trusting that your soldiers will not attack." King Weylind stood, facing Essie's brother, in the center of Linder Island, the tiny rock island in the Hydalla River, which formed the border between Tarenhiel and Escarland.

While the rock made a convenient place for diplomatic meetings since it was neutral territory, it wasn't as comfortable of a place for allies to sit down and plan a war, especially without all the preparation they had done for the previous meeting on the island.

Essie gritted her teeth. That was assuming her brother and brother-in-law didn't start a war arguing about which side of the border should host the war planning session. Last

1

time, it had taken months to arrange the meeting to everyone's satisfaction.

Farrendel didn't have months. Every moment they delayed was another moment he had to spend in the hands of his troll captors.

"If we agree to this alliance, then I'm going to be marching an army across your kingdom. You're going to have to trust me with a whole lot more than your own safety." Averett crossed his arms as he glared back at the elven king.

Behind her, Essie's other two brothers, Julien and Edmund, shifted, as if they were about ready to march over there and help Averett glare at Weylind. Jalissa, Essie's elf sister-in-law, huffed, though Essie was not sure if it was because of Averett or Weylind.

Essie shifted the gun she had slung across her back, its weight growing heavy against her shoulder. Enough of this. If they wanted to bicker, they could do it once Farrendel was safe. "Really, you two. We're all family here, more or less. We all want to get Farrendel back, and we all want to defeat the trolls. Averett, Weylind, if the two of you could stop posturing like a pair of peacocks, then maybe we could get somewhere."

Weylind's gaze snapped to her, and Essie wasn't sure if the hardness in his gaze was because of Farrendel's capture, her tone, or the fact that she'd dared address him as her brother-in-law without his title.

Essie glared right back. She still wore the tatters of the green elven dress she had worn to the ball in Escarland. She was spattered with blood and grime. She'd had to leave her husband behind to escape with vital information about the traitors in both Escarland and Tarenhiel, and in that escape she'd seen one man die and killed another herself. She couldn't care less what Weylind thought of her at that moment.

Averett shifted, his mouth tipping into a tight, wry smile. "You're right, of course." He turned back to Weylind. "Look. We both agree that we need to work together to defeat the trolls. Neither army alone is going to be able to attack Kostaria and rescue Farrendel. It's going to take cooperation and compromise. Now, I propose that we take this meeting to the deck of your steamboat, which will remain docked here at Linder Island. Is that an acceptable enough compromise?"

Weylind studied Averett, as if searching for whatever treachery Averett might be planning.

Essie resisted the urge to thump Weylind over the head with the butt of her gun. "I know you don't trust him. But do you at least trust me when I say he isn't planning anything?"

Weylind tipped his head, the hardness in his expression cracking. "I apologize, isciena. Very well, I will host this meeting on board."

In that moment, Essie saw the pain in Weylind's eyes. Yes, Weylind was being all hard and grumpy right now. But that was a sign of his protective worry for Farrendel. He'd been just as grumpy when he'd been worried she would break Farrendel's heart.

"I know you're worried about Farrendel. We all are." Essie refused to let her voice break. Right now, she had to focus on what she could control. "But my brothers aren't the enemies here. Now, you're going to be hosting the king of Escarland. Please try to be gracious."

That made Weylind's mouth twitch in something that

looked suspiciously like a smile before he replaced it with his hard mask once again.

But Essie had been married to Farrendel long enough to recognize the brief flashes of emotions elves tried so hard to hide.

"I understand your suspicion. The Escarlish haven't given you many reasons to trust us in the past." Averett's voice remained calm, his shoulders relaxed. He gestured to the Escarlish guards standing behind Edmund, Julien, and Jalissa. "With your permission, I will station my guards on the wharf where they will have a view of the deck. I trust that you mean me no harm, but it would reassure my guards."

"That sounds reasonable." Weylind spun on his heels. "If you would follow me, we can continue this discussion on my ship."

After waving to the Escarlish guards and their siblings to follow, Averett fell into step beside Essie as they trailed after Weylind. "I'm sorry you had to be the level-headed one, Essie. You've already gone through too much in the past day."

Yes, she had. And the nightmare she now found herself in wasn't going to end anytime soon. Wars weren't fought overnight. Would they be able to take this war to the trolls fast enough to keep Farrendel alive?

They had to. There wasn't another option.

At least she could be certain Farrendel was alive. If she closed her eyes and concentrated hard enough, she could feel the warm, crackling sense of Farrendel deep inside her chest through the elven heart bond.

He was unconscious now. Or perhaps in some kind of

drugged state. She couldn't tell through the connection of the heart bond.

Either way, the trolls were taking him farther and farther away from her. Would she ever see him again? Or would—

No, she refused to let herself even think it. Farrendel would survive, and they would rescue him.

Within a few minutes, Essie found herself on the deck of the elven ship surrounded by all three of her brothers, Jalissa, and Weylind. The Escarlish guards remained on the wharf with the ship's deck in rifle range. Not that their intervention would be needed.

The few elven guards Weylind had brought scurried around the deck as they fetched a table, chairs, and refreshments. Apparently, now that Essie had called him out on it, Weylind actually intended to be gracious.

Once Essie had them calmed down, snacking on cold venison and cheese, and sitting down at the same table, the negotiations for the new treaty went as smoothly as could be expected. This new treaty would be a mutual defense treaty, with plenty of provisos and legal lingo and all stuff that Essie only cared about marginally as long as they helped her get Farrendel back.

This time, there were no professional diplomats present to read over the hastily assembled treaty to make sure nothing was amiss. Both Edmund and Julien read it over, and Essie figured if it passed Edmund's inspection, then there couldn't be anything too disastrous in the wording.

Averett must have thought so too since he pulled a pen from his shirt's pocket. A carved wooden pen that Essie had given him less than a week ago, made by a friend of Farrendel's in Estyra.

Essie swallowed at the lump in her throat. Everything

had been so happy that day she and Farrendel had given gifts to her family. Awkward, yes, as Farrendel and her family got to know each other. But also filled with so much laughter and joy and everything she wanted to get back.

Averett signed with a flourish and held the pen out to Weylind.

Weylind took the pen, turning it over in his hands. He had to recognize the elven craftsmanship. Leaning over the table, he signed the treaty as well.

This time, there was no fanfare. No celebration. No wedding to make it official.

Weylind set down the pen and faced Averett, waiting.

Averett crossed his arms. "I need to return to Aldon to officially declare war on Kostaria and mobilize Escarland's army. But I would like to send both of my brothers to Estyra with you. Julien can work with your army's leaders to formulate a plan on how to transport Escarland's army through Tarenhiel with minimal disruption, while Edmund..." Averett trailed off, glanced at Edmund.

Edmund smirked, relaxing against the back of his chair.

"Edmund can assist in scouting Kostaria's borders." Averett said it almost too slowly, too diplomatically. He was trying so hard not to say outright that Edmund was a spy that it nearly made Essie smile.

Nearly. Everything was far too serious for smiles.

Weylind's brows lowered. "My scouts have their jobs well in hand. They can move far more easily without a human tagging along."

Essie resisted the urge to roll her eyes. Trust Weylind to get all huffy and offended. He'd only managed to be civil for an hour.

"I'm sure they are excellent scouts and perform

admirably." Averett's tone remained even. "But your scouts are unfamiliar with the Escarlish army's current weapons and only some of our tactics. They don't know what terrain they need to look for or what hurdles my army might face that yours doesn't or vice versa. Edmund does."

Weylind's mouth thinned as he too glanced at Edmund.

Edmund grinned and folded his hands behind his head. Even when he was attempting to look innocent, he still looked far too clever for his own good. Essie couldn't fully blame Weylind for being a little apprehensive about letting Edmund run amok in his kingdom.

When Weylind turned his gaze back to Averett, his jaw was tight. "And I suppose, while he is scouting the northern border, he will also be noting Tarenhiel's defenses?"

There was nothing too accusatory in the words. It was all in the tone, the hardness to Weylind's eyes.

Essie tensed. Would Weylind see every move her brothers did in the worst light possible? Of course Edmund was going to note Tarenhiel's defenses...as a way to help shore them up, not as the precursor to an Escarlish invasion.

For a moment, Averett just met Weylind stare for stare. Then, of all things, he let out a huff, rolled his eyes, and leaned his elbows on the table. "Oh, come off it. Stop getting your elven knickers in a knot and think rationally for half a second."

Weylind's jaw fell open. "I beg your pardon?"

Essie bit her lip, trying—and failing—to keep a straight face. Apparently Averett had decided to use her tactic of calling Weylind out on his huffiness.

Beside her, both Edmund and Julien had adopted their far-too-serious-and-about-to-pull-a-prank faces. Jalissa gave a soft snort before coughing delicately behind her hand.

Averett wagged a finger beneath Weylind's nose. "I just offered to send both my brothers unprotected into your kingdom only hours after you harangued me about not protecting your brother while he was in my care. I'm making them perfect targets for your retaliation and placing faith in you that you won't. So don't act like you're the only one taking a risk here."

Weylind's mouth worked, but he couldn't seem to put together the words. Essie wasn't sure she had ever seen the elven king look so much like he had swallowed a bug and didn't know how to spit it out in a dignified manner.

"Furthermore, I just spent the past week with your foremost warrior, who already has one royal assassination on his record, wandering my halls with full access to observe my own security measures. I placed the life of my family in his hands several times and gave him the full trust of a brother. So do stop with your puffed up, offended dignity. I'm not buying it." Averett jabbed Weylind in the chest to punctuate those last words.

Weylind stilled, his mouth hanging open, as if he couldn't believe Averett had dared to cross his personal space boundaries. He glanced at Essie, almost as if begging, *He is your brother. You deal with him.*

Essie smirked and crossed her arms. No way was she stopping Averett now.

"And another thing." Averett barreled on with all the enthusiasm of a runaway train engine with a full boiler of steam pressure. "We're both going to get an eyeful of each other's defenses, armies, strategies, and tactics by the time this is over. Yes, you're taking the greater physical risk as you'll be allowing me to march my armies across your kingdom. But you'll also have my top generals and the best part of my army within your borders where you could just as easily turn on us. You may not have the numbers, but you did hold Escarland's army at the border for five long years while also fighting a second war with the trolls. I'm not so naïve as to think that you aren't formidable, especially inside your own forests."

Weylind finally managed to close his mouth and regain some of his dignity. Enough for his expression to relax from outright hostility to cautious interest, his posture straight and leaning forward as if intrigued in spite of himself.

Averett tapped the signed treaty still sitting on the table between them. "So, yes, this alliance is going to take an incredible amount of trust. And, yes, if this ends badly, there's a good chance we could take each other out long before the trolls get to us. But if this succeeds, our two kingdoms could come out of this with a strong bond that will stand both of our kingdoms in good stead for many years."

Weylind gave a slight nod to this. "We are facing either mutual trust or mutual destruction."

"Exactly." Averett nodded and pointed at the treaty again. "Thanks to my sister, I know you. I know you're a king who cares about the welfare of his people and who loves his brother very much. I am also a king and a big brother. I understand the burdens of duty you face. Now, if my chatty, overly optimistic sister and your shy, skittish brother can make their marriage work, then surely the two of us can manage to work together long enough to see this war through to victory. What do you say?"

Averett stuck out his hand across the table, as if he were a merchant haggling over a bargain in the market.

Weylind stared at the offered hand for several long seconds. Averett didn't withdraw it. Perhaps Edmund had warned him that it might take Weylind a few moments to figure out how to react to such a human gesture.

With a slump to his shoulders, Weylind turned to Jalissa and switched to elvish. "What was your impression of them?"

Jalissa glanced at Essie's brothers, her gaze lingering longest on Edmund. Probably because she realized Edmund could fully understand this conversation, since he spoke elvish. Finally, Jalissa turned to Weylind. "They are surprisingly honorable and good-hearted, for humans."

A month ago, those words might have been said with derision. Now, Jalissa's tone held a warmth, almost a teasing.

Essie had to resist the urge to lean over and hug Jalissa.

Edmund's mouth twitched. Averett remained still, hand outstretched across the table, while Julien sat straight and regal, as if he knew he was being evaluated even if he couldn't understand what Jalissa and Weylind were saying.

The hint of a smile dropped from Jalissa's face. "And Farrendel likes them."

Essie clenched her fingers beneath the table until her nails bit into her palms. She swallowed back the rising lump in her throat, her chest aching again.

"And we like him," Edmund stated, in Escarlish.

Weylind's gaze snapped to him, though Essie didn't think he should have been surprised. They had pretty much established that he was a spy, and Averett hadn't been at all concerned sending him off with an elven scouting party.

Averett waggled his fingers. "I'm willing to drag my entire kingdom into a war for the sake of my new brother-in-law. If that doesn't prove my sincerity, I don't know what does. So how about it? Friends?"

Weylind stared at Averett's hand yet again before pointing and asking in elvish, "What does he expect me to do now?"

"It is a human custom for greetings and farewells and sealing bargains. It is apparently a varied, all-purpose custom similar to ours." Jalissa made the mouth to forehead gesture.

Essie smiled, though it still felt strained. "I know. It's unsanitary. But you're supposed to grip his hand and shake."

Had it only been a week since she'd had the same conversation with Farrendel? She'd been filled with so much hope and optimism and excitement at seeing her family again. The week had been one of the best in her life...until yesterday tore her heart out.

Farrendel wasn't dead. She had to keep reminding herself of that. While he was alive, there was still hope. No telling what shape he might be in or how long it might take, but as long as he was alive, they could—and would—rescue him.

As long as he wasn't dead, she wasn't going to mourn like he was.

With a curl to his mouth that was probably disgust, Weylind reached out and shook Averett's hand. Not a hearty handshake by any means. But it was a start. "Very well. I will allow both your brothers into Tarenhiel. But I wish for your sister to come as well. I believe her presence may be necessary to smooth tensions when they arise."

"Essie?" Averett turned to her. "It's up to you. I have no wish to push you if you do not feel up to it."

She was scraped raw from the inside out, and nothing sounded better than one of her mother's hugs and a good cry with her sister-in-law Paige, Averett's wife and Essie's longtime friend.

But after that, she would end up stuck at Buckmore Cottage missing Farrendel and frustrated that there was nothing she could do to hasten the glacial pace at which bureaucratic matters in Escarland moved.

In Tarenhiel, she could be useful. She was the person who best understood how to meld elven and human cultures since she had been doing just that for the past three months. Julien would need her help to find his way around Ellonahshinel, at least for the first while. And she wasn't about to miss Julien's and Edmund's first visit to Estyra. At least, she assumed it was Edmund's first visit. If he had been there before, that trip was classified and officially didn't exist.

It would hurt being in Estyra without Farrendel. She had been there alone before during the times Farrendel had been called away to fight raiding trolls.

But even though he had been going into battle, she had never truly doubted he would return. He was Laesornysh, an elven title meaning *Death on the Wind*.

This time, he wasn't coming back unless she went and got him.

She raised her chin, meeting Averett's gaze with as much bravado as she could muster. "I'm fine, Avie. I'll go to Estyra with Julien and Edmund. They'll need me to show them around."

Edmund rested his arm around her shoulders. "We'll take care of her."

"All right." Averett nodded, shifting like he wanted to give her a hug. "I'll come to Tarenhiel myself just as soon as I can, assuming that is acceptable to King Weylind. It would probably be best if I were there to keep the army leadership in hand."

"It is acceptable to me." Weylind nodded. "Mutual trust or mutual destruction."

In other words, if Weylind was going to put himself on the line inviting Escarlish army officers to Estyra to plan the invasion, then Averett needed to be at risk as well. Neither side would start anything with their kings present. At least, that was the idea, anyway.

Jalissa straightened her shoulders. "In that case, I will return to Aldon with the Escarlish king. We need an elven representative in Escarland to answer any questions that might arise."

"We would be happy to continue to host you, Princess Jalissa, and will gladly accept any assistance you can provide." Averett gave her a regal nod.

Edmund smiled past Essie toward Jalissa, but something in his expression wasn't as relaxed as it normally was.

Essie resisted a frown. Edmund had been flirting with Jalissa from the moment she'd arrived, but was it more serious than Essie realized? It was hard to tell with Edmund. Or with Jalissa, to be honest.

But at this point, neither of them would probably pursue anything. All of them would be too busy planning and carrying out this war.

With Tarenhiel and Escarland working together, the trolls wouldn't know what hit them.

ONE DAY EARLIER...

T his was not going as planned.

Melantha, princess of the elves of Tarenhiel, fumed. It would have been so satisfying to scream or stamp her foot or somehow release this rage boiling her blood and heating her skin.

But an elven princess did not scream or pound her fist or in any way display such uncomely emotions. Elven princesses were serene. Calm as the still water of a morning lake.

Not the roiling, seething storm Melantha was and had been for nearly as long as she could remember.

If that human princess had not gotten away, none of this would have happened. Melantha could have gone back to her family, put on a proper show of mourning for the loss of her brother and his human wife, and start the process of finally building a life free of the scandal of Farrendel's illegitimate birth.

Instead, she stood at the border of Tarenhiel and the trolls' kingdom of Kostaria, and there was a very good chance the trolls were not going to let her go.

Prince Rharreth of the trolls gripped her elbow, steering her from the platform that formed the end of the train line across Tarenhiel toward the thin stretch of evergreen forest separating the train platform from the Gulmorth River, the foaming stretch of water that separated Tarenhiel from Kostaria.

"There is a guard post ahead. You will never get through with only three of you." Melantha had to trot at an undignified pace to keep up with the troll's long stride. Perhaps if he released her arm long enough to fight, she could disappear into the forest and return home.

The troll just glanced down at her, his eyes a hard dark blue against the gray of his skin. His white hair was cropped short, revealing his tapered ears. He plucked a mountain goat horn from where it hung on his belt and blew into it. A deep, sonorous note rang through the forest.

A similar horn answered a moment later from the other side of the dense stand of spruces and pines.

The troll prince halted her a few yards short of the trees. He spoke with a thick accent, but the troll dialect was still close enough to elvish to be understandable. "I don't believe the guard post will be a problem."

That meant the trolls had crossed the border and killed the elves at the post. A raid. The very thing she had sacrificed Farrendel to the trolls to prevent.

Melantha yanked her arm free of his grip. "You promised peace. You promised no more raids."

"Once we had Laesornysh." Prince Rharreth crossed his arms. "We are not in Kostaria yet."

She glared. That was not the bargain she had struck, and he knew it.

The tramping of boots came from the forest a moment before a line of trolls marched from the trees. At their head strode a tall troll wearing a circlet formed of carved deer antlers gilt with gold.

Melantha stumbled back a step. What was the troll king doing here at the head of a small army? This was not at all what she had bargained for.

The troll king's gaze snapped to Prince Rharreth. "Did you secure him?"

"Yes." Prince Rharreth motioned behind him.

One of the remaining trolls who had traveled with Prince Rharreth hauled Farrendel's limp form from the train, his hands bound with stone behind his back. The stone wrapped around his arms up to his shoulders. The troll dumped him on the ground in front of the troll king.

The only reaction from Farrendel was a moan. The trolls had used a chemical they had been given by the humans to keep him unconscious during the train ride across Tarenhiel.

Melantha looked away. The pang in her chest could not be guilt. She refused to let it be guilt.

It had been far easier to agree to this plan when she had thought she would simply walk away at the Tarenhieli-Escarlish border, and Farrendel would just be...gone.

The last surviving troll marched Thanfardil from the train. Thanfardil's dark blond hair was still spattered with dirt and the blood from a shrapnel cut along his scalp. Thanfardil had been the elf in charge of the train schedules in all of Tarenhiel. He had recruited Melantha for this mission and convinced her that the trolls would leave Tarenhiel alone once they had been avenged.

King Charvod of the trolls swept his gaze over them. He did not remark on the fact that he had sent a force of twelve trolls, and only three had returned. Perhaps, as they had been sent to capture Laesornysh, three was more than the troll king had been expecting to return. "Have you already disposed of the human princess?"

Melantha grimaced. Farrendel's human wife—a second cause of scandal—had gotten away. She was not supposed to. She, even more than Farrendel, was supposed to be dead.

Prince Rharreth bowed his head. "Laesornysh was not taken down easily. During the fight, she got away."

"I see." King Charvod's thick brow lowered, his dark eyes flashing against his pale, gray skin.

Melantha swallowed. She needed to get out of here while she still could. She straightened her spine. "You have Laesornysh, as we agreed. If that will be all, I will take my leave."

She spun on her heels, intending to march off into the forest if she had to. As the train was still filled with the dead trolls Prince Rharreth had insisted on taking with them, she could not take that, even if Thanfardil could also get away to conduct it for her.

A hand closed over her arm, yanking her back to Prince Rharreth's side. He glared at her. "Where do you believe you are going? Your brother knows you betrayed your kingdom. You have nowhere left to go."

Surely that was not the case. Would Weylind really believe the word of a human over Melantha?

But this was Farrendel. Weylind was oddly attached, considering Farrendel's inconvenient existence continued to taint his reign and their father's legacy.

"Then their identities have been compromised." King

Charvod gestured from her to Thanfardil. "They are no further use to us."

Wait, what did that—

King Charvod grabbed a rifle from the troll nearest him, pointed it at Thanfardil, and fired.

Even as the gunshot echoed, Thanfardil staggered, blood blossoming. He collapsed in a limp heap on the ground.

Melantha pressed her hand over her mouth, unable to completely stifle her shriek. When she glanced up from Thanfardil toward King Charvod, she found the black, smoking muzzle of the gun pointed at her.

Her heart raced. Was she about to be killed? Unceremoniously. Callously. She trembled, her knees barely holding her upright.

Prince Rharreth gripped her arm. "She is still—"

Farrendel leapt from the ground, stumbling a few steps. With a flash of magic and a crack of stone, his hands were free, his face twisted in a grimace. He swiped a knife from King Charvod's belt and plunged it toward the troll king's chest.

At the last moment, a shield of troll magic stopped the knife and flung Farrendel back. Farrendel rolled and came up in a swaying crouch, knife gripped in his hand, a few lightning bolts of magic crackling around him. Blood dripped from both of his wrists.

King Charvod raised the rifle again, aimed, and fired three shots in quick succession at Farrendel.

Farrendel's magic blasted all three bullets before they touched him. He sent a burst of magic at the two trolls who had survived the fight on the Escarlish shore, blowing them off their feet.

Melantha tried to get her shaky legs to move. She needed

to run. To use this distraction to get out of there before King Charvod turned that rifle on her once again.

Ripping her arm from Prince Rharreth's grip, she turned, hiked up her skirts, and stumbled into a run. She only made it three steps before someone grabbed her arm.

Prince Rharreth dragged her back. Something metallic and sharp poked her back hard enough to pierce her dress but not hard enough to nick her skin. An icy wall of magic sprang around them.

"Let me go." She struggled, trying to elbow him or stomp his foot. But she might as well have been fighting a rock for all the reaction she received. "This is not what I was promised. I thought you trolls claimed to value honor."

"You are an elf who betrayed her own brother to torture and death. I'm treating you with all the honor you deserve." Prince Rharreth's deep voice raked over her, as if she was the villain there, and he found her actions disgusting, even though they benefited his kingdom.

He turned her so that she faced Farrendel, the knife moving into her line of sight, the tip pointed at her face. The magical shield remained around them, preventing Farrendel's weakened magic from reaching them.

Prince Rharreth raised his voice. "Cease struggling, Laesornysh. Unless you wish your sister scarred."

Heart hammering in her chest, Melantha struggled to tear her gaze away from the tip of the knife only inches away from her right eye. Why would Farrendel turn himself in for her? He would probably think it would serve her right if she were scarred—as he was—after what she had done.

There was that inconvenient pang in her chest again. The one she had been working so hard to ignore.

Farrendel met her gaze, his silver-blue eyes pained. He

could turn and run. Attempt to escape. Get back to his human princess.

Prince Rharreth touched the tip of his knife to her cheek. She flinched and sucked in a breath, even though he had not drawn blood. Yet.

Farrendel closed his eyes, his shoulders slumping. He sank onto his knees, his magic cutting off, as he set the knife on the ground.

"He has far more honor than you do." Prince Rharreth spoke low enough only Melantha could hear. He eased the knife back so that it was no longer touching her face, though the tip still hovered an inch from her cheek.

Why would Farrendel do this? Willingly sacrifice himself for her?

It stabbed that pang deeper inside her chest.

The two trolls Farrendel had blasted sprawled unmoving on the ground. A third troll lay to one side. He must have gone down while Melantha had been attempting her escape.

King Charvod handed the rifle back to the troll next to him, then stalked over to Farrendel. The troll king touched one of the ropes of stone around Farrendel's upper arm, and the stone tightened, binding Farrendel's hands behind his back once again. More stone sprang from the ground, wrapping around Farrendel's chest and waist.

Farrendel flinched, but he did not resist.

"Laesornysh of the elves, you have been accused of the murder of the late King Vorlec, my father." The troll king picked up the knife from the ground.

"He killed my father." Farrendel's words came between gritted teeth.

"Your father was killed honorably in battle. You murdered my father with a nighttime assassination." King

Charvod grabbed Farrendel's hair and yanked his head up to face him. "There is no honor in that."

"Was there honor in torture? Or in shooting my father in the back when he held no weapon as he rescued his son?" Farrendel's silver-blue eyes flashed, even if they remained slightly unfocused, as if that human drug was still keeping him hazy and disoriented.

Melantha squeezed her eyes shut, seeing again her father's body, arrowshot and still, laid out for the funeral she had planned. Heard again the shake to Weylind's voice as he told the family what had happened.

And Farrendel...his body scarred and his mind broken, refusing to leave their father's side until the burial as if he felt it his duty to stand guard.

And she had given Farrendel back into the hands of the trolls who had killed their father, killed her mother.

Why would that stab in her chest not leave her alone?

"Then you admit your guilt?" King Charvod's hand tightened on the knife, yanking Farrendel's head back farther.

Farrendel glared, still swaying. "No."

Melantha struggled against the troll prince's grip. It had been one thing to betray Farrendel and close her eyes and heart to what that really meant. It was another to stand there and watch it happen. Especially after Farrendel had given up a chance at escape to keep her from being hurt. "Do not—"

The knife flashed down. But instead of red blood spurting, it was silver-blond hair that parted, coming away in the troll king's fist.

Farrendel stiffened, his eyes widening.

King Charvod held his fistful of Farrendel's hair in front

of Farrendel's face. "I have heard this is a symbol of dishonor for you elves."

Farrendel stared at his hair in the troll king's hand, as if he could not believe what had just happened. His shorn hair hung in ragged strands across his forehead and around the tips of his ears.

The troll king tossed Farrendel's hair onto the dirt and ground it beneath his heel.

For a long moment, Farrendel continued to stare. Then, his body stiffened, and when he lifted his gaze to the troll king, his silver-blue eyes simmered. He did not speak, his gaze all the more unnerving for his silence.

After a moment, the troll king looked away and kicked Farrendel, sending him to the ground once again.

Prince Rharreth's grip tightened on Melantha's arm as he lowered his knife and turned to his brother. "The elf king's army will not be far behind me, and we need time to carry our honored dead across the river."

King Charvod sighed, as if annoyed to be reminded of his responsibilities as king. He pointed at several of the trolls behind him. "Take Laesornysh to the boats. The elven princess too." His gaze lifted to Melantha, and his mouth twisted into a smirk. "It seems she will provide leverage over both her brothers."

Melantha dug her heels into the ground as Prince Rharreth shoved her forward. "Farrendel was right. You have no honor. You promised peace."

"I promised that we would not invade your kingdom." Prince Rharreth handed her off to a waiting troll. "I didn't say anything about luring the elf king into attacking us. He and Laesornysh have held us off for years in this forest where they are strong. But now your elven army will be forced to fight in our mountains where we are strong."

Last time Tarenhiel had been forced to invade Kostaria, Melantha's father had been killed. Would Weylind be killed this time? Would Melantha have any family left when this was over?

CHAPTER

THREE

E ssie stood near the gangplank of the elven ship as Averett gave last, hushed instructions to Edmund and Julien before departing. Weylind gripped Jalissa's shoulders as they also spoke in lowered tones.

This parting would only be for a week at most. Not that long when it came to mobilizing armies. But far too long when each day meant Farrendel was imprisoned that much longer.

Essie wrapped her arms around her stomach. Even if Escarland's army managed to march into Tarenhiel within a week, it could still take another week, optimistically, to assemble the joint elven-human army at the border with Kostaria.

Then it was anyone's guess how long it would take to invade. As no one knew where in Kostaria Farrendel had been taken, everyone was assuming their goal would have to be Gror Grar, the trolls' mountain fortress that guarded their capital city of Osmana. Even if Farrendel wasn't being held there, they would have to conquer it to end the war they were about to start.

Jalissa stepped away from Weylind, her head held high. With a glance toward Averett, Weylind turned and stalked toward the ship's bow. It might have looked angry, but Essie had been with the elves long enough to recognize when an elf bolted because he was done with interacting with others and needed a moment to breathe.

Essie crossed the distance to Jalissa and hugged her. Even though Jalissa wouldn't admit it, Essie knew how hard this must be. Jalissa had begun to settle in at Aldon, but she would return there with only her guard. No Farrendel and no Essie to help smooth her way.

Instead of flinching away, Jalissa hugged her back, gripping tightly. Perhaps Jalissa was more willing to admit her emotions than Essie had assumed.

After a moment, Jalissa stepped back and gripped Essie's shoulders. "Stay strong, isciena."

Essie nodded. "You too. And if you need anything, don't hesitate to ask my family. Paige and Mother will try to smother you if you let them."

Jalissa nodded. Hopefully she would reach out to Essie's family rather than stay miserable by herself. They were all aching deep down right now in this strange state of missing Farrendel and grieving him, yet trying to cling to hope at the same time.

After one last squeeze to Essie's shoulders, Jalissa stepped back and strode down the gangplank. Her silent elf guard fell into step behind her as they joined Averett's guards waiting for him on the wharf.

"Essie." Averett wrapped Essie in a hug. "I will join you in Tarenhiel with the army just as soon as possible."

"I know." Essie swallowed at the tightness in her throat. She wasn't ready to say goodbye to her family just yet. She hadn't even had the chance to give Mother, her sister-in-law Paige, and her nephews Bertie and Finn actual goodbyes.

She would still have Julien and Edmund with her in Tarenhiel. At least, when they weren't busy scouting or planning a war.

Averett released her and gently tapped her nose. "I don't know how that heart bond works, but if you get a chance, you tell Farrendel we're coming for him. We're all coming, and we're going to get him out of there just as soon as we can."

"I'll do my best to let him know." It was a bond of the heart, not the mind. So far, telepathy hadn't been a side-effect. But, perhaps, she might be able to communicate the emotions. Even that might be a stretch. What she had experienced so far had been more like impressions.

But perhaps Farrendel felt the heart bond more than she did. She had gotten that feeling the times she and Farrendel had talked about the heart bond. And, Jalissa and Weylind had been surprised when Essie had to concentrate to feel the heart bond.

Averett tapped her nose again. "Don't lose hope."

It was hard to cling to hope, knowing the torture Farrendel was most likely enduring.

But if Farrendel could feel her emotions through the heart bond, then she did not wish to further burden him with her own despair. She wasn't going to hide that she missed him. That she worried for him. But she wanted him to feel her determination.

He wasn't dead. And he wasn't going to be any time soon if she, her family, and his family had any say about it.

Averett stepped back. "I'll arrive in Tarenhiel in a week. Hopefully less."

"Will you be able to mobilize the army that quickly?" Essie didn't want to get her hopes too high.

"Yes. I am king, after all. There are times when my commands do mean something." Averett's mouth tipped into a slight smile, though Essie could see the weary lines around his mouth and eyes.

These past couple of days had been hard on all of them. Her brothers had just started to bond with Farrendel, only to have him ripped away.

With a last smile for her, Averett turned and strode down the gangplank.

Essie stepped back as one of Weylind's guards drew in the gangplank and the ship began to pull away from the wharf. As Essie had no wish to watch the Escarlish shore grow smaller behind them, she made her way to the bow.

There, King Weylind sagged against the rail, his shoulders more slumped than Essie had ever seen.

A part of her didn't want to approach him. She was exhausted down to her bones after two days and a night with little sleep, an escape, and the ache of missing Farrendel. Not to mention, Weylind had not always been the kindest to Essie. His grumpiness had been out of love for Farrendel, but that didn't make Essie all that eager to walk up to him.

But he was hurting as much as the rest of them. Once they reached Estyra, he would have his wife Rheva to lean on.

Until then, he was more alone than Essie was. She had two of her brothers with her, currently standing by the stern peering over the rail as they tried to figure out how the magical propulsion worked.

Weylind had no one. His brother was captured by trolls. His sister Jalissa was returning to Escarland to help the war effort there. His other sister Melantha had turned out to be a traitor and was currently missing. Presumably she had either gone with the trolls or she had fled. She couldn't have returned to Tarenhiel once her treachery was known.

That left only Essie, the sister-in-law he'd never really wanted.

With a deep breath, Essie marched over and leaned against the rail next to Weylind. For once, she couldn't find the words to say anything.

Weylind let out a long, slow breath, the strands of his black hair falling to hide his face. "Your brother is a good man."

That was not at all what Essie had been expecting. "Yes, he is. He will keep his word. The Escarlish army will fight on your side in this war."

Weylind straightened, staring at the Tarenhieli shore, green with its deep forest. "For the past months, I have been wary, waiting for your brother to reveal that the marriage alliance had been a trick. And yet, it turns out it was my sister, not your brother, who dealt in treason and lies."

Even Essie could hear the pain in Weylind's voice. She remembered Farrendel telling her once that elves didn't lie. She hadn't been sure at the time if that was a custom they held to or if they were truly incapable of lying.

It turned out elves could lie. At least, Melantha had maintained lies for years.

Essie wasn't sure how to comfort Weylind. What comfort was there to be had when a sister betrayed a brother to torture and death? There wasn't a bright side. There wasn't even a villain to hate. There was just a double loss, a double reason to mourn.

Instead, Essie decided to focus on her family, on the growing respect she'd heard in Weylind's voice. "I know this might be hard to believe, given how he died fighting your people, but my father was a good man and a good king. He had great respect for elves, even as he went to war against you. While I don't remember him much, I know Averett and Julien especially have always looked to his example."

Weylind nodded, still staring at the shoreline of trees. "I wonder if his war might have been more justified than we elves would wish to believe. As the centuries have passed, we have lost some of the nobleness of character and mightiness in battle that made us worthy allies. There are stories of warriors of the past with magic much like Farrendel's. It was not the rare thing back then that it is now." Weylind turned to her. "And your brother has the making of the noble kings of old. He is young, but I believe he will be a worthy ally."

"Would I be too human if I said I told you so?" Essie's smile was brief and wobbly.

It felt wrong to joke and smile while Farrendel remained captured by the trolls. Yet, it would be weeks before they would be able to rescue him. If she spent those weeks in melancholy, she would break long before they got him back.

As hard as it was, she needed to figure out a way to live with this ache. To keep going, one step at a time.

Perhaps it would be easier in the morning, once she'd slept through the night on the train to Estyra.

Weylind's shoulders slumped once again. "I am sorry, isciena. Farrendel would have good cause to tell me the same thing regarding you."

Essie blinked at Weylind. In her exhaustion, had she heard him wrong? Surely King Weylind hadn't just apologized to her? Again?

Sure, he had been hard on her at times, suspicious of her motives for marrying Farrendel and worried that she would break his brother's heart. But she had never expected him to apologize.

"Thank you. It was hard there, at first, when everyone was so suspicious of me." She shrugged. "But if all of you hadn't been so hard on me, I'm not sure Farrendel would've dug in his heels as fiercely as he did out of sheer stubbornness to prove you wrong."

"Farrendel does not pick his battles lightly." Weylind shook his head, his black hair sliding across his shoulders.

Essie ducked her head, hot tears filling her eyes in a sudden rush. But she refused to cry here with King Weylind. They were making progress, but not enough that she wanted to break down in front of him.

But, for the first time since she had met him, she felt like she truly understood him. Weylind had always been first a king, then a brother. When the late elf queen had been killed, Weylind had been the one to take on the duties of the kingdom while his father had been grieving. When Farrendel's illegitimate birth had been revealed and their father had all but stepped down as king to raise him, Weylind had again been asked to be king, even though his father yet lived.

Weylind had acted as the king so that their father could focus on Farrendel. It had been what was best for Farrendel, but it would have been a great burden to place on Weylind, even before his father had died young, for an elf.

From the moment Farrendel had been born, Weylind had

never had the chance to relax and spend time with his brother apart from the duties of the kingdom. If he sometimes came across as a king giving commands even in his personal relationships, it perhaps could be forgiven.

The ship eased next to the wharf on the Tarenhieli shore. It took a few minutes to secure the ship to the pilings and lower the gangplank, but then they were disembarking, crossing the small stretch of ground, and boarding the elven train, a sleek silver thing that ran along rails of tree roots.

Essie sagged onto the seat in the elven train. The seating car featured two long benches on either side with banks of windows behind them and a silver domed ceiling.

Had it only been a week ago she'd taken this train with Farrendel and Jalissa? Essie hadn't been able to stop chattering on that trip, too excited to sit still at the thought of introducing Farrendel to her family.

Now, she couldn't work up the energy or willpower to smile. All her bones ached, her muscles shaky. She'd been abducted from Winstead Palace at just about midnight when she and Farrendel had slipped from the ball. As the train carrying her and Farrendel and their captors to the border clattered through the night, she had dozed against Farrendel's shoulder. But it had been a light doze, and she had been in constant danger and worry since.

Edmund and Julien took seats on either side of her while Weylind sat across from them. No one spoke as the train eased into motion.

Essie propped her head on her hand and stared out the window, the trees blurring. Farrendel's private sleeping car was probably still attached to this train. She could curl up in that bed and sleep.

But she didn't want to be alone right now. Nor did she

want to be alone in a place belonging to Farrendel. Her heart already ached too much.

Julien started a conversation with Weylind that had Weylind pulling out a folding table to set up in the aisle while Julien spread out a map.

Edmund wrapped an arm around Essie's shoulder. "You can sleep, if you want. I can tell you're tired."

Essie leaned her head against his shoulder. Edmund's shoulder was more comfortable than Farrendel's, which was all bones and angles. Yet, Essie would've rather been curled up against Farrendel.

She squeezed her eyes shut, hot tears burning beneath her eyelids. "I just miss him so much."

"I know. We'll rescue him." Edmund wrapped both arms around Essie.

Would they? How long would it take? What would the trolls do to Farrendel in the meantime?

More tears burned behind her eyes, but she refused to let them fall. She could not break in front of everyone. She needed to be strong.

"It's all right to cry." Edmund held her closer.

She sniffled and allowed a few hot, silent tears to trickle down her cheeks.

WHEN THEY ARRIVED IN ESTYRA, all of them had gotten some sleep during the night, though Essie doubted any of them had slept much. Weylind's shoulders sagged, lines cutting into his face, as if he carried the weight of both kingdoms on his shoulders. He looked like he could use a hug, but even Essie wasn't daring enough to try it.

As they disembarked, Julien and Edmund gazed about, wide-eyed, much as Essie had done when first arriving in Estyra. Elves strolled the meandering paths between the massive trees. The shops were tucked beneath gauzy green awnings while more shops were higher in the trees with bridges connecting them. Broad leaves shaded the forest floor, yet grass still grew lush and thick on the paths.

"This is beautiful." Julien turned around even as he kept walking. "But I can see why the logistics of bringing the Escarlish army through Tarenhiel might be tricky if this is their biggest city."

Edmund nodded, his gaze sweeping back and forth, taking in everything.

As they strolled through Estyra behind King Weylind, some of the elves stopped and gestured in greeting to him. A few called greetings to Essie, and she waved, though her smile felt brittle as a leaf in autumn.

But most of the elves stared at Julien and Edmund, then either shrugged or scowled. If having three humans in Estyra bothered them, they were going to panic when the rest of the Escarlish military leaders descended with Averett to plan the invasion of Kostaria.

At one of the side paths, a tall, blonde-haired female elf hurried onto the main trail. She halted in front of Essie, her deep blue eyes filled with pain.

"Illyna." Essie wasn't sure she could face Farrendel's friends. Had they heard he had been captured by the trolls again? All because of human traitors who had handed him over for money.

"I heard. I am so sorry, Essie." Illyna stepped forward and hugged Essie. A full, human-style hug. Not just the elf version of a hug of gripping each other's shoulders. "If you need anything…"

"I'll let you know. Thanks." Essie gave Illyna one last squeeze before she stepped back.

Illyna gripped one of Essie's shoulders. Her other arm, which ended in a stump just below her elbow, dropped to her side. "Farrendel is strong, and he has you to live for. He will fight to survive this."

Essie swallowed and nodded. The ache of too many emotions filled her chest, too much of a jumble for her to concentrate enough to feel the heart bond. All she could do was nod.

Illyna released her and took another step back.

After Essie introduced Illyna to Julien and Edmund, Illyna headed back to her shop while Essie hurried to catch up with Weylind, who had paused to wait for them.

Before them, the forest opened up to the small cleared space that surrounded Ellonahshinel, the massive tree that formed the elven palace.

Both Edmund and Julien halted in their tracks as they took in the sight of the majestic tree towering before them. Rooms were built into the tree trunks while gold gilding lined the massive branches.

"This is Ellonahshinel. The Heart of the Forest." Essie better understood the warmth that had filled Farrendel's voice when he'd first brought her home to Estyra and she had seen the elven palace for the first time.

Ellonahshinel wasn't merely a place the way Winstead Palace was. It was a living tree, precious and cherished by all elves, and something that could be killed and lost if Tarenhiel was invaded.

They climbed the winding staircase grown into the roots

and trunk of Ellonahshinel until they reached the entry hall. Doors branched from this room in all directions.

Unlike last time, there wasn't a line of Farrendel's family waiting to greet them. Not even Queen Rheva, Ryfon, or Brina were there.

Essie couldn't help but be grateful. She didn't want to keep up her brittle smile through stilted greetings. Right now, all she wanted to do was retreat to her rooms. She had slept some on the train, but not enough.

With a nod to Weylind, she led Julien and Edmund onto one of the broad branches that formed meandering paths between the treehouse-like rooms of the palace. Her brothers followed, silently gaping at everything around them.

They didn't balk at walking on the branches until, like she had the first time she was here, they hesitated when the branches went from safe, twenty-foot-wide roads to a mere four feet.

"Our rooms are right over there." Essie gestured at the treehouse on the far side of the branch. "It's not as scary as it looks."

Julien glanced from her to the branch and back again. "You're not scared of falling."

"I got used to it." Eventually. It had taken Farrendel a lot of coaxing to get her to cross that branch the first time.

She refused to let herself ache at the memories.

She strolled across the branch, then waited on the porch that ran around the outside of the main room. Her brothers inched across, arms spread to help them keep their balance.

Once inside, she gave them a quick tour. The main room was nothing besides a small kitchen area of cupboards and a table with two chairs while the other side held various cushions on the floor for relaxing. The far side of the room had three doors. Two guest rooms and the room she had shared with Farrendel for all of two nights before they had left for Escarland.

She pointed Edmund to the far room, then Julien to the one in the middle, the room that had been hers for most of her three months here. "I think some of my things might still be in that room. I'll fetch them in a little while."

She didn't wait to see his reaction. She retreated through the door to her and Farrendel's room. Her knees wobbled as she climbed the staircase, crossed the porch, and entered the bedroom.

The bed beneath the window looked as if it had been grown of branches out of the wall, still piled with the mound of blankets Essie had hauled into the room since Farrendel liked to sleep with the window open no matter how chilly the night breeze. The clothing shelves were nearly bare of items, as she and Farrendel had taken most of their clothing with them to Escarland.

But more than missing clothing and personal items, this room felt empty. Even though Edmund and Julien were in the rooms a short walk away, Essie sank onto the bed, lonelier than she could remember being in her life.

This place didn't feel right without Farrendel.

She curled onto her side. His pillow still had the minty smell of his shampoo.

Farrendel. How were either of them going to survive the weeks it was going to take to rescue him?

She reached for the heart bond deep inside her chest. It took a few moments of concentration before she felt it. That crackling sense of magic that held the impression of Farrendel.

He was still alive. She could tell that. There was a

lingering sense of pain, though not sharp. Perhaps he was still asleep or unconscious. Yet, he'd been like that for hours now. Were the trolls keeping him sedated? Perhaps they were using the same ether that Mark Hadley and Lord Bletchly had used to capture Essie and Farrendel in Escarland. She couldn't sense enough through the heart bond to say for sure.

Don't give up, Farrendel. We're coming.

CHAPTER
FOUR

Melantha curled in the corner of the frigid train car as it shook and shuddered down the tracks as if about to fly off and go careening down the mountainside toward a fiery crash at any moment. How did the trolls survive these train rides? Surely this was not safe.

But Prince Rharreth leaned against the wall in the center of the train car, arms crossed as if unperturbed by the rocking vibrations. He had been like that ever since they had hiked, or been hauled, across the border and deep inland until boarding this rickety excuse for a train. Rather than join his brother King Charvod in whatever the trolls considered a royal train car, Prince Rharreth had insisted on being locked in this windowless, heatless boxcar with the prisoners.

Farrendel lay on the far side of the train car from Melantha, bound with stone and seemingly still unconscious under the sedation of that human drug. Stone shackled him to the floor of the car, and Melantha was almost jealous. At least he was not in danger of rolling every time the car tipped dangerously.

As the train lurched around what Melantha could only guess was another precarious turn above a precipitous drop, she braced herself as best she could against the steel wall, her fingers burning with the icy chill. She clamped her jaws shut to stop a shriek. She might be a prisoner, but she still had her dignity. Barely.

The trolls had played her for a fool. A royal, naïve fool. The trolls never intended to uphold their end of the bargain. All those fine words about feeding their starving people had just been an act, a reason they had given her as they pretended to want peace, if only they were given the minor appeasement of revenge on Laesornysh.

They had never wanted peace. That dratted human princess Elspeth had been right all along. The trolls just wanted Farrendel out of the way before they started a war to crush Tarenhiel once and for all.

Melantha had been used. Again. Just like she had been years ago when Hatharal, her betrothed, had only wanted to marry her for her title. He had walked away the moment the scandal of Farrendel's birth and acceptance into the royal family made the prestige of Melantha's title meaningless.

But this time, it would cost not just her dreams but her entire family. The trolls would not stop with just Farrendel. They would kill Weylind. Melantha's sister-in-law Rheva. Her nephew and niece Ryfon and Brina. Jalissa, if she did not flee to Escarland. Their grandmother Leyleira. Anyone and everyone who had ever meant something to Melantha.

In trying to save her family from the decades of scandal and heartache that had plagued them, Melantha had doomed them all. She made everything so much worse.

The wheels squealed, and the entire train gave such a hard, slamming lurch that Melantha thunked against the front wall despite her best efforts. Even Prince Rharreth staggered a step under the force.

With a prolonged screeching that had Melantha pressing her hands over her ears, the train came to a juddering halt.

Prince Rharreth stepped away from the wall, his face in hard, unperturbed lines. "We're here."

Melantha peeled herself from the floor, using the wall to help her stand on shaking legs. "And where is here?"

"Gror Grar." Prince Rharreth grabbed her arm, yanking her forward as the large cargo door scraped open, revealing a squad of trolls dressed in leather armor and carrying Escarlish weapons, though Melantha was not sure if they were rifles or muskets or some other human-made atrocity.

Her knees buckled, and Prince Rharreth all but carried her to the door. Gror Grar was the legendary fortress of the trolls. Supposedly impenetrable, only one elf in living memory had ever successfully breached its walls and come out alive.

She glanced over her shoulder to where Farrendel lay in chains. This time, he would not breach the walls and kill the troll king. He was a prisoner to be subjected to torture while being used as bait to lure Weylind to his death.

Prince Rharreth gripped her arms and swung her off her feet. She shrieked and kicked, but his grip remained solid. She was passed from him to the trolls on the ground as if she were nothing but a sack of cargo.

When she was set on the ground, Melantha drew herself straight, gathering the last shreds of her poise. "Unhand me."

The two trolls gripping her arms did not budge. Their gray skin might as well have been made of the stone of the surrounding mountains.

King Charvod marched up to them with more troll soldiers flanking him. He climbed into the train car, reappearing a few seconds later with Farrendel dangling limply from his grip. "Behold! The great Laesornysh of the elves!"

The troll soldiers stomped their feet and gave their howling war cries.

King Charvod tossed Farrendel from the train car, and the troll soldiers let him land hard on the ground.

Melantha winced, finding herself taking a step toward Farrendel before she caught herself. Why the concern now? A few days ago, she had hated him enough to try to have him killed. And yet, now, seeing him like this...being caught in this nightmare with him...

It had a way of shining a light into a part of herself she was not sure she wanted to acknowledge. If she looked too closely, she was not going to like what she saw.

King Charvod jumped from the train car, strode to Farrendel's still form, and kicked him hard in the ribs. "Stripped of your magic, you are nothing. Just a weak, pathetic elfling."

Amid the laughter of the soldiers, King Charvod hauled Farrendel to his feet and dragged him along, surrounded by the jeering soldiers.

Was Farrendel even conscious? A part of Melantha hoped he was not. Better he remain senseless and never remember these insults hurled at him.

She should not care. She had betrayed him to the trolls, knowing this was the cruelty he would face, even if she had shied away from dwelling on anything besides the hope that her life could finally go back to the way it was before her mother had been killed. Back when her family had not been scorned because of their acceptance of an illegitimate half-brother.

Another stab of that churning pang in her stomach had her hunching over. What would Dacha think about all this?

Did she even need to ask? Her father would have been horrified. He had loved Farrendel as much as he had Weylind. Dacha had sacrificed years of his life to make sure Farrendel had the best childhood he could give him. And he had died to rescue Farrendel from the trolls.

How could Dacha have put his illegitimate son over the happiness of the rest of his children? That was the question that had been simmering inside her from the moment he had been killed.

Yet, had he? Dacha would have sacrificed just as much for her or Jalissa or Weylind. Had he not been angry on her behalf when Hatharal had broken their betrothal? He had been there for all her growing up years. Those beautiful years when both Macha and Dacha had been alive and she, Weylind, and Jalissa had spent many happy summers at Lethorel.

Prince Rharreth's grip tightened on Melantha's arm, and he marched her forward after the army of trolls.

Melantha gritted her teeth and trotted to keep up with him. A blast of wind cut through her thin, silk dress, sweeping up off the rocky terrain only sparsely broken by tufts of grass and other brush that Weylind or Jalissa could name, as they had studied such things for their plant growing magic. Mountains stretched toward the horizon as far as she could see.

As they rounded the end of the train, the view of a flat plateau spread before her. Deep gullies stretched on all sides of the plateau except one. Behind them, the train tracks wound up the one sloping side while in front of her, a stone bridge curved over the crevasse.

On the other side of the bridge stood Gror Grar. Its walls and towers rose out of a mountain as if they had been grown like that. With the trolls' stone magic, they probably had transformed a mountain peak into the spiraling towers and mighty walls before her.

Beyond Gror Grar shone the lights of the capital city of Osmana, tucked onto the side of a distant mountain guarded by walls and the fortress of Gror Grar standing in the way.

Melantha shivered and hugged her arms over her body as best she could with Prince Rharreth gripping her elbow. Would she ever leave Gror Grar? Or would both she and Farrendel die there behind those cold, stone walls?

She was hauled across the bridge and into the fortress itself. All the stone surrounding her sent a dull throb to her temples.

In the courtyard, hordes of trolls had gathered with King Charvod in a cleared space in the center, shouting.

The trolls at the edges of the cleared space were shoving and kicking Farrendel as he staggered, arms pinned to his sides with stone. The trolls had stripped Farrendel of his shirt and boots, leaving him in only the Escarlish trousers. His gaze was wide and hazy, as if he was still groggy and drugged.

Melantha struggled against Prince Rharreth's grip. "You have to stop this."

Prince Rharreth stared down at her with cold, dark blue eyes. "Why? He is my kingdom's greatest enemy. We have no reason to spare him any indignity after the numbers he has killed."

She gritted her teeth. "You value honor, especially in

battle. You might hate him as your enemy, but surely you value his strength as a warrior. Treat him with the decency of an honored enemy. This...this is just barbaric."

"Perhaps. But it is deserved." Prince Rharreth dragged her through the crowd of trolls until they broke through the circle.

Shoved from behind, Farrendel tumbled to the ground, lying still.

Prince Rharreth stared down at Farrendel with an impassive expression before he lifted his gaze to King Charvod. "You have paraded Laesornysh before our people as you wished. Now we should kill him, as is honorable for a defeated enemy."

Melantha tried to wrench her arm from the troll prince's grasp. "No, do not—"

He shook her. Not hard, but hard enough to cut off her words. The glare he sent her clamped her mouth shut.

This was what she had wanted when she had betrayed Farrendel. A quick execution by the trolls, an easy elimination of a decades-long problem.

Yet, now, when the time came, why did her stomach churn? Why was she protesting?

"I wish to keep him alive a while longer. He should suffer for our people he has murdered." King Charvod aimed a kick at Farrendel's ribs as the troll soldiers around them cheered and howled more battle cries.

Farrendel curled on the ground as much as the stone wrapped around him would allow. Why was he not fighting back? Were the stone bindings and troll magic lacing them enough to keep his magic locked from his reach?

"It is too great a risk to keep him alive." Prince Rharreth

remained as stoic as the stone walls around them. "His brother believes we have him captured. He will come regardless of whether we keep Laesornysh alive or kill him now."

"Actually, we must keep him alive, since you let his human wife escape. They share one of those elven elishinas, and she would feel it if Laesornysh were killed." King Charvod sent a sharp look at his brother before turning to Melantha. "Isn't that right, elf princess?"

That was one of the tidbits of information she had shared with the trolls through Thanfardil. Still, Melantha stared back and said nothing. She had no wish to continue helping this troll king who had lied to her so grievously.

"I see you aren't talking." King Charvod shook his head. "Too late for guilt now. Your brother already knows you are a traitor. He won't come for you."

Melantha pressed her mouth into a tight line. Would Weylind come for her, if he realized she had been taken by the trolls as well?

After what she had done, he might decide to let the trolls have her, and good riddance.

King Charvod gestured down at Farrendel. "Look at him. He is fully in our control. I am counting on your magic to keep him contained. Unless you believe your magic isn't strong enough for one elfling?"

Prince Rharreth bowed his head. "My magic is strong enough, especially here."

"Exactly." King Charvod pointed at Farrendel. "Take him to the dungeon and see that he is properly secured. Then meet me in my quarters. I have some questions for our elven princess."

Melantha swallowed as Prince Rharreth released her.

Several troll soldiers surrounded her, cutting off any hope of escape.

Even if she ran, where would she go? She was now hundreds of miles into Kostaria. She had no food. No water. Nothing but the thin dress she wore.

While Prince Rharreth dragged Farrendel to his feet, the troll soldiers shoved Melantha forward, following as King Charvod led the way toward a pair of double doors set into the main tower of Gror Grar, which looked more like a mountain peak than a tower.

As she stepped inside, the cold and the stone shivered into her bones, sharp with the tang of troll magic. Her headache pounded harder behind her eyes. Easing a hint of her magic into her fingertips, she rubbed at her temples and soothed the headache away as subtly as she could.

For some reason, it seemed important to keep the trolls from knowing that she was not as susceptible to the stone as Farrendel was. Since she retained more of the use of her magic, she could heal herself from the minor physical discomfort caused by proximity to stone.

The soldiers escorted her up a set of stairs, through winding passageways lit with flickering torches, and finally pushed her through a door embossed with a likeness of the carved, antler crown of the troll king.

Inside, a few frayed rugs covered the floor while a few worn cushions covered the stone chairs in what looked like a sitting room. A fireplace to her left held a crackling fire while a door to her right probably led to the bedroom. Slim windows filled the far wall, providing glimpses of the vast mountains stretching in all directions. It would have been breathtaking, if she had not been marched there as a prisoner.

King Charvod halted in the center of the room and waved toward the soldiers. "Thank you for escorting her. You may wait outside."

With a click of their boots on the stone, the troll soldiers left, closing the door behind them.

Leaving Melantha alone with the troll king.

King Charvod reclined on one of the chairs. "Please. Have a seat."

Melantha perched on the edge of one of the stone chairs as far away from King Charvod as possible. This felt like a trap.

The troll king's icy blue eyes studied her before he gestured at the room. "You have a choice, Princess Melantha. Either I can have you escorted down to the dungeons or you can spend your time enjoying the hospitality that Gror Grar has to offer."

If this was Gror Grar's best, then it was sorely lacking. All but a few of the poorest of homes in Tarenhiel had more luxuries than this.

Even if this place held all the wealth in the world, it would not disguise the fact that King Charvod was attempting to bait a trap. Melantha gathered the poise she had learned as a princess of the elves. "And what would be the price of that hospitality?"

"Nothing much. Certainly nothing more than what you have already done." King Charvod shrugged, as if what he was about to ask her was nothing to raise her concern. The light from the windows highlighted the hard lines of his square jaw. "All you would have to do is give us a few more pieces of information. The size of your brother's army. His likely strategy. The kinds of magic he will unleash now that he no longer has Laesornysh to fight at his side."

Yes, she had given the trolls information about Farrendel and his human wife. But she had done her best never to betray true military information to the trolls. All of the weapons smuggling had been Thanfardil's doing, not hers. She was not fully a traitor. Not really.

And she was not about to start now, especially not after the trolls had played her for a fool once already. She was not about to help them kill Weylind, Jalissa, and the rest of her family, even if it meant Melantha would suffer in a troll dungeon.

She drew herself straight. "I will not give you any information. I am no traitor."

King Charvod smirked. "Are you sure your brother sees it that way?"

"Which brother?" The question popped out before she caught herself.

"You're going to claim him as your brother now?" King Charvod snorted, his fingers clenching on the stone armrests on his chair.

It was a little late to start claiming such filial connection. Melantha hugged her arms over her twisting stomach. What was Prince Rharreth doing to Farrendel down in that dungeon even as she was sitting here?

"You really should re-think your position." King Charvod flattened his palms on the stone armrests of his chair. Icy magic swirled from his fingers and into the stone, traveling through the floor, before bursting into her chair.

Tendrils of stone reached out and circled her body, clamping her to the back of the chair and pinning her arms to her sides. She caught her breath at the pain as the troll magic touched her skin. Still, she gritted her teeth and faced King Charvod. "No."

A knock sounded on the door, then it opened. Prince Rharreth strode inside, though he halted almost immediately, his gaze flicking to her, then to his brother. "I was under the impression she would not be tortured."

"She is still an enemy. An elf." King Charvod stroked the arm of his chair, as if he itched to send more magic into the stone. After a moment, he shook his head. "Do not give me a lecture on honor. She will not be harmed as long as she does nothing foolish. You won't act foolishly, will you, elf princess?"

Melantha glared back and kept her mouth shut. She had already given these trolls too much ammunition to use against her family.

"Or unless her brother acts foolishly." King Charvod leaned back in his chair, nodding as if agreeing with whatever debate he had been having in his head. "Lock her in a cell not far from her brother. It will be easier to fetch her if Laesornysh needs to be persuaded to cooperate."

Prince Rharreth raised his eyebrows. "I thought you said my magic would be enough to contain him."

"It should be, but it never hurts to take extra precautions when it comes to Laesornysh." King Charvod stood and turned his back to them. "Take her away. I need to see to the preparations for war."

War. Against her family and her home.

Melantha did not resist as Prince Rharreth used his magic to release her from the chair and hauled her to her feet. Being locked in the dungeon was exactly what she deserved.

H is toes were cold.

He was in pain as well, head pounding, agony flaring all through his body, but he had expected the pain. Not the cold toes.

Farrendel blinked, his eyes gritty. It took several moments for the blur of darkness and orange light to focus into a stone ceiling above him, lit with torchlight stretching from the barred window set in the door, reinforced with stone and troll magic.

Not that he could reach the door. He lay spread-eagle on the floor, pain flaring from all the places the magic-laced stone pinned him down. Agony cut not just on top of his skin where the stone wrapped around his wrists and ankles, but also at points where the stone pierced through him.

He could turn and lift his head, relieving the ache where the back of his head had rested against the stone floor for far too long, but when he tried to shift, agony flared through his shoulders. He could wiggle his fingers, but stone held each of his wrists.

He was missing his shirt, his bare back pressed against the cold stone beneath him. Glancing down, he moved his bare feet, his boots and stockings also missing, but the stone around his ankles kept him from moving any more than that.

At least the trolls had left the Escarlish breeches he had been wearing when captured. If he had known he was going to be stuck in them this long, he might have thought longer before he had worn them for that ball.

Except...He closed his eyes, remembering the way Essie's smile had brightened her eyes. It had been worth it to make Essie smile. Especially considering the way the evening had ended.

Essie...He squeezed his eyes tighter, chest aching. He could still feel her, the heart bond filled with weight and grief instead of the warmth and cheeriness he usually sensed from her. She slept, a fitful restless sleep, that gave him the impression she had cried herself to sleep.

Would he ever see her again? Or would he die here, pinned like a bug to the floor?

He was stuck in his own nightmare. Stone and pain and crushing darkness.

Memories haunted the darkness. His and Essie's capture by the Escarlish traitors. The train ride. Melantha's betrayal. The troll king. Thanfardil dying and a gun pointing at Melantha. Shouting trolls. Kicks. Stumbling over icy stone in his bare feet.

And...and...

The troll king cutting his hair.

Farrendel's stomach churned, his breathing growing more ragged. Surely that was a nightmare. It could not have been a real memory. Surely not.

But as he turned his head, he felt the shortened strands brush his forehead. He could not see the strands around his shoulders or feel them caught beneath him as he should have if his hair was still long.

The trolls had cut his hair.

It would just be the beginning of the degradations he would suffer. Right now, they owned his body. They could do whatever they liked to him, and he would be absolutely helpless.

His heart pounded harder, a deeper darkness closing in at the edges of his vision. Too much stone. He could feel the weight of all the stone stretch far above him, hammering into his skull. Too much darkness wrapped around him, suffocating.

He needed to move. He strained against the stone, crying out as raw edges of pain cut deeper with his movements. Blood warmed the stones beneath him.

He had to get out. He flailed for his magic, and pain scorched through his head, flaring in his wrists.

Somewhere, far away, Essie stirred. The impression through the heart bond changed from sleep to waking awareness in a snap, filling him with a wave of her emotions. Tears. Worry.

Farrendel squeezed his eyes shut and forced himself to relax, lie still, and breathe deeply. Panicking was hurting Essie. She was already burdened enough without having to feel his despair through the heart bond.

For Essie's sake, he had to pull himself together. It would not be fair to her to expect her to carry the weight of his anguish along with her own. For her, he needed to be as mentally strong as he could manage.

Despair and hope to die. That was his first instinctual

reaction, scarred into him through too much pain. He had fought and won a lot of battles, all while not caring whether he lived or died.

There on the train, he had told Essie he intended to fight to the death rather than face torture again. He had despaired. Given up on any hope of a future. Probably because it was a future he had never fully grasped, not the way Essie had.

Essie had not despaired. She had clung to hope, even in the face of his hopelessness.

This was not a battle he could win with despondency. This pain was only the beginning of torment and humiliation. He would never survive the weeks ahead if he broke now. Nor would Essie survive if she had to carry such unrelenting despair for him.

In the end in that battle at the Escarlish border, he had chosen Essie rather than a quick death. Hope rather than despair. A future of torture for a chance to return to her.

For the past three and a half months since marrying Essie, he had begun to hope. But he had still held back, fearing he would break if he dared to dream of a future, only to have it snatched away when the worst happened.

Well, the worst had happened. And yet he was not broken.

What was a little pain? Torture? It was nothing he had not faced and survived before. It was just a few weeks. What was that compared to the decades—no, centuries—he could have with Essie if he lived through this?

If he survived, he was going to stop holding back and instead fully trust her with every shattered piece of him. He would dream of a future and build a life worth living instead of apathetically existing from day-to-day.

Far away in either Escarland or Tarenhiel, Essie was crying. She did not cry like Jalissa or Melantha, their nearly silent tears trailing an elegant sheen down their cheeks. No, Essie's tears were loud with blotchy, red cheeks, puffy eyes, and drooling, wet sniffles.

How dare the trolls make Essie cry. He did not care what they did to him. But they had hurt Essie by capturing him. They would hurt her even more every time they hurt him.

The heat added strength to the core of raw steel inside him. Farrendel clenched his fists. "I chose this. I chose you."

His words echoed against the cold stone of the ceiling. Essie could not hear them. She was far away. Though, perhaps, she could feel the sense of them from the strength welling in his chest. She stopped crying, and he could feel her internally reaching for the heart bond.

One of the last things he had told her was that he intended to die. He could not let her continue to think that. She needed to know he was going to fight with every shred in him to get back to her.

"I chose this." Farrendel shouted the words this time, even though there was no one there to hear him. "I chose you, Essie. Do you hear that? I chose you, and I am going to survive this."

There was the warmth he remembered flooding through the elishina.

This strength was intoxicating. He glared up at the stone ceiling, the cold darkness barely broken by the torchlight, and shouted with all the breath left in him, straining against the stone pinning him to the floor. "I am Farrendel Laesornysh, and I am going to survive! Do you hear that, troll king? I do not care what you do to me. I am going to survive."

He could not control what the trolls did to him. He could not move more than his fingers and toes. But he could control his mind, mostly. And with his mind, he would win this battle.

Essie probably thought he was out of his head with pain, thanks to the rush of determination and exhilaration she must be feeling from him.

He collapsed back onto the floor, the stone searing his wrists and shoulders. His head pounded as if stabbed with a knife while his throat ached, his mouth far too dry.

But it had been worth it. Instead of giving in to the despair, he was ready to fight.

Perhaps Essie sensed as much through the elishina. She seemed to be trying to tell him something, her own determination sharp and raw. Maybe she was trying to reassure him that help was coming, as long as he was strong enough to wait for it.

Weylind would come for him. Of that much he was absolutely sure.

Essie's brothers would come too. Averett, Julien, and Edmund had accepted him as he had never expected they would, even though he had only spent that one week with them. Strange how his trust in them was just as unshakable as his trust in Weylind, perhaps even more so. After all, his new Escarlish family had not betrayed him the way his own family had.

Farrendel forced himself to breathe evenly, relaxing his muscles and lying still against the stone. This was not going to be over quickly. He needed to prepare himself for that reality, accept it, and deal with it.

More than that, he had to keep his wits about him. If he

saw an opportunity to escape, he would have to take it. When rescue came, he would help any way he could.

Last time, he had been too weak and broken to aid his father, and in the end, his father had died because of it. Now, Farrendel was older, wiser, than he had been fifteen years ago. A seasoned warrior, not the boy captured after only a few battles. This time, he would be ready so that none of his rescuers paid the price for him.

Yes, he was captured. But he was also strategically placed behind enemy lines. Maybe even inside the trolls' fortress. He would have to figure out how to take advantage of that.

Essie, tell our brothers I will be ready.

She would not be able to understand his exact words, but perhaps enough of the meaning would come through anyway.

Something like determination came from Essie, and it almost felt like she was reaching for him, as if they could somehow hold hands across the distance.

How was it possible that he could still feel the elishina even though his own magic was blocked? He would have expected that it too would be blocked by the stone and troll magic.

But the magic of the heart bond was something deeper and far more mysterious than even the powerful magic he wielded. It could not be blocked by something as simple as stone.

Whatever he faced, he would not do it alone.

A shiver passed through him, not caused by the cold in his toes. How much would Essie feel through the heart bond? From talking with her, Farrendel had gathered that she did not feel the heart bond as constantly as he did, though she had experienced other effects, like learning elvish far faster than normal, that he had not. Yet she had awakened because of his panic earlier.

Would she feel something as intense as torture through the heart bond? Torture, he could handle. But if Essie suffered along with him...that was something he could not bear.

Was there a way he could block the heart bond somehow? He had to try if he was to protect her from this.

What would happen if he could not protect her? If the torture pushed him close to death, would the heart bond try to keep him alive, as it had when he had nearly been killed in that troll ambush? What if the trolls killed him, and it killed Essie along with him?

He could not allow that to happen. Whatever happened, he had to protect Essie.

Something clanked farther in the dungeon. A door creaked open. Boots tromped on stone in the passageway, along with a lighter, scuffling sound of a smaller person being hustled along.

A door grated, closer this time. Someone gave a muffled cry before the door thunked closed. The booted footsteps turned in the direction of Farrendel's dungeon door.

Farrendel drew in a deep breath, bracing himself. Was the torture about to begin? Already? He had barely gathered his mental defenses in preparation.

Something scraped before the door swung open. The troll prince, Prince Rharreth, strode inside, ducking to avoid hitting his head on the top of the frame. The torchlight cast shadows across his hard face. In one hand, he held a bowl that wafted a faint hint of steam into the air, bringing with it a savory smell.

Food. Farrendel's stomach clenched again. When was the

last time he had eaten? In the haze of the drug they had used to keep him unconscious for the trip across Tarenhiel and Kostaria, he could not remember if he had been fed. Perhaps, unconscious as he was, they had only managed to force a little water down his throat to keep him alive.

Prince Rharreth flicked his gaze over him before he knelt beside him. Setting the bowl aside, Prince Rharreth touched one of the stone bindings around Farrendel's wrist.

Pain flared, and Farrendel gritted his teeth against it. This was merely the troll checking that the bindings were secure. The real torture had yet to begin. Still, he imagined himself shutting an iron door between him and Essie, locking the heart bond deep inside his chest.

Prince Rharreth drew a canteen from his belt and uncapped it. "You should drink."

He held it to Farrendel's mouth, and Farrendel gulped at the cool water, struggling not to choke.

This was not a kindness. If the trolls wished to keep him alive to torture him and use him as bait for Weylind, then they needed to give him enough sustenance to survive. He had no need to fear poison. A quick death from poison was the last thing the trolls would want.

Seeming to judge Farrendel had enough, Prince Rharreth withdrew the canteen, picked up the bowl, and dug out a small crust of bread. He dipped the bread in the broth. This close, Farrendel could tell that the broth was watery with only a few small pieces of vegetable. Hardly palatable, but, at this point, Farrendel did not care.

When Prince Rharreth shoved the crust toward him, Farrendel nearly refused to bite into it. Torture was probably coming. How likely was he to end up vomiting up this meal from the pain?

But he needed food if he was to survive, and he would not feel like eating later.

He tore a bite off with his teeth, the crust hard even with the broth soaking it. He refused to think about the humiliation of lying here, being fed bite by bite. The trolls did not dare loosen his bonds even for him to feed himself.

Concentrate on the things he could do. Right now, he needed to gather information.

As Prince Rharreth's magic was strong, he was the logical choice to check Farrendel's bindings. Yet feeding a prisoner was something that could have been delegated to someone else while Prince Rharreth stood by and watched in case Farrendel caused trouble. But it seemed that the troll prince took his duty to guard Farrendel so seriously that he did not trust anyone else, even to see to Farrendel's basic care.

As Farrendel chewed another bite of the crust, he remembered the way Essie had chatted with their captors, trying to learn as much information as she could.

Farrendel could not manage her effortless chatter, but perhaps he could ask enough questions to gain vital intelligence. Talking to this troll was not as intimidating as talking when Farrendel actually cared about what the other person thought of him.

As the troll dipped the last bite of bread into the bowl, swiping it along the sides to soak up the last of the watery broth, Farrendel took a deep breath and forced himself to speak. "Where am I?"

Prince Rharreth's dark blue eyes flicked to him, searching his face as if contemplating the repercussions of answering. "The fortress of Gror Grar."

Farrendel refused to let that shake him, even though it sent a punch to his gut. Last time he had been captured, he had been held in a cave in the camp of the troll army not far from the border. Even though it had cost his father his life, that raid was a simple matter compared to a rescue from Gror Grar.

He would not be rescued until the war was over. He had known rescue would take time, but marching across Kostaria and taking Gror Grar could take weeks. Maybe months, if the trolls fought Weylind to a stalemate.

His breathing caught, his chest constricting.

No, he refused to give in to the panic. Weylind would not be fighting alone. He would have Averett, Julien, and Edmund and, if Essie's determination could be believed, the might of the Escarlish army. Rescue would come.

He must not have been as successful at hiding his thoughts as he had hoped. Prince Rharreth held the last bite of bread out to him. "Don't hope for rescue. This fortress has stood for a thousand years and never been breached."

Farrendel took the bite and chewed. No, this fortress had never been breached. But the trolls had never faced humans armed with the weapons Escarland now had in their possession. The humans were known for building fortresses, only to have another army come in and bombard that fortress to rubble.

Essie's brothers would figure out a way inside, if anyone could.

Besides, what Prince Rharreth said was only partially true. This fortress had never been breached *by an army*. But Farrendel, by himself, had slipped inside and killed the late troll king.

The defenses had probably been strengthened since then. But it proved that a small group could slip inside, if that was the route Weylind and Essie's brothers decided to go.

Yet, getting in was one thing. Leaving after rescuing Farrendel would be a different matter.

Farrendel swallowed the bite. Now that he had eaten, his stomach grumbled, hungry for more. He ignored it. That was all the troll was likely to give him for the day.

How should he respond to Prince Rharreth? Had the trolls realized yet that Escarland and Tarenhiel would ally to fight Kostaria?

Nothing had been official before Farrendel's capture, and neither the Escarlish traitors nor the elven traitors would have known to report a deepening alliance. If anything, the elven traitors' hatred for humans and the human traitors' hatred for elves would have made them believe Escarland and Tarenhiel would never become allies, and that was what they would have reported to the trolls.

But Essie had promised that she would make sure their brothers worked together to free him. That promise was enough for Farrendel. Escarland and Tarenhiel would fight alongside each other in this war. He was betting his life on it.

Probably best just to change the subject. He had no wish to give away something the trolls did not already know. The point of talking was to gain information, not give it.

"Where is..." Farrendel had to swallow the last of the gritty bread from his mouth. "Where is my sister?"

Did he want to know the answer to this question? The last time he had seen Melantha, she had a knife to her face as Prince Rharreth threatened her. Had she ever been in danger? Or had that just been for show to recapture Farrendel? His mind had still been so hazy and drugged, he was not sure how much had been real and what had been pretense.

How much was she still cooperating with the trolls? She

might hate Farrendel, but surely she would not aid the trolls against Weylind, her full brother, not a half-brother born illegitimately. She had betrayed Farrendel because she believed the trolls' promises of peace for Tarenhiel and because she wanted her family to return to the way it had been. Neither of those things would happen now.

Prince Rharreth eyed Farrendel, his square jaw hard. "You ask after her? After what she did?"

"She is still my sister." Farrendel's chest tightened at Prince Rharreth's evasive answer. "What have you done to her? Is she all right?"

Was she a guest of honor in an opulent suite, plotting with the trolls on how best to torture Farrendel? Or was she the person Prince Rharreth had locked up before coming to Farrendel's cell? What if she was also pinned with stone and suffering?

"If you hurt her..." Farrendel strained against the rock binding him to the floor. What he would not give for even a crackle of his magic.

"You will do what? Assassinate me as you murdered my father?" Prince Rharreth's mouth curled, his face as hard as the stones around them. With his pale gray skin, he looked like he could fade away into the stones of the wall behind him. "You are in no position to make threats."

Farrendel forced himself to lie still. He should not display this much care for her. It would hand the trolls another weapon to use against him. "It seems you are just like your father. He enjoyed torturing helpless victims as well."

Prince Rharreth's eyes flared, and his jaw worked. Gathering the bowl, he stood and brushed off the knees of his trousers, his leather tunic creaking. At the door, he paused and glared over his shoulder at Farrendel. "Enjoy today, elfling. My brother will extract from you the blood of all of our people you have killed soon enough."

Farrendel gritted his teeth, even as the crust of bread and watery broth he had eaten churned in his stomach. Weeks of torture. That was what he was facing.

But not today. The trolls probably intended for him to stew in the darkness and stone and pain to weaken him before they started the torture.

Without another word, Prince Rharreth strode from the cell, and the door slammed shut behind him. His bootsteps marched down the corridor before another door creaked open and shut in the distance.

Quiet descended on the passageway for several long heartbeats. Then, Melantha's voice echoed through the darkness. "Farrendel? Are you there?"

That was Melantha in the other cell. She did not sound like she was in pain.

Should he answer her? What if the trolls had put her down there so that she could attempt to regain his trust? Maybe they thought he would spill Tarenhieli military secrets and planning to his sister.

"Are you all right? Farrendel?" Melantha's voice rose, as if strained with worry.

Was she pretending? Or was that concern real?

No, he could not allow himself to be taken in. Better to believe she still hated him than to fall for her trick again.

Still, it might be worth playing along. Maybe she and the trolls would tip their hand and give Farrendel information or something else he could use.

Besides, it was either lie here unmoving, slowly going insane by himself, or he could converse with Melantha.

"I am fine. They have not hurt me yet, besides the

restraints." Farrendel closed his eyes. Somehow, the darkness was better if it was of his own making. If only he could pretend away the headache and the piercing stone as easily.

"I am sorry."

Sure she was. She was probably just sorry that her treachery had been revealed and she had been forced to come here with the trolls instead of returning to her home in Tarenhiel.

Perhaps he did not want to talk to Melantha after all. He would rather go back to trying to talk to Essie through the elishina and clinging to the hope she gave him.

As the minutes dragged on and he did not respond, Melantha did not try to talk to him again.

He did not need her to keep his sanity and cling to hope. Even if his entire family were to turn on him, he still had Essie and her family. He would have a home in Aldon no matter what. Thanks to Essie, he had plenty of reasons to hope.

Besides, the trolls had made several glaring tactical errors. They had intended to spark a two-front war, a war the elves could not have won with both Escarland and Kostaria armed with Escarlish weapons. It would have been the end of Tarenhiel.

Instead, thanks to all the trolls' machinations, Escarland and Tarenhiel would fight this war united against Kostaria. On their own, the elves of Tarenhiel had never been strong enough to take the fight to the trolls and defeat them once and for all. But with the might of the Escarlish weaponry and numbers on their side, this war could finally be over. No more fighting. No more killing. Freedom to finally dream of a future with Essie.

Not only had the trolls started a war, but they had started a war they could not win.

That made Farrendel's capture the trolls' biggest mistake. His capture would incite and unite all four of his brothers in a way nothing less could have. They would not rest until they had marched their armies all the way to Gror Grar, rescued Farrendel, and utterly defeated the trolls.

He just had to live long enough to be rescued.

E ssie swiped at her face, pushed herself upright, and released her tight mental grip on the heart bond. As much as she wanted to stay curled in bed all day clinging to the connection she had with Farrendel through the heart bond, that wouldn't accomplish anything toward the goal of getting him back.

After taking a long, hot shower, she considered the shelves holding the few clothes she and Farrendel had left behind when they had visited Escarland. She dressed in her own trousers, but she put on the light green tunic of Farrendel's she'd borrowed when she'd first traveled to Estyra. It still smelled like him, like a forest with the minty hint of his shampoo.

There were probably going to be official meetings that afternoon and evening, but she didn't care. It helped to keep something of Farrendel's close, even if her eyes burned with more tears and a lump ached at the back of her throat.

But she had cried enough tears that day. If Farrendel could stay strong and determined while captured, she could do so here in the safety of Ellonahshinel. Besides, she did not want to burden him with her sadness when he was the one facing torture.

After checking that the puffiness had faded from her eyes and the redness from her cheeks, she made her way down the stairs and entered the main room.

There, Edmund and Julien were sitting on some of the cushions, papers and maps spread between them on the floor. Both of them looked up as she entered.

"Did you have a good nap?" Julien's mouth tipped into an attempt at a smile. It faded quickly.

"Yes." She had slept. That was the main thing. She navigated through the mess spread across the floor. "Though I spent more of that time trying to communicate with Farrendel through the heart bond. He's awake, and more aware than he's been for nearly two days. I think they were keeping him drugged or something earlier."

"How is he doing?" Edmund set aside the paper he had been reading.

"Better than I expected. He seems determined to fight through this." Essie sank onto the one cushion not being used by either her brothers or their papers.

Julien rested an elbow on his knee as he leaned forward to better meet her gaze. "He's a fighter, Essie. He'll do what it takes to get back to you. Just keep letting him know that we're coming."

"I already did." She had to swallow back that pesky lump in her throat. She was strong, and she had no choice but to carry on. It was what Farrendel would want her to do. She forced a lighter tone into her voice as she peered at the explosion of paper. "Planning?"

"King Weylind was good enough to send a servant

with some maps and intelligence reports for us to look over. We're due for a meeting in less than an hour." Edmund scribbled something on a paper after consulting a second paper, written in elvish. "Glad you woke up in time. We weren't sure if we should wake you or let you sleep."

"Wake me, if it comes up again." Essie wasn't sure what she would add to the discussions besides act as peacemaker, but she didn't want to miss a single one. Not when Farrendel's life depended on the outcome.

Julien glanced at his pocket watch. "How long do you think it will take us to reach the meeting room? King Weylind said it was somewhere below the library but above the grand hall. Do you know where that is, Essie?"

"I think so. I can at least get us to the general area." Essie had never been called into the meeting room or study or whatever Weylind had to run Tarenhiel. Did elves accumulate the same amount of paperwork that human rulers had to tackle?

But she had passed the general area with its bustle of servants and flurry of courtiers and other activity.

After she helped her brothers pick up all their maps and notes and paperwork that they had already managed to produce in the few hours they had been there, she led the way from the treehouse toward the main part of the elven treetop palace.

Her brothers edged across the branch just as cautiously as before. She would have found it humorous, and she even turned to comment on it, her hand reaching to clasp Farrendel's, before she felt the emptiness beside her.

Farrendel wasn't there to laugh with her over her brothers' hesitation. He wasn't there to make a dry comment about the way she had clung to him on her first time across this branch.

She drew in a breath, willing the pain to stay deep inside her chest. Now was not the time to break. She had promised Farrendel that she would make sure her brothers and his brother worked together to rescue him. She would not let him down.

"This is a rather out of the way set of rooms, isn't it?" Julien's shoulders relaxed as he reached the wider branch.

"Farrendel likes his privacy." Essie refused to feel the stab of pain inside her chest.

"I can see why he took to Buckmore Cottage." Edmund's eyes darted about as they walked deeper into the heart of Ellonahshinel. Before the day was out, Edmund would have a mental map of this palace.

When they reached the section of the tree King Weylind had indicated, it was an easy matter to follow the bustle to the room where the elven king ran Tarenhiel's government.

The room was already filled with King Weylind and a few other elves Essie only vaguely recognized, guessing they were the elf equivalents of generals or military tacticians. More elves lurked by the wall. The scouts, perhaps? Maps were spread out over a long table in the center of the room while a desk with a chair had been grown into the wall. King Weylind's desk, presumably.

"I see the meeting started without us." Edmund grinned and sauntered inside. He set his bundle of papers on the end of the table.

King Weylind glanced up from his hushed consultation and gave both of her brothers one of his dark, disapproving eyebrow looks.

Her brothers were going to have far too much fun

pushing King Weylind's buttons. This was either going to be very entertaining or very frustrating.

Julien spread his own map on the table. "Let's get to it, then. I'm Prince Julien, and this is my brother Prince Edmund. I'm going to be helping with the initial logistics of bringing the Escarlish army into Tarenhiel while Edmund will be joining your scouts."

Two of the elves lurking in the shadows glanced at King Weylind while the last one stared at Edmund.

King Weylind heaved a large sigh, for an elf, and tipped his head in a nod. "That is correct." He gestured toward the three elves in the shadows. "Prince Edmund, these are my top scouts. Your train north leaves tonight."

Edmund nodded and sidled across the room toward the scouts. He was soon in conversation in elvish with them. Two of them seemed like they were fine scouting with a human in tow, but the third elf all but crossed his arms and glared daggers at Edmund.

Oh, well, Edmund could handle himself.

Essie found a seat next to the table as Julien, King Weylind, and his generals started in on the technical discussion. As Julien didn't speak elvish, Essie translated when the elves lapsed into elvish. It seemed at least one of the generals was not as comfortable speaking Escarlish as King Weylind and Farrendel were.

Julien pointed at the map. "I was thinking it would be best to have the Escarlish army set up multiple camps along here away from the border. I don't think we should muster the full force of our armies at the border until we are ready to attack. We might as well not give away that we are allies until the last possible moment. Even if Kostaria learns Tarenhiel and Escarland have become allies, they may assume we would never work this closely together."

One of the generals crossed his arms. "A valid assumption."

Essie winced. No one knew exactly how it would go once they brought the Escarlish army into Tarenhiel. Fifteen years ago, the Escarlish army had fought long and hard along the Hydalla River only to fail to gain so much as a toehold in Tarenhiel. The Tarenhieli army had fought just as hard to keep them out. It would be strange for everybody, to suddenly be inviting the Escarlish army into Tarenhiel and trying to work together.

"Exactly. By spreading out the army, I believe we can minimize the strain on your infrastructure, though it will mean much of your northern forests will feel the Escarlish presence." Julien glanced from King Weylind to the elven generals.

King Weylind frowned. "We will not allow your army to roam our forests at will."

"We don't expect you to. We'll muster into orderly camps and our commanders will be expected to maintain strict discipline. There will still be incidents. There always are, even when the Escarlish army is inside Escarland. But the accelerated pace of this war will keep the men from becoming too restless." Julien drew in a deep breath. "Besides, my brother Averett and I would like to propose that you station divisions of your elven army alongside our divisions to begin the process of intermingling the two armies."

Essie straightened in her seat. She hadn't heard this part of the plan yet.

King Weylind stiffened. "Intermingling? So that you can

divide our armies and weaken us before an ambush inside our own borders?"

Julien crossed his arms. "We have a treaty. We are not going to ambush our own allies."

King Weylind met Julien's gaze. "This plan would give you that opportunity, if you wished it."

"We do not." Julien didn't look away. "And Averett will keep in line those that might."

"It would be a foolish choice to attempt such an ambush. Your armies would be scattered and weakened as well." One of the elven generals glanced from King Weylind to Julien. "But I do not know why you wish to attempt such integration. Your armies will be under your command while our armies will be under our command. We will settle on a strategy together, but we will fight under our own kingdoms' banners."

"That's true. But, I do believe integrating the two armies will be our best chance for victory." Julien gestured around them. "Each of our armies has strengths that can balance the other's weaknesses. Escarland's army has devastating firepower and weapons unlike anything you have seen before. We can provide long distance fighting beyond what you can accomplish with your archers. Escarland's army, however, does not have the magical abilities that your armies have. We need your warriors to provide the countermeasures to the trolls' magical attacks. You are also the better close combat fighters, though we have the advantage of numbers."

"I see." The general nodded, but the set of his mouth didn't soften. "But do you believe it is necessary to begin integrating now? Our peoples were at war not that long ago.

Fighting may break out among our peoples if they are stationed too closely together."

"That's actually the other reason I believe we should begin having our soldiers interact now. They won't work together on the battlefield as a team if that old hatred lingers. Our armies need to train together. They need to learn to depend on each other and trust each other enough to go to battle together. It will be rough. There probably will be a lot of internal fighting that the commanders will have to deal with. But better we get all that internal fighting out of the way before we are in a battle for our lives in Kostaria." Julien glanced between the two elves, then gestured at Essie. "We just need to give them a reason to rally."

Essie wasn't sure if she should smile or blink away tears or what. Right now, she just felt too numb. What sort of expression should she wear as the human princess missing her elf prince? How should she look when trying to rally both peoples to get Farrendel back?

ESSIE GLANCED around the table in the royal dining room. In some ways, this wasn't much different from her first time dining with her new elven family. The vaulted ceiling of the dining room soared, held up by pillars made of living branches. The long table filled the center of the room while the elven servants set the plates before them in serene efficiency.

But in many ways, this time was very much different. Not Farrendel's absence. He had been absent during her first dinner with his family.

This time, Farrendel wasn't the only one missing. Jalissa

was missing, still in Escarland. Melantha was also missing, and her empty seat made everyone shift awkwardly and talk around her absence. Perhaps it would have been better if they had filled that seat or moved it or something.

Beyond Melantha and Farrendel missing, Edmund and Julien sat in two of the seats at the end of the table near Essie. Julien conversed with Ryfon on Escarlish military techniques while Edmund chatted with Brina about Escarlish cities.

It was the most conversation this table had probably seen in a long time. Before Essie had left, Ryfon and Brina had barely begun to open up to her after the troll ambush near Lethorel. But now, it seemed King Weylind's somewhat more welcoming attitude—and the deepening ties with Escarland—had relaxed the tension.

Perhaps Essie and her brothers felt safe compared to the betrayal that had ripped apart the elven royal family.

Essie picked at her food and tried to participate in the conversation between Queen Rheva and Farrendel's grand-mother Leyleira.

Eventually, Queen Rheva joined Brina and Edmund's conversation while King Weylind joined Ryfon and Julien.

Leyleira turned to better face Essie. Due to all the missing family members, Essie had somehow ended up next to Leyleira.

With a soft smile, Leyleira patted Essie's hands. "How are you holding up?"

"As well as can be expected." Essie forced herself to smile. Leyleira had always been kind to her, even though her words often felt like a test. What would Leyleira read into Essie's words and expression this time?

A flare of pain shot through Essie's chest. She gasped, but the pain faded quickly. Farrendel again?

Leyleira's gaze studied her. "Anything you wish to ask?"

What did Leyleira want her to ask? Or expect her to ask?

There was one thing...Essie hadn't been sure who to ask about the heart bond. But surely Leyleira would know, if anybody would. "How much will Farrendel be able to sense through the heart bond? I know it connects us, but besides the explanation of how it forms and how I saved Farrendel's life with it, I don't know much about it. No one really seems to talk about what having a heart bond is like. Farrendel and I have talked about it, and I know he feels it differently than I do, and I don't know if all elves feel it like that or..." Essie swallowed back her nervous chattering. "Or, well, I don't know. How much can he feel?"

Leyleira's mouth twitched with something almost like a smile, though it faded quickly. Good. At least Essie had asked the right question. Leyleira glanced around the table, everyone else still distracted with conversation, before she turned to Essie. "We elves do not often discuss our elishinas publicly. Often not even with close family. An elishina is considered something private."

Essie suppressed a sigh. This was another one of those elven propriety things. Seriously, it was amazing the elves managed to actually reproduce, considering all their rules of propriety.

Leyleira's hint of a smile was back. "Unless, of course, that elishina becomes as obvious as yours and Farrendel's. Then everyone talks about it unabashedly. I do not know what it is about elishinas between humans and elves that capture our imaginations so."

The elves' greatest love story was of a human, Daesyn,

and the elf princess Inara, who formed a heart bond that kept Daesyn alive when he should have died, much as Essie had kept Farrendel alive after that troll ambush.

"So glad we can provide plenty of gossip for the elven court." Essie grimaced and rubbed her chest. The magic of the heart bond, normally so warm with the sense of Farrendel, had gone cold. It was still there. Not empty as it would be if Farrendel had died. But like an iron wall had been put up between them.

What did it mean? What was happening to Farrendel?

"Not gossip. An inspiration. The stuff of legends and stories." Leyleira's deep brown eyes were soft, the gray streak in her dark brown hair giving her bearing a regal wisdom. "As to your questions, every elishina is different. Some manifest as simply a bonding without any particular strength and magic, perhaps because they have never been tested. Others, like yours and Farrendel's, are incredibly strong."

Essie swallowed, that iron wall still in her chest. "Jalissa said that Farrendel's father and the late queen shared a heart bond."

The faintest hint of lines crinkled around Leyleira's eyes and mouth. "Yes, they did indeed."

And, if Essie were to guess right, Leyleira had shared one with her late husband, though she probably wouldn't talk about that one.

Weylind cleared his throat, turning toward them. His dark eyes focused on his plate, the line of his jaw hard. "He felt it, that day, when she died. She was not killed instantly."

"She wasn't?" Essie hadn't heard the details of how the late elf queen had been killed. Farrendel didn't talk about her much. Understandable, as she wasn't his mother, and the late queen's death had been the start of the cracks that tore the family apart.

Still, it was unexpected that Weylind would bring it up. He was not the most forthcoming of her elven family members, and this was his mother he was talking about.

Leyleira's eyes saddened. "Lorsan had not been with her that day. She had gone ahead, visiting with distant cousins of hers who lived near the border with Kostaria. Lorsan planned to join her in a few days. When her party was ambushed, Lorsan felt her pain, until she cut off the heart bond. For the rest of his life, Lorsan carried the guilt that he failed to save her, even though there was nothing he could do. I believe it is one reason why he mourned so hard and so deeply for her."

The late elf king had mourned his wife so desperately that it had eventually led him to seek solace and a single night of forgetfulness with Farrendel's mother.

"I think...I think Farrendel might be doing something like that right now. I don't know. The heart bond doesn't feel as warm and vibrant as it normally does." Essie rubbed at her chest again. "But what did you mean that he felt he failed? Was there something he could have done?"

Was there something she could do to help Farrendel?

Lines dug into the corners around Weylind's eyes, making him appear older than Essie had ever seen him. "It is possible that, when one person in a heart bond is killed, the other can also die if they try to save them. There are times death is inevitable."

Leyleira raised an eyebrow at Weylind, something in her tone firm. "Have I taught you nothing? You are supposed to comfort her, not frighten her."

"She should know the dangers. It is her life at risk, as well as Farrendel's." Weylind crossed his arms.

"Do you really believe Farrendel will allow anything to happen to her?" Leyleira reached out and patted Essie's arm. "Farrendel is strong, my dear. Do not give up hope."

"My parents were strong too." Weylind's words were murmured, so low Essie wasn't sure they were meant for her.

Essie's fingers went cold. The heart bond had always seemed like such a good thing. But it had dangers, especially with Farrendel in the hands of the trolls who hated him.

She had saved his life during that ambush. Had that really been less than two weeks ago? So much had happened since then.

She had so naively saved him with that heart bond. If the healers hadn't been there to stabilize Farrendel, what would have happened? Would she have let go in time to keep from dying along with him? Or would he have been aware enough to save her by severing the bond that made her heart keep his heart beating?

Let the sacrifice be my choice this time. That's what Farrendel had told her on the train when they'd been captured. He didn't want anyone to be killed trying to rescue him. That would include Essie trying to save him through a heart bond.

If it came to it, Essie would be hard pressed not to at least attempt to save him, even if she didn't want to die. She didn't want to lose him. It would gut her.

But she also didn't want to make her family grieve both her loss and Farrendel's. And his family would need her to be there for them after all the losses they had already sustained.

But it wouldn't come to that. It wouldn't. Farrendel would pull through this. They would rescue him, and everything would be fine.

Except that Farrendel was already blocking her. Yet, Essie didn't think he was dying. Surely she would sense if he was dying.

Was he trying to spare her the pain he was feeling? Was he already undergoing torture?

The little she had managed to eat churned in her stomach. She didn't want to think about the torture he must be enduring. Here she sat eating a fine meal, safe in Ellonahshinel, while he was suffering enough pain to feel the need to keep it from her.

Essie pulled her shoulders straighter. "It won't come to that. I'm sure of it. Farrendel will pull through this. We'll get to him in time."

She refused to doubt that. Would Farrendel feel it through the heart bond if doubt took hold and her hope wavered? For his sake, as much as for her own, she could not give up hope.

Leyleira nodded and made a small gesture to the others in the room. "With humans and elves working together as they have not done in centuries, I am certain this war will be nothing like the trolls expect."

Essie glanced back at the others. Her brothers were still animatedly talking as the elves listened. Edmund caught her eye and gave her a subtle wink. Yes, they were doing their best to ingratiate themselves to the elves. Either that, or they were going to talk the elves to the brink of insanity. But if Essie hadn't managed to do that yet, Julien and Edmund combined wouldn't manage it.

She turned back to Leyleira. "Now about my original question…"

"Yes." Leyleira's smile was both soft but also a touch knowing, as if Essie's impatient prompting was what she had been angling for all along. "With my Ellarin, I could sense impressions. I would know if he was thinking about me or sending thoughts my way, even if it was more a sense than actual words. No matter where he was, I could always feel him there."

Essie sighed and rubbed at the woodgrain of the table-top. That was pretty much what she felt, though hers was less a constant presence in her chest than what it sounded like the elves experienced. "I guess actual telepathy would have made things far too easy. I just wish I could talk to him."

"Then do so. He may not be able to understand the words through the heart bond, but he will sense you are thinking about him. Maybe an impression of the words will carry through." Leyleira's smile faded once again. "Perhaps it is a hope he desperately needs."

Essie nodded and gazed around the table once again. *Farrendel, you would've loved to see this.*

SEVEN

Melantha huddled against the back of the cold, stone cell, pressing her hands over her ears. Tears filled her eyes, even as the stone pounded a headache behind her temples.

Shouts of pain echoed from somewhere down the dungeon's passageway.

Farrendel. They were torturing Farrendel.

What had she expected when she had betrayed him to the trolls? She had been so angry for so long. It had been easy to direct that anger at him, to focus on how much better life would be once the scandal of his existence was wiped from her family's life.

Yet, sitting here now, all those reasons were ripped away in the reality of what her betrayal meant and would cost. She had never truly wanted this.

Another scream of pain, then silence. Had Farrendel passed out? Had they killed him?

What had she done? How could she have done this? She

pulled her knees to her chest, gasping at the force of the sobs that begged for release.

She must not cry. An elven princess did not indulge in such hysterics.

But that was her little brother being tortured. And she had been the one to put him there.

Boots tromped past her cell. She stifled her mouth against her folded arms, muffling her sobs. She could not allow these trolls to see or hear her emotions.

The footsteps faded down the passageway. The silence stretched for far too long.

Melantha pushed to her feet, approached the door, and peered through the bars. Torches provided weak light for the passageway, either side lined with dungeon cells just like hers with one cell at the far end. That was the one where she suspected Farrendel was being held. "Farrendel?"

She waited a long moment, but he did not answer her. Was he ignoring her? Or was he still unconscious? As the trolls had not carted a body past her door, he must be still alive.

Melantha sank to the ground by the door, her fists clenched. Her chest burned, and she longed to lash out and punch something. A door. A wall. One of the trolls who had been torturing Farrendel.

But an elven princess did not display that much emotion. Instead, she just simmered in constant, unrelenting anger with no way to release it.

The door into the dungeon grated. Melantha scrambled to her feet, peering from the window of her cell.

Prince Rharreth strode down the passageway once again. He halted outside her cell's door. "Step away from the door."

Melantha backed away from the door, clenching her fingers into fists. It would be so satisfying to spring at him and claw his eyes out. For one moment, she let herself indulge in such thoughts.

But only for a moment. Then she huffed a breath and wrapped her arms over her stomach, her shoulders hunched.

The door grated, and Prince Rharreth stepped inside. He carried a bowl in one hand and a knife in the other. He did not bother to close the door behind him. As much as Melantha wished she could dart past him and escape, it was impossible.

If only she could use her magic to attempt an escape. She felt the faint threads of her magic coursing through her. Her head ached from the stone, but she was not as cut off from her magic as Farrendel was.

Her magic was not crackling and destructive the way Farrendel's was. Nor could she control plants the way Weylind and Jalissa could.

Melantha had healing magic. Long ago, when she had trained with the best healer in Estyra, she had taken an oath never to use that power to harm anyone. Healing magic, after all, could just as easily be turned to killing magic.

The elven oath was a magical one, and the stories said that any healer who broke their oath of healing to harm another would die.

Yet, was this circumstance dire enough that she should risk breaking that oath? Should she turn her magic on this troll and attempt to escape, assuming she did not die or become too injured to move?

No, before she did that, she needed to find out how they had Farrendel secured and if there was a way she could break him out. She might have put him here, but she had no intention of leaving here without him. Not after listening to his screams.

Prince Rharreth eyed her, as if trying to decide if she was going to bolt. Nodding, as if satisfied, he held out the bowl.

She did not take it. "What have you done to my brother? Is he still alive?"

His brows shot up. "Now you are concerned about him?"

He had a right to question her rapid change of heart. But being locked up provided ample time for self-reflection. More than that, how many screams did it take for a person to realize what a horrible sister she was and what terrible mistakes she had made?

She had never truly been angry at Farrendel. She could see that now. Over the years, he had simply become the convenient target for all the anger she had bottled up inside. Now that she had other targets—namely, this troll prince before her and his torture-happy brother—her anger at Farrendel had disappeared.

Even now, heat simmered in her chest. It was so tempting to stand there and scream until she no longer shook with the force of everything she kept inside.

Instead, Melantha clenched her fists and stared Prince Rharreth down. She did not have to explain herself to him of all people.

He snorted and set the bowl of watery soup on the floor. "He asked about you. After everything you did to him."

Even though he had just come from helping his brother torture Farrendel, Prince Rharreth was looking at her as if she was the disgusting, villainous one of the two of them.

"Please. Take me to him. I can heal him." Melantha stepped forward, her fists still clenched. If only she could just blast her power down the corridor and heal Farrendel from a distance without having to beg for this troll's mercy for Farrendel. But she had to be touching a patient to use her magic.

"Why would I allow you near a prisoner you wished dead not long ago?" Prince Rharreth eyed her and crossed his arms.

"I would not…" She trailed off. She had betrayed Farrendel to this. What else had she expected?

And yet, now that she was here, she could not stand by and listen to his screams without being moved. She was not so cold, so angry, so hateful that she could not have all her delusions stripped away beneath a cold dousing of reality.

She had done wrong. Very, very wrong. She could not undo it. But, perhaps, she could do something to make it better, even if she could not make it right. "I could not. My healer's oath would prevent me from harming him, even should I wish it, which I do not."

Prince Rharreth shook his head, his eyes cold. "Eat your supper."

He spun on his heel and left her cell, the door slamming shut behind him, the lock clanking into place.

Melantha tiptoed across her cell and peered through the bars. The barred door at the entrance clanked shut behind the troll prince. At the far end, no noise came from the direction of Farrendel's cell. Was he unconscious? The troll prince had implied Farrendel was still alive. It seemed a quick death was not in the trolls' plan.

She sank down against the door to her cell and picked up the watery broth. It had gone cold, sitting on the floor of her cell. She forced herself to drink it anyway, sopping it up with the crust of bread that had been stuck on the bowl's rim.

When she finished, she rested her head on her hands. What a mess she had made. Of her own life. Of Farrendel's life. Why had she ever let herself be convinced that this course was the right one?

Nothing in her life had been right from the moment her mother died. Melantha had mourned, but then...then she had been angry.

Angry with the trolls for killing her mother. Angry at her father for falling apart as he mourned, instead of dealing with the grief the way she and Weylind had been forced to do. Angry that her father's betrayal of her mother's memory had ended with the scandal of an illegitimate brother abandoned on their doorstep. Angry with her betrothed for leaving her at the first sign of scandal, showing how little he had truly cared about her. Angry with the trolls for taking her father from her too. Angry with her father for dying and leaving them. Angry with Farrendel for being so...Farrendel. Broken and scarred and possessing such deadly magic that made him both revered and disdained. Angry that he had made everything worse by marrying that human princess, even if it was in the name of peace.

So much anger. It would burn a hole through her chest if she let it.

She buried her face in her arms and, for once in her life, she gave in to the urge and vented her anger in a muffled scream.

EIGHT

E ssie sat in a corner of the meeting room, listening as Edmund and the elven scouts outlined what they had learned. Judging by the way all of them alternated in their telling, with Edmund throwing in a few laughing jokes along the way, he had gained the trust and even friendship of the elven scouts.

She shouldn't have worried about him. Edmund could charm his way into anywhere, even as he cataloged the layout, defenses, and weaknesses at a glance.

From Edmund's report, King Weylind, Julien, and Edmund moved on to discuss the progress on the Tarenhieli transportation system. With Thanfardil, the elf in charge of the train system of Tarenhiel, revealed as a traitor and found dead at the border, the elves' transportation system had been in a bit of chaos. All of Thanfardil's underlings had been temporarily suspended as the elves sorted through those who were loyal and those who weren't.

As she sat and listened, she thought all of that in Farrendel's direction. Perhaps she shouldn't. If he could understand her words, then she was giving him information the trolls would torture him to obtain, if they realized he had it.

But she didn't think he felt any more than the impressions she sensed. Hopefully the sense of planning would be enough to give him hope.

He needed it. He'd been slamming that iron wall between them in the heart bond more frequently over the past day.

A whoosh signaled the door to the meeting room gliding open. Essie didn't bother glancing over her shoulder. It was probably yet another elf scout or elf army officer bringing another report to add to this meeting.

Hands settled on her shoulders. "What did I miss?"

"Avie!" Essie shot to her feet, spun, and flung herself into Averett's hug. "It's only been three days. How did you get here so quickly? I thought it would take at least a week for Parliament to ratify the new treaty, authorize going to war, and prepare the army."

Averett's mouth tipped into a smile. "I am the king. When I want something to get done, it happens."

"Oh, yes. Because playing the king card has worked so well with Parliament before." Essie shook her head and gave another squeal and hugged him yet again. "I'm just so glad you're here."

"Are you not happy to see me?"

Only when she spoke did Essie finally notice that Jalissa had entered the room behind Averett. Essie waved a hand over Averett's shoulder. "Yes. I'm so happy to see both of you."

"So I gathered." Averett chuckled and turned her to face the rest of the room. Edmund and Julien were both smirking, while all the elven generals and scouts were giving her various versions of the raised eyebrow, scandalized look she got far too often from the elves. Weylind, however, looked like he was trying to suppress a smile, even as he gave her his own raised eyebrow.

"Oh, right." Essie gave the entire room a wry smile. Apparently shrieking loudly was a good way to interrupt a tactical meeting. "As you can see, my brother, King Averett of Escarland, has arrived."

Averett patted her shoulder one last time, then stepped forward. "My army is mustered at the border and just awaits word that Tarenhiel is ready to host us."

Weylind tipped his head in a nod. "We are ready, though a few of the preparations will take a few more days. You are here earlier than expected."

Somehow, Weylind managed to sound mildly affronted. As if Averett arriving early was a bad thing.

Essie resisted the urge to roll her eyes. Elves.

Averett strolled forward and worked his way between Julien and Weylind to stand next to the table. "After one of their own turned out to be a traitor, Parliament was rather motivated to cooperate. Charles Hadley's testimony decrying his own son's traitorous activities and listing the number of weapons given to the trolls turned out to be particularly compelling. And the army has been prepared to rally at the border in case of an elven invasion for the past twenty years. It was simple to revise the plan to a peaceful march across Tarenhiel."

Essie wormed between all the elven warriors to find a place next to Edmund. Now that Averett was here, the plans could go from mere plans to actual action.

Averett nodded to Weylind. "It will take time to gather

enough steamboats and elven ships to shuttle all of my army and supplies across, but we might as well start the process. I, for one, do not want to delay."

"Nor do I." Weylind clenched his fists and glanced at Essie.

Essie pressed her hand over her chest. The iron wall was still up, but at least that meant Farrendel was still alive.

For now.

ESSIE STEPPED from the train into the bustle of an army camp, following King Weylind. Spread out between the massive tree trunks were rows upon rows of Escarlish army tents made from a dull brown canvas. In a small clearing before the train's stop, several officers oversaw a group of soldiers drilling, their muskets clacking first against their shoulders, then into their palms as they moved between positions.

It was impressive, especially considering this was only one of several regiments camped in the deep forest below the Tarenhieli-Kostarian border.

Essie adjusted the rifle hanging from its strap across her back and eased to the side to give Averett room to disembark.

Weylind halted at the edge of the train platform, a moss-covered mound of dirt several feet higher than the surrounding forest floor. His mouth flattened as he surveyed the encampment.

Essie halted next to him. "It must be a strange sight, seeing the Escarlish army camped in your kingdom. Your armies fought hard to keep the Escarlish army out of your kingdom fifteen years ago."

Weylind's shoulders lifted with a deep breath. "It is a disconcerting sight. But necessary."

For Farrendel's sake, Weylind was willing to go to great lengths. Essie would have hugged him, but he probably wouldn't appreciate it.

Averett halted on Weylind's other side. "We are allies. I know this isn't a comfortable alliance yet, but we're getting there. By the time this war is over, we're going to get so used to fighting alongside each other that it will be inconceivable to fight against one another."

Weylind raised an eyebrow, as if he didn't believe that. But he did not bother contradicting Averett either. That was progress, perhaps.

As the servants unloaded the few belongings they had taken along, Essie surveyed the camp again. Several large tents had been set up near one of the largest trees. The command tents, and royal tents for Essie and her brothers.

It seemed strange to sleep in a tent here in Tarenhiel. She glanced upward, scanning the lower branches of the trees. She didn't see any of the elven treehouses here, though that was not surprising. They had picked largely uninhabited areas of northern Tarenhiel for the three large encampments and their surrounding smaller camps. It would be hard enough keeping the peace between the Escarlish soldiers and the elven warriors. They didn't want to risk any incidents with local citizens.

Would the elven army grow temporary shelters once they arrived? If they did, she might request one for herself.

Behind them, the train pulled away from the station, on its way to whatever the elves used to turn their trains around to send it down the parallel track back to Estyra.

Averett hefted the small bag of personal items he'd taken

with him on the train. "Let's get settled in. I believe the next train is due in about an hour."

The next train would be carrying the first of the elven army assigned to this encampment. Everyone would be mustered with all due pomp and circumstance then.

Essie nodded but hesitated, glancing at Weylind. Besides the few elven servants and the lone guard who had come with them on the train, Weylind was one of the few elves there. A stranger inside his own kingdom right now. "You are welcome to take your ease in our tents, Your Majesty, until your army arrives."

Weylind glanced at the tents, his lips pressing even tighter together.

Something in his stance reminded her of Farrendel. At times, Weylind could be just as shy and reticent as his younger brother. He had just gotten better at hiding it over the years.

After a moment, Weylind shook his head. "I believe I will begin growing my quarters."

"Then I guess we might as well walk in the same direction." Essie took a step, then turned back to him when he didn't follow. She pointed at the large trees that sheltered the Escarlish command tents. "I'm assuming you're going to be camping out in the trees above Averett's tent. A show of solidarity among the leaders, or something like that. Also, it would probably be safer for both concerned if Averett's tent was the one at the base of your tree and your quarters were above his tent. Not to mention easier to fetch both of you in case an incident does break out."

Weylind eyed her, glanced around as if searching for Farrendel to fob her and all her talking off on him, then sighed. "Very well."

She wasn't sure if she had won him over through her logic or if he simply agreed to halt the flow of her words. Either way, she had gotten him moving in the right direction rather than frozen on the train platform gawking at the Escarlish army camped within his borders.

As they strode from the platform toward the command tents, several of the Escarlish soldiers bustling about halted to gape at King Weylind. Thankfully, none seemed too hostile. Just curious and in awe of the elven king striding through their midst.

Essie could barely wait for the first of the elven army to arrive. An army of elves was bound to be impressive all on its own, but if she had learned anything about elves in the past few months, it was that they were not above making a grand entrance when it suited them. She suspected their arrival at the Escarlish encampment would be one of those times.

Weylind made a soft, throat-clearing noise. "Is Farrendel still..."

"Alive." The sense of the heart bond was nearly a constant presence in her chest now. Was this what the heart bond had always felt like to Farrendel? "But..."

Essie rubbed her chest. For the past few days, she had felt the way he was slipping away from her. He was dying. Not physically, though she could tell he was in pain. No, this was his mind and heart slowly dying, hardening. No matter how much encouragement she sent his way, he was turning cold. As cold as he'd been the day she'd met him.

The iron wall slammed shut between them. Essie winced and caught her breath. She suspected Farrendel blocked her whenever he was being tortured. Just because she couldn't feel his pain didn't make it that much easier knowing every time he was suffering.

Weylind halted and turned to her. "Is something wrong? You have gone pale. Should I call for a healer?"

Essie grimaced and leaned against the nearest tree. How much should she tell Weylind? Though, he might understand more than her brothers would. "I'm getting better at sensing Farrendel though the heart bond. He's figured out how to block me when he's being tortured, but it still means I know when it's happening."

"They are torturing him right now, are they not?" Lines grooved deep into Weylind's face. His fingers fisted, and deep green magic swirled down his arms. The grass around his feet grew several inches.

"Yes." Essie swallowed and wrapped her arms over her stomach. She was normally the overly optimistic one. She could find a silver lining in anything.

But how could she find a silver lining in Farrendel's torture? All she wanted to do was rescue him as quickly as possible and end his suffering.

"I see." Weylind nodded and swept his gaze over the sprawling encampment once again. He straightened his shoulders. "We will rescue him, isciena."

Essie nodded, also taking in the bustle of the Escarlish soldiers setting up camp.

Farrendel was the reason Weylind was even allowing the Escarlish army in Tarenhiel. Perhaps they could have formed an alliance against the trolls if Farrendel hadn't been captured. But it wouldn't have looked like this. Because of Farrendel, Weylind was willing to risk far more than he would have considered any other way.

Farrendel, I hope you know just how much your capture has deepened this alliance.

If there was a silver lining in his capture, this was it. The Tarenhieli-Escarlish alliance would not have made this much progress without it.

As Weylind wandered off to select his tree for his shelter, Essie located her tent, made of deep green canvas with the royal standard flying above it. Inside, a rug covered the lush grass with a cot along the back wall, a small wood-burning stove set in the center with a pipe going through a hole in the ceiling, and a trunk with her things had been set along the sloped wall by the end of the cot.

Essie set her bag on the cot. The tent appeared empty and lonely. She pressed a hand to her chest, even if the iron wall remained between her and Farrendel. As long as she had the heart bond, she wasn't entirely alone.

An hour later, Essie stood at the edge of the train platform next to Averett with King Weylind standing on Averett's other side and several of Escarland's generals standing next to her. Behind them, this division of Escarland's army stood in stiff rows, awaiting the arrival of the elven army.

Essie blew out a long breath, trying to ease the tightness in her stomach and chest. Why was she so nervous? Everything was going to be fine. The soldiers on both sides were disciplined enough that they weren't going to just break out in fighting.

That still didn't stop her nerves. This moment needed to go just right. It would set the tone for the entire alliance and war. If all went well, the other elven armies would start arriving at the other two main encampments tomorrow.

Essie shook herself and refocused on the train tracks. Was that a blur of silver glinting far off in the trees?

Moments later, the silver elven train glided into view, easing to a stop alongside the platform.

Essie pasted on her smile and swiped her hands on her trousers yet again.

The doors on the train cars opened, and the first of the elven warriors marched from the train. Polished armor winked in the sunlight while oiled leather shone between the pieces of armor. Bows and quivers full of arrows stuck out over shoulders while some of the elves wore short, curving swords on their backs and others had longer swords strapped to their waists.

As they marched from the train, the warriors stepped to the side and lined up in precise rows in the cleared space facing the Escarlish army. All of them wore identical, serene expressions.

Essie caught her breath as the tall, graceful warriors continued to march from the train. There was a deadly beauty to the way the elven warriors moved, their long hair flowing over their shoulders and down their backs.

While she had seen Farrendel leave for war, she had never seen him fully battle ready. Every time she had seen him fight, it had been during ambushes when he was not wearing his full armor. He must be an impressive sight when going into battle.

She did her best to try to send an image of what she was thinking to him. All she got was a puzzled feeling. Guess her imagination didn't exactly translate across the heart bond.

When the last elven warrior stepped from the train, Averett and Weylind strode forward so that they stood between the two armies facing each other.

Averett gestured. "I know this is an unusual sight. Our two kingdoms were enemies not that long ago. Yet today, we are allies. From this day forward, we will fight alongside each other, and we will claim victory together."

Weylind waved back and forth and repeated the speech in elvish. He must have added to the speech because after several minutes, he switched to Escarlish. "When my brother married an Escarlish princess, I was doubtful such a union would promote anything besides more bitterness. Instead, their union has drawn our two kingdoms together. They proved that we do not have to be enemies. Through this war, our alliance will be tested. But it is my hope that it will prove as strong and enduring as the love my brother has formed with his princess."

Essie smiled and gave a little wave as some of the Escarlish soldiers gave a cheer. The elven warriors didn't so much as twitch.

It was a good sign the Escarlish soldiers were cheering the elven king. Surely his own soldiers were cheering internally, even if they didn't show any outward emotion.

Seeing the two armies together gave Essie hope. Not just that they would get Farrendel back, but that they would get him back as quickly as possible.

F arrendel closed his eyes, the better to block out his
pounding head, his aching body.

Essie was chattering again.

He could not tell what she was saying, but he knew that,
somewhere far away, she was talking to him. If he held still
and closed his eyes, he could almost imagine they were back
in their rooms in Estyra, the moonlight streaming through
the windows as they sat on the cushions on the floor. Her
head resting on his shoulder, her hand in his, as she sleepily
chattered about nothing and everything until the words
silenced into deep breathing.

And yet, even as she chattered and he strained to
remember the feel of her at his side, her presence became
more distant, more dreamlike, by the day.

Five days. That was how long he had been captured, as
near as he could figure. Time lost all meaning, with no
sunlight, no way to track its passing besides the daily visits
of the troll prince bringing food and water and the troll king
bringing torture.

Five days. That was how long he had been captured last time. Five days, with rescue on the sixth night.

A part of him almost believed he had never been rescued. That the last fifteen years of his life had been nothing but the fevered dream of a mind long tortured.

Yet, his father's death had been all too real. The blood on Farrendel's hands could not be dreamed away.

And Essie was real. Even without the heart bond existing, warm and taunting him with the life now out of his reach, he would know she was real. Because he never would have dreamed a talkative human princess with her flaming red hair and freckles. He did not have enough of an imagination to have conjured her.

She was real. But so very far away. A wisp slipping from his grasp with each passing day.

But, perhaps, he never had truly escaped. He had returned again and again in his nightmares. The nightmare had just become reality.

Five days. And so many more to go before he could even begin to hope for rescue.

Would there be a rescue? Even if Weylind and Essie's brothers rallied the armies of Tarenhiel and Escarland and the armies cooperated together enough to fight a war, would the trolls let him live long enough for rescue a second time?

No matter. Essie was out of their reach. Even if that meant she was out of his reach as well. Not that she would recognize him now.

"Farrendel? Are you awake? Are you all right?" Melantha's voice echoed down the passageway. "Farrendel?"

She had taken to calling out to him every hour or so. Occasionally he would respond. Most of the time he did not.

Farrendel clenched his fists and ground his teeth. "I am alive, if that is what you are asking."

The longer he was here, the more torture he endured, he began to understand how it was possible to hate a sibling.

Melantha had to be working with the trolls. Even though they had used her to recapture him, they had not used her since. They had not threatened to torture her and had not tortured him with her screams. If she had been spared, it could only mean that she was working with them or had somehow bargained for her safety at his expense.

Something rattled, then clanked down the hall. Two sets of boots tromped closer across the stone.

His eyes snapped open, even as he let a hard, savage strength flow into his muscles. With a swift thought, he slammed an iron door on the heart bond, locking away Essie's chatter and cutting her off from what was to come.

The door to Farrendel's cell opened, and King Charvod marched inside, his carved, antler crown resting on his forehead. His short-cropped white hair gleamed in the torchlight while his gray skin was the same color as the stones behind him. His dark blue eyes burned.

Prince Rharreth shut the door behind him and leaned against the wall. Ever the observer. He never participated in the torture himself, but he never stopped it either.

The troll king halted next to Farrendel, his boots inches from Farrendel's ribs as he loomed over him as if trying to make him feel small and vulnerable.

It would not work. Such feelings had died days ago.

Farrendel bared his teeth and glared. What he would not give for a sword in his hand and magic crackling over his fingertips.

King Charvod slammed his boot into Farrendel's ribs. "It

has been five whole days. Why has your brother not attacked yet? What is he waiting for?"

Pain flared along Farrendel's ribs, but not enough to even draw a moan from him. A kick was hardly considered pain at this point.

Of course, King Charvod would expect Weylind to have attacked by now. A quick rally of the army. An attempt at a swift rescue. A repeat of last time, down to its deadly end and a fallen elven king.

But King Charvod had revealed his hand too soon, and now he no longer had spies in either Escarland or Tarenhiel to tell him what was happening. As Jalissa, and not Melantha, had been the sister sent to Escarland, King Charvod had no way to know how much Essie's family had embraced Farrendel, nor how willing Essie's brother Averett was to go to war to help Tarenhiel.

Farrendel might have worried about the delay, but he had the heart bond. He had felt the way Essie had gone from grief to determination to chattering hope. Surely she would not seem so lively, so hopeful, if the alliance between their brothers was not going well.

No, this delay was not something for him to fret over. It meant Weylind was wisely waiting for Averett to gather Escarland's army so that together they could assault Kostaria. Would the combined forces be enough to carry them all the way to Gror Grar itself?

"Answer me!" King Charvod knelt and rested a hand on the stone floor, though he did not yet unleash his magic. "If you don't, I will break you."

Farrendel stared back. Then, of all things, he laughed.

Not a laugh of happiness or joy. He had forgotten how to do that kind of laugh decades ago. No, this was a laugh of hatred and wry contempt, filled with knowing what the troll king did not.

He could not break what was already broken.

That was something no one truly understood. Not even Essie had realized the truth.

Farrendel had not broken from the torture the last time he had been captured. Back then, just as he did now, he had the hope of rescue. He had clung to it with all the innocence of a boy whose father had never failed him.

He had hardened when his father had died in his arms. In those cracks, something else seeped inside to replace the innocence. Anger. Bitterness. Hatred.

He had broken the night he had killed the troll king in this very fortress. How many others besides Weylind realized the troll king had been his first? Blood spilled not on a battlefield, not protecting his family or his kingdom, though he had given that excuse to himself even as he made the decision to so coldly kill for the first time.

And under that shame, with blood on his hands and the last of his innocence gone, he had shattered.

"You laugh?" King Charvod gripped Farrendel's jaw, yanked his head to face him. "You know the pain I can inflict."

Farrendel had to choke back another laugh. Physical pain was the least of all forms of torture. It could be endured and, eventually, ignored. King Charvod could inflict all the agony, mental torment, degrading humiliation, and mutilation he wished, but he could not truly touch Farrendel.

Because, the truth was, King Charvod had lost the only weapon that could truly harm Farrendel the moment Essie had successfully escaped. Farrendel could endure anything as long as Essie remained out of King Charvod's reach.

King Charvod still had Melantha. But even then, he had miscalculated in revealing her treachery too soon. It had been a blow. One that sent Farrendel reeling on top of the initial bewilderment of his capture.

But King Charvod could have used Farrendel's trust in her to make him freely talk. Or bond him further by having her tend him, only to turn on him.

No, this could have been much worse in the hands of a more experienced and calculating torturer. Instead, King Charvod wielded physical pain with all the clumsiness of a man who would himself break under such torment and could not conceive of someone who would not.

Farrendel glanced past King Charvod to where Prince Rharreth still leaned against the wall by the door, his face impassive and hard as the stone behind him. If Prince Rharreth ever stopped observing and started helping King Charvod, the torture would be worse. Much worse. Prince Rharreth was, after all, the one who figured out how to use Melantha to recapture Farrendel at the border.

Farrendel dragged his gaze back to King Charvod's burning, dark eyes. "You really are inept at torture."

It probably was not smart to goad him, but goading King Charvod into causing pain felt like the little bit of control Farrendel could grasp.

King Charvod made a growling sound and his fingers dug into Farrendel's jaw. "Inept? I will fill this fortress with your screams."

Farrendel yanked his chin free of King Charvod's grip and lashed out with his teeth, the only weapon left to him. He managed to bite King Charvod's thumb and clamped down as hard as he could.

King Charvod shouted and yanked his hand free, ripping his skin on Farrendel's teeth.

Farrendel spat out the taste of blood. A small wound to inflict. But it was far too satisfying to have drawn blood.

King Charvod gripped his thumb, blood welling. When he turned to Farrendel, his eyes burned. "You will pay for that."

Farrendel braced himself and drew in a deep breath. The last decent breath he would get for the next while.

King Charvod pressed his hand to the stone floor. The temperature of the room dropped, and magic flared.

Spikes of stone drove into Farrendel's body. Deep. Far too deep. Pain tore through him, even as he tried to hold back his screams.

Perhaps, this time, he had goaded King Charvod too far.

E ssie strolled through the encampment, gazing about at all the activity. In one of the cleared spaces beneath the spreading branches of a humongous tree, a group of Escarlish soldiers and elven warriors drilled together. Other groups practiced in other sections of the camp.

It looked like everyone was getting along...on the surface. But Averett and Weylind had both been called away to different parts of the camp to settle disputes while Leyleira and Julien had rushed off to one of the other encampments. It had been nearly a full-time job to keep everyone peacefully training together instead of fighting.

"Princess!"

Essie turned at the call, finding a young soldier skidding to a halt before her, panting. She smiled at him to put him at ease. "Yes, soldier?"

"The chief surgeon sent me to find you or one of your brothers. He needs you to settle a...discussion he has been having with the elf healers." The soldier pointed back the way he had come.

Even the healers were at odds? Essie huffed out a breath. At this rate, they were going to be so busy arguing, they were never going to get around to attacking the trolls. "Very well. Lead the way."

She hurried after him as he trotted past training soldiers and past her inventor friend Lance Marion as he fiddled with one of the Escarlish guns. She waved as she walked by, but she wasn't sure Lance even noticed. Finally, they reached a long white tent. Inside, rows of cots were set up. A few were even occupied, thanks to accidents while training and a few scuffles between humans and elves.

In the center, the elves' healer, a tall, brown-haired elf, faced the chief surgeon, a short, stumpy man with bulging arms. Behind each of them, their various helpers, nurses, other healers, and surgeons, lined up as if preparing to battle.

Time to calm this situation. The last thing they needed was for their entire medical staff to wipe each other out. Essie strolled into the tent and pasted on her best princess smile. "What seems to be the problem, gentlemen?"

"I refuse to—"

"He won't—"

"Human medical practices—"

"Pointy-eared, stubborn elves won't—"

Essie held up a hand for silence. With both of them talking at once—very nearly shouting at once—she couldn't make out exactly what was going on. "Please. One at a time. Healer Nylian, please go first."

It was probably best to start with the elf healer. If she started with the Escarlish surgeon, the elf would feel like she was giving preferential treatment to her own people by letting the surgeon tell his side first. While the surgeon was more likely to be patient and wait to tell his story second since he would believe she would listen to him.

The elf healer, Nylian, crossed his arms and glared at the surgeon. "I refuse to work with the human healers. Your medical practices are antiquated. My people's knowledge and skills are far superior."

"Because you have magic. That's basically cheating." The surgeon crossed his bulky arms and didn't budge an inch under the elf's stare, which had grown even colder after that comment.

"Far, far superior." Nylian turned away, as if dismissing the surgeon and all the human medical staff.

"It isn't like I want to work with you either. Pointy-eared..." Maxwell, the surgeon, glanced at Essie and cut off the last word. Probably some kind of swear word or a demeaning word about elves.

Essie suppressed her grimace. With these kinds of attitudes, working together wasn't going to happen anytime soon.

"Then you can tend your people with your primitive methods, and I will tend my people." Nylian waved a hand in the air, further dismissing all the humans in the room.

That could be a possible compromise, but not one Essie wanted to employ. That was the kind of ignoring each other that their peoples had been doing for the past decade and a half. If good was to come out of this war, then it had to bring their peoples together. And that started with the little things, like forcing a bunch of healers to work together... and like it.

Essie plastered on a bright smile. Time to do what she did

best. "That would be one way to do it, but that would not be the best use of the unique talents of both sides."

"Both sides? It is not as if the humans have anything to offer."

Elves and their annoying superiority complex.

Before Nylian could object, Essie took a step forward. "On the contrary, we humans do have much to offer. No, we don't have healing magic. But that has pushed us to develop our surgical techniques. We have come a long way from the leeches and bloodletting of past centuries. We have scalpels designed to do as little damage as possible during surgery." Essie met Nylian's gaze. "Why should you or your healers waste time digging out musket balls and performing those kinds of surgeries when that is exactly what the human surgeons have trained for?"

"I see." Nylian turned back to Maxwell and the other human surgeons. His gaze now had a gleam of something that might have been grudging consideration. "I could see how that would be...beneficial."

"Exactly." Essie's smile became more genuine, though no less bright. She couldn't believe this was actually working. "And, Maxwell, the elven healing magic is really amazing. I have seen them heal near fatal wounds in mere seconds. Working alongside the elves, you will learn much from their knowledge of the body. It could lead to medical break-throughs we can't even dream about now."

Maxwell still had his arms crossed, but his posture relaxed. "So, we turn the medical care into a factory assembly line."

She wouldn't have put it that way, but that was the idea. "Kind of. But it would be most efficient to work in teams where the elven healers use their magic while the human surgeons take care of whatever manual surgical procedures need to be done. It might also be best if the human surgeons took care of minor cuts and injuries while the elven healers conserve their magic for the most dire wounds. That will save the most lives."

When the battles came, there would be a lot of wounded. The healers and surgeons would need to become an efficient team otherwise it would cost lives.

She stayed in the healers' tent a while longer, working with Nylian and Maxwell for some of the particulars on what each group would handle and the size of the teams and stuff like that. She took notes so that she could arrange messages to the other two encampments so that this policy could be implemented there too.

After finishing with the healers and surgeons, Essie made her way to the far corner of the healers' tent. There, Illyna and several other elves mixed salves, which the healing elves would infuse with their magic. It would allow minor wounds to be treated in the field without expending magic at the time, saving the magic for more critical wounds.

Essie stopped next to Illyna. "How is it coming?"

Her jaw set, Illyna used a pestle strapped to her forearm to grind herbs and ingredients in a mortar. "We will have plenty of salve by the time the armies move out. I just wish I could go with the army to help rescue Farrendel."

"Every little bit helps, and this is no small thing. Thanks to you, the elven healers will be able to conserve their magic. That will save lives." Essie smiled and waved at the tent. "Thanks for all your hard work. Truly. It means a lot."

"It is the least we could do." Illyna reached out with her hand and squeezed Essie's shoulder. "Farrendel has been a good friend to all of us. He stuck by us when few others would. We will do whatever it takes to get him back."

"I know." Essie squeezed Illyna's shoulder, then stepped back.

After talking to a few more of the elves in the tent, Essie left and made her way toward the mess tent since it was nearly lunch time.

"Essie!" Edmund jogged up to her. "Jalissa and Leyleira are waiting by the command tent for me to bring back food. Want to help carry all the trays?"

"Sure." Essie fell into step with him. "Do you think it will be chicken or—"

The iron wall slammed across the heart bond, cold and hard. Essie hunched, pressing a hand to her chest.

Edmund gripped her elbow, steadying her. "Are you all right?"

"I'm fine. It's Farrendel." Essie straightened, forcing herself to take a deep breath. "They're torturing him again."

Edmund's expression held no trace of his usual smile. His fingers clenched over the hilt of the elven dagger belted to his waist. The same dagger Farrendel had given him. "How is he holding up? Can you tell?"

"He's..." Essie wasn't sure how to explain the impressions she felt. Or how much she should tell Edmund. "He's going hard. Cold. I guess it's to be expected, but he feels more like Laesornysh than my Farrendel."

Edmund didn't try to reply. What was there to say to something like this?

The iron wall crackled, then crumbled, tearing a wave of agony through Essie's chest. Stars burst across Essie's vision as darkness crowded in. She curled over her stomach, fighting to breathe. Her lungs burned, and it felt like her heart might tear itself apart at the rate it was beating.

"Essie!" Edmund's voice was distant, barely audible past the ringing in her ears.

Her lungs were tearing. She struggled to draw in another breath.

Farrendel...

ELEVEN

T he door to Melantha's cell slammed open. With her hands pressed tightly over her ears, she had not heard the tramping of boots down the passageway nor the locking bar lifting.

Prince Rharreth marched inside, grabbed her arm, and hauled her to her feet. "I hope you meant what you said about healing."

Melantha had to trot to keep up as he dragged her along with him from her cell. What was going on? Only seconds before, the dungeon had been filled with Farrendel's cries of pain.

Prince Rharreth turned in the direction of Farrendel's cell, his stride long and hurried. Melantha had to just about run to keep up with him, nearly tripping several times as she had never quite gained her balance. His grip on her arm was firm, tight enough that she could not wrench free, but not painful.

Her heart was pounding, her shoes scrambling on the

stone in an off rhythm to the troll prince's steady, swift stride.

The door to Farrendel's cell stood open, and Melantha was thrust inside before she had a chance to take a deep breath or steel herself for seeing her brother again after betraying him to this torture.

He lay on his back, pinned to the stone floor. A steady trickle of blood ran from him to a drain in the corner. His eyes were squeezed tightly shut, his body shuddering as he choked in wet gasps, a thin film of blood coating his lips.

A punctured lung. Melantha tore from Prince Rharreth's loosened grasp and crashed to her knees beside Farrendel. Lying on his back as he was, he was suffocating. He would die within a few minutes if she did not do something.

She pressed a hand to his chest and reached for her magic, ignoring the faint throbbing at her temples caused by all the stone around them. Her magic surged in her chest, down her arm, into Farrendel.

Pain jolted her arm, and she snatched her hand back as if burned. Farrendel thrashed, a moan escaping between his ragged gasps for breath.

All the stone and troll magic inside him had reacted against her magic, causing him more pain instead of helping.

But, even in her brief flare of magic, she had sensed enough of what was happening inside him. It was not an image, exactly. More a detailed impression so that she knew the state of his bones, his blood, his internal organs. And knew how to craft her magic to fix the damage that had been done.

Glancing over her shoulder, she pointed to Farrendel's right rib cage. "The stone needs to be removed. Now."

King Charvod stood a few feet away, arms crossed, something almost like a smirk on his face as he watched Farrendel struggle to keep breathing. Prince Rharreth shifted, glancing at his brother.

Melantha gritted her teeth. Prince Rharreth had dragged her here. He was not allowed to just throw up his hands and ignore what needed to be done. "Unless you want him to die right here, right now, it needs to be removed."

Prince Rharreth pushed from the wall and knelt next to her on the floor. He rested a hand on the stone next to Farrendel, and an icy white glow spread from his fingers into the floor.

Farrendel cried out again, and Melantha pressed her hand to his shoulder, though she was not entirely sure why. It was not as if she needed to hold him down. He was already thoroughly pinned. Nor would he wish comfort from her.

If only there was a way she could ease this pain for him. If her magic reacted that painfully to troll magic, his must be worse.

Could she help? If she could work her magic alongside the troll magic, as if using her magic as a shield between the troll magic and Farrendel...

It was worth a try. She called on her magic again, this time easing it into Farrendel far more cautiously than she had before.

Pain flared up her arm, behind her eyes, but she gritted her teeth and kept going. With her magic, she sensed the active troll magic and coated it with a layer of her own. Her whole body was throbbing now, but Farrendel's thrashing had stilled, though he still struggled to breathe.

Prince Rharreth removed the stabbing stone from Farrendel's body. When he drew out a few of the other daggers of stone piercing Farrendel, Melantha refrained from commenting. She had not asked him to do that, and she did not want to draw attention to it with King Charvod watching.

Instead, she drew on more of her magic and sent it into Farrendel's lung. Troll magic still sizzled against hers, but she pushed the pain aside as best she could, shielding Farrendel from the war of the two magics.

She cleared his lung of blood, steering the blood back to the vessels where it belonged, then knit the tear the stone had caused.

Farrendel stilled, gulping in a deep, non-choking breath. He turned his face and spat, probably trying to clear the taste of his own blood from his mouth.

Melantha rocked back onto her heels and withdrew her hand. She was shaking, her head throbbing.

"Well done, Melantha." King Charvod's voice rumbled behind her, sounding far too smug for someone who had nearly killed his prisoner with his over-enthusiastic use of torture. "Your aid has been invaluable once again."

Wait, what? Melantha stiffened. The way he had worded that sounded like she had been complicit in this.

Farrendel's eyes snapped open, flashing a deadly silver-blue and filled with more anger than Melantha had ever seen him direct at anyone, much less at her. "You should have let them kill me. It is what you wanted."

The snarl in his tone, the venom in his voice, stabbed at her. She opened her mouth, but her words caught in her throat. What defense did she have? She had wanted him dead. She was complicit, even if not quite the way King Charvod had made it sound.

But she had just proved to King Charvod that she would

heal Farrendel and save his life if necessary. That meant King Charvod could push his torture farther, take Farrendel even closer to death, than he would dare without a healer present.

And he had just implied to Farrendel that she was willingly and knowingly helping to make the torture worse.

Before she could think of a response, Prince Rharreth dragged her to her feet. She was nearly at the door before she thought to struggle. "Wait. No. It is not like that. I did not..."

But Farrendel had his face turned away from her, his fists clenched.

King Charvod followed them from the cell, slamming the door and the locking bar into place.

Heat burned in Melantha's chest, down into her hands. She screamed and clawed at Prince Rharreth. "Let me go! Monster! I am not helping you hurt him!"

Prince Rharreth wrapped an arm around her, pinning her arms to her sides as he hauled her down the short stretch of passageway. He shoved her into her cell. Before Melantha had a chance to regain her balance, he had slammed and locked the door.

Melantha gripped the bars and shook the door as hard as she could, filled with the longing to break something. But the stone did not budge. As ever, the burning rage had been denied an outlet. Another scream built in her chest, then tore out her throat past her gritted teeth.

Healing was such a useless power. Sure, she could save Farrendel. But she could also be used against him, turned into a weapon of his torture. What she would not give for the fiery crackle of his magic. Then she could blast this door off its hinges, tear down the walls of this dungeon, and kill all who stood in her way.

The door at the far end of the corridor slammed and locked into place.

With one last shake of the bars, Melantha forced herself to calm with deep, steady breaths. Giving in to her rage helped no one, and only gave the trolls another reason to scorn her.

She had to be calm. Calm as a forest lake. Calm as a bird soaring on a steady breeze. Calm as a perfect elven princess ought to be.

When her heart rate returned to normal, the heat subsiding back to its background simmer in her chest, Melantha gripped the bars set into the window of her cell's door and peered in the direction of Farrendel's cell. If she listened closely, she could just make out his breathing, still ragged, still pained, though not with the choking gasp of earlier. "Farrendel?"

A hitch to his breathing, but that was her only answer.

Had she really expected him to talk to her after King Charvod had implied she was helping them torture Farrendel? On top of the betrayal she had actually done?

You are not my brother. Her own words echoed in her ears as she leaned her forehead against the cold stone bars. Callous. Cruel. So despicable even the trolls despised her, even though they had been willing to use her treachery for their own ends.

"I am sorry, Farrendel." More, broken sincerity filled those words than the last time she had said them two days earlier. How many times would she have to say them before he believed she meant them?

Still no answer. Perhaps nothing she said now would erase her earlier words.

With her eyes squeezed shut, she could all too easily

picture the look on her father's face if he had been alive to know what she had done. The hurt. The anger. The way he would draw back from her. The same look Weylind, Rheva, Machasheni Leyleira, and Jalissa were sure to give her if she ever saw her family again.

Their father had died to save Farrendel's life, and, in her anger, Melantha had turned that sacrifice vain and empty by placing Farrendel right back into his tormentors' hands.

She could not undo what she had done. But she would not allow her father's sacrifice to be in vain. Somehow, she would make sure Farrendel survived this, no matter what it cost her. Perhaps it would be best if she died here. Better for her family to mourn her after she had given her life to save Farrendel's than for them to try to decide what to do with a living, traitorous sister.

Leaving the bars, she stalked across the room and sat on the one wool blanket she had been provided. She needed a plan.

About an hour later, the door at the end of the passageway opened again, and Prince Rharreth strode inside, carrying two bowls of the stew that seemed to be the only thing the trolls served their prisoners. He set one bowl on the floor outside her cell while he opened the locking bar.

Melantha stood a few feet from the door, back straight, her hands clasped in front of her where he would be able to see them. This was a battle she intended to win, and that started with appearing cooperative and meek.

He held the bowl of stew out to her.

She did not take it. "Prince Rharreth, I respectfully request to be allowed to tend to my brother."

He raised a thick, white eyebrow at her. "Why should I allow this?"

She kept her tone even, her face serene. She had a lot of practice hiding her inner turmoil. "My healing was rushed earlier. I should examine him to make sure there is not more internal bleeding that I missed earlier."

Prince Rharreth studied her face with his dark eyes, and she had a feeling he was seeing right through to her true motives.

So what if he did. Melantha clenched her hands. He could refuse her. If he were as cruel as his brother, he would.

But she did not think he was that cruel.

"I am a healer. I cannot break stones with my magic. I cannot free him. I have taken the oath of a healer, a magical binding so strong I would likely die myself if I attempted violence against you or anyone." Melantha let some of her anger seep into her voice as she pointed in the direction of Farrendel's cell. "All I can do is provide him with a little comfort. Surely you will not deny him that. You claim to be honorable, but can you truly call it honor to torture even an enemy like this? You would not keep a rabid animal in the deplorable conditions that my brother is currently suffering."

Something flashed through Prince Rharreth's eyes a moment before he glanced away from her. His broad shoulders were tense beneath his leather jerkin.

Melantha suppressed her reaction. She had guessed right. Prince Rharreth did not approve of Farrendel's treatment. "And you call me despicable. At least I am willing to do something."

His jaw tightened, his fingers flexing on her bowl of stew. "Very well. I will allow you to examine him."

She resisted the urge to breathe a sigh of relief. She could not let him see how much she wanted this or that it was just the beginning of her plan.

Prince Rharreth thrust her bowl at her, and this time she took it. He spun on his heels. "Come."

She snatched her blanket from the floor, draped it over her arm, then hurried after the troll prince. She paused to retrieve Farrendel's bowl of cooling, watery stew from the floor, then quickened her pace as much as she could without sloshing the stew. It would not do to waste even a drop when they were already given so little.

Prince Rharreth unbarred Farrendel's cell door and waited for her at the door, his expression stony.

This time, Melantha took a moment to take a deep breath and brace herself before stepping inside.

Her deep breath had not been enough. Last time, she had been in too much panic to notice the details. This time, the smell struck her first. The trolls so feared Farrendel they did not even allow him to take care of the most basic of needs.

She would not allow herself to flinch. She was a healer. This was, after all, what she had trained for. She had managed to fake compassion well enough to fool her instructors into training her and allowing her to take the oath even though her heart had never been in healing. Surely she could manage it when, for the first time, she truly felt compassion amid all the burning anger.

When she stepped through the door, Farrendel's gaze flicked to her, enough for a glimpse of pain, before swinging back to the ceiling, his jaw hardening. "Melantha, if you ever loved me at all, then, please, do not help them torture me."

So much pain in those words that even his attempt at coldness could not hide it.

With her freely walking inside under Prince Rharreth's escort, it must appear as if she was willingly working with the trolls. But she had known it would take more than simply helping Farrendel once for him to trust her again.

Melantha knelt next to him, set the bowls aside, and spread the blanket over him. Held unmoving on the stone, he would be cold. "I know you do not trust me, but I am here to help."

He did not thank her. Nor did he look at her. If anything, he turned his face farther from her as if he could not even stand to see her in the corner of his eye.

Calling on her magic, she reached out and rested her hand on Farrendel's forehead, letting her magic seep into him, relieving the headache she could sense pounding at his temples. Most likely the result of being surrounded by so much stone.

With her magic, she had been able to heal her own headache. But Farrendel could not heal himself and he had always been more susceptible to the stone than the rest of them were.

Some of the tension in Farrendel's jaw and the tightness around his eyes eased. But he kept his face turned away from her.

She moved her hand from his forehead to his shoulder and poured more of her magic into him, making sure she weaved her magic between the troll magic and Farrendel to prevent paining him further.

She could not heal him completely. Not with the amount of stone still lacing through him. But she could heal as much damage as possible.

By the time she pulled her hand away, her fingers shook with the amount of power she had expended. Her head pounded, and she did not have the magical strength to heal herself.

But the way Farrendel's tense muscles eased made the expenditure of her power worth it. He would rest easy for a few hours, at least.

Melantha sat back on her heels and glanced over her shoulder. Prince Rharreth remained leaning against the wall by the door. Guarding her in case she should try an escape, but not interfering.

Behind her, the two bowls of stew remained with two small chunks of bread jammed on the rim. With Farrendel still not looking at her, she poured some of the stew from one bowl into the other. She would have given Farrendel all of her portion, but she would need to eat something, even a reduced portion, to maintain her strength and continue to heal Farrendel. As long as Prince Rharreth allowed it.

Setting both bowls in front of her, she dipped Farrendel's bread into his stew. "I know you do not want to take anything from my hand, but you need to eat."

Farrendel blew out a long breath, then faced her. "I am used to being fed by an enemy."

It should not sting. Not after what she had done.

But she still had to blink and stare down at the bowl for longer than necessary before she held out the piece of bread to him.

It might have almost felt like a family meal, if not for the tension and the fact that she alternated between feeding herself and feeding Farrendel as if he were yet again the child she had helped raise.

That brought another stab of pain. When had she started

to resent him, then hate him? When he had been little, she had been almost like a mother to him. She was old enough that she could have had a son Farrendel's age, had Hatharal not delayed the marriage, then ended things.

It had hurt, in those early years, to hold Farrendel close and think about the children she had been denied. When had that pain turned to anger and that anger turned on Farrendel instead of the betrothed who had left her?

Why had she never been grateful that Farrendel's birth had shown her the truth about Hatharal before she had actually married him? Hatharal had never truly loved her. Not if he had been so willing to break it off at the first sign of trouble.

Love was what their father had shown in enfolding Farrendel into the family no matter the scandal and scorn it had caused.

Would Farrendel's Princess Elspeth love him in that way? Or would she falter at the first sign of trouble?

No, Melantha might not have bothered to get to know her new human sister, but Princess Elspeth had proven to be incredibly loyal and resilient.

Melantha picked up the last piece of her bread and gave it to Farrendel after sopping up the last of his larger portion of soup. As he chewed, she struggled to think of something to say. This tense silence gnawed at her.

What could she say? From his stony silence, he had no wish to converse with her.

Prince Rharreth pushed away from the wall, taking a step toward her. Her time was up. If she was going to say something, she needed to figure out what it was and how to say it now.

She rested her hand on his shoulder again, his skin still

cold even after the warmth her magic had lent him. "I am sorry. This...this is not what I meant to happen."

Farrendel's gaze snapped to her, ice blue and filled with fire. "What did you intend to happen? A quick execution rather than torture? That hardly makes your betrayal any better."

She flinched, rocking back on her heels. The venom in his tone stung. But what else had she expected?

A part of her had almost expected him not to be angry with her. Farrendel so very rarely became angry. Nor had she intended to be there when he did. The whole point had been for her to walk away and simply move on, as awful as that made her.

"No, I guess it does not." Her throat thick, she picked up the bowls and hurried out the door, keeping her head down. She left her blanket, though Prince Rharreth was unlikely to let Farrendel keep it long.

At her cell, she handed back the bowls, then retreated to the back wall of her cell as Prince Rharreth locked her inside. She did not look at him. Certainly did not want to give him cause to talk to her. Talking would betray the tears choking her throat.

The troll prince had been right this whole time. Of the two of them, she was the monster.

Perhaps she had always had her broken betrothal backwards. Maybe her betrothed had not walked away because he could not stand the scandal of Farrendel's illegitimate birth. But, instead, he had glimpsed her anger, her growing bitterness, and had seen that marriage to her would be miserable.

That meant the problem had never been him, but had always been her.

After all, a sister who would knowingly betray her innocent brother to torture and death had to be a despicable person indeed. Not someone that anyone would want to be stuck with in a marriage.

In the end, she had lost everyone. Even if rescue came for Farrendel, it would never come for her. There could be no rescue, no return to her family, no forgiveness. Not for her.

CHAPTER

TWELVE

Farrendel wiggled his fingers, then his toes. For the first time in five days, his toes were verging on warm underneath the blanket Melantha had left and the troll prince had yet to return to take.

Also for the first time in five days, he was pain-free. As long as Melantha's magic lingered, the pain would be banished. A brief reprieve.

Why had she done it? Was it out of guilt? Was she...?

No. Farrendel dashed away that line of thinking. He could not allow himself to believe she had a change of heart. If this turned out to be a trick, it would hurt that much worse if he let himself hope.

It had to be a trick. He did not dare trust Melantha again. After all, she had spent a century pretending she loved him as a sister. This could just as easily be another deception.

Perhaps the trolls thought it would be another cruelty to make him think his sister had a change of heart, only to lump a second betrayal onto the first. Maybe they thought he would reveal something of Weylind's battle plans to Melantha, and she would pass them on to the trolls.

Still, a part of him hoped. After what she had done, why did he still want her kindness to be real? Why, even now, did a large part of him want to forgive her?

Weylind had once told him he loved far too easily. Back then, it had been a warning not to fall in love with Essie too quickly.

Yet Essie had not been the one any of them should have been worried about. It turned out the one Farrendel had loved too easily was his own sister.

Farrendel wiggled his toes against the warm wool of the blanket. A trick. Just a trick. But he would enjoy these comforts while they lasted. A warm blanket and no pain, even if he still was pinned and unable to move.

He eased the barrier on the heart bond. As soon as he did, a flood of emotion poured into him from Essie, and he did not need to hear the words to sense her tears and worry.

How much had she felt? His block had faltered for a few moments when the shock of the stone piercing him had shaken his senses. It must have been bad enough for her to tell he had nearly died.

I am fine. I am not dead. He was not sure how much she would be able to sense, but hopefully the impression of the words would carry through. He did not wish to worry her more than he already had.

Could she tell how much better he was now? Would she sense the lack of pain at the moment? It was not much, but he wanted to savor the feeling with her. He had not thought he would get even this much relief until he was rescued.

He had the impression she was reaching for him,

mentally holding him as close as she could through the bond.

As he reached for her, he felt the warmth of the bond and...something else. He frowned and blinked up at the stone ceiling above him. Was that a crackle of his magic?

He tugged on the power, easing it into his right hand. When he craned his neck, he could just see a faint blue, shimmering glow beneath the blanket by his hand.

He halted the crackle. If Prince Rharreth returned soon to retrieve the blanket, Farrendel could not let him suspect this.

This had to be an unintended consequence of Melantha's healing. Somehow, her magic must have been blocking the stone and the troll magic enough for him to access his power. It was still a small amount, crushed as it was beneath so much surrounding stone and nearby troll magic, and it would disappear the moment her magic faded from his system.

If Melantha's healing was just a manipulative trick, then it had gone badly awry for her and the trolls. Thanks to her, Farrendel could access his magic.

What could he do with it? It was not strong enough nor would it last long enough to free him or take on Prince Rharreth.

If Melantha's visit had been a trick to lure Farrendel into trusting her again for some nefarious purpose, then she would be back. She would heal him again, and when she did, he would gain access to his magic again. If he could figure out something to do with his power, then he would use her visits against her and the trolls. He would not be just the helpless victim awaiting rescue.

Perhaps, when rescue came, this time he could fight back.

He could make sure his rescuers did not pay the price the way his father had.

Could he store his magic? It was not a concept he would have thought of a few months ago. But in Escarland, he had met Essie's inventor friend Lance Marion, who worked with human magicians to store magic in devices to power machines. It had taken an afternoon of experimentation, but Lance had successfully figured out a way to store Farrendel's magic in a device like he did with the magic from human magicians.

Farrendel glanced around the cell. Nothing but stone around him. Not even iron chains dangling from the wall.

Lance had needed some kind of high-grade metal for the device to store Farrendel's magic. Even if there were iron chains rusting in the corner, they probably would not work.

The stone would not hold his magic. It would just fizzle out.

Farrendel blew out a breath. He had brief access to his magic, but he could not do anything with it. Within an hour or two, Melantha's magic would dissipate from his body, and he would be back to pain and lack of magic.

Lack of all magic...except the heart bond.

The heart bond wasn't exactly a thing. But could it store his magic somehow?

How would pushing his magic into the heart bond affect Essie? She had speculated once that the heart bond might make her immune to his magic, but they had never tested that idea. There was not a safe way to experiment.

If she was not immune, then what would adding more magic to the heart bond do to her? He would not risk her, not even for the chance to escape. He did not even have a way to ask her permission before he experimented with this, if he decided to attempt it.

A heart bond was a mysterious magic. Elven scholars had been debating exactly what it was for millennia.

But it had given rise to many of their marriage customs. The eshinelt, the green paint used during the blessings and vows of the wedding ceremony, had magic from the bride and groom mixed into it, which was believed to encourage a heart bond to form. That was the theory behind it, anyway.

Since Essie did not have magic, the eshinelt Farrendel made for their wedding contained only his magic.

If that magic was the spark that the heart bond used to form, then the magic of the heart bond was his originally. If his magic was already integral to the heart bond and tied to Essie, then surely the addition of more of his magic would not hurt her.

He would be careful. He would ease only a little bit of his magic into the heart bond this time. If his hunch was right, Melantha would be back. He would have more chances to store more magic...if this worked.

Essie, I wish I could ask you first before trying this.

She must have sensed a question through the heart bond. He felt an impression of a question in return.

Farrendel flexed his fingers. This would have been so much easier if elishinas resulted in true telepathy. He tried to send thoughts about what he was going to try, but it was not an idea that could translate to vague impressions.

Gripping the crackle of his magic, he drew it deep into his chest. It crackled next to the warmth of the heart bond, but nothing else happened.

Farrendel huffed a breath. He had to make this work. Already, the faintest hint of pain throbbed at his wrists.

Using his magic was making Melantha's magic disappear from his body faster.

Somewhere, he could feel Essie still questioning. Would she figure out what he was trying to do?

He had to get this right. This tiny crackle of his magic was fragile.

Yet, if he could store this magic, he could prevent history from repeating itself. No one would die on his account.

He gripped the crackle of his magic tighter with one mental fist, the heart bond with the other, and drew the magic together.

Something burst inside his chest. He gasped, magic sparking across his vision. He blinked and took a moment to catch his breath.

When his senses finally sharpened, he felt for his magic.

The crackle had lessened, but was still there, melded into the warmth of the heart bond.

He had done it. What he had done, exactly, only time would tell. Would he still be able to access this magic once Melantha's magic wore off?

Essie. Was she all right? He felt for her through the heart bond. Even through the additional crackle of his magic, she was still there. The wave of impression he sensed from her was filled with confusion, but not pain.

His experiment had not hurt her. He breathed a sigh of relief. This had worked, and it had not hurt Essie.

He flexed his fingers, feeling the tingle of his magic. He was not going to be helpless this time. By the time he was rescued, he would be able to fight back.

No matter her reasons for pretending to help him, Farrendel was looking forward to Melantha's next visit.

CHAPTER THIRTEEN

E ssie glanced around the command tent, crowded with both elven and human generals going over their plan of attack one last time. Weylind and Averett stood at the center, though now that the debates had all been laid to rest during earlier discussions, they were mostly there to give their royal approval to the plan.

The tent flap was thrown open, and Edmund's tousled brown hair popped through first before he straightened and grinned. "What did we miss?"

Jalissa followed him and gave him a quelling look, as if she thought that opening line inappropriate for the seriousness of battle planning.

Leyleira strode in behind Jalissa, glanced around, and raised her eyebrows. "It would seem we are precisely on time."

Julien was the last to enter. He glanced around the tent before he worked his way through the crowd to where Essie stood. He wrapped her in a one-armed hug. "How are you holding up?"

"All right." Essie wasn't sure how to describe how she was feeling. Mostly, she was impatient to start the battle and rescue Farrendel. And yet, the invasion of Kostaria would mean war. It would mean bloodshed and death and many lives lost. How many would die to make Farrendel's rescue possible? How many wives and mothers and sisters would mourn so that Essie didn't have to?

It wasn't fair, in the end. Essie shouldn't ask that sacrifice.

Except that she wasn't the one doing the asking. Averett and Weylind were.

This invasion was about more than rescuing Farrendel. It was about eliminating a threat to both Tarenhiel and Escarland. If they did nothing, Kostaria would continue to attack Tarenhiel, and probably Escarland as well due to the alliance.

Julien squeezed her shoulders and didn't let go, perhaps sensing she needed his continued comfort. "How is Farrendel holding up?"

"As well as can be expected." How much should she tell Julien? They had all been so busy she hadn't managed more than snatches of conversations with anyone. "Ever since yesterday, he's been optimistic. More than he had been earlier. He's still captured, but something changed. I don't know what."

That was the frustrating thing about the heart bond. The details were always rather vague, no matter how hard she concentrated.

But something had changed. She was sure of it. Only a few hours after Farrendel had nearly died, his pain had suddenly vanished for a while, and she'd started to get a determined, optimistic impression, and the heart bond had taken on a crackling edge.

Whatever had happened, she was grateful. The anger and distance she had sensed from him before hadn't exactly vanished, but they were not as overwhelming as before. They were more controlled, raw-edged and dangerous.

A few days ago, he had simply been surviving. Enduring.

Now, he was still surviving. Still enduring. But also possibly plotting to kill everyone in sight. He was definitely planning something.

Whatever he was planning, she tried to send him as much of their own plans as she could through the impressions of the heart bond. Maybe he could time his plan to theirs.

"That's good, isn't it? Especially after…" Julien gestured toward her, his eyes going worried once again.

She had worried all of them when she had collapsed and passed out, before Farrendel had blocked the heart bond once again. By the time he had released the iron wall across the heart bond, he had gone from nearly dying to as pain-free as she had sensed from him since his capture.

It was almost as if he had been healed by elven magic. But that didn't make sense.

Surely Melantha wasn't doing that, was she? But she was the only elf healer that Essie knew about who could be with the trolls.

Was this some plot on the part of the trolls? Were they having Melantha patch Farrendel up after the torture sessions so that they could just torture him worse?

The sense that she got from Farrendel was far too relaxed for Melantha's healing to be a part of the torture. As if he believed she was truly helping him. Or, at least, hoped she might be.

And that worried Essie. If this was some kind of trick and Melantha intended to use it to hurt Farrendel yet again...

Essie wasn't sure if Farrendel could survive a second betrayal.

What did that have to do with the crackle to the heart bond? Farrendel was probably causing it. But how? What was he doing?

Farrendel could sometimes be frustratingly reticent, but at least when they were together, he would communicate. This lack of true communication gnawed at her. When she got Farrendel back, she wasn't going to take his short answers for granted again.

Julien was still looking at her, expecting an answer.

"Yes, it is. But I'm still worried about him. I just..." Should she share her worries that Melantha might be helping him? Or setting him up for another trap of some kind? "I just wish there was more we could do."

"I know." Julien nudged her. "I think Averett wants us over there."

Essie glanced up. Averett was waving toward them. Jalissa, Leyleira, and Edmund all crowded around the table by Averett and Weylind, displacing a few of the generals.

Julien shouldered his way through the crowded tent, and Essie followed in his wake. Tall, broad-shouldered brothers were handy for some things.

When she reached the table, she squirmed into a spot next to Edmund. He gave her his own one-armed hug while Jalissa leaned around him to give Essie a small smile. Across the table, Leyleira nodded to her.

Averett tapped the map laid out on the table, indicating

the ridge along the Gulmorth River that separated Tarenhiel and Kostaria. "We march out tomorrow morning to arrive at the ridge by evening. We'll stay hidden in the trees until dawn. Julien, you will be going with your army and will fight with our east flank. Edmund, you have the western flank."

"Machasheni." Weylind glanced to Leyleira beside him. "We wish for you to take over command of the support forces here at this camp. The wounded will be evacuated to here to be stabilized before being sent to Estyra or Aldon on the train."

Leyleira nodded, the streak of gray in her hair shining in the lamplight.

"Jalissa and Essie, you will come with us and stay behind at the ridge here with the support personnel." Averett tapped the center of the line. "The triage for the wounded will be here, and you will need to make sure our supply line stays clear. Once we are in Kostaria, we plan to move quickly, and we will have to be careful we don't outpace our supply line."

Essie bit her lip, studying the map. She knew letting her and Jalissa be at the site of the initial battle was already closer to the fighting than her brothers would wish her to be. Yet...She drew in a deep breath. "I need to go with you when you take Gror Grar."

"What? Not a chance." Averett turned and gripped her shoulders. "I know you'll want to be there when we rescue Farrendel, but you aren't a soldier."

"I know. And I don't intend to fight. Not like that. But..." She glanced over her shoulder at Weylind. How much would the elves wish her to say? Especially in front of the mixed group of generals.

Weylind met her gaze before turning to her brother. "Averett Daresheni, she needs to come."

"What?" Averett spun. "Would you wish to place your sister in that kind of danger?"

"No, I would not. But, for the sake of our brother, she needs to be there." Weylind braced himself with his hands on the table. "It is because of the elishina."

"That heart bond thing?" Averett huffed. "It's becoming more trouble than it's worth."

The generals were shifting. The human ones were glancing at each other, as if wondering how to ask to be dismissed. The elven generals eased toward the door as if intending to sneak away.

Essie touched Averett's arm. "If the rest of the planning is done, maybe we should discuss this in private?"

It was probably her fault for bringing it up in front of others in the first place.

"Right." Averett drew himself straight and gestured to the generals. "You're dismissed. Please prepare the men for marching out tomorrow."

Weylind gave similar instructions to his elves.

The generals nodded and marched outside until only family remained in the tent.

Averett crossed his arms. "Now explain what you mean about why you need to be there and what it has to do with the heart bond."

Julien studied her without Averett's ire while Edmund was glancing from Essie to Weylind, his forehead scrunching as if he was most of the way to figuring it out on his own.

Essie wrapped her arms over her stomach. "If Farrendel is badly injured, I can keep him alive with the heart bond long enough for the healers to save him."

She wasn't going to mention that there was a chance that if he was hurt badly enough, the attempt would kill both of them.

"I might be able to save him from a distance. The heart bond has strengthened over the past week or so, or maybe I've gotten better at sensing it. I don't know." Not to mention that strange crackle. Essie stared down at the table. "But I'm not sure if that would work or if I would be strong enough that way or if I'd be able to pull back if..." If hanging on too tightly meant she would die along with Farrendel.

That might sound all romantic in stories, but real life was more complicated. Dying with him would just mean both families would be mourning two people instead of one. Nor would Farrendel wish for her to die that way.

"But you might not have to be there." Of course Averett would latch onto that.

"It would be a lot better if I was." She glanced from Jalissa to Leyleira to Weylind. Surely one of the elves could explain it much better than she could. "I'm not asking to be put in the front lines. You'll have healers and medical staff staying behind the lines in the battle. I'll stay there."

"That won't mean you'll be safe. Armies are routed and overrun all the time." Averett touched her arm. "If you were killed during the battle, it would shatter Farrendel. He would not wish for you to be hurt trying to rescue him."

No, he wouldn't. He would want her far away and safe.

She had to balance the risk to herself and the risk to Farrendel. If she could stay as safe as possible and be able to help Farrendel, then it would be worth it.

"There is another reason she should come." Weylind shifted. "Gror Grar is large, and the dungeon tunnels winding into the mountain are extensive. When we attack, we might not be able to reach him before they kill him if we wander the tunnels blindly. But there is a chance Elspetha will be able to sense where he is."

She could? Essie closed her eyes. Was she imagining that she could tell the general direction Farrendel was in? It was such a subconscious thing, she had not even noticed it. Yet, hadn't she always found herself turning in that direction when she thought about him?

"This just gets better and better." Averett waved a hand, his arms still crossed tightly across his chest. "Not only do you want her at risk behind the battle lines, but now you want to send her into danger during the attack on the fortress of Gror Grar."

Essie scowled and crossed her own arms. "This is my choice, Averett. If I can help save Farrendel, then I want to try. You'll have until the assault on Gror Grar to come up with a plan to keep me as safe as possible."

"Of course. That makes it so much better." Averett's scowl deepened.

Julien stepped to Essie's side. "She'll have all of us along."

"We'll keep her safe." Edmund rested his elbow on her shoulder. "What could go wrong when she has all three of us guarding her?"

"Four of us." Jalissa stepped to Edmund's side. "If Elspetha is going, then she will need another female along with whom to share a shelter."

Essie grinned. "I'll be happy to have you for a bunk mate."

That made Weylind scowl and cross his arms.

Averett raised his eyebrows. "See. Not so easy accepting that your sister is determined to put herself in danger, is it?"

Essie elbowed him. "You don't have to rub it in."

"Yes, I do. It's the one thing I can do to make myself feel better." Averett's mouth twitched as he fought to stay frowning instead of smiling.

Essie wrapped her arms around Edmund and Julien. This was it. Tomorrow, they would launch the attack. One step closer to getting Farrendel back.

FOURTEEN

When Prince Rharreth allowed her into Farrendel's cell the next day, Melantha ate her meal next to Farrendel, trying to make conversation. As he was still giving her frosty silence, it was not working.

After they had eaten, she convinced Prince Rharreth to let her haul buckets of water from the spring of water that trickled from the rock wall in an alcove just on the other side of the door to this wing of the dungeon.

While Prince Rharreth led her there, she was able to get a glimpse of more of the dungeon. Not much. Just more tunnels branching off into the darkness. But at least she had learned they were deep in the warren in the mountain that formed the trolls' dungeon.

Not exactly helpful information, but surely Farrendel would find all information she could gather useful. If she could not bribe him into speaking to her by helping him, maybe she could with information.

Two buckets sat next to the pool formed at the base of the

steady trickle of water. Convenient for trolls fetching water for prisoners. Or washing out dungeon cells after torturing their latest victim.

Prince Rharreth leaned against the wall, eyeing her, as she dipped first one bucket, then the other into the water. When she hefted both of them, he did not offer to help.

As she passed him, both hands laden with full buckets, she gritted her teeth and glared. "I am not going anywhere. You could help. Unless it is beneath your dignity as a proud troll warrior."

His dark eyes remained hard as they focused on her, his mouth tight. "I am not prey to be baited."

Melantha huffed and resisted the urge to roll her eyes. That was a human expression she would not deign to employ, even if it was tempting. "Fine."

She marched through the door to the dungeon corridor. Prince Rharreth remained where he was. No sense for him to tramp back and forth when she could not go anywhere, nor could Farrendel so much as move.

The door to Farrendel's cell stood open, and Melantha maneuvered her way inside carrying the two buckets. Her shoulders already ached, and she let out a breath of relief when she set them down.

Farrendel's gaze flicked to her, and his brow furrowed.

Melantha picked up one of the buckets. "You may wish to close your eyes. And hold your breath."

Farrendel squeezed his eyes shut, his face twisting. It was almost comical.

Except...he used to make that same face when he had been a toddler, waiting for Melantha to rinse the shampoo from his hair.

A pang stabbed her chest. For all the pain of those years,

there had been good times. When had Melantha forgotten that?

She splashed the first bucket on Farrendel. He gasped and peeked up at her through the water trickling across his face. "That was cold."

"Sorry. It is from a spring here in the dungeon." Melantha hefted the second bucket, paused long enough for Farrendel to close his eyes again, before she dumped that one on him as well.

She trekked back to the spring, glared at Prince Rharreth, filled the buckets again, and tottered back to Farrendel.

It took several more trips before Farrendel was somewhat clean and the dungeon cell no longer smelled. Melantha's shoulders strained. Her arms hurt. Blisters formed on her fingers from the buckets' rope handles.

She returned to the spring and set the buckets down where she had found them. Facing Prince Rharreth, she crossed her arms, as much to give her shoulders a rest as to look tough. "Would it have killed you to help? You claim to care about honor. What is honorable about the way you and your brother are treating Farrendel? Is it honorable to torture someone and deny him the ability to so much as feed himself? You could at least give him some decency or care."

Prince Rharreth pushed away from the wall. "I let you take care of him, didn't I?"

He had. Why? It was not what he should have done. Not if he were wise.

And she had needed to do it. Had Prince Rharreth realized that? Why would he bother trying to help her? She was his enemy, as was Farrendel. His prisoners.

"Come." Prince Rharreth led the way back down the dungeon corridor. Probably to lock her back in her cell.

He opened the door to her cell and gestured.

She stepped inside but halted. "Could I bring my blanket to Farrendel? He will be cold."

Prince Rharreth stilled for a moment before he nodded. "Very well."

She grabbed her blanket from the pile of straw in the corner where she had slept after Prince Rharreth had returned her blanket to her the day before. She also grabbed a large handful of the straw.

Prince Rharreth did not comment as she hurried past him.

When she stepped into Farrendel's cell, Farrendel's teeth were chattering, his body shivering as much as he could while pinned as he was.

That water must have been colder than she thought. She had worked up a sweat while carrying it, but he was pinned to the cold stone floor with no way to get himself warm.

Melantha dropped to her knees beside him and rested a hand on his shoulder. His skin was icy beneath her fingers. Even though she had already expended magic to relieve his pain, she poured more magic into him, trying to give his body some warmth.

When some of his shivering lessened, she spread the blanket over him and glanced over her shoulder at Prince Rharreth. "Could I stay with him a while? I would like to make sure he stays warm enough. I do not believe your brother would appreciate it if he died from the cold."

Prince Rharreth's mouth thinned, but he nodded. "Very well. But just in case..." He pressed his hand against the wall. Icy magic flowed across the stones, and the stone by Melantha's ankle reached up and wrapped around her.

She hissed in a breath at the cold of the stone and the troll magic touching her, but she kept herself from making more of a reaction. Farrendel had stone wrapped around him and piercing through him. She could hardly complain about a single stone shackle holding her in place.

When the stone had formed a shackle with a short length of stone chain, Prince Rharreth lifted his hand from the wall, and the flow of his magic cut off. "I will return this evening."

He spun on his heel and strode from the dungeon cell. The door clanked shut behind him, the locking bar grating into place.

Melantha held up her smile as she listened to the sound of his footsteps fading down the corridor. She had done it. Somehow, she had talked him into not only allowing her to help Farrendel, but also letting her stay with Farrendel for several hours. Progress.

When the sounds of footsteps faded, Melantha turned back to Farrendel.

He was studying her, his gaze less hard and angry than it had been on her previous visits, though the wariness remained.

"Here, lift your head." Melantha gathered the handful of straw. When Farrendel lifted his head, she tucked the straw beneath for a pillow. "There." The back of his head must be sore from lying against the hard stone. He probably had bruises all along his back from lying in the same position against rock for so long.

Melantha settled beside him, tucking her legs beneath her to keep her own toes warm. The stone chain rattled as she moved, the shackle cold against her skin. She rested her hand on Farrendel's shoulder again, pouring more of her magic into him. A headache formed at her temples, but it was not as bad as the one the day before. "Are you staying warm enough?"

"Yes." His gaze flicked from her to the ceiling. But at least he had answered her.

"I am sorry the water was so cold." Perhaps it would have been better to skip sluicing him off with icy water. But she remembered how Farrendel could not stand to be dirty. Even as a child, he had not liked to leave his hands dirty after playing.

Silence fell. Melantha stared upward at the ceiling, a circular pattern of stones. It was interesting, but not something she would wish to stare at day in and day out.

If only there was more she could do. If she could help Farrendel escape, perhaps it would in some way make up for the fact that she had gotten him captured in the first place. It would not exonerate her. It could never earn back her place in her family. But perhaps a small measure of forgiveness could be gained.

But how could she help him escape? Her healing magic was powerful, but it could not break stone. Perhaps she could risk breaking her oath and kill with her magic. But if she died in the attempt, she could gain Farrendel nothing.

She drew her knees up and hugged them to her chest. So much pain and guilt now joining the ever-present anger. If she did not think of a way to release the storm building inside of her, then she was not sure what would happen when she could no longer suppress all of it.

Farrendel released a breath, and he turned his head toward her. "Why did you do it?"

One of the shortened strands of his hair had fallen across his forehead, but Melantha resisted the urge to sweep it behind his ear as she had done when he had been a toddler and his hair had been barely longer than it was now. But Farrendel would not appreciate such a gesture. Instead, she rubbed at one of the forming blisters on her fingers. "I know how you like to be clean. I know it is not much, but it was something I could do to make you more comfortable." She grimaced at the slight shiver that still ran through him. "More comfortable once you dry off and warm back up."

Farrendel shook his head. "Not that. Why did you betray me? Betray our kingdom?"

She had told him, back when he had been captured, that she had betrayed him for the good of the kingdom. That she had believed the trolls when they had promised that all they wanted was to avenge the old king, and they would leave Tarenhiel in peace once Farrendel was dead.

But that was not the reason, she knew that now. That was the excuse she had talked herself into believing. It was the delusion she had used to quell her conscience, telling herself it was better to sacrifice one elf to save the entire kingdom, when, underneath, her real reason had been that she had wanted a convenient way to get rid of her own brother.

There was no good reason she could give him. Because there was no good reason to do what she had done. And bad reasons only sounded like excuses in the end. She could not give any reason that would make her actions forgivable, especially not by Farrendel.

But she was not asking him to forgive her. He would not. After all, she would not—could not—forgive herself.

Melantha hugged her knees to her chest and stared at the wall rather than look at him. "I was so...angry. At everything and everyone. At Father for dying. The trolls for killing him. My betrothed for leaving me."

147

"At me for existing." Farrendel's tone was soft, but impassive enough that she could not tell his emotion from it.

"Yes." She rested her chin on her knees. "You became the target of my anger. You were the only one left to hate. Everyone else was gone or dead."

It was such a bad, bad reason for betrayal.

"In the end, I solved nothing. I am still so angry. I do not know what to do with this constant simmering. I just want to lash out and fight and hurt something. Or someone." She dug her fingers into her hair, ignoring the way the greasy, dirty strands clung to her fingers and scalp. "Hardly the proper attitude for a healer."

When she finally found the courage, Melantha lifted her head and glanced at Farrendel. He was studying her, his expression impassive. What was he thinking? That she was an even more horrible sister than he had believed?

She huffed out a breath and shook her head. "Growing up, I wanted to be an elven warrior like Father and Weylind. I was so disappointed when I came into my magic, and it turned out to be healing magic. I begged Father to allow me to avoid taking the healers' oath and fight as a warrior, but he refused. He said that all killing hurts the soul, but killings when an elf can feel the heart stop with magic tears a mind the most, and he would not see that happen to me."

"Father was wise, in that." For a moment, Farrendel's silver-blue eyes filled with pain, but not the physical kind of pain that she could heal.

"I envied you. I think I still envy you. Your magic is what I always wished to have." Melantha could imagine crackling power filling her fingertips, blasting into her enemies. It would feel so good to have the power to lash out that way. Maybe then the fiery pain in her chest would ease.

But, perhaps, with that kind of magic, she would have become even more of a monster than she already was. All that anger would only lead to more anger.

She gave in and brushed the strand of hair from Farrendel's face. He flinched, but when he met her gaze, he was not glaring. Just hard and cold. She pressed her lips into a small smile. "It was probably better you were gifted with such deadly magic instead of me. I would have enjoyed the destruction and death far too much. You have a good heart, and your love for our people—not anger—controls your magic."

"All except once." Farrendel's fingers clenched into fists, his eyes squeezing shut. "I understand killing anger. All I thought about was vengeance when I killed the troll king."

Melantha nodded. She had felt that same anger when their father had been killed. She just had not had Farrendel's chance to do anything about it. She had cheered when he had returned and told them what he had done, though by then he had been far from jubilant.

Such vengeance had long reaching consequences. Would their situation with the trolls have been different if Farrendel had not killed their king?

The war would have dragged on longer. The trolls had only ended the war because their king had been killed. But would this second war have happened? King Charvod was much like his father. He enjoyed torture and death. He would have pushed for war regardless.

But Prince Rharreth was different. He hated Farrendel because of the assassination, but he would not condone this kind of torture in other circumstances. He did not fully condone it now. Would he have been less hardened against her people if Farrendel had not killed his father? Or if his father had been killed on the battlefield rather than assassinated?

"I wanted to be a healer."

"Pardon?" Melantha turned back to Farrendel. Had she heard that right?

Farrendel's mouth twitched in a hint of a sad smile. "When I was young, I wanted to be a healer."

How had Melantha forgotten that? How he used to play healer and pester her with questions about what it was like to actually be a healer. She had spent those times brushing him away, still trying to come to terms with the fact that her magic forced her to become a healer instead of a warrior.

She smiled and touched his hand. "You would have made a good healer. You have a healer's heart far more than I do."

He had a loving, protective heart. It would have made him an excellent, caring healer, just as it made him a terrifying warrior.

"Perhaps." Farrendel's gaze swung to the ceiling, but it no longer seemed like he was ignoring her with the gesture. "While I do not enjoy killing, I enjoy the thrill of testing myself and claiming victory. I am, perhaps, more a warrior than a healer after all."

Melantha focused on the floor. She was not a warrior. Not really. She had attempted to kill her own brother. Worse, she had not even had the courage to do it herself. Instead, she arranged to have him killed by the trolls.

She had thought getting rid of him would solve all her problems, as if he was merely an inconvenience she could do away with, the circumstances of his birth making him less worthy of life.

But, she saw now, she would have realized her mistake

soon enough. She would have missed Farrendel, the guilt of his death gnawing in her chest the rest of her life. She would have been haunted by the brother she had killed to make her life a little easier.

Was it possible to change? To change her heart and the direction of her life? Or was it already too late? Had her choices cost too much and made her irredeemable?

CHAPTER FIFTEEN

F arrendel stirred from a doze. With Melantha's magic banishing the pain and the blanket keeping him warm, he had let himself sleep. He needed the rest, since he got little of it during the night.

A faint vibration traveled across the floor a moment before Farrendel heard bootsteps in the corridor.

He blinked and turned his head to find Melantha curled up on the floor a foot away. Close enough to tuck her slippered feet beneath the blanket she had spread over him, but not touching him. "Melantha?" He would have nudged her, but he could not move enough to reach her. "Someone is coming."

Melantha stirred, swiped at her face, and pushed herself into a sitting position. "Is it Prince Rharreth? Or someone else?"

If King Charvod walked in and discovered how lenient Prince Rharreth had become, he would not be pleased. Farrendel suppressed a grimace.

The locking bar grated, and the door creaked open.

Prince Rharreth strode inside. He wore the same leather jerkin and black trousers as he had earlier in the day. His short white hair spiked above his tapered ears.

Melantha clambered to her feet, then gestured down at Farrendel. "You usually come before your brother in the morning, so I would like to leave my blanket with Farrendel tonight. You can bring it back to my cell in the morning. You would not wish for him to weaken from cold."

Prince Rharreth glared, but Melantha did not back down.

Farrendel hardened his expression. It would do no good to let Prince Rharreth know how much he wanted that blanket. Or how much he was weakening toward Melantha. If all her help was a trick, then he should not let either of them know how close he was to losing his wariness.

"Very well." Prince Rharreth's thin-lipped, hard expression did not waver, giving Farrendel no hint to the reasons behind his actions. Why was he so willing to let Melantha help him? Did Prince Rharreth disapprove of the torture?

That was something Farrendel could leverage. Maybe. Though, figuring out people's motivations was more Essie's thing. Farrendel spent most time around people bewildered.

Prince Rharreth pressed a hand to the wall, and the stone shackle fell from Melantha's ankle. With her head high, Melantha glided from the dungeon cell. Prince Rharreth followed a moment later.

Farrendel flexed his fingers and stared at the ceiling. If only he could ask Essie what she thought of Melantha's actions. She would be able to tell if it was a trick or if it was genuine.

That foolish part of him so desperately wanted Melantha to be sincere. She was his sister. No matter what she had done to him, she was still family. As much as he had to keep his guard up, he could not hate her. No, worse. He was pretty sure he was most of the way to forgiving her.

If he was not careful, he would end up trusting her before this was over.

The door creaked again, and Prince Rharreth's heavy tread tromped back into the dungeon cell.

Farrendel flicked a glance toward the troll prince as he knelt. An icy flood of troll magic rushed through the stone piercing Farrendel. He sucked in a breath, gritting his teeth at the renewed rush of pain, though Melantha's magic managed to dull it somewhat.

He forced himself to breathe deeply and steadily until the pain subsided.

Prince Rharreth stood and turned to leave.

"Why would you allow her to help me?" Farrendel needed to probe for the answer. He was not sure Prince Rharreth would tell him the truth, but he had to ask anyway.

Prince Rharreth faced him once again, crossed his arms, and studied Farrendel.

Farrendel was not sure what he would see. Desperation, perhaps.

After a long moment, Prince Rharreth's shoulders rose and fell, as if in a deep breath. "This is not how I would have chosen to deal with a prisoner."

Farrendel huffed out something that might have been a laugh in different circumstances. He twisted his fingers as much as he could, pointing at himself. "You do not have a choice for me. Nothing less would hold me."

"If it were up to me, I would not have taken you prisoner. I would have killed you as due a vanquished enemy." Prince Rharreth rested a hand on the sword belted at his hip.

"I see." As Farrendel had decided he would rather

survive for Essie, even if it meant enduring torture, he was almost thankful Prince Rharreth had not been the one in charge. Almost.

"Nor would I use torture, even for the elf that killed my father." Prince Rharreth's gaze hardened, his mouth thinning. "But I can understand why my brother would wish to."

"He is much like your father." It was probably not wise to bring up the late troll king, but this had started with him. The late troll king had been the one to order the raids that killed the elf queen. He had tortured Farrendel and killed his father.

It had been wrong to hunt him down and kill him out of vengeance. The horror of so deliberately shedding blood still plagued Farrendel's nightmares. But there were times he struggled to feel truly sorry he had killed his tormentor. Perhaps he was only sorry he had not found a better way, a more honorable way, of going about it. It was likely that, had Farrendel waited, he would have had the chance to kill the troll king on the battlefield.

"Yes." Prince Rharreth glanced away, the only acknowledgment that he was likely to make that his brother had the same enjoyment of torture that their father had.

As the recipient of their torture-happy ways, Farrendel could vouch for that aspect of their personality.

With one last glance in Farrendel's direction, Prince Rharreth stalked from the dungeon cell. The door thunked shut behind him, the bar sliding into place. At this point, that sound was almost comforting because it signaled a few hours of being left alone.

Farrendel stared at the ceiling, the patterns of the stone overhead memorized by now. He waited until even the echoes of footfalls faded before he accessed his magic. With Melantha there for most of the day, he had not dared store the magic in the heart bond in case she sensed what he was doing. Nor had he been sure he could draw on his magic without letting a few crackling bolts slip free.

Hints of magic crackled around his fingertips under the blanket. It was so tempting to use the magic to crack the stone binding him. It would be such a relief to move a hand or arm or curl onto his side for the night to relieve the throbbing bruises on his back.

But the trolls would notice if his bonds were broken, and it was not yet time to make his move. As much as it hurt to lie here, he had to be patient. His chance would come, and this time he would be ready for it in a way he had not been fifteen years ago.

Essie, I am going to pour more magic into the heart bond.

He sensed her pausing, questioning, waiting.

When he drew his magic into his chest this time, it was easier to pour it into the heart bond than it had been before. He paused several times, making sure the impression from Essie remained as before without the slightest discomfort. All he sensed was confusion. If only he could explain exactly what he was doing.

By the time he had poured all the scraps of his magic he had been able to pull thanks to Melantha's magic, his wrists throbbed, and his head pounded.

Now concern tinged the impression from Essie.

I am fine. Just... He was not sure what he was.

If only this could be over. He could be home with Essie, either at Estyra or Aldon. Either would work. Anywhere but here. What he would not give to be safe. And free of stone and pain and daily torture.

Would he ever truly be free? Even after rescue, he would find himself back here in his nightmares. Parts of his mind were still trapped in the torture of fifteen years ago.

Farrendel forced himself to take a deep breath and unclench his fingers. One battle at a time, otherwise the future would overwhelm him.

First, he needed to face tomorrow. More torture. More pain. Another healing by Melantha.

What was he going to do about Melantha? Did he dare trust her? Was she helping him out of guilt or a reawakened sisterly love? Or was this all yet another betrayal? Her healings allowed King Charvod to torture Farrendel even more each day than he would have been able to otherwise. But if she truly did want to help, what was she supposed to do? Sit by and let him suffer?

Nothing in her actions could prove her true motivations. He did not know what to believe anymore.

What he would not give to have Essie's opinion, though he was thankful she was safe and far away from this dungeon.

He needed to figure out if he could trust Melantha, and soon. A plan was beginning to take shape, and he might need her help to implement it.

If he guessed wrong, then his plan was already doomed to failure.

CHAPTER SIXTEEN

E ssie crouched deep in the line of trees. Between the dense pines, the rows of soldiers and elves crowding the space in front of her, and the shields Averett had insisted on placing around her, she could barely see the edge of the crevasse. She couldn't see the Gulmorth River, though its roar filled the early morning while a mist hovered in the gorge.

Across the way, the scraggling pine trees and scrub brush of the Kostarian side remained quiet. Too quiet? Were they expecting the attack?

They had to be. From the moment they had captured Farrendel, they would know Tarenhiel, at least, was coming. Did they know yet that Escarland would also participate in the invasion?

Her stomach knotted. How many people were about to die on both sides of that river? Perhaps Essie should have stayed farther behind the lines as Averett had wanted.

Jalissa tucked in closer to her and pressed her hand to the ground, though she did not use her magic yet. None of the elves had, since they would not wish for the trolls to sense the use of magic and alert them to their presence.

"Are you as nervous as I am?" Essie kept her voice low as she glanced at her elvish sister-in-law.

Jalissa's face was set. Almost blank. But when she glanced at Essie, a glimmer shone in her eyes. "Terrified."

It was more than Essie had expected her to admit. But they had not had much of a chance to talk since their heart-to-heart on the train after Farrendel was taken. It seemed the bond they had formed then was still holding strong.

Today's goal was to cross the river. That was all. But that one task could take all day.

If they even succeeded in this first attempt. What if they failed and had to try again? How many times would Weylind and Averett try an invasion of Kostaria before the cost became too high? The cost would already be far too high as it was.

We're coming, Farrendel.

She resisted the urge to rub at her chest. That crackling feeling to the heart bond was getting strong. At times, it almost felt like she was constantly filled with static, though she had yet to shock herself when she touched things. It wasn't an uncomfortable or painful feeling. Just strange. Especially since she wasn't sure exactly what it was.

A signal must have been given. With a creaking of large wheels, squads of Escarlish soldiers pushed the large artillery guns forward. The long cannons would be able to lob explosive charges and grapeshot across the crevasse toward anyone who might be hiding behind the trees and rocks on the far side.

Men with large iron shields rushed forward to help protect the artillery men. It took several men to move the heavy wood and iron shields, which only provided a modicum of protection. But they would be better than nothing if the trolls guarding this stretch of the border were armed with the Escarlish weapons the traitors had provided them.

A few elves rushed forward as well and crouched behind the shield bulwarks.

The other side of the river remained still. Were the trolls there? Surely they had to be guarding their own border.

Essie gripped the stock of the rifle resting next to her. Her black trousers and tunic would keep her hidden in the shadows while her hair hung in a long braid down her back. Even behind the shield, dressed for war, she felt vulnerable. Her skin crawled, knowing each moment the bullets might start flying.

How did those soldiers march forward so bravely, crouching exposed on the edge of the crevasse?

A boom shattered the stillness, vibrating through the ground. One of the guns rolled back a few feet with the force of firing. A cloud of smoke drifted on the morning breeze, filling the pines with the scent of burnt gunpowder.

More guns fired, the roar turning into a solid, unending sound rolling across the river.

Essie pressed her hands to her ears, the ground trembling beneath her.

Under the cover of the artillery fire, the elves crouching in the forest in front of Essie pressed their hands to the ground. Ahead, Weylind's dark hair bent as a green glow filled the forest around him, illuminating Averett crouched beside him.

Next to Essie, Jalissa pressed both palms to the ground. Magic flowed around her fingers and into the ground.

A crackling groan filled the air, like that of flexing tree branches in a storm, barely audible under the thunder of the cannons.

Roots burst from the side of the gorge, thicker than Essie's waist. They launched themselves across the space.

Before the roots reached the far side, a sheet of ice poured from the far side and coated the wall of the gorge. The roots slammed into the ice and halted.

Was that an automatic defense magic? Was something like that even possible? Or were there trolls huddled behind those rocks controlling that magic?

More Escarlish soldiers hurried forward, carrying another large bulwark. Behind them, soldiers rolled forward one of the repeater guns. They pointed the gun at the wall of ice and worked the crank.

A repeated crack, higher pitched than the boom of the cannons, rang in Essie's ears. Chips of ice flew into the air, obscuring the other side in a haze of mist and the smoke of gunfire.

In all the booms of the cannons and reverberating crack of the repeater gun, Essie wasn't sure when the additional gunfire began until one of the Escarlish soldiers by the repeater gun fell, red blossoming at his shoulder.

A stiff, cold wind blasted across the gorge. A blizzard of snow filled the air, obscuring the far side from sight.

A wall of green light flared on the Tarenhieli side. The elves by the artillery were on their feet now. The light of magic pulsing around their hands varied in color from dark green to a green-blue to a lighter yellow-green. While none were as powerful as Farrendel, together, they formed a wall protecting the rest of the elves and the Escarlish soldiers.

With a blast of elven magic, they pushed back the trolls' blizzard.

As the snowflakes and smoke and magic cleared, Essie could just make out the far side of the gorge. The roots the elves had grown had snaked past the ice through gaps and holes the Escarlish soldiers had formed with the repeater gun.

Sweat beaded on Jalissa's forehead as she poured more green magic into the ground. When Essie peeked around the shields, she spotted Weylind also lit with green as he expended magic.

The roots grew, solidifying into a broad branch. From the branch, more branches shot up along the sides, forming railings, until a living arched bridge spanned the chasm.

Although she couldn't see farther than this one section of the gorge, more bridges like this should be sprouting all along the line.

Essie's mouth thinned in a tight line. The railing on the bridge had been her contribution to this plan. She'd told Weylind to make sure the elves knew to grow railings on the bridges. While the elves wouldn't balk at dashing across a branch across the gorge, the Escarlish soldiers would hesitate if asked to do so without the reassurance of railings.

But at that moment, she couldn't feel more than a slight satisfaction. It had been her contribution...the better to send Escarlish soldiers charging toward their deaths.

With the constant barrage of the artillery providing some distraction while the elves wielding their magic provided cover, a mixed squad of elven warriors and Escarlish soldiers dashed forward in formation across the open area and onto the bridge.

"Look out!" Jalissa pressed Essie to the ground as rocks

hurled from the other side of the gorge. Most were aimed at the warriors and soldiers on the bridge, but some were directed into the trees.

Saplings sprang up in front of Essie, then curled over her and Jalissa until they were protected beneath a dome of wood.

Something rattled against the barrier Jalissa had grown.

Essie peeked between the sheltering saplings. On the bridge, men and elves fell, but those left continued to press forward. At intervals, the Escarlish soldiers knelt and fired their repeating firearms. While they reloaded, the elves behind them loosed arrows, arching them into the trees on the far side.

When they reached the end of the bridge, the soldiers fired a volley. Then, the elven warriors bounded over them, swords flashing as they raced forward. The ring of steel on steel came from the far side as the elves clashed with the troll defenders.

Snow and rocks flew, obscuring the far side once again. Green and blue elven magic flashed against it. The booming artillery fell mostly silent, except for the points farthest from the bridges where they wouldn't risk hitting their own men and elves.

Weylind sprang to his feet, his sword flashing in his hand, and charged forward. A contingent of elves charged in his wake with a powerful grace. As he reached the far side, green magic surrounded Weylind. Roots burst from the ground, tossing aside the boulders and rock defenses the trolls huddled behind. He vaulted over the remains of a wall, spinning and slicing with his sword.

"I've never seen Weylind fight before. Not like this, anyway." Essie glanced at Jalissa.

"He was our strongest warrior, before Farrendel came into his magic." Jalissa's fingers still glowed as she poured her magic into the ground. "Who do you think trained Farrendel?"

Essie hadn't thought about it much, though it made sense. By the time Farrendel became Laesornysh, his father was already dead. Training Farrendel would have fallen to Weylind.

With a shout, the Escarlish army officers led their men in a charge across the bridges, now that the elves cleared the way. More repeater guns were wheeled across the bridges.

From that point on, the fighting became too heated and chaotic for Essie to follow. Partway through the day, she and Jalissa eased from their spot until they were farther behind the lines. There, they joined the effort gathering the wounded and loading them onto the ambulance wagons to travel to the encampment where Leyleira oversaw the hospital.

As the sun set, Essie sat on a stump, worn thin. Blood spattered her clothes and coated her hands. When had that happened? She had been so busy wrapping wounds, spreading the balm Illyna and the other elves had prepared, giving the injured drinks of water, and trying to lift their spirits with a smile.

Footsteps crunched on the pine needles in front of her. She blinked up, taking a moment to recognize the person standing in front of her. "Avie?"

He knelt in front of her. Dried blood coated the left side of his face from a cut across his cheek. "We gained a foothold on the far side. It will be a difficult night, but we don't intend to let them push us out."

Essie glanced around. Weylind stood a few yards away, hands gripping Jalissa's shoulders. "Julien and Edmund?"

"They're fine. They're going to camp on the far side with the army." Averett's mouth tilted wryly. "But the generals are insisting that kings and princesses should remain on this side for tonight."

Ah. At least Essie wouldn't be sitting safely behind the line all by herself. "I guess today was already costly enough."

"Yes." Averett slumped onto the ground next to her stump. "I remember the way Father looked when he returned for brief visits during the last war. He had aged. He didn't smile quite the way he used to."

Would this war make her brothers smile and laugh less? She had already seen the lasting damage war had caused to Farrendel.

She drew in a deep breath, reaching for the heart bond. It was late, and Farrendel seemed to be dozing. She didn't want to wake him if he had found some sleep.

All she wanted to do was lean against Farrendel's shoulder, his arms around her.

Averett hugged her, but it just wasn't the same. Not at all.

CHAPTER SEVENTEEN

T he door to Farrendel's cell slammed. He stared at the ceiling, refusing to glance toward the troll king's icy presence. It was best to ignore King Charvod as long as possible.

Heavy footfalls clomped to Farrendel's side. King Charvod loomed into Farrendel's line of sight. The troll's gray, square jaw was hard, his dark eyes burning. He knelt and pressed a hand to the stone next to Farrendel's shoulder. "Escarland has invaded alongside the elves."

If Farrendel had not been burying his emotions, he might have let some of his satisfaction slip at that news. Essie had done it, making sure their brothers got along enough to organize the invasion. They were coming. Farrendel just needed to hold on.

King Charvod gripped Farrendel's chin and forced Farrendel to look at him. Behind King Charvod, Prince Rharreth leaned against the wall by the door, his face impassive. King Charvod's fingers dug painfully into Farrendel's skin. "What are their plans? How do they intend to take

Gror Grar? Not that they will get close. We will push them back over the Gulmorth soon enough."

Not only had Escarland and Tarenhiel attacked, but they had successfully crossed the Gulmorth River. If the trolls could not stop them with the river between them, then surely the Escarlish and Tarenhieli army would have no trouble continuing to push them back. The next large obstacle would be Gror Grar itself.

"What is their plan?" King Charvod's fingers dug hard into Farrendel's jaw. Magic flared around his hand a moment before pain surged through Farrendel's chest.

Farrendel gritted his teeth and squeezed his eyes shut, biting back a cry of pain. He would not give King Charvod the satisfaction.

The magic cut off, and Farrendel gasped in a breath past King Charvod's grip on his chin. Someone like one of Essie's brothers would have made a sarcastic comment. Probably something about how he had been a little busy being captured and tortured when Escarland's and Tarenhiel's generals had made their plans for war.

Instead, Farrendel glared up at King Charvod. "I do not know. I was already your prisoner when they formed their alliance."

"But you are Tarenhiel's elite warrior. You must have some idea of their plans." King Charvod sent another burst of magic into the stones.

This time Farrendel could not fully swallow the cry of pain. Warm, sticky blood dribbled against his back from where the stone had pierced him. "Escarland's aid will change any strategy I would know."

He could be certain of only one thing regarding plans. His brother and Essie's brothers would be coming for him.

Something of his thoughts must have shown on his face. King Charvod's face cracked with a sneer. "You think they will rescue you, as your father did before. They might try, but even with Escarland's help, their army will break against the walls of Gror Grar."

The fortress perched on a steep mountainside with only a single bridge leading to the gate. The inner keep of Gror Grar was built into the mountain with a warren of tunnels, not just for the dungeon but for the inner chambers of the troll king and his family.

Could Weylind take the fortress? Even with the powerful weapons Essie's kingdom had invented?

"Besides, I have you." King Charvod grinned as he sent another stab of stone into Farrendel. "When your brother arrives, intending to take the fortress, I will pin you to the walls and let him hear you scream before you die."

Farrendel tried, but he could not stop a cry of pain this time. His head pounded, and he had to clench his hands to stop himself from unleashing the magic he had conserved over the past few days.

Even if they could take Gror Grar, could they reach Farrendel before King Charvod killed him?

Unlikely. Very unlikely.

"How much will your brother be willing to negotiate to spare you?" King Charvod's grin showed his teeth. They were not pointed, but they should have been for how feral his grin was. "And while he is negotiating, he will come close to the walls where a bullet to the heart or the head will end him quickly enough. Another elf king killed on Kostarian soil."

Farrendel could picture it all too clearly. Weylind would be cautious. But if Farrendel was pinned like a bug on the wall of Gror Grar, his blood dripping down the stones, Weylind would lose his caution. He would be desperate.

It was so tempting to grasp his magic and blast it through the troll king's heart.

If he did that, then he would never see Essie again. Prince Rharreth would kill him only seconds after King Charvod died.

The truth was, Farrendel only lived because King Charvod wanted him alive for torture.

If Farrendel could take out King Charvod, would it matter if he died as well? Was that the kind of sacrifice his father would have made?

But Farrendel had promised Essie to survive. He wanted that life, the life he had tasted so briefly during those three months with her.

Perhaps he should not kill King Charvod just yet. He should conserve his magical strength and make sure that, when he made his move, he would be able to kill the troll king and defend himself. After all, King Charvod had all but promised he would come for Farrendel when Weylind attacked. That was the moment when Farrendel would make his move.

By then, Escarland's and Tarenhiel's combined army would have proved they could defeat Kostaria. They would be in a position of strength to negotiate a peace with Prince Rharreth. If Farrendel killed King Charvod now, not only would Farrendel end up dead, but Weylind and Averett would only have just stepped foot in Kostaria. Prince Rharreth might not even negotiate for peace. He might choose to push them back and continue the war rather than admit defeat.

No, Farrendel needed to bide his time.

"Are you even listening?" King Charvod growled. "Perhaps a shot to the heart is too quick for your brother. Perhaps I should give him a taste of what you have suffered before he dies."

"I will...kill you...first." Farrendel glared at King Charvod. It took all his self-control not to reach for his magic.

King Charvod slapped his hand to Farrendel's chest and shoved his magic through Farrendel into the floor, drawing on the stone.

Farrendel's breath seized. He could not breathe, could not think, as another wave of pain slammed into him. Pain and blood and screams until, finally, black nothingness.

SOMETHING cold and wet touched his mouth. Farrendel groaned. His head hurt. His chest hurt.

"Farrendel. Can you hear me?"

Essie?

No, not Essie. She was far away.

A warm, soothing magic flowed through him, brushing away the pain in his head and his chest.

Not Essie. Melantha.

He cracked his eyes open. Her black hair blurred against the ceiling for a moment before she came into focus.

She tucked a hand beneath his neck, lifted his head, and pressed a cold tin cup to his mouth. "Try to drink a little."

He sipped at the cold water. It hurt as it settled into his stomach.

How badly had the troll king hurt him this time? Even Melantha's magic was struggling to heal him.

He reached for the crackle of his magic. Still there, tucked with the warmth of the heart bond. He kept much of the shield in place, keeping Essie from feeling the pain he was still in.

Melantha laid his head back down. She pressed her palm to his forehead. "Just lie easy for a few minutes."

More warmth soothed his aching muscles and bones. Farrendel drew in as deep a breath as he could manage. As he did, the truth settled more deeply into his chest.

He needed Melantha's help to make this plan work. He would need her magic, her strength, for he would have no strength left when it came time to act.

But did he dare trust her? If he trusted her, and she betrayed him again...

He would lose Essie forever.

Yet without Melantha's help, he definitely would not return to Essie. He would end up pinned to the wall of Gror Grar.

He forced his eyes open. "Melantha?"

"Yes?" She leaned over him. Her black hair straggled, unwashed. She shifted her hand from his forehead to his shoulder, pouring another wave of magic into him.

He could feel the crackle of his magic as her healing magic flooded through him. "Why are you helping me now?"

"How could I not?" Melantha fussed with the blanket thrown over him. "I know there is nothing I can say or do to make up for what I did. But I am sorry. I never should have..."

He wanted so badly to believe her. Perhaps that was a reason he should be more wary. Was he merely deluding himself that she was truly sorry?

He was not sure what to say in response to her. He squeezed his eyes shut and listened. He could not hear anyone in the dungeon corridor, nor could he sense anyone with the little bit of magic he allowed himself.

But he could not confess this secret without being sure. Not that he could be certain she would answer him truthfully if she was still working with the trolls. "Have the trolls left?"

"Yes, they have been gone for some time now." Melantha adjusted her position on the floor, rattling the stone shackle on her ankle. "They were arguing as they left. King Charvod is leaving tonight to lead the army, and he ordered Prince Rharreth to stay here to guard you and prepare Gror Grar's defenses. Prince Rharreth was not happy with this arrangement. He seemed to imply that he is the stronger of the two of them and, as the prince, should be the one with the army while King Charvod should remain here. King Charvod was not pleased by this dissent."

Would Melantha have told him that if she was working with the trolls? Then again, Farrendel had no way to know if she had truly overheard an argument or if she was making it up for some nefarious purpose.

But if she was telling the truth, then Farrendel would have a few days' relief from the torture. Prince Rharreth would not torture him. He would probably largely ignore him. He might even leave Melantha with him all the time, which would allow him to regain physical and magical strength even more quickly. Not to mention, give him and Melantha time to plan, if he decided to trust her.

"How soon do you think Prince Rharreth will return?" Farrendel might respect Prince Rharreth more than his brother, but the troll prince was still loyal. He would halt Farrendel's plans if he overheard them.

"Not for a while. Maybe not even at all tonight." Melantha shook her head and tucked her toes beneath the blanket near Farrendel's arm. "You were in a bad way when the two of them left. Prince Rharreth stomped back only moments after King Charvod left, all but dragged me and my blanket from my cell, and plopped me in here. I think he barely remembered to shackle my ankle before he hurried off. Probably to argue with his brother some more."

It would make more sense for Prince Rharreth to lead the army. But Farrendel could not help but hope that Prince Rharreth lost the argument. Not only would it spare him a few days of torture, but with Prince Rharreth here, King Charvod would be the easier of the two for Weylind and Essie's brothers to fight.

Melantha touched his arm, and Farrendel flinched, his mind conjuring memories of King Charvod's hand and icy magic tearing through his chest. He hissed a sharp breath and tried to force his heartbeat to slow.

"I am sorry." Melantha withdrew her hand and hugged her knees to her chest. At that moment, she looked small and scared. Nothing like the strong, aloof sister he knew. A shiver shook her fingers before she buried them in her skirt.

She had given up her blanket and poured her magic into him to keep him warm.

He was going to trust her. It might be a mistake. But he had to risk it.

"Melantha?" Farrendel flexed his fingers, his heart beating harder. Was he really going to do this? If she turned him in, it would take away the last shred of control he had over his situation. "Can I trust you?"

"Yes." She said it quickly. Too quickly? He could not tell. But she met his gaze unwaveringly. "What I did was wrong. So very wrong. I will not betray you or Tarenhiel again. Right now, I just want to do whatever I can to get you out of here."

It was what he wanted to hear. Did she know that? Was that why she said it?

Was he about to be tricked again?

Then again, what did he have to lose? If she tricked him, he would die. But if he did not trust her, he was just as likely to die.

"I hope you are telling the truth." Farrendel drew in a deep breath. This was it. "I have a plan, and I will need your help. But I am not sure I should trust you with this."

"I can see why you would hesitate." Melantha hugged her knees tighter, her black hair scraggling down her back and over her shoulders. "I have had a lot of time to think, lately. I have realized how disappointed—no, more than disappointed—Father would be with me. Mother, too. She would have liked you."

"I would not exist if she had lived." Their father never would have betrayed her. He had loved her too deeply. Farrendel bit back the ache in his chest. It had been too easy as a boy to imagine that the kind, loving person that everyone talked about would have extended that love to him, despite how he had been born.

Much like how Essie's mother had taken him into the family, even though he had ended up married to her daughter because of a treaty. The memory eased the pain. Whatever the pain that still lingered in his own family, Essie's family had shown him healing was possible. Perhaps his family would find a way toward the happiness her family had built after the death of her father.

Assuming he and Melantha survived this.

Melantha reached, as if to rest a hand on his shoulder, but drew her hand back. "I still miss my mother, dreadfully. But, being here has reminded me of how much I am thankful you exist. You are my..." She hesitated. "You are family."

It stung, that she still would not claim him as her brother. But a part of him trusted her more because of it. It would have been suspicious if she had been too quick to assert he was her brother after what she had said while betraying him.

The last bit of tension faded from his muscles. Perhaps he was making a mistake. But this was his choice, and maybe, if he chose wrong, he would die before learning the truth. He would rather die believing his sister actually loved him. "Did you hear their plans for me? And Weylind?"

Melantha grimaced. "Yes. Hard not to when King Charvod was shouting."

"I cannot allow King Charvod to go through with his plans. Not only do I not want to die pinned to the wall of Gror Grar..."

Melantha's grimace twisted her face even more. "Understandable. I think King Charvod is going crazier the longer he has you in his clutches."

Something Farrendel had seen in the late troll king as well. "But I especially do not want Weylind to be killed trying to rescue me like Father was. Nor do I wish to put any of Essie's family in danger. Whether King Charvod parades me out during the attack or if Weylind sends a small party into this dungeon to attempt a rescue, it will be a trap. Anyone trying to rescue me will be killed."

"And you have a plan to prevent that? How can I help?" Melantha leaned forward, her hands fisted in her skirt.

Did she sound too eager? As if she had been playing up until this moment to get him to spill his secret?

No, he had chosen to trust her. He was not going to doubt himself now. Of course she was eager. She was also stuck in this dungeon, and, even though she had resented Farrendel, she loved Weylind as a brother. A brother with whom she shared a father and a mother. She would not wish to see Weylind killed.

"I do not plan to be here when King Charvod comes to kill me." Farrendel drew on his magic and let a few bolts twine around his fingers.

Melantha gasped and flung back the blanket covering his hand nearest her. She gaped at his fingers. "You can use your magic."

"Thanks to your healing magic. When you coat the stone and troll magic with yours, it stops their effect on me, and I am able to access my magic." Farrendel drew his magic back into his chest, easing it into the heart bond. That was something he was going to keep to himself. He might have decided to trust Melantha, but it would be best if she did not know everything. "I believe I can break the stone pinning me and free myself."

"Really?" Melantha stopped hugging her knees and sat forward, her eyes wide. "Then what are we waiting for? Break the stone, and we can get out of here while the trolls are distracted."

It soothed his suspicions that she was so eager. Perhaps it helped prove that she was just as much a prisoner as he was. Her cheeks were sunken, her cheekbones sharp. Her dress hung on her frame, her fingers knobby. If she was helping the trolls, then she was being forced in some way. Surely no one would go to such lengths as to starve herself and be locked up in the dungeon with him if she was here out of her own free will.

Farrendel shook his head. "We cannot leave now. You and I are both weak, and we have no supplies. Doubtless, the trolls have blanketed Kostaria in ice and snow to slow down Escarland's and Tarenhiel's armies. Without supplies, we would not get far. Even if we could, we have the entire troll army standing between us and safety."

"Oh. Right." Melantha sighed and slumped. "So what is the plan?"

This felt all too similar to the conversation he had with Essie on the train. The plan was essentially the same. Waiting for the last moment, believing that to be the right time, instead of acting right away.

Perhaps he and Essie should have attempted the leap from the train. They might have survived without too much damage, and he would not have ended up here, locked in the trolls' dungeon.

But Essie would not have learned about Melantha or Thanfardil. How much worse would the war have been had Thanfardil remained in charge of all of Tarenhiel's train system? He could have alerted the trolls to every movement of troops and supplies. He could have sabotaged Escarland's army as they tried to transport all their weapons across Tarenhiel.

And, without this, Melantha would have gone on hating Farrendel. She might not have continued to aid the trolls, but she probably would have given them enough information to kill Farrendel on the battlefield. He might have ended up here anyway.

It had been the right decision to wait there on the train. Waiting was the necessary choice now.

"We have to wait until Escarland's and Tarenhiel's army attacks Gror Grar." Farrendel stared at the ceiling, steeling himself. It sounded so appealing to break the stone now, end this pain, and take his chances in the rocky, icy wilds of Kostaria.

"You wish to wait until then? Is that not risky? That is when King Charvod plans to drag you out onto the wall. Or possibly kill you here. Or otherwise use you as a trap for Weylind." Melantha went back to hugging her knees.

"I know." Farrendel flexed his fingers, telling himself he needed to bide his time. He would only get one chance to escape. "With your magic, I might be able to access enough of my magic to help from the inside. It will be difficult for Weylind to take Gror Grar, unless someone were to blow the gates out from the inside. Or maybe part of the wall."

Melantha huffed and shook her head. "I never realized your plans were so grandiose. You do not want just to escape. You wish to take down the entire fortress."

"King Charvod cannot pin me to a wall if I knock the wall down first." He took too much satisfaction from the thought. This place was getting to him. "But I will settle for causing some minor problems and distractions as we make our way to Weylind. The primary concern is escaping alive."

"Of course." Melantha patted his hand. "I will do every-thing I can to make sure you get home."

Her fingers were cold. Without a blanket, dressed in a silk dress as she was, she must be freezing.

"Thank you." Farrendel tried to shift, but the stone pinned him too tightly. All he could do was wiggle his fingers. "If Prince Rharreth is not likely to return tonight, then you should share the blanket. The nights are growing colder."

"Perhaps Prince Rharreth will let me haul more of the straw from my cell into here. Maybe I can even convince him to let me stay here. It would be easier for him to care for both of us at once." Melantha settled onto the floor next to him, her back to him, and tugged a corner of the blanket over herself. She rested her head on her arm. "How long do you think it will take Weylind and the army to get here?"

"I do not know." Farrendel shifted his head, trying to find a more comfortable spot on the small padding of straw Melantha had given him. Realistically, it would probably take weeks. The ice and blizzards that the trolls would hurl at the army would make going difficult, and he could not begin to guess what it would take to move Escarland's army over the treacherous Kostarian terrain with all their large weapons.

But he desperately hoped it would not be that long. Surely Weylind would have guessed how the trolls would fight back, and he would have planned for it. And Essie's brothers would have figured out a way to counteract the ice for Escarland's army as well.

He reached for the heart bond. Somewhere, Essie was trying to sleep. But she was cold. Why was she cold? Surely she was not in Kostaria. Her brother Averett would not have wanted her anywhere near the fighting.

But she would come for him. Because of the heart bond, she might have been able to talk her brothers into it.

Another reason he needed to escape on his own.

CHAPTER

EIGHTEEN

T he blizzard howled above the thick branches of the shelter Jalissa had grown from the scrub brush that grew between the rocks of the windswept Kostarian wilderness.

Essie shifted. The grass and scrub brush padding Jalissa had also grown insulated them from the cold of the ground and was far softer than the rock. But it was still so cold. She tucked her face deeper into the blanket. Her nose was cold. Her fingers were cold. Even dressed in thick clothes and under the blankets allotted to her and Jalissa, her bones still ached with cold.

The blanket shook with a shiver, but Essie wasn't the one shivering. She half rolled to peer over her shoulder at Jalissa. "It's hard to sleep when you're shivering."

"Yes." Jalissa pressed her hand to the wall of the shelter, and more leaves and branches filled in the cracks to make their shelter more snug. "I hope the warriors do not freeze tonight."

Essie nodded. The elves had expended as much energy as they dared to grow shelters like this for most of the men, both elves and humans. But a portion of the men had to stay alert and patrolling to make sure there would not be a night attack. Nor could most of the shelters be as snug as the one Essie shared with Jalissa, since a door needed to be left for the Escarlish soldiers. According to Essie's brothers, they were using the canvas from their tents to block the worst of the wind.

Essie shifted closer to the center of the shelter. She and Jalissa had left space between them, but perhaps it was time to stop worrying about personal space. "If we sleep back to back, we'll stay warmer."

Jalissa immediately shifted and put her back to Essie's. It took a few moments, but Essie felt warmer.

In the shelter her brothers were sharing, they were probably sleeping in a pile to stay warm, though they would not admit it to anyone.

For some reason, the thought made her giggle.

Jalissa glanced over her shoulder. "I do not see anything funny."

"Sorry, thinking about my brothers unwillingly snuggling to stay warm. Do you think your brother will deign to join their pile out of desperation? He doesn't have anyone else."

Jalissa snorted out something like a laugh. "If he does, it will be because your brothers dragged him there too forcibly for him to resist. Though, I almost hope they do. I hate to think of him shivering alone on a night like this."

The branches above them creaked as another gust of wind howled down from the nearby mountain.

Essie wormed deeper into the blankets. "I've slept

outside before, but this is a lot colder than family camping nights, that's for sure."

"It will probably become even colder before we reach Gror Grar." Jalissa also burrowed into the blankets.

Essie grimaced at that thought. Each day had been a hard-fought battle, and not just against the trolls. The trolls had used their magic to blanket their kingdom with snow and ice. Slogging through it wearied the men even before they reached the battle, while they struggled to stay warm during the night. The mule teams strained to pull the artillery guns forward, even though they had been put on sled skis to make moving them easier, while the few steam-powered transports for the weapons often got stuck on the rough terrain and had to be levered free.

Those same steam-powered vehicles had to have their boilers stoked all through the night to keep the engines warm. Normally a job the soldiers avoided, but now they all but fought over the duty. Other soldiers stoked the fires that kept the artillery guns warm enough to function properly.

Even the set of train tracks left abandoned by the trolls was too iced over to be of use, even if they could retrofit an elven train to work on the rails.

"Attacking Kostaria in the early fall might not have been the wisest choice." Essie's shivers eased as Jalissa's shared warmth seeped into her.

Not that they had much of a choice, if they wished to rescue Farrendel. Besides, back in Escarland, the trees had not even begun to turn their autumn colors yet. Summer still lingered with warm days and only mildly chilly nights.

"It would not have mattered. They would have blanketed their kingdom in snow regardless. They have few crops to worry about killing in the summer." Jalissa tensed, then raised her head. "Grab your rifle."

Essie reached for the gun she had tucked alongside her under her blankets, keeping it warm and ready. "Another night attack? What direction?"

Then she heard the shouting, the reports of muskets, and the clash of bladed weapons.

Jalissa pointed at the wall of the shelter by their feet. "That is from behind our lines."

Meaning, the trolls had somehow circled around to attack from the rear. A rear guard was stationed around the perimeter, protecting the noncombatants and healers, but it would not be many.

Essie pushed to her knees. "We need to get everyone to the safety of the front lines."

"The trolls might be attacking there too." Jalissa picked up her bow and quiver of arrows.

Good point. "It should still be safer than staying here."

The shouting grew louder, closer. Jalissa grimaced. "Very well. We should hurry."

That was a given. She and Jalissa might be able to hold their own against a few trolls. But neither of them was a trained warrior.

Jalissa slung her quiver across her back and glanced at Essie. "Ready?"

As she was already fully dressed and wearing her coat, Essie looped the strap of her ammo pouch over her head and gripped her rifle. Her stomach knotted, but she forced herself to smile. "Yes."

Pressing a hand to the wall, Jalissa's green magic seeped into their brush shelter. The branches withdrew, opening a door.

An icy blast pelted Essie's face with globs of snow. She blinked, squinting into the blizzard.

Figures dashed across the camp. Elven healers, the Escarlish surgeons, and a few soldiers ran through the snow, headed for the safety of the front line. Behind them came a tight knot of trolls, their white hair and gray skin nearly blending into their blizzard.

Essie clambered to her feet and dashed across the snow. When she could get a shot past her fleeing men and allies, Essie dropped to a knee and lifted her rifle. She drew in a deep breath, held it as she lined up her shot, then released a part of her breath to steady her hands. Her finger gently squeezed the trigger.

A troll went down, blood staining the snow.

She couldn't let herself think about the fact that she had just taken another life. Stomach churning, she levered the rifle to chamber a round and lined up for another shot.

Jalissa halted next to her. The bow thrummed. An arrow plunged into the throat of another troll.

"Rally to the princess!" A command called in Escarlish. A few of the fleeing Escarlish soldiers halted and veered their path toward Essie.

As she fired again, wounding a troll in the arm this time, a few Escarlish soldiers flopped to the ground beside her, raising muskets.

"Stand by the princess!" This shout was in elvish. The elven warriors on the rear guard formed up next to Jalissa.

Essie couldn't tell, thanks to all the swirling snow, but her and Jalissa's small force seemed pitiful compared to the numbers racing toward them.

Except for the cold and snow, this was too much like that

ambush. Had it really only been a mere two and a half weeks ago?

But this time, there would be no Farrendel to blast the trolls back with his magic.

A few more physicians and elven healers fled past, loaded down with stretchers. Trying to save the wounded too injured to flee on their own.

Essie and Jalissa just needed to buy some time for the others to get to safety. Once the attack at the rear was reported, reinforcements would come, probably with Weylind and Averett leading the charge.

Would they come in time?

Essie banished all such thoughts from her head and focused on another target. She needed to get off as many shots as she could before the trolls got too close for her gun to make a difference.

She fired three shots before she had to pause and reload. With the gloves making her fingers thick and the snow blasting her with cold, she fumbled with the cartridges. Too long. This was taking too long.

The trolls rushed forward. Muskets and repeating rifles fired next to Essie, but only a portion of the shots struck targets. The rest were deflected with troll magic or missed altogether. Jalissa and the elves rained down arrows, but many were blown off course by the howling wind.

A few of the trolls paused long enough to raise their own repeating rifles. One of the soldiers not far from Essie cried out. She gritted her teeth. It was the most painful of ironies that her soldiers were being killed by Escarland's own weapons.

She finally managed to shove the last cartridge into the gun. She levered the bolt to chamber the first round, raised, and fired. The trolls were close enough now she hardly had to aim.

Should she give the order to retreat? Did they even have enough men to make a defensive retreat? If they simply fled, the trolls would cut them down as they ran. More soldiers tended to be killed during panicked retreats than were killed in the actual battles.

No more time. The trolls were too close.

She reached for the heart bond, thankful Farrendel wasn't blocking her. She wasn't sure how to communicate goodbye to him. Was this goodbye? After all she had done to try to get him back, she certainly hadn't planned on dying in the snow during a night ambush before ever reaching Gror Grar.

Farrendel's concern flooded through her, along with the growing crackle in the heart bond that felt a lot like his magic.

I wish you were here. I wish you could unleash a wave of power to blast them back. Essie raised the rifle again for one last shot before the trolls reached them. This was all too much like those last moments of that ambush, when she had glanced at Farrendel, thinking she was going to die. She tried to will that same feeling she'd had, meeting his gaze then, through the heart bond to him now. She found herself reaching for that simmer of power, as if in a desperate attempt to draw on it.

The crackle built, humming in her ears. The warmth of the heart bond filled her chest. No, not just the heart bond. She gasped, struggling to breathe past the power filling her.

Some instinct, or perhaps it was a nudge through the heart bond, made her drop her rifle and raise her hands, as if warding off the oncoming trolls.

Sizzling blue power blazed in front of her before blasting outward, hurling the trolls several yards backwards.

Essie gaped at her hands. That had been Farrendel's magic. Had she done that? Or had he done it through her? How had he managed to decipher the impressions she'd sent him enough to guess what she needed?

"What was that?" Jalissa gripped Essie's shoulder, staring down at her with wide eyes. "Was that..."

"I don't know." Essie fumbled to pick up her rifle, then dropped it again. She wasn't sure what she should be doing with her hands. Raise them for another blast of magic? Start firing her rifle again?

The sense of a question came from Farrendel. Asking if she was all right? Or if she needed more power?

Yes. Maybe. She didn't know. How did she even go about telling him what she needed?

A few of the trolls had clambered to their feet. One raised a rifle, aiming it straight at Essie. Even with the yards separating them, that black muzzle gaped round and deadly, about to spew its lethal projectile.

Essie flung out a hand in the direction of the troll, squeezing her eyes shut as if that would make him disappear or miss or make the bullet hurt less as it tore through her chest. She tugged on the crackle in the heart bond. *Farrendel!*

Another crackle of magic built in her chest before exploding outward with jarring force. Essie gritted her teeth at the sulfuric sizzle that filled the air. Her scalp and arms prickled as if all of her hair was attempting to stand on end beneath her hat and coat.

A bolt of blue magic plowed into the troll, cutting through him and the troll behind him before blasting into a wave of energy that knocked the few trolls that had regained their feet back to the snow.

She wasn't in control of this magic. The thought tightened her chest, her breathing coming in gasps. How did she stop it? Control it? She sensed the well of power that magic had come from, and the sheer vastness made her stomach heave.

Was this what Farrendel sensed when he unleashed his magic? No wonder he used as little of his magic as possible, as if he feared what would happen if he lost control over it.

And she didn't even have his level of control over this power. Somehow, Farrendel was channeling his magic through her. He wouldn't know what the battle looked like or what was truly needed.

Boots crunched on the snow behind her. She didn't have the strength to turn to look.

But she didn't have to. She recognized the voice shouting orders. Averett.

Another question from Farrendel.

No, no. Make it stop. Please. Too much.

She wasn't sure how much of that he understood. Her mental voice was screechy with panic even to herself.

The crackle cut off instantly. The normal warmth of the heart bond returned, filled with worry.

Essie wanted to vomit. Or perhaps curl in the snow and pass out. Her head still buzzed, though that could be from her hyperventilating instead of all the magic that had poured through.

She forced herself to draw in a deep breath, then let it out slowly. Her head cleared, the cold air steadying her.

The worried impression from Farrendel had grown even more pronounced.

I'm fine. She tried to relax and send the relief of being alive to him instead of the panic of having magic unexpectedly blast from her hands. She glanced up to the fighting in front of them. Averett's soldiers and Weylind's warriors had pushed the trolls back, and it looked like the trolls were retreating, fading back into the snow and the mountains. *I'm safe. Well, for now.*

Farrendel relaxed, though some of the crackle of his magic still simmered in the heart bond.

Thank you. Essie wasn't sure he would sense it. Even locked in the trolls' dungeon, he had managed to save her.

Except, they had never done something like this before. How could he possibly wield his magic through her? Did she perhaps partially draw on the magic through the heart bond? That heart bond magic was half hers, after all, in some shape or form. Farrendel might be the one with magic, but it took two people to form a heart bond. He couldn't have done it on his own any more than she could have.

The bigger question was, could she wield his magic again?

And did she want to?

If she could, then this could be the tipping point in pushing the trolls back to Gror Grar. But that would mean she would have to fight like Farrendel. On the front lines. Causing bloodshed.

It went against her nature. She wasn't a warrior. She didn't want to become one. Perhaps she was willing to take up a gun when backed into a corner. Or to fight her way to Farrendel to rescue him.

But to fight like her brothers did?

The noise of battle ahead of them died away. A figure dashed toward them through the snow. When he sank to his knees in front of Essie, it wasn't any of her brothers, but Farrendel's.

Snow coated Weylind's long hair, though he wore a fur hat to keep his head and ears warm. His dark eyes searched Essie's face. "Was that Farrendel's magic I saw as we were running here? It felt like his."

"Yes, it was." Essie shivered at another blast of the icy wind. Now that the power of Farrendel's magic had faded, she became aware of the cold once again. Over Weylind's shoulder, she spotted Averett trotting toward her. "But maybe let's discuss it somewhere warm?"

Weylind rose to his feet. "Very well. Come."

Jalissa gripped her bow and tromped through the snow after Weylind.

Averett halted in front of Essie and held out a hand. "Was that what I thought it was?"

"Yes, it was, and no, I have no idea how it was possible." Essie took Averett's hand and let him pull her to her feet.

Soon, she found herself crawling through the narrow door into her brothers' shelter, this one much larger than the one Jalissa had grown for her and Essie as it also served as the command center.

Inside, she counted four bedrolls, not just three. Perhaps Weylind really had moved into here with her brothers for warmth. Or maybe there just wasn't enough scrub brush to make two shelters.

Weylind already sat on one of the bedrolls, the one set the farthest from the other three. Jalissa lowered herself onto the bedroll next to him.

Essie sat on one of the other bedrolls. This explanation would have been so much easier if she knew exactly what Farrendel had done on his side of things. As of right now, her explanation boiled down to a big *I don't know* that probably wasn't going to satisfy anyone.

A few seconds later, Averett crawled inside, brushing snow from his shoulders. "I sent for Edmund and Julien."

Good. She would be able to give her non-explanation to all of them at once.

Averett settled onto the blanket next to her. "I should have asked earlier. Are you all right?"

"Yes, I'm fine. Not a scratch." Essie wrapped her arms around her stomach. The panic of so much magic coursing through her was fading, leaving her muscles aching and her eyes heavy. Though, the exhaustion could be because it was the middle of the night, and she hadn't been sleeping even before the nighttime raid.

He wrapped an arm around her, and she leaned against his shoulder. It would have been far nicer to lean against Farrendel's shoulder. But before Farrendel, her brothers had been her shoulders to lean against and cry on. That didn't change, even though she was married.

"You don't sound fine." Averett's arm around her tightened.

"Just tired." Essie sighed. It was warm, leaning against him. "Maybe we should bunk with all of you. It would be safer. And warmer."

"You snore."

"I do not. I breathe loudly." She tried to keep her tone light, but it was hard, remembering that same teasing argument with Farrendel. Farrendel, at least, had a leg to stand on. He slept as silently as a rock as long as he wasn't having a nightmare. Essie's brothers, though, were just as noisy as she was. "It's not like any of you sleep silently either."

Across the way, Weylind glanced at them and gave a tiny

huff. It was the elf equivalent of an eyeroll. If he had been camping in here with all three of Essie's brothers, then he would have been subjected to the full force of Averett's nighttime lip smacking, Julien's snoring, and Edmund's... well, Edmund was mostly silent, except for when he talked in his sleep.

The cold swirl of snow blowing through the opening to the shelter made Essie peel her eyes open as Julien and Edmund crawled inside. The tent canvas fell back over the opening, keeping out the rest of the howling wind.

"What's this I hear about a family meeting?" Julien glanced around before sinking onto the bedroll closest to the door. "A full, both families meeting, I see."

"What happened?" Edmund jabbed a thumb over his shoulder. "Besides the sneak attack to our rear lines. If this was only about that attack, then I would expect we would be having this meeting with the generals. They weren't too happy to be put off."

"This is important." Averett glanced from Edmund to Weylind across the shelter before peering down at Essie. "You'd better explain. I just caught a glimpse of it."

"A glimpse of what?" Julien's frown deepened as he glanced from Jalissa and Weylind to Essie, as if guessing this had something to do with elves.

Where did she even begin to explain? With the blast of power?

No, she should go back farther than that. She couldn't leave anything out. Maybe, if she gave as much information as possible, Weylind would be more forthcoming instead of mysterious with any conclusions he came to.

"For the past few days, I've felt a...crackle to the heart bond. Like Farrendel's magic." Essie sat up straighter. It seemed more appropriate to sit properly instead of slumped against Averett when giving a report.

"And you didn't mention anything?" Averett pulled back and turned to her.

"We were all a little busy planning for war and invading Kostaria and fighting for our lives through this blizzard. Besides, I wasn't even sure that feeling was unusual. It isn't like anyone handed me an instruction manual on heart bonds." She resisted the urge to glare at Weylind and Jalissa. This all would make so much more sense if elves weren't so tight-lipped about their magic. "All this reaching for Farrendel through the heart bond has made me more sensitive to it. I thought I was just sensing his magic in him, nothing more."

Across the shelter, Weylind was frowning, but he didn't deign to comment. Jalissa met Essie's gaze and just shrugged. As Jalissa had never been married and experienced a heart bond herself, she probably didn't have anything but stories to add.

Did Weylind have a heart bond with his wife Rheva? No one had said anything one way or the other. But as their cryptic grandmother Leyleira had mentioned, elves didn't talk about personal matters like heart bonds unless forced to. Or if that heart bond reached legendary status. Then they had no problem talking about it.

"Then, tonight, when those trolls attacked, Jalissa and I were rallying the defenders and trying to give the healers and wounded time to escape. Things looked desperate for a moment there, and it reminded me of the ambush outside of Lethorel. I reached for the heart bond, for Farrendel. I'm guessing Farrendel sensed enough through the heart bond to know I was in trouble." Essie shrugged and waved her hands in front of her. "Next thing I know, his magic is blasting from me. I'm not sure if it was him or me or both or how he even deciphered enough through the heart bond to figure out what I needed. Communication is hardly precise."

Averett faced King Weylind. "Do you have any thoughts on how such...magic-sharing is possible? It won't hurt Essie, will it?"

"I am unaware of such a thing happening before, though I suppose it is not out of the realm of possibility." Weylind cleared his throat and glanced at the ceiling of their shelter.

Essie glared at him. "What does that even mean? And no cryptic answers this time. I don't care if it is a sarcastic answer you would give to a two-year-old as long as it's understandable to magicless humans."

Weylind raised that eyebrow at her again.

Essie planted her fists on her hips. The gesture lost something since she was sitting down, and she managed to elbow Averett in the ribs. "Come on. Spit it out. This isn't the time for your elven sense of propriety."

Weylind's shoulders lifted in the restrained, elven shrug. "As I said, I have never heard of those with an elishina sharing magic like this before. But there is much even we elves do not know about elishinas. And an elishina between a human and an elf with Farrendel's magic is bound to be more unpredictable than most."

That wasn't much more helpful than his first comment, but at least Weylind was trying. Somewhat.

"I guess it makes sense. I mean, if we're sharing enough life essence or magic or whatever for me to keep his heart beating while he's grievously wounded and for him to extend my life by several centuries, that's already a lot of sharing going on. What's a little magic on top of all that?"

Essie leaned her elbows on her knees. Now that she thought about it, she wondered why she hadn't thought of it before. Perhaps because it would have sounded crazy, if she hadn't already done it.

"Most of the time in an elishina, both already have magic and have no need to reach for each other's magic." Weylind gestured to her. "But in your case, you do not have magic while Farrendel…"

"Farrendel has enough magic for both of us." She probably hadn't needed to say it out loud. Everyone there had to be thinking it.

"Indeed." Weylind glanced around the shelter, at Essie's brothers listening but not interrupting, before he focused back on her. Some twist to his mouth or hitch in his breathing suggested he was struggling to find words. But at least he was trying to accommodate her by being more forthcoming. "Each elishina is as unique as the individuals bonded by it. No one can predict exactly how it will manifest. It is known elishinas can be strengthened through ordeals, especially when the elishina is still new."

So being young and in love made the elishina do such crazy things that even the elves didn't dare predict what could happen? That was…comforting.

"But that doesn't answer my question." Averett pointed at Essie. "Will it hurt her?"

"If Farrendel's magic was going to hurt her, it would have done it while surging through her." Weylind's voice was back to matter of fact.

Essie nearly snorted. So reassuring to know how worried her brother-in-law was about her.

"Guess that answers the question of whether I'm immune to his magic." Accidentally wielding his magic against charging trolls probably wasn't easier—and definitely not safer—than sticking her hand into his magic to test it, but at least she knew.

"There's one big question no one has thought to ask yet." Edmund broke into the conversation, glancing to Essie before focusing on Weylind. "How does Farrendel have the ability to use his magic? I thought the whole reason he was captured was that the trolls had a way to block his magic. If he can use his magic, does that mean he has escaped somehow? I think that would be rather important information to know before we march to Gror Grar."

Right. Essie had told her brothers some of what she could sense through the heart bond, but she hadn't shared all of what she suspected.

But Edmund's gaze was still focused on Weylind, as if he thought Weylind would have the answer.

Weylind lifted his shoulders in a small shrug once again. "I do not know."

All eyes turned to Essie. She breathed out a sigh. "I don't know either. Not exactly. I know...I know he was tortured shortly after we invaded Kostaria. He blocked me through the heart bond for a long time that day. He hasn't been tortured since."

Was the invasion keeping the trolls too busy to torture Farrendel? If that were the case, then Essie would endure ambushes every night if it would spare Farrendel.

She had been staring at her lap, but when she raised her gaze, she caught the hopeful looks. As much as she wanted to hope, she didn't want to hope without reason. "I've still caught hints of pain, and I think I would have sensed more...elation if he had escaped. He's still a prisoner."

Averett's expression fell back into a frown. Julien's jaw tightened with a grim slant to his mouth.

Edmund waved his hand, as if he wasn't sure what gesture to make in response. "Then how…"

Essie peeked at Weylind and Jalissa. She wasn't sure how they would react. "I think…I think Melantha has been healing him."

Julien crossed his arms and glowered. Edmund reeled back, jaw working.

"What?" Averett straightened. "Why would she help now?"

Her brothers had never actually met Melantha in person, yet they were angry on Farrendel's behalf.

Across the shelter, Jalissa wrapped her arms over her stomach and curled inward, as if in pain.

For a moment, Weylind's face twisted, as if he could not figure out what expression to wear. Pain. Grief. Anger. He finally settled on a blank mask, much like Farrendel's. When he spoke, his tone was cold. "Are you sure? If it is true, is it another trick?"

Essie's heart ached. It must be a particular pain, to have to hold such anger for a sister they still loved. "I don't know. I'm not even sure Melantha is helping him. I just know his pain disappears, as if someone is healing him, and the crackle of his magic is strongest during those times. But…let me check. Maybe I can confirm with Farrendel that it is Melantha who is helping."

She closed her eyes, focusing on the heart bond. How could she communicate her question through strong emotions?

Her skin prickled under all the gazes focused on her. She grimaced, though she didn't open her eyes. "If you all could not stare at me while I'm doing this. Go back to discussing Melantha's motives or something. Or perhaps discuss that ambush. Something. Anything."

The gazes swiveled away, and low voices soon filled the shelter. Essie kept her breathing even, doing her best to ignore them and not get drawn into the conversation.

Perhaps, if she focused on a strong memory of Melantha, it would carry enough emotion and sense of Melantha for Farrendel to understand.

The one memory that stuck in her mind...she didn't want to send that one to him. The last thing she wanted to do was make him relive the moment of Melantha's betrayal.

But that memory would convey what she wanted to ask. Maybe.

Farrendel? She could sense that he was still awake. Perhaps he had still been worried for her after what had happened. *Is Melantha there and helping you? Melantha.*

Before she could talk herself out of it, she thought of Melantha standing in front of them, denying that Farrendel was her brother.

Even through the heart bond, she felt Farrendel stiffen, as if he'd felt again the emotions of that same memory. Essie winced. Perhaps she shouldn't have tried to use those particular emotions.

After a moment, a sense of hard determination replaced the pain, followed by an impression of gratitude that definitely felt like it was directed toward Melantha.

Essie frowned and squeezed her eyes shut again. What was Farrendel trying to tell her? Was this an answer to her question?

It hurt, but she had to confirm her guess was correct.

Melantha. She thought of the memory of Melantha's betrayal again.

No.

She didn't hear the word, exactly, but the impression came through so strongly from Farrendel, she couldn't mistake it. She felt the determined edge as Farrendel all but shoved a sense of gratitude toward Melantha at Essie. *No. Melantha.*

I understand. She wasn't sure he would sense her mental nod, but some of the urgency from him faded, replaced by a sense of exhaustion.

It was the middle of the night, and it probably had tired him to use his magic through her like that.

Get some sleep. I'm fine. Essie tried to send him the sense of holding his hand, leaning against his shoulder.

He relaxed enough that Essie's tight muscles eased as well.

When she opened her eyes, the conversation had trailed off. She squirmed. Hopefully she hadn't been muttering to herself while trying to communicate with Farrendel.

Averett had his head bent, peering at her. "You get a strange look on your face when you're talking to him, you know."

"And you make facial expressions along with whatever silent conversation you're having in your head. Just in case you were wondering." Julien waved a hand at her face.

Great. Essie would now spend her time wondering just how strange she looked when she attempted to talk to Farrendel through the heart bond.

"Anyway..." She straightened her shoulders and faced all of them. "If I'm interpreting the emotions we were sharing back and forth correctly, then, yes, Melantha is helping Farrendel. And I think he trusts her."

Weylind rubbed a hand over his face, exhaustion drawing lines around his eyes and mouth that Essie had never seen on him before. Next to him, Jalissa slumped, eyes focused on her hands in her lap.

Averett's jaw tightened. "Will she betray him again, do you think?"

Weylind released a breath and stared at the ceiling, as if he couldn't face them. "I do not know. She is our sister. I had no wish to believe her capable of this kind of betrayal the first time. Now...I am no longer sure of what she might be capable."

Jalissa curled into a tighter ball, her face in her hands.

So much pain and brokenness in that family. Even though she was exhausted and wanted to curl up next to Averett again, Essie forced herself to her feet. She crossed the shelter, sat next to Jalissa, and put an arm around her.

Getting Farrendel back would help, but Essie wasn't sure what it would take to heal this rift. A rift that had started over a hundred years ago with the elf queen's death.

NINETEEN

Farrendel listened to the sound of Prince Rharreth's retreating boots as he left the dungeon corridor after giving them food, checking Farrendel's bonds, and taking Melantha back to her cell for a few minutes for privacy.

"Is he gone?" Melantha once again sat beside him, her ankle shackled to the floor.

Farrendel stretched his magical sense, just a hint of it, until he could feel Prince Rharreth leaving the dungeon. He tried to follow the troll prince's progress through the twists and turns of the dungeon, but he lost him quickly, not daring to tap too much into his magic. "Yes, he is gone. And I think, after the corridor we are on and that room with the spring that you mentioned, it is a left, then a right. But I lost a sense of him after that."

"That is more than we knew before." Melantha gave a sharp nod, before grimacing. "I wish I had paid more attention when they were dragging me down here. But it all blurred together."

"It is understandable. You observed more than I did." Farrendel retraced the route he had just observed with his mind, adding in the details that Melantha did remember. For the past few days, they had spent their time plotting the details of their escape. When the moment came, they would be ready to take it.

"You were drugged and unconscious. You were not in a position to observe anything." Melantha's scowl deepened for a moment before smoothing. She raised her hands and tapped her fingers for a moment, as she did when mentally going through a checklist. After a moment, she sighed, her hands falling to her lap. "There is not much we can plan, is there? It is frustrating."

He had been planning for this escape for longer than she had, and he had more opportunity to prepare.

With Prince Rharreth leaving them together for most of the day, Farrendel had been able to store a great deal of his magic. Though, he was no longer sure if he was storing the magic or had simply figured out a way to access his magic through the heart bond.

And last night when he was able to use his magic with Essie…that was something rather unexpected. He had been glad Melantha had been asleep at the time. There were some secrets he would keep to himself. He had decided to trust Melantha, but he was still going to be cautious.

"No, there is not much we can plan." Farrendel flexed his fingers to relieve some of the urge to move. With Melantha's magic keeping away the pain of the stone, he was only mildly uncomfortable due to being unable to move and lying on rock. By the time he was rescued, his muscles would be weak from lack of use.

"How do you have so much patience when you are the

one…" Melantha gestured at him. "All I can think about is getting out of here."

"I have had practice with this sort of thing." Farrendel took his own restlessness, squashed it, and locked it behind one of the iron doors in his mind containing the things he did not think about. Pain was locked behind one. Previous torture behind another. "It is best not to think too much and simply exist."

Melantha rested her chin on her knees and studied him for a long moment. "I understand that, now. Better than I would have before. I am sorry that I am the reason we are here, but I am glad we have had this time."

Farrendel opened his mouth, but he could not formulate a reply. He was glad of this time, yes. But the emotions Essie had stirred toward Melantha last night had reminded him once again of the reason he needed to be wary. Melantha had experienced a change of heart, but only because she had ended up a prisoner as well. If the trolls had treated her as a princess, giving her a luxurious room where she would not have seen Farrendel's suffering, she would have put him from her mind and never had a twinge of guilt over what she had done.

Something tugged at his senses, and he stilled, glancing past Melantha toward the door. "Prince Rharreth is returning and…" His stomach sank. "King Charvod is with him."

"What?" Melantha's eyes widened as she glanced from Farrendel to the door, then down at herself. She leapt to her feet and tugged on the shackle as if she could rip it from the stone.

She needed to get out of there. If King Charvod found her in here, found the blankets, and figured out how much

Prince Rharreth had helped them, then Farrendel was likely going to be punished for it.

"I will break the chain." Farrendel gathered his magic. He had not intended to use it now. If King Charvod or Prince Rharreth sensed him using his magic, then they would bind him even tighter in stone.

But they would do that anyway if King Charvod discovered Melantha here.

"Wait." Melantha knelt again and pressed both hands to his shoulders. Her magic flooded into him, almost painful with its intensity as it coated every bit of stone and troll magic holding him down.

Farrendel choked in a breath, forcing himself to reach for his magic even through the blast of her magic. He twisted his hand and directed a bolt at the chain holding Melantha to the floor.

The chain snapped near the floor.

Melantha snatched both of the blankets, then glanced around, probably to check that she had not left anything else lying around Farrendel's cell.

After dashing across the cell, she stood on her tiptoes, stuck her arm through the barred window, and stretched.

Lying on the floor, Farrendel could not see how close she was to reaching the locking bar. He would help with his magic, but the trolls would notice if the dungeon door were blown off its hinges.

With a soft scream of frustration, Melantha lunged. The locking bar thunked, and she stumbled as the door swung open. She raced out.

It was not soon enough. Farrendel squeezed his eyes shut, sensing King Charvod and Prince Rharreth in the corridor. Melantha gave a short cry. King Charvod's voice thundered outside Farrendel's cell.

Farrendel gathered as much of his magic as he could and flung it into the heart bond. Thanks to Essie using his magic, he was certain all this magic in the heart bond would not hurt her.

Somewhere far away, he sensed her mentally starting. A sense of confusion and fear flooded back from Essie, but he did not try to decipher more as he walled away all emotion.

The door flung open, slamming into the wall. King Charvod strode inside, gripping Melantha's upper arm. He tossed her inside, and she stumbled, falling to her knees beside Farrendel.

Farrendel clenched his fists. He must not react. Otherwise, he would give away that he had access to his magic, and it was not yet time to act.

Though, it might not matter. They would wonder how Melantha had broken that chain, and they might have been close enough to sense Farrendel's use of magic to break it.

King Charvod glared first at Melantha, then focused on his brother. "Why have you allowed her to stay here?"

"A small compassion for a captive, nothing more." Prince Rharreth's face remained blank, but his gaze flicked to the broken chain dangling from Melantha's ankle. He would know he had left Melantha more secured than she was now.

King Charvod rounded on his brother. His hand lifted, almost as if he planned to strike his brother, but he halted and instead jabbed Prince Rharreth in the chest. "Thanks to your *compassion*, some of his magic was used during the fighting on the front lines."

Prince Rharreth started, his gaze flicking to Farrendel, before his jaw hardened. "How is that possible? No one can use their magic in a place without being there in person. Are you sure it was his magic? Magic like his is rare, only appearing every few generations, but perhaps the elves discovered another who can wield a similar magic."

Farrendel gritted his teeth, noticing Prince Rharreth did not say it was impossible for Farrendel to use his magic at the moment. With the broken chain, Prince Rharreth had to suspect.

"It was his. I recognized the taint of it." King Charvod's mouth curled. "If there is a way to launch such an attack from a distance, I'm sure this murdering elf could discover it."

Farrendel glared, hardening his expression to his most dangerous mien. He had to keep the trolls' focus on himself. They must not, under any circumstances, guess he had wielded his power through Essie.

Next to him, Melantha tucked herself closer to his side and gripped his hand. The way she positioned herself, it was almost as if she wished to shield him from the trolls. But surely that was not the case. She had been helping him, but would that extend to placing herself in danger for him?

"Then I have failed you." Prince Rharreth bowed his head.

King Charvod scowled and stomped closer to Farrendel and Melantha. He grabbed Melantha by her hair. She cried out as King Charvod lifted her to her knees. "What did you do? It must have been something you did. He would have done something before now if he could have."

Farrendel clenched his fists hard enough to hurt. He must not react. He must not.

"What did you do?" King Charvod shook Melantha harder by her hair. "I shall have you punished for this."

She cried out, eyes squeezed shut, her feet scrambling to try to gain her balance.

Farrendel could not sit by and watch this. Besides, they already knew he could use his magic. There was no reason to hold back.

He gripped his magic and shoved. Blue bolts of power surrounded him, snapping through the restraints around his wrists. He raised an arm and blasted power toward King Charvod.

A shield of troll magic sprang up before King Charvod, but a few sparks of Farrendel's magic glanced off the troll king's hand.

He released Melantha, and she slumped to the floor.

Farrendel gritted his teeth, a headache pounding at his temples even through Melantha's lingering magic inside him. "Do not touch my sister."

Troll magic surged through the stones around him. Tendrils of the stone floor reached up, trying to grasp his arms and pin him once again. The stone around his legs, waist, and chest tightened.

He pushed back with his magic, holding the stone back. The floor trembled beneath him, shaking with the force of so much magic hurled about in such a tiny space.

Melantha lifted her head and met Farrendel's gaze. Slowly, she shook her head and mouthed, "The plan."

This was not the plan. He could fight. Perhaps he could keep them from pinning him down for a time. But they would win, as this was their home and he was weakened. Fighting now would just deplete the magic he had saved for when the time came to escape.

If he wanted to live and return to Essie, then he could not fight now. He had to save his magic and pretend he was still weaker than he was. If the trolls suspected his true strength, they would kill him here and now.

Melantha shook her head again, her eyes wide and pained.

Farrendel released his magic and slumped to the floor, as if the effort of holding back the stone and troll magic had used the last of his strength.

The stone surged around him, binding him to the floor. He cried out as stone stabbed through his shoulders.

King Charvod grabbed Melantha's upper arm and hauled her to her feet. "You will regret turning on us and helping him."

"Don't punish her. He is her brother, after all. The failing was mine." Prince Rharreth's hard expression did not change. "I will accept your punishment."

King Charvod jabbed a finger at his brother again. "Oh, you will face my punishment as well. You have betrayed your brother and your king in aiding Laesornysh."

Head high, Prince Rharreth marched from the cell first, followed by King Charvod dragging Melantha with him. Just before the door slammed shut, King Charvod glared over his shoulder at Farrendel.

That glare held a promise. Prince Rharreth and Melantha would be punished first, but Farrendel would feel every bit of their pain, and then some.

He swallowed and stared at the ceiling. If King Charvod's rage was any indication, it would be surprising if he survived the night.

CHAPTER
TWENTY

Melantha clawed her way through the blackness and waves of pain. For several long moments, it took all her will to simply breathe. With each inhalation, another spike of pain shivered down her back.

Straw prickled against her cheek. She peeled her eyes open and blinked several times, trying to get her mind to function past the pain.

She lay on the pile of straw against the back wall of her cell. Both blankets were missing, and a cool draft brushed against the skin of her back.

Her back. She bit her lip at the pain and the memories. Shackles pinning her to the wall. King Charvod wielding the whip laced with troll magic.

A whip. She had not realized such instruments of torture were still employed in these modern times. Surely such things had been banished to history.

But she should have known King Charvod would still keep something like that, just in case.

He had used it not just on her, but on his own brother as

well. She squeezed her eyes shut against the memory of several trolls pinning Prince Rharreth to the wall as he bore his brother's punishment.

Only when Prince Rharreth had been wounded and weak had King Charvod turned the whip on her. King Charvod had still had to order Prince Rharreth restrained, then eventually knocked unconscious to prevent him from stopping her punishment.

She shifted, and stone rattled. Frowning, she tilted her head and peered at her hands. Stone shackles bound her wrists. Cold stone rested against her ankles. It might not be as restricting as Farrendel's bonds, but she was bound more than she had been.

Gathering her strength, she pushed onto her elbows. Tears sprang to her eyes at the pain flashing through the raw welts and bleeding slices on her back.

With all this stone around her, would she be able to heal herself? The stone shackle had not impeded her ability to heal Farrendel.

It took several more moments of effort to push herself all the way to sitting. She leaned a shoulder against the wall, her head spinning, blackness bursting in front of her eyes. She forced herself to breathe deeply, steadily, until some of the dizziness faded.

Wincing, she rested her right hand on her left arm and reached for her magic. At first, she could only grasp a sliver of it. She squeezed her eyes shut, concentrating.

It was not the stone making it difficult but her pain. Gritting her teeth, she dug deeper and dredged up her magic, sliding it through her skin and into her back.

The pain faded, though the weakness remained. Loss of blood, most likely. And she had poured a great deal of her magic into Farrendel before she had been dragged away.

Was Farrendel all right? What had King Charvod done to him while she had been unconscious?

Melantha staggered to her feet and tottered toward her door. With her arms and feet shackled, she could no longer reach the window in the door. She eased to the side, trying to see down the corridor.

What if King Charvod was still there? She would not wish to call out to Farrendel if anyone would overhear.

No, the corridor was too quiet. If King Charvod was still there, there would be cries of pain.

"Farrendel? Can you hear me? Are you all right?" She waited, holding her breath to hear any faint reply.

Nothing.

What if Farrendel was dead? It would have been wiser for King Charvod to kill him—to kill both of them—long before now. Would King Charvod risk Farrendel regaining his magic again and keep him alive to enact his original plan to kill Farrendel in front of Weylind?

"Farrendel?" She called louder this time, unable to erase the edge of panic straining through her voice. She had reminded him not to fight. To be patient and wait for the right moment. What if that had been the right moment? Maybe not the right moment, but the only chance they had?

He could not be dead. If he died now, it would be her fault. All her fault.

"Farrendel!" Her fists clenched as she strained against the shackles, heat building in her chest. If King Charvod had killed Farrendel, then she might just find out what happened to an elf healer who violated her oath and used her magic to kill. At least she could take King Charvod down with her.

"Melantha?" His voice was so faint Melantha had to turn her ear toward the window to hear it. "Are you all right?"

He sounded like he was barely breathing, yet he was asking if she was all right? "I am fine." She hesitated. For some reason, she did not want to tell him that she had simply healed herself and the pain was already gone. Not when she did not have a way to heal him and take away the pain he was in. "And you? Are you all right?"

He was not. She could hear that much in his voice. But she had to ask, regardless.

"Well enough."

His answer would have been convincing, if his words had not broken with a moan.

"I am sorry. I should have moved faster. I should have..." She would have leaned her head against the bars of the window, but she could not reach. What could she have done? There had not been time to get from Farrendel's cell to her own cell before they had been discovered. Perhaps she never should have convinced Prince Rharreth to allow her to stay with Farrendel, but she could not make herself regret the past few days.

"Not your fault." Farrendel sounded barely conscious. What had they done to him while she had been drifting on that haze of pain?

Still shaky on her feet, she sank to the floor at the edge of the reach of her chains. She would rather have curled up on the straw, but she would not be able to hear Farrendel from there. "If King Charvod is this afraid, then surely it will not be long until Weylind is here."

Farrendel did not reply. Had he passed out again? How badly was he hurt?

Melantha clenched her fists, breathing past the rising

heat in her chest. If only she could blast this cell door off its hinges and heal Farrendel. Then she would march out of here, track down King Charvod, and...

And do what? It was not like she was a warrior. She would probably die as well if she used her magic to kill instead of heal.

It might be worth it.

CHAPTER
TWENTY-ONE

E ssie wrapped a bandage around the arm of a wounded elf. It was just a shallow gash, and the elf would probably be back in the fight the next day, once the balm Illyna had helped make healed the injury.

Tying off the bandage, Essie gave the elf a smile. "There you are."

He gave her a return smile. "Linshi, amirah."

She glanced around, the setting sun casting shadows from the rows of shelters grown on the rocky ground. Over the past two days, the constant blizzards and ice had dissipated, leaving clear skies for the first time since they had invaded Kostaria.

No more wounded waited for tending. The day's fighting had been light. Perhaps too light? The combined army was approaching Gror Grar. Shouldn't the fighting be getting harder, not easier?

"Essie."

She turned to find Averett striding toward her, though

with a hitch in his step. She hurried to him. "Are you hurt? Why are you limping?"

"I'm fine. Just a scratch on my calf." Averett's smile was framed with tired lines.

It was more than that. Now that she was closer, she spotted the blood, both brown and dried, red and glistening. "You should let me tend it."

"I'm fine. Really." Despite his words, Averett sank onto the rock where the elf warrior had been sitting a moment before. "I sent Edmund with a few elven scouts. He probably won't be back until late. They are hoping to scout most of the way to Gror Grar and back."

"And Julien?" Essie eased off Averett's boot and rolled down his sock, wrinkling her nose at the stench of his foot. A long gash cut through his calf muscle. It would need stitches by one of the physicians, but Essie could at least wash it and bandage it to tide Averett over until he could pause long enough to get it tended.

"Helping Weylind set up the shelter for tonight." Averett winced as she took a rag and dabbed the injury.

Ever since the ambush on the rear lines, Jalissa and Essie had been bunking with Weylind and Essie's brothers, curtaining off a corner to give themselves some privacy. Averett and Weylind weren't happy about having Essie and Jalissa closer to the fighting, but nowhere in the encampment was truly safe.

"Are the trolls still falling back? We gained a lot of ground today." Essie dabbed at the wound, making sure she got all the dirt out. She wasn't sure when she had lost any squeamishness over blood and sliced muscle, but it no longer bothered her.

"Yes. I think the trolls left fighting us are simply making

a defensive retreat, delaying us while the rest of them retreat to Gror Grar and rally those defenses." Averett rubbed a hand over his face. "While I'm glad it means we'll arrive at Gror Grar all the sooner, I am concerned what we will find when we get there. Is Farrendel..."

"Still alive. But..." Essie resisted the urge to rub at the cold feeling of the heart bond in her chest. For the past two days, he had been nearly constantly blocking her. The only time he didn't block her was when he was sleeping or unconscious. "Still not good. I think we need to hurry."

She wasn't sure what had happened. After a week of being nearly relaxed and pain free, Farrendel had suddenly gone back to the torture and pain of those first few days before Melantha had begun helping him. Had Melantha been killed? Or had she betrayed Farrendel again, and that was why he was so listless and pained?

But it had started the day after Farrendel had used his magic through Essie. Had the trolls figured out that was Farrendel's magic that night?

With Farrendel blocking her, she couldn't attempt to ask him.

"We're only a day from Gror Grar." Averett patted her shoulder. "He only needs to hold out a little longer."

Her hands shook as she wrapped a bandage around Averett's leg. As she finished, she pasted on a smile and stood. "You can put your boot back on. I'll pass out if I'm subjected to the stench of your sock much longer."

"Ah. Yes. Bathing and washing socks hasn't been on the top of our list for the past two weeks." Averett sniffed at his armpit. "You might want to avoid hugs as well."

As she didn't smell much better than he did, she might risk it, if Farrendel took a turn for the worse.

THE COLD BREEZE swirling into the shelter and the low murmur of voices woke Essie from a light doze. She had struggled to sleep, knowing Edmund was out there scouting and Farrendel was drifting in and out of consciousness.

As Jalissa stirred next to her, Essie eased out of her bedroll and slipped through the curtain separating their section of the shelter from the rest.

An elven lamp, glowing with a white blue light instead of the yellow of a flame, sat in the center of the shelter. Essie's brothers gathered around a piece of paper along with Weylind. Edmund was pointing at something, but he glanced up as Essie wedged into the circle between Averett and Julien.

Essie glanced over the paper. A rough sketch of the terrain around Gror Grar? "I'm glad you arrived back all right."

"No trouble. It looks like even more of the trolls have retreated into Gror Grar. We'll have little resistance on the final march tomorrow." Edmund shook his head and bent over the paper again. "It will be Gror Grar itself that will be difficult. Its mountain is steep and made up of shale on many of the sides. We will have no cover on the approach, even if we try to take the army up the sides. A frontal assault across the bridge would be even worse."

"We will consult with the generals tomorrow. The final decision on tactics will be theirs, anyway." Averett leaned his elbows on his knees, head bent. "But if anyone has any ideas, I'm sure they would love to hear them."

Essie bit her lip. Should she mention this? "Up until a few days ago, I know Farrendel was planning something. I think he meant it to coincide with our efforts. There's no other reason he would wait to put it—whatever it is—into action. We might find we have help on the inside of Gror Grar."

Weylind bent his head, his hair hiding his face. "Farrendel was unable to help last time he was rescued. I do not think we should count on his aid."

"He is stronger this time." Essie had to believe that. She wasn't sure she could bear it if she believed Farrendel had given up.

On the train, he had been determined to fight to the death rather than face torture. But something must have changed. Either he had been captured even while trying to fight to the death or he had surrendered, deciding to survive and live for her. Surely, if he had made that choice once, he would do it again. He would survive. He would push through this. And he would be ready to fight back when the time came.

TWENTY-TWO

E ssie sat on a rock outside of the command tent, only half listening to the murmur of voices behind her. All around, the Escarlish-Tarenhieli army set up camp and fortifications.

The fortress of Gror Grar loomed on the mountain before them, the dark granite walls, limned with snow, blending in with the gray of the surrounding mountain.

The fortress cut into the mountain itself with a bridge spanning the gorge and connecting it to the plateau. The peak of the mountain formed the tallest tower of the fortress while the outer walls rose from the steep cliffs. No army could approach except by the bridge, where they would be mercilessly cut down by the defenders.

Farrendel was in that fortress. She could feel it.

But how to get to him? Gror Grar was just as intimidating as the elves had said it would be.

Edmund appeared next to her. "You look pensive."

"Back from scouting already?" Essie held her breath. She hardly dared hope he'd found something.

"I think I have a way in." Edmund held out an arm. "I might as well tell it only once."

Essie hopped to her feet and fell into step with Edmund. As they entered the tent, the generals gathered around the table glanced up. Weylind and Averett stood side by side on the far side of the table, and, next to them, stood...Lance.

Lance Marion, an inventor specializing in using magic to power machines, cradled a magical power cell to his chest in a sling, as if he was carrying around a baby instead of a piece of machinery.

No, not just any power cell. Essie spotted the faint blue light and the crackle to the power as she stepped closer. This was the one Lance and Farrendel had worked on that afternoon in Aldon where they had successfully stored some of Farrendel's magic.

As his gaze flicked to her, Lance smiled and gave her a nod. She had seen him around the camp, helping fix the steam vehicles and various weapons, but she hadn't had a chance to talk to him. Everyone had been too busy surviving.

Edmund strode to the table and pointed at the sketch of Gror Grar laid out on the table. A much better sketch than the one last night. "I found the back way in."

"The back door?" Essie wedged herself next to Edmund. She found Julien on her other side.

"Of course. Every fortress has a back way out. No one wants to be stuck in a dead-end corner, not even if that corner is a supposedly impenetrable fortress." Edmund pointed toward a spot on the sketch that seemed to indicate the far side of the fortress opposite of the bridge. "As I suspected, they must have been sending out noncombatants to flee deeper into Kostaria in preparation for our arrival. A valid strategy, and they did their best to erase the trail. But they still left enough evidence in the side of the mountain that I could find the entrance."

Really? Essie studied Edmund. She had known Edmund was good at what he did, but where had he gotten that confident experience in this kind of thing? Did she really want to know? Apparently, those were the stories her brothers didn't tell her. Possibly out of their instincts to protect their little sister. But it might also be because Edmund's previous missions were national secrets.

"Excellent." Averett nodded, crossing his arms.

"Yes and no." Edmund jabbed a finger over his shoulder in the direction of Gror Grar. "The entrance is hidden about a hundred feet up the side of a sheer cliff. I suspect that, when they wish to escape that way, they use their magic to form stairs in the cliff side. There was a section of the cliff that was too unnaturally smooth, as if molded by magic. They neglected to replicate the craggy edges of the natural cliffside when they erased their stairs."

One of the Escarlish generals tapped his chin. "It might be possible for a small party to scale that cliff. It would be difficult, but not impossible."

"Exactly." Edmund glanced to Essie. "If a small group of us sneak into Gror Grar during the night, the rest of the army could attack at dawn to provide a distraction. If Farrendel is in bad shape, we will sneak out the back way again, thus avoiding any trap the troll king will have planned for whoever attempts to rescue Farrendel. But if Farrendel thinks he can use enough of his magic to assist us, then we'll go out the front, attacking the trolls from inside their own fortress."

Lance patted the power cell with Farrendel's magic.

"And the rest of us will have blown the gates off the fortress by then."

Essie raised her eyebrows at him. "That's what all of you were discussing before we came in?"

"Oh, yes." Lance patted the power cell again. "We managed to contain Farrendel's magic, but it is still highly unstable. Pack enough gunpowder around it and light a fuse, and this will explode with enough force to take down half of Gror Grar's walls, no matter what kind of magical reinforcement the trolls have put on them."

A few of the Escarlish generals grinned. The elves didn't deign to do something as undignified, but a few of them indulged in twitching smiles.

"Don't use all the gunpowder. I couldn't get a good look at it from the ground, but I think the trolls blocked off their escape tunnel with stone." Edmund shrugged, as if a tunnel sealed with stone wasn't a big deal. "It won't be thick, since they will want to be able to open it again in a hurry if needed. It will be a simple drilling and blasting operation, though we'll want to wait until the bombardment of the main gate starts before we blow the door."

Essie eyed Edmund. Drilling and blasting? Simple? What had Edmund been doing on all those spy missions?

The elven and Escarlish generals gathered around Lance, discussing the best ways to construct the magic-and-gunpowder bomb and plant it at the base of the gates.

Weylind and Averett edged around the table until they had joined Edmund, Julien, and Essie.

Averett rested an arm on Essie's shoulders. "I really wish you didn't have to go with the rescue party. If something happens to you, I would never forgive myself. Neither would Farrendel."

"I know." Essie didn't want to imagine what Farrendel would do if he lost her after suffering that torture. Farrendel had never lost control of his magic, but that might do it. Still, she couldn't leave him there. "I'm our best hope for getting to him in time. You could end up wandering that fortress for days trying to find him, and King Charvod would kill him long before that."

"I know." Averett's arm tightened around her shoulders before he released her.

"We'll be with her." Julien gestured between him and Edmund. "And I'm sure our small group will still have plenty of handpicked, elite soldiers along. Maybe even a few elf warriors?" He glanced at Weylind.

Weylind crossed his arms. "Of course. I will be going as well."

Essie's brothers shared a look before Averett faced Weylind, jaw set. "No, you won't. You and I will be with those attacking the main gate."

"Farrendel is my brother. I cannot..." Weylind's voice cracked, and he cleared his throat as if to pretend that moment of emotion hadn't just occurred. "I cannot leave him there."

"I understand. But it's what the troll king will expect. If he doesn't see you attacking the main gate, he will know you are elsewhere trying to sneak into the castle. It would place Farrendel and those sneaking into Gror Grar in danger." Averett met Weylind stare for stare. "But if the troll king sees you attacking the front gate, he will think that is the main attack. Instead, we are the diversion."

Weylind's shoulders slumped. "Very well." After a moment, he straightened, his gaze hardening as he focused on first Julien, then Edmund. "I am once again trusting you with my brother's life. Do not fail to protect him a second time."

"We won't." Julien nodded sharply.

Jalissa stepped closer, her face drawn. "And if Melantha is there...I know what she did, and she might not want to leave. But if she is locked in that dungeon with Farrendel, could you please rescue her, too? She is still our sister."

If Essie closed her eyes, she could still hear the sharp stab of Melantha coldly telling Farrendel, *You are not my brother.*

Yet, Farrendel seemed to believe Melantha had been helping him. If Melantha was helping him now, then Essie would rescue her, if just for Farrendel's sake.

Essie rested a hand on Jalissa's arm. "If she's there with Farrendel, we'll get her out with us."

"But Farrendel will be the priority." Julien grimaced and glanced between Weylind and Jalissa. "I don't think we'll have time to search the dungeon looking for Melantha if she isn't kept near Farrendel. Essie should lead us to Farrendel, but we won't have a way to find Melantha."

"I understand." Jalissa hugged her arms over her stomach. After the week of fighting across Kostaria, her dark brown hair hung limply over her shoulders. Essie had offered to braid it, but Jalissa hadn't yet been ready to tie back her hair.

Averett glanced around at them. "Edmund, Julien, Essie. You should try to get some rest. You'll need to leave several hours before we begin the attack to reach the far side of Gror Grar at the right time."

Essie resisted the urge to swipe her palms against her trousers. Soon. Just a few more hours, and then she would finally be on her way to rescue Farrendel. *Hold on just a little longer, Farrendel. Just a few more hours.*

She wasn't sure Farrendel sensed what she was telling him. He was blocking her again, the heart bond cold as icy steel between them.

ESSIE ADJUSTED the strap of her rifle where it lay across her chest. The rifle's weight settled against her shoulder, a reminder that this mission was dangerous. Her mouth was dry, her heart racing. They hadn't even left the encampment yet, much less reached Gror Grar. How did Farrendel face this kind of fear walking into battle again and again? Did it get easier after the first time?

She stifled a yawn. The stars still twinkled overhead on this clear, cold night, and would remain there in the dark sky for several more hours until dawn broke.

Averett and Weylind exited the command shelter, where they had been consulting with the generals one last time. Averett strode over to Essie and hugged her, tight and long.

Essie leaned into him, drawing on his strength. It was tempting to stay there in camp, as her brothers wanted her to do. It would be safer. Less frightening.

But Farrendel was in that looming fortress ahead, and she was their best chance to get him out alive. Not to mention, it would be safer for the rescuers to move quickly through the dungeon tunnels.

She forced herself to step out of Averett's embrace and smile. "I'll be fine, Avie. Julien and Edmund will look after me. And, once we find Farrendel, he won't allow anything to happen to me."

Averett returned her smile, though his was strained as if the action pained him. He didn't remind her that Farrendel most likely wouldn't be in any shape to help them. He didn't have to. She could feel Farrendel's pain even as he slept fitfully.

Julien and Edmund strolled toward them, packs slung over their backs and ropes hanging over their shoulders.

Averett patted Essie's shoulder, his eyes glinting in the starlight. "Stay safe, Essie."

"I will." Essie blamed the cold night air for the husky, choked sound of her voice.

Averett moved off to Julien and Edmund. There was a lot of grinning and back-slapping. No emotional goodbyes or anything like that. But it didn't need to be said. They knew.

With a cleared throat, Weylind approached Essie. His dark eyes were filled with more emotion than Essie could remember seeing on him. He gripped Essie's shoulders. "Bring my brother home. Please."

Essie patted his hands, but that didn't seem like enough. She stepped forward and gave Weylind a quick hug. He remained as stiff as a tree through it, but hopefully he understood that it was the best human gesture she could give him at that moment. "We will."

Three Escarlish soldiers jogged out of the darkness, bowed to Averett, then saluted Julien. After Julien returned the salute, all three of them relaxed. Something in their smiles said they had worked with Julien before. Good. If Julien trusted them, then Essie could too.

A few moments later, three elves glided from the darkness. They nodded to Weylind before glancing toward Edmund. Essie was pretty sure they were the elven scouts who had gone with Edmund scouting the border.

Julien glanced at the group. "Looks like everyone is here. Let's move out."

"We will give you two hours until we start the bombard-ment." Averett patted Julien's shoulder one last time. The information was nothing new. They had gone over this mission several times over the past few hours. All of the details were drilled into their heads.

"We'll be in place." Julien nodded first to Averett, then Weylind. Then he shouldered his pack and led the way. The Escarlish soldiers fell into step behind him.

Essie hurried to fall into line. She didn't want to take up the rear, even if she was the slowest of all of them. Not that her brothers were likely to let her lag behind.

Edmund came after Essie, with the elven scouts after him. At this time in the morning, few were moving about the encampment yet. Most of the soldiers were still sleeping, catching the last bit of rest before they were roused for battle. A few of the commanders were already up, going over the last few items for the plan while the artillery men were also awake, quietly moving their cannons and stores of ammuni-tion into place under the cover of darkness.

Julien led the way to the faint trail going down the plateau, out of sight of Gror Grar. Still, they didn't talk as they wound their way into the gorge.

Essie tried to keep from kicking stones loose or making noise, a difficult task in the near darkness. She tried not to glance to the edge, where nothing stood between her and a long drop to the bottom, a bottom she couldn't even see in the darkness. Only the stars provided illumination.

Edmund and the elves behind her glided down the trail without a sound. The soldiers ahead of her crunched on the gravel, but even they didn't make a lot of noise compared to the usual Escarlish soldier. They must be specially trained. Not surprising, given they were on this mission.

By the time they reached the bottom, Essie's thighs burned from holding herself back against the steep downward incline. But she would not complain. They still had a long way to hike that night, and that was just the beginning. Who knew what would be demanded of them once they reached Gror Grar?

At the bottom, Edmund took the lead. He led them in the shadow of the cliff wall, sticking as close to the jagged stone as possible. Since they couldn't light a lamp or a candle or any light that would give them away to any trolls watching from the walls of Gror Grar, they were left to stumble in the dark.

At least, Essie was stumbling over rocks and pitfalls she couldn't see in the near darkness. This whole sneaking into the fortress was a lot less glamorous than she had expected. She struggled to keep her breathing steady. Edmund was setting a fast pace, and she was breathing hard. She might have to join Farrendel in his morning exercise sessions, if she was going to participate in sneak attacks.

Though, once she got Farrendel back, hopefully she wouldn't have to. He would be safe, and Weylind and Averett would have taken the fortress and forced the trolls to surrender.

She would focus on that. Not on the winding gorge or the deep darkness shrouding them. Tonight, they would get Farrendel back.

After hiking for what felt like three hours, though was probably more like one, Essie glanced up and caught her breath. The jagged towers of Gror Grar loomed far above, the wall a flat, menacing presence far above them.

Essie swallowed. It had looked formidable facing it across the gorge. But she had been surrounded by two armies. Now, it was just the nine of them, hiding in this gorge like mice compared to the might of Gror Grar above.

She reached back and gripped the stock of her rifle where it rested by her thigh. No matter how intimidating, she had to go in there, for Farrendel.

Edmund led them around the mountain where Gror Grar perched until the wall disappeared as it melded into the mountain itself with the mountain's peak forming the tallest tower of the fortress.

Finally, Edmund halted and pointed upward. "Here." He kept his voice low, even if they appeared to be alone.

Were they alone? Would the trolls have someone watching this back entrance?

Essie pressed her back to the cliff, trying to hide her panting breaths. For once, the cold seeping through her coat felt good.

Julien halted next to her, pulled out a pocket watch, and checked the time in the faint light. "We have about forty-five minutes until the bombardment starts. Essie, you should rest."

She didn't want to be the weak member...but she was. There wasn't anything she could do to change that. But, she could at least not be a burden.

Resting was the sensible thing to do. She would only get in the way of those trained for things like this, and she would need her strength for the next part of their mission.

Edmund talked quietly for a moment with the three elven scouts. Moments later, he and the elves melted into the darkness, probably to scout the area.

Julien and the three Escarlish soldiers set to work opening packs and laying out equipment. One soldier set out a large bundle and unrolled it, revealing numerous iron spikes tied to the canvas and padded to keep them from rattling. Julien took their various lengths of rope and began sorting through them.

Essie found a seat on a nearby rock. "Is there anything I can do to help?"

"Not at the moment." Julien pulled a bundle of paper-wrapped sticks from his pack. "Unless you want to help me inspect these blasting sticks?"

"Blasting sticks?" Essie's voice squeaked, and she cleared her throat. "Are those for the back door, if the trolls have it locked up tight?"

"Yes. These will blast it to pebbles." Julien turned over each stick in his hands. Essie wasn't sure what he was looking for, but he must have been satisfied for he gently set each stick onto the padding of his pack.

Good thing she hadn't realized her brother had been toting around volatile explosives while they had been hiking through that gorge in complete darkness. She might have been a lot less bored and a whole lot more worried.

This was why they had to wait for the bombardment to start before they made their move. The sounds of hammering the spikes into the rock to climb the cliff would be audible on the quiet night, and blowing off the door definitely would be. Hopefully the trolls wouldn't realize that one of the explosions had come from the back instead of the front.

Edmund appeared out of the darkness, followed by his three elven shadows. He pointed over his shoulder. "No one's around, and they couldn't detect any recent use of troll magic that would indicate someone is hiding nearby. Arlanor here found a place a few yards down where he thinks he can scale the cliff and reach the ledge by the hidden door without needing the spikes."

Julien glanced past Edmund toward the elf he'd pointed at, a shorter elf with lighter hair, though Essie couldn't make out the exact color in the darkness. "Are you sure? If you fall, you won't have a rope to catch you."

Edmund turned and repeated the words in elvish.

Arlanor glanced up at the cliff, then shrugged. "It is not that tall."

Even after living in their treetop palace for three months, Essie wasn't quite that cavalier about heights. But she could see how the elves wouldn't find a hundred-foot cliff that daunting after they had grown up wandering treetops hundreds of feet in the air.

"If he is willing to risk it, then let's try it. If we could have the line secured and start planning where to place the blasting sticks, we'll be able to start drilling as soon as the bombardment starts." Julien glanced at Essie. "Even fifteen minutes might make a difference."

Essie clenched her fists, trying to breathe normally. It was a risk, waiting to enter until the cannons started firing. The troll king might order Farrendel killed the moment the bombardment started. Or he might have Farrendel brought from his cell and used as a shield to stop Weylind and Averett from firing on Gror Grar. If either of those things happened, they would never get to Farrendel before the trolls did.

They were gambling that the troll king would wait to either kill or fetch Farrendel until the actual fighting at the gate started, trusting the walls of Gror Grar to hold against puny cannon fire in the meantime.

Essie reached deep inside for the heart bond, but

Farrendel was either asleep or unconscious. Would she even be able to tell if the trolls took him from his cell if he remained unconscious?

"Yes. I think we need to hurry." She didn't try to explain. Perhaps she didn't have to. The glints of expression on the elven faces grew more sober.

"Here, take this." Julien held up one of the coils of rope in one hand, then a hammer and spike in the other. "And these if there isn't a good place to secure the rope up there."

Arlanor's mouth twisted, like he wanted to grimace at all the stuff he'd have to carry with him, but whatever emotion he had been about to express, he stifled it beneath a hard mask. He looped the rope over his shoulder, then secured the spike and hammer under his belt at the small of his back.

After studying the cliff for a few moments, Arlanor selected a section a few yards down and started climbing.

Essie held her breath. She'd seen Farrendel climb trees easier than she climbed stairs, but she didn't know Arlanor well enough to trust his abilities.

For the first twenty feet, Arlanor scurried up the cliff like a squirrel. After that, he took a few more seconds before he made each choice of handhold and foothold. Some of the grips were nothing but tiny fingerholds.

In less than five minutes, Arlanor reached the ledge. He edged along it until he reached the section above the smoothed over stairs. After several moments of inspection, he disappeared from view from below.

Did that mean the door had been left open? Or had he simply crouched on the ledge and they could no longer see him because of the angle?

A few moments later, the soft thunks of the hammer hitting the stake echoed down to them. It wasn't as sharp as

Essie would have expected, so Arlanor must have muffled the hammer strikes somehow. Perhaps he'd used his tunic or something to pad the stake.

The hammer strikes ended, and a minute later, the rope launched over the edge and dropped down to them. Arlanor reappeared, and he descended the rope hand over hand.

When he settled on the ground, he turned to Edmund. "The door is sealed."

"Not unexpected." Edmund nodded, then turned to Julien. "We'll need the blasting sticks."

Julien nodded and tugged on the rope. "I hope that rope is secure enough to hold me."

After a quick consultation, Arlanor scampered up the rope, followed by Edmund and Julien, both carrying more ropes and gear. In a few minutes, more ropes dropped down from the ledge, rigged with climbing harnesses. The blasting sticks were secured in a padded pack and carefully carried up to the ledge.

Edmund returned to the ground. "There's enough room for everyone up there, and it might be dangerous to be down here once we set off the blasting sticks. Ready for this?"

Not really, but Essie took a deep breath and faced the cliff. She could do this. It wasn't like she would fall. Not once she was all harnessed up, and she had Julien at the top and Edmund at the bottom looking after her.

Edmund held out the harness for her and showed her how to put it on. Straps pulled tight against Essie's thighs and around her waist. Not the type of harness she could have worn in a dress.

"Keep your feet planted against the cliffside and walk as Julien pulls you up." Edmund checked the knot connecting the harness to the rope. He raised his hand and gave a thumbs up.

Julien, after peering over the edge, gripped the rope and began pulling, hand over hand.

Essie's feet lifted from the ground. She gripped the rope, spinning in the air.

Edmund grabbed the rope, steadying her. "Lean back. Center your weight in the harness."

Her heart racing, Essie leaned back, settling her weight more firmly in the harness. She swung toward the cliff, and she planted her boots against the cold stone.

As Julien pulled, Essie walked up the cliff, her rifle hanging heavy against her back. She refused to look down, though she was probably immune to deep drops after strolling around Ellonahshinel.

When she reached the top, Julien held her steady while one of the Escarlish soldiers held out a hand. Essie took it and was hauled onto the ledge.

The ledge was about ten feet deep and extended for about fifty feet along the mountain side. It was plenty big for all of them, though it felt smaller as no one but the elves wished to go anywhere near the edge.

At one end, an opening cut into the mountain, but it was blocked by a flat stone wall about a foot inside the mouth of the cave. Beside it, Julien and the Escarlish soldiers had laid out the small, steam-powered drilling machine that would bore holes into rock for the blasting sticks.

Edmund and the remaining two elves climbed the ropes and knelt on the ledge. After a glance at the stars, Edmund eased next to Essie. "Should be only a few more minutes until the bombardment starts."

As if on cue, the first rumble blasted through the night air, followed by three successive booms.

Essie found herself giving Edmund a small smile. "I think your clock is a little off."

"Avie is early." Edmund glanced at Julien.

After checking his pocket watch and shrugging, Julien held up the steam-powered drilling machine. "He's early. But I don't mind moving up our schedule."

Essie gripped the stock of her gun. Time to get Farrendel back.

TWENTY-THREE

Melantha shoved herself to a sitting position, her arms shaking from lack of food and water. It had been three days since anyone had come to her cell for any reason, though King Charvod had stopped to gloat a few times as he passed to and from Farrendel's cell. She hadn't seen Prince Rharreth.

Farrendel. He had been far too quiet in the past hours. How long had it been since she had gotten a response to one of her shouts?

A distant noise caught her attention. Melantha cocked her ear and held her breath to listen. What was that? It must have been loud, for her to have heard it down in the dungeon.

Another boom. Vibrations—so small she would not have felt them if her hands had not been pressed to the cold stone floor—shivered up her arms.

What was that? It must have been some kind of...explosion.

Another distant explosion. Another shudder.

Melantha stared at her hands on the stone, her mind hazy. Those explosions meant something. Something she was supposed to remember.

The Escarlish army had explosive weapons. She had heard that somewhere, though she had never heard them in action before. But that could be the only explanation.

And that meant the Escarlish army was out there, attacking the castle. Presumably, the Tarenhieli army was with them. Weylind was out there.

This was the moment Melantha and Farrendel had been waiting for.

Melantha crawled as close to the door as the stone chains would let her. Her throat hurt, but she forced herself to shout as loudly as she could. "Farrendel! Can you hear me? Farrendel?"

No answer.

"Farrendel!" Her voice creaked, but she managed enough volume that he should have heard her.

Was he awake and simply too weak to reply? Or was he unconscious?

He could not be dead. Surely King Charvod wanted Farrendel and Weylind to suffer too much to have allowed Farrendel to die in his cell.

Unless King Charvod had not realized he had pushed Farrendel's body too far. He had been weak. Tortured. Then left for three days without food or water, all alone except for King Charvod's torture.

What if Farrendel had quietly died in that cell, all alone? Abandoned?

No. He had been too determined to live to return to Essie. He must be still alive.

Yet, he must be in no shape to put his plan into action. Too weak without her magic to break his bonds and escape.

She had to get to him. Before Prince Rharreth or whatever troll King Charvod sent came down here to kill him.

But how? She did not have magic capable of breaking the chains holding her to the wall.

She yanked on the chains. They would not budge.

How could she be this helpless? She was a princess of the elves. The daughter of a long line of kings. She could not—would not—be this helpless.

With another yank on the chains, she gave a short scream. If only she had magic like Farrendel's where she could blast through these chains, these walls, this castle.

Even if she had magic like Weylind's or Jalissa's, maybe she could have broken the chains.

What good was healing magic? It was nearly useless. Sure, she had kept Farrendel alive this long because of it. She had helped him regain the use of his magic temporarily.

But she could not do anything herself. She could just help others do things.

Another scream. Another pound of her fists on the stone. She wanted to do something great. Herself. Not through someone else. But by herself.

Now was not the time for self-pity. She had work to do and a brother to save.

Melantha stared at her hands, at the stone shackles clasping her wrists. If she could not break the shackles, could she slip her hands free? Elven hands were slimmer than troll hands tended to be, though the trolls would know that. They had practice shackling Farrendel.

But her chains were not tight and embedded into her skin like his were. These chains had been done hastily, and not by

Prince Rharreth who knew her better than the other trolls did. Perhaps the troll who had formed the shackles would not take into account that her hands were even smaller and slimmer than a male elf warrior's hand.

Squeezing her thumb to her palm, she shoved the shackle with her other hand. After several minutes of straining, the shackle popped free, leaving bloody gouges across her hand behind. The second one popped off with a few more minutes of effort.

Melantha stood, the shackles still rattling against her ankles. The shackles halted her several feet from the door. Even leaning forward, she could just brush her fingertips against the stone of the door.

This would not work. She had to free her ankles as well as her hands if she were to reach the door.

Melantha plopped onto the floor and removed her thin shoe, then her stocking. Even then, when she pulled on the shackle, she could not get it over the heel of her foot, no matter how she worked it back and forth. She even tried lubricating her ankle with spit, but she could not get the shackle close to slipping free.

Melantha heaved a sigh that sounded more like yet another scream and stared at that shackle. In the distance, the booms were growing more constant, more insistent. Surely King Charvod would not hold off on sending someone for Farrendel for much longer. She had to get herself free.

She had taken an oath that she would not cause harm with her magic. But, would that oath stop her from rearranging the bones in her ankles temporarily in order to escape? She would not be using her magic with the intent to harm, even if she would be hurting herself in the process.

Another boom, this one louder, shook the floor beneath her.

Melantha drew in a deep breath. She had no choice on this. To free herself, she would have to break her own ankles. She could heal the bones afterwards, and she probably could dull the pain. Maybe.

Calling on her magic, she pushed a soothing burst of magic through her foot and ankle, numbing her skin, muscle, bones.

Gritting her teeth, she gathered more magic and for a moment simply held it, ready.

She could do this. She had to do this. No matter how much it might or might not hurt. To rescue Farrendel, she had no choice.

With a deep breath, she shoved her magic into her ankle, grabbed hold of the bones, and snapped them.

Pain shot through her, first in her ankle, then spreading into her chest and head. Melantha gasped, black spots dancing in front of her eyes.

Her stomach roiling, ankle throbbing, she reached for her other shoe, her hands shaking. Somehow, she peeled off her shoe and her stocking.

This time, she did not bother trying to numb her foot first. With a growl, she grabbed her magic, shoved it into her ankle, and cracked her bones.

Fiery pain exploded in her ankle, spreading up her leg until her whole body seized with it. All she could do was whimper, under too much pain to even scream, as a few hot tears coursed down her cheeks.

Blackness danced across her vision. Somehow, she had ended up curled on the floor, even though she did not remember lying down. She tried to breathe through the agony, but it squeezed deep inside her chest.

No matter how much it hurt, she needed to gather her strength and push through this. If she waited too long, her ankles and feet would swell, and she would never get the shackles off even after breaking her own bones.

With shaking hands, she reached for her ankle. She must not be weak. Not now. More tears coursed down her cheek as she shoved the stone shackle over her shattered foot.

Her stomach heaved as she shifted to reach her second ankle. This one was the foot she had broken first, and it had begun swelling. She pushed, but the stone shackle got stuck partway off.

Melantha groaned with the pain. She was so close. Just a little bit more pain. After the beating she had endured, surely she was tough enough for this.

With a deep breath, she shoved on the shackle. It clattered to the stone floor, free of her ankle.

She had done it. She was free.

Gathering her magic, she pressed a hand to her leg and let her magic flow into her bones. It would take some time for her magic to heal herself after the damage she had done. Hopefully the trolls would not come for Farrendel while Melantha was still lying there on the floor, helpless to even walk.

Just a few more minutes. That was all she needed.

TWENTY-FOUR

T he whine of the rock-cutting drill cut off as the Escarlish soldier finished the last hole in the stone.

Essie lifted her hands from her ears and craned her head around Julien to watch as one of the other Escarlish soldiers stuffed a blasting stick into each of the holes. He then uncoiled all the fuses and tied them together and to one longer fuse a few feet from the door. He then laid out this longer fuse for about ten feet.

About forty feet away, Essie was huddled against the cliff side between Julien and Edmund. The three elves crouched behind Edmund. One of them tapped Edmund's shoulder. "Should I shield us when that explodes? I do not like the look of the slope above us."

Edmund glanced at the shale above them. "Neither do I. But whatever happens, no magic unless we are all about to die. If there's a chance the trolls will sense the use of magic back here, I don't want to risk it."

The elf nodded and sent a glare upward, as if daring that slope to come sliding toward them.

Essie leaned closer to Julien. "This is safe, right? There isn't going to be a rockslide?"

Julien's muscles tightened. "Keep your head down. And be prepared to run."

That was...not comforting. Not at all. Was this the kind of thing her brothers did all the time? They were far too calm for the circumstances.

The soldier lit the fuse, then raced to where everyone else was huddled. Julien turned and put an arm over Essie. "You might want to plug your ears again. And keep your mouth open."

"Keep my mouth open?" Essie tucked herself into a tighter ball.

"For the shock wave from the explosion. It shouldn't be bad enough to burst our eardrums, but best not to take the chance." Julien shifted so that even more of his body covered Essie's. Next to them, Edmund tucked close to Essie's other side, further protecting her.

Essie plugged her ears and let her mouth hang loose. With her brothers pressing so close, she couldn't watch the fuse. The only warning she had was a tightening of Julien's arm.

A boom tore through the air, shaking the stone beneath her. A fist of air pummeled Essie so hard her breath caught in her lungs. When she tried to gulp in a breath, it clogged in her throat.

She couldn't breathe. She couldn't.

Julien's arm wrapped around her waist and dragged her to her feet. Shale peppered Essie's back, rattling off the barrel of her rifle. A cloud of dust and smoke enveloped them, stinging her eyes. She probably would have been coughing, except that she had yet to force her lungs to take a breath.

Then they were inside a dark tunnel, piles of rubble at their feet. Essie slumped against the wall and finally drew in a breath of the dusty air choked with the acrid stench of the explosives.

The others piled inside, even as a deeper rumble started outside. More of the shale mountainside poured onto the ledge.

"Is everyone here?" Julien glanced around, his mouth moving as if he was counting heads. After a moment, he nodded. "Ah. Good. Everyone's here. Let's get moving. Someone might have figured out that blast came from the rear instead of the front gate."

Two of the Escarlish soldiers lit lamps. As much as they did not want to give away their position, they also wouldn't make good progress if they stumbled around these tunnels in the dark.

One of the elven scouts took the lead with Edmund padding behind him.

As Julien set out after them, with the Escarlish soldiers following, Essie hurried to keep up. The other two elves glided behind her. Until they reached Farrendel, they would be severely outmatched if they ran into any trolls with strong magic. Even after they rescued Farrendel, would he be strong enough to help?

The dark tunnel sloped upwards. It was nearly pitch black, even with the two lamps casting pale orange circles around them. Edmund and the leading scout elf disappeared into the darkness ahead.

Essie's chest tightened, and she forced herself to breathe normally. Her heart beat so loudly in her ears that she couldn't even hear her own footsteps, much less anyone else's.

Calm. She needed to remain calm. And focus on Farrendel.

Concentrating, she felt the heart bond, warm and still crackling with Farrendel's magic. She reached for it, mentally holding it tightly, and sensed...

She sensed Farrendel. He was somewhere ahead of them. And above them? On a higher level, that must be it. At least the tunnel still sloped upward, so they were going in the right direction.

After taking a few turns, the tunnel opened into a large chamber with four tunnels branching off it. Edmund and the elf scout waited in the center of the room.

Edmund gestured at the branching tunnels. "Essie? Can you tell which way we need to go?"

Essie closed her eyes, double-checking the direction. She pointed at the tunnel on the far left. "He's in that direction, but still on a higher level than we are."

Julien studied the tunnels. "It appears that tunnel on the far left goes down, and not up. While Farrendel might be in that direction, we might have to wind our way through the tunnels to reach him. There probably isn't a tunnel that goes directly there."

"I had the same thought." Edmund waved to the elven scouts and switched to elvish. "Let's each take one of these tunnels. Go down them for two minutes or so, then come back."

With nods, each of the elven scouts loped down three of the tunnels. Edmund took the last one.

Julien glanced over his shoulder to Essie. "I take it they are scouting?"

"Yes. They'll be back in about five minutes." Essie turned in a circle, checking that her senses were correct. Yep.

Farrendel was to their left somewhere. *We're coming, Farrendel. Hold on just a little longer.*

"Very well. Everyone at ease." Julien sat, took out his canteen, and sipped.

Essie sat next to him and took a small sip from her own canteen. But not too much. It would be a long time before they would be safe and anywhere near a latrine.

Until then, she had never realized how long five minutes could feel. She tapped her fingers against the stock of her gun, glancing between the tunnels.

Arlanor, the elf sent down the far-left tunnel, returned first. He glanced at Essie and pointed down the tunnel. "This tunnel goes down to a large storage chamber with a pool of water and a few crates of food."

Essie repeated what he'd said for Julien. She'd barely finished when the other two elves returned, followed by Edmund.

Edmund pointed back the way he'd come. "This tunnel continues to the right before branching into other tunnels."

"This tunnel is the same, but to the left." The elf who had scouted one of the middle passageways nodded to the one he had scouted.

"Mine was the same, though it seems to continue straight," the other elf added in elvish.

Once Julien had the report translated, he frowned as he studied the four tunnels. "Let's take the upper one that goes to the left. It should take us in the right direction."

As they set out again, Essie kept her grip on the heart bond, following her senses. They were getting closer to Farrendel. She could feel it.

MELANTHA PULLED herself to her feet. Her bones still ached, but she could walk. After tottering the few steps to the door, she strained to reach through the bars. Her fingers brushed the locking bar. With a growl, she stood on her tiptoes, her still-healing bones in her feet screaming with pain, and gained a few more inches.

She grasped the locking bar and hauled with all her might. Arm shaking with the strain, she lifted one end of the bar free. It toppled from its other bracket and tumbled to the floor with a loud crack, thankfully covered by the rumble of yet another booming gun somewhere in the fortress above.

As she reached to push the door open, the gunfire died away, and other noises took its place. The outer door to this dungeon corridor grated open, followed by the tramp of heavy bootfalls.

Melantha peeked through the bars. A squad of six trolls marched down the passageway. Her stomach churned. They were here to take Farrendel to his death, and any moment now one of them would notice the locking bar of her dungeon cell lying on the floor.

What could she do? She was too late to get to Farrendel, and she could not fight one troll by herself, much less six.

But she could not allow them to hurt Farrendel. Weylind was here, and rescue was so close. All Melantha had to do was delay these trolls long enough that help could arrive for Farrendel. It did not matter if she died in the attempt, as long as Farrendel was freed.

With a scream, she rammed into the door, flinging it open. The trolls had paused in front of her door, one kneeling to pick up the fallen locking bar. The dungeon door smashed into his face, sending him sprawling on the floor with blood spurting from his nose.

Melantha did not wait for the rest of them to gather their wits. Still screaming like she had lost her mind, she leapt on the back of the nearest troll, clawing at his eyes. Thanks to her healing training, she knew the places to scratch and bite where it would cause the most pain.

The troll howled and tried to yank her from his back. Still, she hit and kicked and flailed. She would hold out as long as she could, conserving her magic. If help did not arrive in the next few minutes and it looked like the trolls would get past her to hurt Farrendel, then she would do her best to touch all of them and break her healer's oath. Perhaps she would die, but she would take all of these trolls with her.

As long as Farrendel survived, it would be worth it.

So close. So very close. Essie's heart pounded, and it was all she could do not to go tearing ahead to reach his side as quickly as possible. After all this time, she almost had him back.

Edmund and the elf scout returned. "The tunnels are lit ahead."

"We must be getting close." Julien doused the lantern he held, as did the Escarlish soldier with the second lantern.

A scream shattered the stillness of the tunnels, coming from the direction where Essie sensed Farrendel lay.

"Double time." Julien broke into a steady jog, the other soldiers keeping pace with him.

Essie hurried to keep up. Even a jog felt too slow, though it would be reckless to charge full speed into an unknown situation.

After going around a bend, the end of the tunnel was blocked with a metal, barred gate. Peering over her brothers' shoulders, Essie could see that their passageway opened into a large chamber with water seeping into a pool at one end. Several passageways branched from the chamber, all of the tunnels barred with metal doors and lit with torches, though the door to one of the tunnels stood open.

Another scream rang out, far closer now.

That scream didn't sound like Farrendel. Thanks to his nightmares, she knew what his screams of pain sounded like. This scream was higher pitched. More feminine. Melantha?

Essie struggled to keep her breathing even. Was it possible for her heart to pound any harder? What she wouldn't give for some of Farrendel's magic to blast this door out of their way, but he was unconscious and the crackle in the heart bond lay dormant.

Edmund took out some tools, reached through the bars, and inserted the lock picks. After a minute of fiddling, something in the lock clicked open. Edmund nudged the door, and the hinges gave a grating groan.

Julien led the way with one of the Escarlish soldiers keeping pace. Edmund and the elves jogged after them, weapons drawn. They charged into the passageway with the open door. A shout rang out, then the clash of swords.

Essie skidded to a halt at the end of that passageway, gripping her rifle.

Melantha clung to one troll's back and shoulders, clawing at his face as if she intended to tear his face off with her bare hands. Her hair straggled down her back, her cheeks and eyes sunken. With the way she was screeching, she looked and sounded like a thing from a ghost story told around a campfire.

Five other trolls had turned and raised weapons, fending off Julien, Edmund, the Escarlish soldiers, and the elven warriors.

Essie raised her rifle to her shoulder, but she couldn't get a shot. Nor would it be wise to fire a rifle in such a confined space.

Two of the trolls went down. The first troll managed to fling Melantha from his back, and she went down, skidding into a wall and lying still. The troll raised his sword, angling it toward Melantha's prone body.

Essie sighed. She couldn't believe she was doing this, but Melantha had clearly been fighting the trolls. Raising her rifle, Essie lined up her shot, waiting until the others were all struggling in a knot against the other wall, before she squeezed the trigger. The report of the rifle battered her ears, echoing off the stones.

The troll went down, blood spreading across his chest.

Outnumbered, the final three trolls were subdued. Julien and Edmund pushed the two wounded trolls into a nearby dungeon cell, locking them in. The cell wouldn't hold them long, as the door was locked with only a bar, but it would keep them out of the way for now and make them easier to guard.

Essie slung her rifle onto her back once again and hurried down the corridor.

Melantha pushed to her hands and knees, glancing at them through a curtain of greasy hair with wild eyes. Hollows dug underneath her cheekbones and eyes while her tattered red dress hung from gaunt shoulders and bony hips. Her feet were bare, and the back of her dress had been cut open at one point, revealing welts and scars still pink and fresh.

What had happened to her? Essie halted in the corridor, staring. She had not expected to feel this much pity for Melantha. Even though Melantha had hurt Farrendel and brought this upon herself, Essie couldn't gloat. Not when Melantha had clearly suffered for those choices.

With one trembling hand, Melantha pointed down the dungeon corridor. "Farrendel is in the last cell at the far end. Please hurry. He has not responded to me at all today."

Essie took a running step down the corridor. Farrendel was down there. He was still alive, she could sense that much. How badly was he hurt?

Julien caught her around the waist before she could pass him. "Let us go first. Just in case…just let us go in first, all right?"

Julien and Edmund weren't sure what they would find in that cell. While she appreciated that they were trying to protect her, this was her husband they were talking about.

Still, Essie nodded and didn't try to run past when Julien let her go.

After giving a quiet order for the soldiers to stay there and guard the wounded trolls, Julien strode down the passageway. Essie trailed after him, and Edmund fell into step beside her.

One of the elves stopped to help—or, perhaps, apprehend—Melantha while the other two padded behind Essie and Julien, their gazes darting about the dungeon.

The dungeon cell at the far end was locked with only a large stone bar, though the door itself appeared to be made from stone fashioned to look like an iron door. It even swung on stone hinges. Definitely a door designed to hold Farrendel.

After lifting the locking bar, Julien opened the door and stepped inside. Essie hurried to follow. Edmund raised a hand, like he wanted to stop her, but he halted.

The interior of the cell was dark, lit only by the torches outside. It was round, entirely stone from ceiling to walls to floor.

The stench slammed into her first. Blood and unwashed body.

But even that wasn't what froze her in place. It was the sight of Farrendel, pinned spread-eagle to the floor like a frog in a science experiment waiting to be dissected. His hair lay in shortened, uneven strands plastered to his temples. Each of his ribs stuck out clearly while blood had dried in a solid brown puddle all around him.

Even though she could sense he was still alive through the heart bond, she stared at his chest for several long seconds, trying to pick out the steady rise and fall of his breathing, though it was so shallow it was barely detectable.

Her stomach churned, and a part of her wanted to bolt back out the door and run far away from this cell. She had known Farrendel would not look like himself. That he would be hurt. But she had not realized how painful it would be to see him like this.

It took concentrated effort to force her legs to move. She knelt next to Farrendel's shoulder where the bones of his collarbone and shoulder jutted against his skin. She gently brushed at a lock of hair on his forehead. "Farrendel, my love. Please wake up."

He didn't even stir at her touch. How far gone was he?

At least the heart bond hadn't immediately connected like it had on the battlefield after the ambush, so he must not be so bad off yet that he needed her to keep his heart beating.

Or he was so close to death the heart bond knew not to try.

Julien set his pack on the ground and pulled out a hammer and a chisel. "You'll have to let me know if trying to break the stone holding him is hurting him too badly."

Essie nodded and rested her hand on Farrendel's shoulder. She reached through the heart bond, trying to reach for him, his magic, something to draw him back to her. But he didn't stir, the heart bond itself feeling cold.

Scuffling came from outside. Melantha's voice. "Please. I can help him."

Two of the elves appeared, holding Melantha upright between them. She stood, but she kept shifting, as if her feet pained her. Her gaze focused on Essie. "Please, let me help. I can give him strength with my magic. He might be able to break the stone himself. He did it before. Please."

The last thing Essie wanted to do was let Melantha anywhere near Farrendel. But Farrendel had been convinced Melantha was helping him, and she had been fighting the trolls in the passageway.

Julien gripped the hammer and chisel as if they were weapons, his body tense. Edmund crouched, hand on his knife.

Essie held out a staying hand to them. Farrendel needed all the help he could get right now, even if that help came from Melantha. "Let her heal him."

The elves released Melantha, and she stumbled forward, falling to her knees next to Essie.

Essie shifted so that she sat closer to Farrendel's head, resting her hand on his forehead.

Melantha pressed both hands to Farrendel's chest. A green light flared around her fingers as she poured her magic into him. "Come on, Farrendel. Remember the plan. We are leaving here together, remember. Please, little brother."

Farrendel stirred, his head shifting beneath Essie's hand. His eyelids fluttered, giving a brief glimpse of his silver-blue eyes. "Essie?"

"I'm here, Farrendel. I'm here."

He let out a shuddering breath. "Do not leave."

"I won't." She rested her other hand on his shoulder. "We're going to get you out of here."

He was still so listless, just lying there. Essie had expected something more. More determination. More of the warrior she knew was in him.

Melantha growled. Her hands flared with an even brighter green, enough that the hair on Essie's arms prickled, before the magic spread into Farrendel.

Melantha slumped. One of the elves caught her before she fell to the ground.

Farrendel's eyes snapped open. His gaze darted first to Melantha, unconscious or nearly so in the elf scout's grip, to Julien, still gripping the chisel and hammer, before finally swinging up to focus on Essie. Farrendel's eyebrows knotted. "Are you really here?" His voice was a rasping whisper.

"Yes." Essie dug out her canteen, uncapped it, and held it to Farrendel's mouth. She carefully tilted the canteen, only dribbling in a little bit of water at a time.

Farrendel managed a few swallows before coughing and

grimacing. He squeezed his eyes shut, drawing in a few deep breaths.

"Is that better?" Essie stroked the hair from his face again. "Now lie still. Julien is going to break the stone holding you down."

Farrendel's eyes flew open again. "You should not be here." He struggled against the stone holding him down. Fresh blood dribbled from his wrists and his shoulders.

Was that stone...impaling him? Essie's stomach heaved, but she forced herself to smile and press on Farrendel's shoulder to keep him still. "Shh. It's all right. Lie still."

"No, you need to get out of here. I cannot let them hurt you. If they find you here..." Farrendel's fists clenched. "This cannot end like last time."

"I know, I know. Calm down." Essie met Julien's gaze. He shrugged, as if he wasn't sure what to do either.

Edmund gestured toward Melantha. "Your sister said something about a plan?"

Farrendel stilled and glanced toward Melantha. Something in his gaze sharpened, alert and focused. "Yes. The plan. Stand back. All of you."

The elf picked up Melantha, slung her over a shoulder, and retreated to the wall. Julien and Edmund rose to their feet, eyeing Farrendel.

Essie hesitated. Now that she had found him, she wasn't ready to step away, even a few feet.

"Go." Farrendel's jaw set.

She needed to trust him. Essie clambered to her feet and pressed her back to the stone wall. Julien and Edmund closed in on either side of her.

Blue lightning-bolt magic flared around Farrendel's

hands. The crackle in the heart bond built, then was yanked from the heart bond. All of it at once.

Essie gasped, pressing a hand to her chest. "I think we might want to close our eyes."

The blue lightning bolts built around Farrendel until it was hard to breathe from all the magic.

Essie squeezed her eyes shut, but even then the blue magic seared against her eyelids. She covered her head with her arms.

Several sharp cracks sounded in quick succession. Farrendel's magic lessened.

Essie lowered her arms and blinked several times past the dazzle of magic. She squinted at Farrendel.

Magic still flowed down his arms, crackling around him. He rolled, pushed himself onto his elbows, then onto his knees. When he raised his head, his silver-blue eyes burned, his expression hard. He rose to his feet.

Essie would have run to him, kissed him, but he was all Laesornysh at that moment, hard and fierce.

Julien gestured at the door. "We should get out of here. We came in the back way, and we can get out that way."

"Where is Weylind?" Farrendel's hands clenched around bolts of power.

"He's—"

A boom shook through the stones around them. Something tugged deep inside the heart bond, and Essie pressed a hand to the wall, her shoulder bumping into Edmund's. She could sense a blast of Farrendel's magic, though it wasn't coming from him.

No, instead, she could feel Farrendel drawing that power to him. A surge of magic flowed through the stones, and the dungeon cell lit blue for a moment as blue lightning swarmed over Farrendel before settling, glowing, around his hands. His stance steadied even more, something in his eyes glowing hard and deadly.

Julien's mouth twisted with something between a grin and a grimace. "I think they set off the bomb at the gates."

"Then we will be going out the front." Farrendel stalked past them, his magic sparking around him. He disappeared out the door.

"Do you think he knows the way out?" Edmund pointed toward the now empty doorway.

Essie shrugged. She didn't know Farrendel's plans as there hadn't been a good way to communicate them through the heart bond. Though, she wasn't sure Farrendel was even sticking to his own plan at the moment.

Melantha was still unconscious, slung over the elven scout's shoulder. If she knew, she wouldn't be telling them any time soon.

This wasn't how Essie had pictured this rescue going. Somehow, she had imagined something more...romantic. Maybe a kiss, though she would have been happy with a hug.

But it was all right. What had she expected, really? They were in the dungeon of the enemy fortress. It was probably an inopportune time for kissing or hugging or anything romantic. Highly illogical to waste time with any of those things, after all.

Later. They would have time for that later. First, they needed to catch up with Farrendel, then they had to finish this once and for all.

TWENTY-FIVE

Farrendel stalked down the corridor, noting the footsteps following him. Edmund, Julien, Essie, and the others. As long as they were behind him, they would be safe. He brushed past the dead troll bodies lying on the floor.

He let his magic flood him, lending him strength. After two weeks of idleness, he probably should not be standing, much less walking. Somewhere, distantly, he felt the weakness in his muscles and body. But with Melantha's magic lending him strength and his own magic filling him, he felt powerful.

Normally, he used as little of his magic as possible, aware of how much destruction he could cause.

But now, everything in him had been stripped raw. Emptied. And he did not care if he destroyed this fortress stone by stone. As long as his family, both human and elven, survived this day, he did not care how much destruction he caused.

He could feel the way the stone still pierced him. Last time, the trolls had kept the stone just beneath his skin. Restraining him, but far from killing him. This time, the stone burrowed deeper, tearing through him with an abandon that told him King Charvod did not intend for him to survive a second time. Farrendel was not meant to survive this rescue.

Fine. Embrace the pain. Embrace death, for he was dead already. If he was not meant to survive, then King Charvod would not survive this day either.

King Charvod had tried, but Farrendel had not broken. He had become stronger. Stronger in the knowledge that pain meant nothing to him anymore. Stronger with the fire that burned in his chest.

Not fire. Magic. So much magic. Perhaps today Farrendel would find out just how much of it he could unleash when he did not care about the consequences.

Farrendel paused in the chamber at the end of the dungeon corridor, the one Melantha had described with the pool of water in the corner.

Which way? Farrendel closed his eyes and stretched his senses. He felt the brush of fresh air from two of the tunnels. The air from one carried the scent of the mountains. The other held a whiff of the Escarlish gunpowder. Shouts and the clash of weapons came from that passage as well, along with the icy tang of troll magic.

Time to tear this fortress apart.

Footsteps hurried down the corridor after him, including Essie's soft patter. He glanced over his shoulder.

Essie's eyes were wide, her brow furrowed. Worried. About him.

A part of him wanted to turn around. Soften. Go to her.

But not yet. Not until he made sure the trolls would never hurt him or his family ever again.

Farrendel gripped his magic harder and strode down the tunnel toward the clash of steel and blasts of power.

Somewhere ahead, boots pounded on stone, headed toward him. Probably a squad of trolls, sent by King Charvod to fetch Farrendel.

Farrendel did not slow his pace. Why waste time with caution?

Eight trolls raced around the bend ahead of him. They skidded to a halt, several of them gathering their magic and hurling it toward Farrendel. Ice crackled along the tunnel walls while the stones of the floor reached for Farrendel's feet.

Farrendel let his magic flood the corridor, melting the ice into clouds of steam and blasting the floor's fingers into pebbles. Then he shoved a blast of power at the trolls and hurled them backwards.

When he stalked past the bodies strewn on the floor, he did not pause to check if the trolls were dead. He did not have to.

The tunnel swerved through several turns, the floor sloping upward. A few chambers opened up with intersecting passageways, but Farrendel followed the echoes of war, growing louder with each step.

A stone door barred his way. Beyond it, the boom of the Escarlish weapons vibrated through the stones beneath his feet while the clash of steel and shouts of fighting rang into the air.

A flick of Farrendel's wrist sent bolts of magic at the door. The explosion shook the passageway. Pebbles pattered against the floor while dust clouded the air.

For the first time in two weeks, Farrendel stepped from the darkness of the dungeon into sunlight. He squeezed his eyes shut. Daylight. It warmed his face, even as a cold breeze blasted his face and clawed through the shortened strands of his hair. When he gulped in a lungful of the smoke and gunpowder filled air, it felt like the first time he had truly breathed in far too long.

The sunlight, the cold air, the snow-covered stone beneath his bare feet...it was almost enough to cool the fire of his magic searing his veins. Sunlight felt like home. The breeze tasted of freedom. And he could savor neither of them. With his magic crackling in every part of the raw emptiness inside him, he could focus on nothing but destruction.

He squinted against the morning sunlight, thankful for the early dawn. Full daylight would have been far too dazzling.

Ahead of him, lines of trolls fought against elves in flashing armor. Magic burst around them, ice and green shields, rocks hurling through the air and roots lashing from the ground. Behind the elves, squads of Escarlish soldiers filled gaps in the elven line or stood back and aimed their rifles at the trolls on the wall tops.

Heads turned toward him. Trolls at the back turned and dashed in Farrendel's direction.

A blast of his magic sent the trolls stumbling back. Farrendel poured more magic into the ranks of the trolls, killing a number of them, hurling most of them from their feet. Even the elves stumbled back from the sizzling sweep of Farrendel's magic.

A blast of icy magic slammed into Farrendel from the

side. He stumbled a step before he steadied and pushed back with his magic, obliterating the troll magic.

Prince Rharreth stood by a door that led into what looked like the main section of the mountain castle. He raised his hands, as if to send another wave of magic at Farrendel.

Not this time. Not again. Farrendel hurled magic at the troll prince, wrapping bolts of power around the troll's arms and body, piercing his wrists much as Farrendel had been pinned. Farrendel shoved the troll prince and held him there, helpless, even as the troll prince struggled against the magic.

Where was King Charvod? Weylind and Averett?

If King Charvod had already killed Farrendel's brother, then this fortress would be razed to the ground.

There. At the far side of the courtyard, King Charvod lunged at Weylind, backed by five other trolls. Next to Weylind, Averett held an elven shield and fended off a troll swinging a mace. The trolls pushed back both the elven and Escarlish royal guards, isolating Weylind and Averett.

King Charvod swung a large, two-handed sword, iced over with magic. Weylind gave a step, but a rock heaved from the ground, tripping him. He raised a hand, a root shooting up to block the sword's swing.

But the root was too small, too weak here in the rocky, icy ground of Kostaria. King Charvod's sword sliced through the root and continued its arc, aimed at Weylind's head.

Farrendel gathered a fistful of power and thrust it forward. A bolt of magic cracked across the courtyard, slicing through King Charvod and punching out a section of the stone wall behind him. King Charvod's limp body fell to the ground even as the wall crumbled with a roar, falling into the gorge below.

Far too much satisfaction burned alongside the magic in Farrendel's chest. King Charvod was dead. He would never pin another elf to the ground and fill them so full of stone they could not move or breathe with the pain of it. Never again.

Magic built around Farrendel as he strode forward. He let it pour from him in waves, crackling on the ground and bursting in the gathering clouds above. He swept away the rest of the trolls around Weylind and Averett, along with more of the wall.

More, ever more magic. It hurt in his chest, his bones, yet still it came. And he let it, sinking into the magic more than he ever had before.

He stalked closer to Prince Rharreth, blasting aside any troll that attempted to stop him. He halted a few feet from the troll prince, his fingers dripping magic. "You will never hurt me or any of my family ever again."

Sweat beaded on Prince Rharreth's forehead as he strained against Farrendel's magic. The troll prince had gathered his magic enough to push Farrendel's magic a foot away from his body, but no farther. He met Farrendel's gaze and held it. "Is that it, then? You're going to kill me?"

Farrendel flexed his fingers, bolts of power twining up his arms. It was tempting to take his magic and drive it through Prince Rharreth's chest.

But the troll prince was pinned, helpless. And he had treated Farrendel with far more honor than his brother had.

Instead, Farrendel poured more magic into the troll prince's restraints, his magic sizzling the ice into nothing. "Surrender. We are no longer in Tarenhiel or Escarland. I do not care if I tear the very bedrock of your kingdom."

"No." The veins along Prince Rharreth's neck bulged,

and a wave of power surged around him. Back at the Escarlish border, the troll prince's magic had been formidable. Then, Farrendel had cared if he burnt himself up with power or if he destroyed all of Escarland by unleashing more power than he could control.

But not here. Here Farrendel just bared his teeth and let the last of his iron control drop. Magic roiled into the air. The ground shook, cracks spiderwebbing jagged lines across the courtyard.

Behind him, Farrendel could sense Essie and her brothers as they stumbled out of the door of the passageway, safely clear of the dungeon tunnels.

Farrendel poured his magic into the ground. It groaned as his magic tore through stone and the magic the trolls had embedded into their fortress. He coated each and every dungeon tunnel, wrapping his magic through the stones that had once held him captive.

A few troll soldiers remained inside the fortress, but no elves or humans. And no noncombatants that Farrendel could sense.

Clenching his fists, Farrendel let his magic tear out the foundations of Gror Grar. A whirlwind of lightning-blue magic whipped around him before he blasted it at the remains of the fortress.

With a mighty groan and the rumble of stone, Gror Grar collapsed, its walls and towers falling into the gorge around the mountain it had been built on. Portions of the mountain crumbled, the stones lit blue and shattered with Farrendel's magic.

Dust filled the air, even as Farrendel's magic crackled through each mote of dust, swirling into storm clouds rumbling with magic in the sky above.

Pinned to the one remaining wall of Gror Grar, Prince Rharreth had stilled, his eyes wide.

Farrendel growled and stabbed a bolt of power through Prince Rharreth's shoulder. "Surrender."

Prince Rharreth flinched and cried out. He gritted his teeth and glared at Farrendel. Magic pulsed around his fingers, but Farrendel's magic crawled over him, sizzling against the troll magic and snuffing it out.

Farrendel grasped for his magic, but it burned through his fingers. A storm built above, flickers of magic dazzling across black clouds. Power poured through him, consuming him even as it threatened to tear him apart.

"Last chance. Surrender. Or I will raze your entire kingdom to the ground." Farrendel channeled as much magic as he could control through his body. Blue lightning coated his skin, coalescing into a massive, glowing sword. With a growl, he drove it into the stone courtyard.

The stone cracked, a jagged crevasse opening as it zigged and zagged across the courtyard of the once mighty fortress of Gror Grar.

The ground shook, laced with glowing blue magic spreading outward from Farrendel. With a rumble, the mountains surrounding Gror Grar shattered, rubble tumbling to earth with ear-splitting cracks.

Still pinned, Prince Rharreth glanced over his shoulder as best he could, his eyes widening. "Please, Laesornysh, pull your magic back. I surrender. Please. I don't care what you do to me, but don't destroy Osmana. There are women and children in there."

Farrendel followed Prince Rharreth's line of sight. With Gror Grar nothing but rubble, the lights of the city of Osmana were now visible, huddled behind a wall farther in the gorge that Gror Grar had once guarded. The wave of Farrendel's magic swept through the ground, opening fissures and leveling the mountains, heading in the direction of the troll city.

In moments, Farrendel's magic would utterly destroy that city, killing every troll male, female, and child huddled inside.

Farrendel tried to yank back on the crashing tide of his magic, but it tore from him, bursting behind his eyes and building into an inferno of magic. He collapsed to his knees under the force of it, feeling the tremors in the ground beneath him.

"Please, Laesornysh!" Prince Rharreth thrashed against the bonds of magic holding him against the stone. "I said, I surrender. Please. Just spare them."

Farrendel shook, magic blazing beneath his skin and sizzling deep into his bones. He could not breathe for the force of it, the stone inside him tearing deeper as it reacted against his magic. He braced a hand against the stone of the courtyard, his body too weak to withstand much more of this.

"I cannot." He shuddered, his senses shredding with the force of the magic coursing through him.

He could not draw his magic back. He had lost control, and now he was going to kill as he had never killed before. Not just enemies on a battlefield. But women. Children. His own family and friends huddled behind him.

Essie. His magic was going to kill Essie.

He had been wrong. This—not the weeks of torture—was his worst nightmare.

TWENTY-SIX

Essie clung to Edmund, bracing herself against the whipping wind so filled with magic it hurt to breathe it, even for her. Her skin prickled as her hair stood on end with the power crackling through the courtyard.

In the courtyard, the fighting had stopped. Escarlish soldiers huddled on the ground, gaping at something to Essie's left. Elves knelt in front of them, raising their hands as if to shield themselves from something. And the remaining trolls...it was hard to tell the dead from the living. All were pressed flat to the ground, bolts of blue power coursing over them.

Another rumble shuddered through the ground. High above, dark clouds gathered, streaked with blue lightning.

Farrendel stood in the middle of a blaze of power, swirling like a tornado of magic around him. The shortened ends of his hair whipped around his head.

The troll prince was pinned to the wall with cords of shimmering blue magic. His jaw was hard, even as sweat dripped down his gray skin. He said something to Farrendel, though Essie couldn't hear it over the roar of Farrendel's magic.

The dark clouds above swirled, lit with blue magic within. Magic flared like a lightning bolt around Farrendel before he drove it into the ground.

Essie staggered as the ground shook, then stumbled as Edmund yanked her back. A foot-wide fissure opened where they had been standing a moment ago.

Magic glowed in the stones of the courtyard. Cries of pain came from the trolls already pinned with Farrendel's magic. Roars filled the air as the surrounding mountains crumbled into dust.

Farrendel dropped to a knee, as if straining under the weight of all the magic.

"He lost control." Essie pressed a hand to her chest, feeling the way his searing magic tore through him. At that moment, he was truly Laesornysh, *Death on the Wind*.

And if someone didn't stop this, then he would kill them all.

Essie straightened her shoulders. It was up to her. After all, she was immune to Farrendel's magic. At least, small amounts of it. She wasn't sure even Farrendel was immune to this much of his magic.

She tugged free of Edmund's grip and dashed across the courtyard, hopping the fissures as she went.

When she was halfway across, Averett raced up to her and grabbed her arm. "Essie, no. You can't go to him. It isn't safe."

"Of course it isn't safe. But it's a lot safer for me than anyone else." Essie held Averett's gaze, even as Weylind dashed up behind him. "I'm the only one who can snap him out of this."

Averett's grip tightened on her arm, as if he would refuse to let her go. "Essie..."

"He needs me, and if I don't go to him, none of us are going to make it out of here." Essie glanced from Averett to Weylind.

Weylind nodded, but his gaze swerved to Farrendel. "Averett Daresheni, she needs to go."

Face twisting, Averett released her arm. He stepped forward, as if he planned to give Essie a hug, but Essie dodged him. She didn't have time to waste. Nor was a hug goodbye necessary. Farrendel would never hurt her. Not even now. Of that she was certain.

Essie staggered across the uneven ground toward Farrendel. He was hunched on his knees under the force of all the magic. Blue bolts of power coursed beneath his skin.

Days ago, Essie had felt the immense power of Farrendel's magic when it flowed through her. He usually only used as little of his magic as possible, fearful of what would happen if he released more than he could handle.

Apparently, he'd had good reason to worry.

The ground heaved, and Essie fell to her knees, scraping her hands on the rough stone. When she glanced over her shoulder, Weylind was hunched, roots springing from the ground to protect all three of Essie's brothers. At the far end of the courtyard, the elven warriors held green shields over the Escarlish soldiers.

When Essie pushed to her feet and hurried forward again, pebbles crunched under her boots, and Farrendel's head snapped up, his hand lifting as if to blast her with magic.

"Farrendel, it's me." Essie kept her voice even, calm. The crackle of magic against her skin escalated from a prickle to an uncomfortable scouring. Yet the magic didn't tear her apart or disintegrate her where she stood.

"Essie." Farrendel's eyes were so filled with magic that the silver-blue of his eyes was no longer visible.

"It's all right, Farrendel." Essie knelt in front of him. After a moment, she reached out and rested her hands on his cheeks. Her skin prickled with magic, but it didn't hurt.

"I cannot let them hurt anyone again." Farrendel's voice was strained. Sparks of power trickled down his cheek. "I cannot."

"I know. But not like this." Essie swiped away one of the magic sparks. It prickled against her finger but didn't hurt. "You're safe, and the trolls are defeated. It's over."

"I do not...I cannot..." Farrendel was trembling beneath her fingers. Magic lit his veins, glowing in the depths of his eyes.

Could Farrendel stop this? Was it possible he had unleashed so much magic, he could not rein it in?

This was too much for him to control by himself. But, perhaps, they could control it together.

"Then give it to me. Do whatever you did to pour your magic into the heart bond before. I don't think I can wield your magic by myself, but I can hold a portion of it while you get the rest under control." Essie tipped his chin so that he was looking at her, hard as it was to hold his magic-lit gaze. All this magic was fueled by his pain and anger after the torture he'd endured. He was stuck in that dungeon still, even though his body was free.

She needed to remind him of love. Happiness. The future they had together.

"It might hurt you." Farrendel lifted a shaking hand, his fingers dripping bolts of magic. He stopped short of touching her.

She clasped his hand, a jolt of energy traveling through her. "It won't." She leaned her forehead against Farrendel's. "Please. It's time to come home."

This time, Farrendel reached out and traced a hand over her cheek. Then, he leaned closer and kissed her.

Magic whirled about them, crackling through her hair and sparking in her chest. Or, perhaps, that was the kiss and not magic. She couldn't tell.

Magic poured into her, bright and sparking. The magic in the air and filling the courtyard coalesced around them until she couldn't see anyone past the bright blue crackle. The light grew so intense she had to squeeze her eyes shut. She clung to Farrendel, even as he pulled back from the kiss. His skin was slick with blood or sweat. Perhaps both.

The fiery power of his magic tore through her, and she struggled to grip it. She gritted her teeth, mentally wrestling with the amount of magic placed in her hands. Forcing herself to breathe, she held onto Farrendel's magic even as he poured still more into her and the heart bond.

It felt as if fire scorched through her veins about to burn her up. Essie dragged in a breath and struggled to stay conscious. She must not pass out. She had to hold on to Farrendel's magic for just a few moments longer.

Then, through the heart bond, she sensed Farrendel's grip on his magic steady, his control shaky but returning. He grasped the remaining magic, drawing it to him. Essie's breathing hitched with the force of the magic contained in the two of them.

The magic surrounding her and Farrendel exploded.

271

Essie was thrown backwards, Farrendel torn from her grip. The moment before she would have struck the ground, the magic in the heart bond flashed out and shielded her, cushioning her fall enough that only her shoulder ached from the impact.

A gigantic boom tore through the sky, then the pressure of magic dissipated like a breeze sweeping away into the distance.

When she peeled her eyes open, sparks of Farrendel's magic drizzled down from the sky like rain before winking out.

Farrendel lay unmoving on the ground several yards. He must have also been blown backwards by the force of the magical blast, though the way he sprawled limply on the ground suggested he hadn't had the magic-protected landing Essie had.

Essie tottered to her feet and dashed toward him, her legs still unsteady.

Weylind raced past her and knelt next to Farrendel, gently lifting him. As Essie approached, Weylind held up a hand. "No, do not touch him. Not yet."

Essie clenched her fists but didn't go any closer. He was right. If she activated the deep connection of the heart bond now, it might make it harder for the elven healers to do their job, since they would have to worry about putting too much strain on Essie. Better to wait until it was absolutely necessary, even though she wanted to hold Farrendel close.

Weylind stood, cradling Farrendel to him. Farrendel lay limp, head lolling against Weylind's shoulder. Weylind strode in the direction of the gates, as if oblivious to everything else but getting Farrendel to a healer.

Essie moved to follow, yet something caught her eye.

Behind Farrendel and Weylind, the troll prince eased to his feet and pressed a hand to his shoulder. She whipped her rifle from her shoulder and raised it.

Averett appeared at her side, a pistol already in his hand. He pointed it at the troll prince. "No sudden moves."

The troll prince spread both hands at his sides, palms up. "I have already surrendered."

Averett's pistol didn't waver. Not that a mere pistol would do much good if the troll prince tried something. Averett reached out with a hand and blindly patted Essie's arm. "Take care of Farrendel. I can see to things here. Edmund, go with them. Julien, with me."

Essie handed her rifle to Julien. He and Averett would need the weapon more than she did. Then, she hurried across the courtyard. Edmund fell into step beside her, his jaw set.

With his long stride, Weylind had already reached the gates and was crossing the temporary wooden bridge that spanned a two-foot-wide gap in the stone bridge. The explosive they had used to splinter the gates must have been strong enough to punch a hole through the bridge.

Even though she was hurrying, Weylind still reached the camp on the far side and disappeared into the hospital tent before Essie had caught up with him. She reached the tent flap and pushed inside.

Wounded lay on cots with nurses bustling between them. Surgical rooms in the back were walled off with curtains.

Before Essie could take more than a step inside, an elven nurse blocked her way. "You need to wash before you're allowed inside."

"But Weylind...Farrendel..." Essie couldn't manage to

talk coherently. She just wanted to push past this nurse and hurry to Farrendel's side.

Arguing would take longer than simply doing as the nurse demanded. Essie stepped to the buckets of hot water and the soap at the washing station just inside the tent and scrubbed her hands, then waited while Edmund did the same. As much as she wanted to hurry on without him, she also didn't want to face whatever lay ahead without one of her family members by her side.

When they were both clean, Essie led the way between the cots to the back of the tent where six surgical rooms were cordoned off with canvas. She heard Weylind's voice in the nearest one, and pushed her way inside.

Farrendel was laid out on the wooden surgical table in the center of the space with two nurses bustling around him, cleaning the blood and grime from his skin. A white sheet draped over his middle and legs, and Essie guessed the nurses had stripped him of the remains of the filthy clothes he'd been wearing.

The head surgeon and healer that Essie had met back in Tarenhiel were huddled next to the table, their heads together as they discussed something between them. Weylind stood next to the table with a hand on Farrendel's shoulder.

Farrendel's breathing was ragged, his eyes squeezed shut, his fists clenched. He was conscious now, if the amount of pain tightening his face was any indication.

While Edmund stayed by the door, Essie crept closer. She didn't want to get in the way, but she didn't want to stand on the outskirts either. She halted next to Farrendel's head at the end of the table. "I'm here."

"Essie." He gasped her name between ragged breaths.

Farrendel's eyes remained squeezed shut, as if to block out the pain.

The elven healer reached out a hand, a glow of magic around his fingers, and pressed his palm to Farrendel's chest.

Farrendel cried out, and the healer snatched his hand away, gripping it as if he had been burned. The healer turned to the Escarlish surgeon and began another discussion in rapid, hushed tones.

Essie should have felt satisfaction that the surgeon and healer were getting along so well, considering this teamwork on the part of the medical staff had been her idea. But her stomach was churning, and she had to grip the edge of the table to keep herself from reaching for Farrendel's hand.

At the door, Jalissa rushed inside, though she halted only a few feet past the entrance, her mouth and eyes wide with a stricken look. Edmund stepped forward and put an arm around her, steering her toward his place by the wall.

After a moment, Nylian, the elven healer, turned to Weylind, his whole body braced as if prepared to be shot for delivering his news. "Weylind Daresheni, I am sorry. But your brother is dying."

Weylind's shoulders sagged, his head bowing as if to hide his emotion from those present. Jalissa gasped, pressing a hand over her mouth. Edmund wrapped both arms around her.

Essie's knees sagged, and she gripped the edge of the table with both hands. No, he couldn't be dying. They'd rescued him. He was supposed to be fine now. "No. No, there must be something you can do."

The healer swung sad, dark brown eyes in her direction. "I am truly sorry. But whoever put that stone into him did not intend for him to survive his rescue. The stone has pierced him deeply, curling around his bones and puncturing organs. There is too much troll magic still inside him for me to keep him alive through the surgery that it would take to remove it. On top of that, I suspect his own magic reacted against the stone, doing even more damage."

The surgeon glanced at the healer before he too turned to Essie. "I'm not sure we could even remove it with surgery. Not if the stone is as embedded into him as Nylian has described. If this stone were a bullet or shrapnel, the normal procedure would be to leave it in. Most people can live a normal life under such cases."

"But he would be in constant pain. The stone would slowly kill him." The elven healer shook his head. "I am sorry. But there is nothing we can do."

Weylind's head remained bowed, his hands braced against the table.

"No. No, there must be something. The heart bond...I can keep him alive during a surgery. It's strong enough. I'm strong enough." Essie reached for Farrendel. She could help him. She refused to let him die. Not like this. Not when she'd just gotten him back.

But Farrendel was shaking his head, his eyes cracked open to slits. "My...choice...Essie..." he gasped, his gaze meeting hers.

His choice. That had been what he'd told her on the train when they'd been captured. He'd wanted the choice to sacrifice to be his, this time.

"The stone is too deep." The healer's tone was gentle, even though he was stabbing Essie's heart. "The attempt would likely kill both of you."

"My choice..." Farrendel gritted out again, his gaze still locked on hers.

He didn't want her to risk herself for him. Perhaps it was her life and her choice to make, but it was also Farrendel's choice to refuse her help. He wouldn't want to kill her along with himself.

Then what could they do? Essie wasn't just going to stand there and watch Farrendel die. Not after how far she'd come to get him back. Not when they had just barely begun to experience happiness together.

If neither the Escarlish surgeon nor the elven healer could remove the troll-magic laced stone killing Farrendel, then there was only one answer. A troll had to remove it. After all, the trolls had put it there. It made sense that only a troll could take it out.

How would they find a troll willing to save the life of the trolls' most feared enemy? And a troll they could trust enough to help Farrendel and not hurt him further?

She met Edmund's gaze across the room and motioned. He said something to Jalissa, then eased her away from him. After he hurried across the tent, he halted by Essie.

The healer and the surgeon had begun another discussion with Weylind listening.

Essie leaned closer to Edmund and whispered, "Fetch Averett. Make sure he brings the troll prince."

Edmund searched her face, then nodded. "Right."

As Edmund left the tent, the Escarlish surgeon motioned to Farrendel. "We should give him something to make him comfortable. Thanks to your elven magic, we have more than enough morphine to spare."

"Morphine." The elven healer's nose wrinkled for a

moment before he sighed. "I suppose such methods are the only means left at our disposal."

At least he'd left out the word *primitive*, even though it was still implied.

The surgeon stepped away and disappeared into a curtained-off section. Essie caught a brief glimpse of crates. That must be the supply closet, if a tent could have a closet.

Weylind turned to the healer. "Are you absolutely sure there is nothing that can be done?"

The healer sighed and shook his head. "If there was something I could do, I would. We should let Maxwell make him comfortable. It may be some time before..." The healer trailed off, as if he couldn't bring himself to say it out loud.

If the trolls couldn't help Farrendel, if this was it, Essie wanted to hold Farrendel's hand. She didn't want to let him go.

But she wasn't sure what the heart bond would do if she touched him. She had to wait and save her strength in case it was needed.

The surgeon returned, trailed by a nurse holding a tray with a glass hypodermic needle partially filled with a clear liquid, a glass bottle, and a few wads of bandages. The surgeon splashed one of the cotton cloths with the liquid in the bottle, an alcohol based on the smell. Essie remembered the process from the inoculations she had received as a child.

When the surgeon swabbed the inside of Farrendel's elbow, Farrendel started and tensed. His eyes flew open, and he focused on the surgeon.

The surgeon picked up the hypodermic needle, held it, and flicked it with a finger several times to make sure there were no air bubbles.

Farrendel's breathing grew more rapid, his muscles rigid.

"It's all right. I've had inoculations before. It will be fine." Essie rested her hand next to Farrendel's head, though she didn't touch him.

"It's just a quick pinch." The surgeon lowered the hypodermic needle and bent over Farrendel.

Farrendel's eyes remained wide. When the surgeon reached for Farrendel's arm, blue magic sparked around his fingers.

"Get back." The elf healer threw an arm around the surgeon's chest and pulled him back.

"Farrendel." This time, Essie didn't hesitate. She rested a hand on Farrendel's cheek, feeling the sweaty warmth to his skin. For a brief second, the heart bond connected, and she gasped as pain shot through her chest.

Then Farrendel placed that iron wall between them, though it wasn't as solid as it was when they were apart. She could still sense his emotions, taste a portion of his pain, though her body wasn't trying to keep his alive.

Placing her back to the others, she leaned over Farrendel and cradled his face in her hands, blocking his view. "Do you trust me?"

Farrendel's gaze searched her face before he nodded, slowly.

"And do you trust that I won't let them do anything to harm you?" Essie traced her fingers across Farrendel's cheek, then brushed aside a lock of his hair.

Farrendel drew in a deep breath, his muscles relaxing. He squeezed his eyes shut. "I trust you."

"Good." Essie straightened, but she kept a hand on Farrendel's cheek. "Go ahead, Maxwell. It's safe now."

The surgeon hesitated, as if he wasn't sure it was as safe as Essie said. After a moment, he stepped forward.

Essie focused on Farrendel's face. She knew the moment the needle slid into Farrendel's arm by the tightening of his jaw. But he kept his magic in check.

"There, all done. It will take a few moments, but you should start feeling a numbing sensation spreading up your arm." The surgeon set the hypodermic needle back on the tray.

Good. At least Farrendel would be more comfortable while they waited for Edmund to return with Averett and the troll prince, though the others didn't know that was what they were waiting for. They all thought they were waiting for Farrendel's death.

After a minute, Farrendel's breathing began to steady, and his muscles relaxed beneath Essie's hand.

The surgeon glanced between Weylind, the elf healer, and Essie. "We should move him. I'm sorry, but we'll need this table for the next patient."

"Not yet." Essie moved her free hand to Farrendel's shoulder, as if to keep the others from moving him. She opened her mouth, but she wasn't sure how to explain. Or if she should. Weylind would surely object.

Beside the wall, Jalissa had sunk to the floor, her arms wrapped over her stomach, her head bowed so that her hair hid her face. Her shoulders shook, though she didn't make a sound.

"Princess Elspeth. I understand why you would be... reluctant." The surgeon glanced at Weylind, as if pleading for him to deal with her.

Weylind stared down at Farrendel. "I know...I know it is hard to accept..."

"No, it's...we need to wait for Averett." Essie couldn't let them move Farrendel. That would mean giving up. Accepting the fact that he was dying.

And she was not ready to stop fighting for him.

"No need to wait." Averett's voice came from the entrance as he pushed the tent flap aside. He stepped into the tent, followed by the tall, gray-skinned, white-haired form of the troll prince.

Weylind stiffened, his hand reaching for the dagger at his belt. "What is he doing here?"

"He is here to help Farrendel." Averett stepped aside as Edmund entered the tent and immediately knelt at Jalissa's side.

"No." Weylind's grip tightened on the dagger. "I will not let him anywhere near my brother. He has already hurt him enough."

"He's also the only one who can save him." Essie pointed at the troll prince. "A troll put the stone in him, and only a troll can take it out."

"We cannot trust him." Weylind's whole body tensed, though he didn't draw his dagger. Not yet, anyway.

"Probably not." Averett turned hard eyes on the troll prince. "But Prince Rharreth knows that treaty negotiations will not go well for Kostaria if he harms the brother and brother-in-law of the Tarenhieli and Escarlish kings. After all, he unconditionally surrendered. Utterly destroying his kingdom without any kind of consideration is still an option at this point."

Prince Rharreth bowed his head, his gaze focused on Farrendel. "Even though he is the elf who killed my father and my brother, I will help him. He has already paid enough for the blood of my family."

Weylind shook his head, fingers flexing on his dagger's hilt. "We cannot trust him."

"Farrendel, what do you think?" Averett's voice was quiet, solemn.

Farrendel held Prince Rharreth's gaze for a long moment, before his silver-blue eyes flicked up to meet Essie's. "I trust Essie."

Essie smiled, but the smile hurt. "You heard him. He trusts me. And this is the only chance we have to save him."

Weylind crossed his arms but nodded. "Very well."

Averett, the troll prince, the surgeon, and the elf healer began discussing how to make it work. Something about the surgeon helping to remove the stone so that Prince Rharreth could direct the stone out in a manner that did the least damage rather than snaking it through Farrendel's body yet again.

Essie only partially paid attention, just enough to stop them if she heard something that didn't sound right.

She cradled Farrendel's face and put her back to the others, blocking Farrendel from seeing anyone besides her. He already remembered far too much of torture and pain. This time, when he remembered this moment, she wanted him to remember only her.

"It's almost over." Essie stroked Farrendel's cheek with her thumb. After the two weeks of capture, the hollows under his cheeks and eyes cut far too deeply. "Just hang on a little longer, all right? Just a few more minutes."

He opened his mouth, like he was going to reply, but his face twisted, and he cried out.

Essie glanced over her shoulder. What were they doing to him?

Prince Rharreth gripped his hand before shaking it, as if

he'd been burned. "Laesornysh's magic is still coursing through the stone. I can still remove it, but it will be difficult." He met the healer's gaze. "You will wish to slide your magic between the stone and his body. That is what Princess Melantha did, and it gave Laesornysh access to his magic. You should be able to shield him from my magic with yours."

The elf healer grimaced, but he nodded. Perhaps he didn't want to protest that he couldn't do it after Prince Rharreth just said Melantha could perform such a feat with her magic.

An icy glow started around the troll prince's fingertips again, but he didn't reach for Farrendel until the elf healer's fingers were surrounded by a green glow.

Essie turned back to Farrendel, stroking his hair. Farrendel stiffened, his breathing growing ragged. How much pain was he in that even morphine and elven healing magic couldn't numb it?

She resisted the urge to glance over her shoulder again. She didn't want to see the surgeon cutting him open, the troll prince dragging stone from his chest. She ran her fingers over his cheek. "I just need you to survive a little longer, Farrendel. Just a little longer, and this will be over."

Through the heart bond, she could sense the effort it took him to breathe, the struggle as he fought to stay conscious.

He cried out, and a wall of pain blasted through Essie. Her vision blurred as she struggled to draw in a breath. Her chest hurt, as if her heart were tearing itself apart with each beat.

Hands gripped her shoulders, keeping her standing. She braced herself against the table and buried her fingers in Farrendel's hair. She squeezed her eyes shut and fought to stave off the wave of pain and blackness that threatened to crush her.

She couldn't breathe. She tried, but she couldn't get her lungs to fill. A buzzing sound filled her ears, her legs buckling beneath her. Only the table and those steadying hands on her shoulders kept her upright.

"Let go, isciena." Weylind's voice was soft and gentle near Essie's ear, and only then did she realize he was the one holding her upright. "We cannot lose both of you."

"No." Essie gasped the word with the last breath in her lungs. She pressed her forehead to Farrendel's. *Please, Farrendel. Breathe.*

"Isciena." Weylind's voice, pained and gentler than she'd ever heard, came from beside her.

"Essie." Averett, his tone both firm and anguished, gripped her arm as if he intended to physically pull her away from Farrendel.

"No." It was nothing but a whimper. She had promised Farrendel she would let go when the time came. That she would let this sacrifice be his choice.

But now that the moment was here, she just couldn't do it. If she could just…breathe…

Farrendel gasped a choking, shuddering breath. Essie gulped in a lungful of air, her legs steadying, the blackness retreating. Her chest ached, but the sensation of having her heart beat for his faded.

Weylind and Averett didn't say anything, but stood there, prepared to keep her upright if she needed them to do so.

But Farrendel kept breathing ragged breaths, punctuated only with a few moans of pain.

Finally, Averett rested a hand on Essie's arm. "They're

done, Essie. Step back and let the healers finish cleaning him up."

She swiped at her face and stepped back. The head elf healer had slumped against one of the poles holding up the tent, and another elf healer had taken his place, along with an Escarlish nurse. The nurse and healer appeared to be spreading salve and bandaging wounds. Why hadn't the elves healed Farrendel completely? Was something still wrong?

Farrendel had slipped into unconsciousness, but Essie could still feel a deep, lingering pain from him. As if he was still badly injured.

The troll prince had his hands at his sides, sweat trickling in rivulets down his temples, though he had stepped back as if to prove he wasn't a threat.

Weylind braced his hands on the table, only moving when the new elf healer spoke to him quietly, and finally nudged him out of the way to continue bandaging Farrendel.

Edmund and Jalissa remained sitting near the wall of the tent, Jalissa resting her head on Edmund's shoulder. It would have been an adorable sight, if Essie hadn't been so worried for Farrendel and if Jalissa's eyes weren't red and puffy.

Essie glanced at the head elf healer and the Escarlish surgeon, trying to ignore the surgeon's red-stained fingers. "Will Farrendel be all right?"

"Thanks to you, yes, I believe he will." The elf healer pushed away from the pole, stepping forward on shaking legs. "We removed as much of the stone as we dared, but he is too weak for us to risk more today. We have stabilized him, at least, though I will be more optimistic of a full recovery once he has rested and gotten some fluids in him."

"But there's still stone in him? Won't that hurt him?" Essie leaned against Averett, thankful that he had put an arm around her shoulders.

"Yes, there is still stone in him, and, yes, it will continue to hurt until we can do a second surgery to remove the rest of it. But, right now, the strain of all the competing magics is too much for him and for you." The elf healer shook his head, swaying as if the movement made him dizzy. "And for us as well. After the troll magic and his magic have had a chance to dissipate and he has regained some of his strength, it should be a simple matter to remove the rest."

The surgeon stepped forward, his fingers now clean. "We will use morphine to keep him comfortable in the meantime."

Essie nodded, letting out a long breath. Surely Farrendel would be all right once he rested and healed.

She rested a hand on his shoulder, feeling the warmth of his skin and the pain still coursing through him.

But he was alive. And he would heal. Eventually.

TWENTY-SEVEN

W hile Essie dashed to the shelter to retrieve her things, Edmund and Jalissa set up Essie's tent, the one she hadn't used for most of the march across Kostaria since she had been sharing a shelter, first with Jalissa, then with all the brothers.

Weylind and Averett went with Prince Rharreth to see to settling down all three armies, finding shelter for the captured trolls whose fortress had been destroyed. They had agreed to meet in several hours to discuss a peace treaty.

By the time Essie returned, her tent had been set up outside of the hospital tent beside rows of other large tents, probably more recovery tents for the wounded. She raced toward it, flung open the tent flap, and smacked into Edmund's chest.

Edmund stumbled back a step, as did she, though neither of them fell. He pointed over his shoulder. "He's stirring."

"Already?" Essie hurried past him.

Farrendel lay on an Escarlish army cot, blankets piled on top of him and drawn up to his chin, leaving only his wan face and shortened hair visible. Jalissa sat next to him, her hands clasped in her lap.

A few feet away, a small wood-burning stove kept the tent warm while a few foldable stools provided extra seating if necessary. The floor of the tent had even been covered with a canvas rug, cutting down on the chill coming from the stony ground.

Edmund held out a hand to Jalissa. "Why don't we fetch some hot broth and some fresh water?"

"But..." Jalissa glanced from him to Farrendel, her face twisting.

"You don't have to go." Essie stepped forward, doing her best to put on a smile. Honestly, she'd rather have a few moments alone with Farrendel. But Jalissa was Farrendel's sister. Essie wasn't going to tear her from Farrendel's side now. It might even do him good to see at least one of his sisters worried about him.

"Let's give Essie some time with Farrendel first. By the time we come back, he will be more awake and ready for visitors." Edmund beckoned with his hand.

Essie tried to pack all of her gratitude for her brother into the look she shot him. Hopefully Farrendel really would be up for visitors, and not just promptly pass out after being awake for only a few seconds. Or he might only toss and turn at the brink of consciousness before sliding back into deeper sleep once again.

With one last glance at Farrendel, Jalissa slowly climbed to her feet and took Edmund's arm. "Very well. He may appreciate food and drink when he wakes."

As if bolstered by the logic that fetching food was the best thing she could do to help Farrendel, Jalissa all but swept from the tent with Edmund hurrying to match her pace.

Essie sank into Jalissa's spot beside Farrendel. He had his face turned away from her, his eyes and mouth tight with pain even in sleep.

She reached beneath the blankets, traced his arm until she found his hand, and gripped his fingers. With her other hand, she ran her fingers through his hair. Even though she'd known the trolls had cut his hair, it was still a shock seeing it so short and ragged. He didn't look like himself, and she ached for him because of it. It was one thing to choose such a drastic change in appearance, but another thing altogether to have it forcibly done against his will.

At least he had her. While she'd found his long hair surprisingly attractive, she loved him. He could be bald, and she'd still love him.

He shifted, murmuring something between cracked lips.

A canteen and a cloth sat on a small end table. Essie wet the cloth, then dabbed first his mouth, then his forehead. "It's all right, Farrendel. You're safe now."

"Essie." His eyes flickered open, his head tilting toward her. "Is this...a dream?"

"No, this is real. We rescued you." Essie held up the canteen. "Would you like some water?"

Farrendel's silver-blue eyes studied her, his eyelids drooping. "You would say that, if this were a dream."

Essie capped and set down the canteen. Leaning closer, she stroked his hair and pressed a kiss to his forehead. "Would I do that in a dream?"

"Yes." If anything, his brow furrowed more.

"How about this?" She kissed him on the mouth. More a

peck, really. His lips were cracked and bleeding, and she didn't want to hurt him.

"Maybe."

She sat back and put her hands on her hips, giving him a fake glare. "Just what kind of dreams are you having about me?"

"Very good dreams." A hint of a smile tugged the corner of his mouth. He lifted a shaky hand and touched the end of her braid, where it had fallen onto his chest. "But...this must be real. I had forgotten how very red your hair is."

From anyone else, that would have been a snide comment. But Farrendel meant it as a compliment.

Normally, she would have made a joking comment about his hair. But she didn't want to remind him of it now. Nor did she think he was ready to joke about its current state.

She didn't know how to approach any of the past two weeks. Would he want to talk about it? Not talk about it? Pretend it never happened?

How was she supposed to love him through this when she wasn't even sure what expression of love he needed right now?

Putting on a soft smile, she picked up the end of her braid and tickled the back of his hand with it. "I had forgotten just how playful you can be when tired. Or, perhaps, that's the morphine talking." She dropped her braid and rested her hand on his cheek instead.

Farrendel's eyes flickered closed, and he leaned his face into her hand. "I survived."

"Yes, you did." A lump formed in her throat. He'd had to fight so hard to get back to her.

"I chose this." Farrendel's voice was soft, so soft she had to lean closer to hear him.

"What do you mean?" Essie traced the line of his jaw, the shape of his ear.

Farrendel's eyes cracked open. "I chose to live. To return to you."

"Thank you for surviving for me." She pressed a kiss to his forehead, her eyes growing wet and a lump forming in the back of her throat. She blinked at the tears, though one dripped down her nose and dropped onto Farrendel's cheek.

His eyebrows scrunched, and he peered up at her. "Are you crying on my face?"

"Maybe." Essie quickly wiped her eyes on her sleeve before she dripped more tears on him. "But they are happy tears." Mostly.

"You do not have to stop. I do not think a few tears will kill me." His eyes fluttered closed again, a small smile tugging the corners of his mouth. His fingers tightened on her hand. "Thank you for coming for me."

"I promised I would." Essie leaned forward and kissed his forehead again.

She wasn't sure if he heard her or not. He seemed to have slipped back into a light doze. That was probably best. He needed sleep.

But after a few minutes, Farrendel roused again. He gripped her fingers with more strength than she would have expected. "Weylind...your brothers...none of them were..."

"They're fine. All of them. No one got hurt this time except you." With their hands clasped on his chest, she could feel the angular ridges of his ribs even through the layers of blankets.

His muscles relaxed, but only for a moment. His gaze snapped back to her. "Melantha?"

What was she supposed to tell him? Last she'd seen, the

elf scout had been toting an unconscious Melantha over his shoulder. Essie hadn't even spared the time to worry about what was wrong with her, much less find out where she had been taken. She probably should have. Melantha was her sister-in-law, after all.

But something must have changed, if Farrendel was so concerned about Melantha. Though, this was Farrendel. He might be concerned even if she was still a traitor.

"She is alive." At least, she was the last time Essie had seen her. If that had changed, she would figure out how to break the news to Farrendel later.

Farrendel sank back onto the pillow, closing his eyes. "She helped me. I would not have survived without her."

"I'm glad she helped you." Essie remembered that time she'd passed out after feeling a wave of pain from him. She'd known he'd nearly died, though she hadn't been sure Melantha had been the one to save him. How much had they bonded during their capture? Essie wasn't sure how she felt about that. All she wanted to do now was protect Farrendel from the sister Melantha had been last time Essie had seen her.

"I was not alone this time. I had Melantha. And I had you," Farrendel murmured. His eyes fell the rest of the way closed, as if he was only partially awake. Perhaps he thought he was talking to her in a dream instead of real life.

Even now, she could feel the pain breaking through the haze of the morphine. All this struggling and moving and talking wasn't doing him any good. He needed rest.

She gripped his hand between hers. "If you want to talk about it, I'm here. But if you aren't ready to talk, that's all right. I'm still here. Either way, you need rest."

The tent flap opened, letting in a blast of cold air.

Edmund stepped inside, carrying a tray laden with food. Jalissa followed, with another tray. Good. They'd brought enough for them and Essie as well.

Until the smell of roast beef and bread filled the air, Essie hadn't realized how hungry she was. Her stomach gave a loud gurgle.

On the cot, Farrendel shifted, his head turning toward her. Essie was going to blame the blast of cold air for rousing him and not her growling stomach.

"Food is here." She touched Farrendel's shoulder. "Are you hungry?"

He shook his head. "No."

"Farrendel?" Jalissa all but dropped her tray on the end table. She fell to her knees next to the cot. She cradled the back of Farrendel's head, then pressed her forehead to his. "Shashon."

It was a more touchy-feely gesture than Essie was used to seeing out of elves. But, perhaps, it was saved for I'm-really-glad-you-survived-torture-and-didn't-die situations. A mere shoulder hug didn't quite do it.

"Jalissa, isciena." Farrendel reached a shaky hand and rested it on Jalissa's shoulder.

Jalissa's shoulders started shaking. She pulled back and swiped at her face. "I…" She trailed off, as if she wasn't sure what to say. It wasn't like she could say he looked well.

Edmund worked his tray onto the small side table until both trays were balanced half-on, half-off the table. "We brought broth for Farrendel. It's in a mug. The surgeon said it would be easier for Farrendel to drink that way."

"Good plan." Essie turned back to Farrendel, reclaiming his hand. "I know you aren't hungry, but could you try to sip a little bit?"

Even though he was an elf and could probably go longer without food and water than a human, he still needed sustenance.

His gaze flicked to her before he nodded. "I will try."

Edmund held out a mug to her, and she dipped the end of her pinkie finger into it to check the temperature. It was warm, but not scalding. Safe for sipping.

Working a hand behind Farrendel's head, she held the mug to his mouth...and promptly splashed far too much broth. Farrendel coughed as broth drooled down his face and onto his neck.

"Sorry. I'm so sorry. I'm apparently not a good nurse." Essie hurriedly set the mug of broth back on the tray, her face heating. Bad enough she got broth all over, but her brother and sister-in-law were also watching.

Farrendel wrinkled his nose and gave her a raised eyebrow look.

Edmund managed to keep a straight face as he handed Essie a cloth. "Remind me never to let you nurse me."

Since she had already thoroughly embarrassed herself, she stuck her tongue out at Edmund as she took the cloth. She washed the broth from Farrendel's face and neck. "I'm so sorry. I'm not good at this."

Farrendel reached a shaking hand toward the mug. "I can feed myself."

There was something about the mix of determination and pleading in his voice. It wasn't that he was offended at her efforts. But it was that he felt like he needed to do it to reclaim a part of himself.

When they'd found him, he'd been pinned to the floor, unable to move more than a finger. He wouldn't have been able to feed himself. Had he suffered a troll forcibly feeding him?

He'd been stripped of all control over even the most basic things. He needed some of that restored to him.

Essie held out the mug, and he gripped it in both hands. With her holding up his head, he lifted the mug to his mouth with his shaking hands and sipped. Essie resisted the urge to take the mug. Farrendel needed to do this himself. But she kept a hand free, in case he looked about ready to drop it.

He managed a few sips, resting the mug on his chest for several minutes between each sip, as if he wanted to pretend he didn't find the mug heavy.

Essie managed to eat her own supper one-handed and kept up a lighthearted conversation with Edmund and Jalissa. When they were finished, Jalissa gathered the trays of food, and she and Edmund headed for the tent flap, Jalissa glancing over her shoulder before leaving as if to reassure herself one last time that Farrendel was really there.

Once it was just her and Farrendel again, Essie turned back to him. He was shivering, his eyes squeezed shut.

Essie gripped his hand. "Do you need more morphine? I can run after Edmund. They can't have gone far, and he can get the surgeon."

"No." Farrendel shook his head, though his jaw remained tight, as if he was clenching his teeth. "Just cold."

The fire in the wood-burning stove was already going merrily, and Essie didn't see any more blankets to pile onto him. As he already had four blankets, he shouldn't be cold.

There was only one thing left to do. She gestured to him. "Scooch over."

His nose wrinkled as he glanced at her. "Scooch?"

"Yes." She lifted a corner of the top blanket. There wasn't

a whole lot of room next to him. Army cots were designed for only one person. But, Farrendel was thinner than the average Escarlish soldier, so that left a little bit of room.

Farrendel squinted at her. "This cot is not intended for two people."

Of course he would manage a full sentence for that. She wasn't going to admit she had just been thinking the same thing.

Wiggling onto the cot next to him was more difficult than she'd expected. She nearly fell off several times, and the cot wobbled. With Farrendel so thin, she probably weighed more than he did right now.

With a little squirming, she managed to tuck herself alongside Farrendel. The wooden side bar of the cot dug into her hip hard enough to leave a bruise, and she wasn't sure what to do with her right arm. She couldn't lie on it because of the wooden bar, and eventually she just tucked it awkwardly against her chest.

Since she didn't want to rest her head on Farrendel's shoulder and possibly cause him pain, she tucked her head next to his. With her left hand, she clasped his, their hands resting on his chest.

She squeezed his hand. "See. I fit."

"Barely." Farrendel shifted. At first Essie thought he was trying to put space between them, but his movement gave her a fraction more room to fit more comfortably against him.

"Are you warm enough now?" Hopefully he was. She was sweating thanks to her coat, the blanket, and the roaring fire in the stove.

"Yes." His voice was quieter, sleepier.

"Good." Essie closed her eyes and snuggled against him.

Except for the boniness of Farrendel's shoulder against her chin, his rank stench after two weeks without a proper wash layered over with the sting of antiseptic, and the cot's bar digging into her, this would almost be comfortable. Perhaps they should have done a lot more snuggling in the past three months when they'd had a chance. Now that she had him back, she was going to make up for that lack.

It would be a few hours until the diplomatic meeting. Surely she would have enough time for a nap.

"I want to go home." Farrendel's murmured words were so quiet she wouldn't have heard them if she hadn't been snuggled up next to him.

She kissed the tip of his ear. "We'll get you home to Estyra just as soon as we can."

Though, how he was going to navigate the branches of Ellonahshinel when he was so weak, she didn't know.

"Estyra. Or Aldon. Both are home."

"Even after what had happened in Aldon?" Essie lifted her head so that she could better see his face. She'd never heard him refer to Aldon as home.

"Yes." He turned his face in her direction, though he didn't open his eyes, as if too tired for that. "It was...nice until then."

She probably shouldn't keep him up with talking. But she couldn't help herself when it came to talking. She snuggled down next to him again. "I'm sure Averett has cleared out all the traitors, and it will be a lot safer the next time we visit. Whenever you're ready. Though, maybe we'll take a few more elven guards next time, and you should wear your swords all the time. No one would blame you. Oh, and we should invite Brina to Aldon. Not right away, of course. But sooner rather than later. She seems really fascinated with human culture. Though, your brother might find that rather appalling."

Farrendel gave a tiny snorting sound. "I missed your chatter."

Essie winced. "Even my nighttime rambling when you are trying to sleep?"

"Yes." His laugh was still in his voice, though it was breathed out on a yawn.

Essie closed her eyes and tried to relax. Light streamed around the tent flap, and her body was telling her that it was still daytime. But she had been up a large chunk of the night. Surely she could use the rest.

She must have dozed at one point. She woke with the brush of cold air on the back of her neck and Averett's voice from behind her. "I see we should have knocked."

Essie tried to roll off the cot, but she had been balanced too precariously. The moment she moved, she wobbled, her feet catching in the blankets, and tumbled to the ground with a shriek. The ground beneath the rug was hard, but Essie landed on her rear end, so the embarrassment hurt more than the landing.

"Told you the cot was too small," Farrendel murmured, though he reached out a hand to her as if to check she was all right.

She patted his arm as she clambered to her feet. "Yes, yes, know-it-all elf. Just admit it. It was worth it."

This time, he didn't even murmur but instead just gave a tiny smile.

Averett was still standing there, smirking. Worse, Weylind was standing beside him, both eyebrows raised as if still hoping someone would provide him with that book on the care of humans one of these days.

Averett crossed his arms as Edmund and Jalissa strode in behind him. "Done being all mushy?"

"For now." Essie stood and stepped aside.

As soon as she was out of the way, Weylind strode across the tent, crashed to his knees next to the cot, gripped the back of Farrendel's head, and pressed his forehead to his. "Shashon."

The depth in that one word. Weylind could be a stubborn pain, but he was a good brother to Farrendel. That wasn't something that could be said for all of Farrendel's siblings.

Averett touched Essie's arm, drawing her a few steps away, and spoke in a lowered tone. "I'm sorry to ask this of you, but the diplomatic meeting is going to start in a few minutes, and I'd like you to come as well. You—and your marriage alliance—are the reason Escarland is even here and invited to be a part of this treaty. I'd rather neither the elves nor the trolls forget that. It would be too easy for them to negotiate between them and leave Escarland out of it."

Essie hesitated, glancing between Averett and Farrendel. More than anything, she didn't want to leave Farrendel's side. If he should take a turn for the worse while she was elsewhere...

But she was still a princess. This was still her duty.

"And I'd like your peace-making skills. We're going to need them." Averett glanced over his shoulder, raising his voice above the whisper he had been using. "Besides, Edmund and Jalissa will stay with Farrendel and fetch us if anything changes."

Edmund nodded. "Of course, we will."

Perhaps it would be better to help with the diplomatic meeting. Farrendel needed his rest, and he was more likely to sleep with Edmund and Jalissa here than with her keeping him awake with her chatter.

Besides, with the heart bond, she would know if he took an unexpected turn for the worse.

When she eased toward the cot, Weylind stood, giving her room. Farrendel had his eyes closed, breathing evenly.

Essie stroked the ragged ends of Farrendel's hair and kissed his cheek. "Rest, my love."

He stirred, but he did not wake.

No matter. While he slept, she would help negotiate the peace treaty to end this war once and for all. Farrendel would never have to fight another battle. He would finally have the peace he deserved.

That thought gave her the courage to turn, take Averett's arm, and leave the tent.

TWENTY-EIGHT

hen Essie crawled through the door into the shelter following Averett, she found that someone had found—or made—a low, round table. Folded bedrolls formed cushions for sitting while paper and pens now lay on the table for drafting a treaty.

Someone had even managed to track down the elven diplomat Sindrel and the Escarlish diplomat Master Wendee. Both of the diplomats had helped negotiate the first treaty between Tarenhiel and Escarland. They sat across the table from the entrance with Sindrel next to Weylind and Master Wendee next to Prince Rharreth, providing a buffer between the elves and the troll prince.

That was exactly what Escarland's role would be in this negotiation.

Prince Rharreth and Weylind sat across from each other in a silence that managed to be both frosty and awkward. Both Escarlish and elven guards lined the walls of the shelter, all wearing the dour, impassive expression of guards pretending not to listen while remaining alert. Compared to this, that first diplomatic meeting between Weylind and Averett had been a friendly affair.

Apparently, the friendliness would be up to her, even if she didn't feel all that perky at the moment.

Essie pasted on a smile and plopped down into one of the two remaining cushion seats around the table. She picked the one next to Weylind, leaving the final spot between her and Prince Rharreth for Averett. "I'm glad everyone was available for this meeting. It is a pleasure to sit down at this table with all of you."

Weylind and Prince Rharreth continued to glare at each other without a flicker to show they'd heard her. Prince Rharreth had one of his arms tucked close to his side, a burned hole in his jerkin above what looked like an injured shoulder. But he didn't ask for aid or otherwise acknowledge that he was wounded.

Essie resisted the urge to roll her eyes. This was worse than trying to wrangle Weylind and Averett before they had managed to bond. Bonding probably wasn't going to happen any time soon between Weylind and Prince Rharreth, but it would be nice if they didn't try to stab each other with their glares.

Averett cleared his throat. "I believe we can start with the framework we used for the peace treaty between Tarenhiel and Escarland and make modifications from there."

"A lot of modifications." Weylind shifted to clench his fists while keeping his arms crossed. "I do not wish to encourage such open trade between Tarenhiel and Kostaria. A ceasing of hostilities is all we require."

"But not all that my kingdom requires." Prince Rharreth's shoulders remained stiff, but he kept his arms loosely resting on the table, both hands in view as if to prove he was not reaching for a weapon or preparing to use his magic. "There was a time when my people and yours were kin. The forest elves aided the mountain elves with their growing magic while we provided stonework and ice. But those days—and the time when we called ourselves elves— are long past."

"Long, long past," Weylind muttered, though his words were loud enough he clearly wanted Prince Rharreth to hear.

Prince Rharreth's expression and tone didn't waver. "In the centuries since the first rift between our peoples, we have done our best to survive in our mountains. But our ground is rocky and hard, and our growing season is short. My grandfather, father, and brother all believed the solution was to annex Tarenhiel and from there have access to Escarland's fertile fields."

So the trolls had intended to attack Escarland all along. Essie highly doubted either of the past two troll kings would have been content to sit idly at the border begging for whatever her father and brother would give them in trade.

Weylind's glare competed with Prince Rharreth's magic for iciness. "We are well aware of your family's aggression."

Essie's smile felt tight on her face. These two needed to talk this out. Perhaps if they shouted at each other and vented all their anger, then they could come to this table with reasonable solutions.

The muscle at the corner of Prince Rharreth's jaw tightened. "While I believe in honor and the defense of the homeland, I don't believe this constant warfare was the way to help my people. In the end, all the ice and snow we used in fighting your people further hampered our growing season to the point that we couldn't grow any crops this year. Very little last year. The game animals are scarce. Frankly, my people are starving. I will agree to much in order to save them from starvation. All I ask for are two things."

Weylind made a soft sound that was the elven version of a snort. "You surrendered. You do not make demands. We do."

Essie would have given in to a snort of her own but, since Weylind was failing to be his usual regal self, it was up to her and Averett to bring dignity and reason to these peace talks. If Weylind would stop acting like an angsty teenage elf, maybe they would get somewhere.

Averett held up a placating hand toward Weylind, then turned to Prince Rharreth. "I would like to hear these demands. I am willing to accommodate reasonable requests."

Prince Rharreth faced Averett, something in his stance relaxing. Though, he still kept his injured arm stiff at his side. "First, I would like to establish trade with Escarland for some of your grains and produce. Tarenhiel is welcome to inspect the shipments as they pass through their kingdom to ensure it is nothing besides food."

Weylind scowled. Essie shot him her best warning look. It wasn't like Weylind genuinely wanted to let the trolls starve. He was just being stubborn enough to argue with everything Prince Rharreth said.

Averett gave a small nod. "What would Tarenhiel and Escarland get out of this arrangement?"

"I believe our magically enhanced ice will last longer in your ice boxes than regular ice. And our stonework would be an asset to the homes of your nobility." Prince Rharreth answered so readily it was clear he'd already thought of this answer long before Averett had asked the question. How long had he been planning peace talks like this? Had he been hoping all along for a chance to negotiate a treaty with Escarland? "As for Tarenhiel, I know you have no need of ice. Nor would you wish for our stonework, though you would have access to it if you found a need. But there would be transportation fees for the trade across your kingdom."

"I have no wish to turn Tarenhiel into a commercial transportation hub. It is not in our way of life." Weylind's crossed arms tightened.

"We could bypass Tarenhiel and establish trade with Escarland through other kingdoms. But that would also mean you would not be able to inspect the goods to know that no more weapons are being traded." Prince Rharreth's gaze remained unwavering. "I am giving you the concession of controlling whatever trade goes in and out of Kostaria. I am putting my kingdom's livelihood in your hands."

"That seems like a fair compromise." Averett added, as if to cut off any objection Weylind might make, "I'm sure we can develop a way to conduct trade across Tarenhiel that would cause the least disruption possible."

"You do not have to be this accommodating." Weylind didn't slouch in his seat—an elven king would never be that undignified—but something about the set to his shoulders said he wanted to slump and glower.

"Yes, I do. Because if we can find Kostaria's version of shampoo, then all three of our kingdoms will be better off in the future." Averett gestured around the table.

Across the table, both Sindrel and Master Wendee had their heads down, scribbling furiously. Master Wendee glanced at Averett, but Sindrel kept his eyes focused on the page as if to pretend he wasn't ignoring Weylind.

Essie would've hugged Averett, if they hadn't been in the middle of a diplomatic meeting. He was doing so well at this meeting. They might actually get out of this without another war starting. With how smoothly this was going, she would be able to get out of here and return to Farrendel soon.

Averett faced Prince Rharreth again. "I have a request of my own, however. All Escarlish weapons which were illegally obtained from the traitors in my kingdom will be turned over to my army immediately. While I am willing to open trade with your kingdom, I am not willing to provide your kingdom with weapons at this time."

Prince Rharreth dipped his head in a nod. "That is reasonable. I believe your army has managed to either reclaim or destroy most of the weapons during your march across my kingdom, and most of the remaining weapons have been buried and destroyed in the collapse of Gror Grar. But I will see to the return of any weapons that still remain in my army's hands as a sign of good faith."

Weylind softly snorted, his arms crossed, but he didn't interrupt to object.

"Thank you." Averett gave a polite smile. He, too, seemed to think this negotiation was going well. "And what was your second request?"

For the first time, Prince Rharreth hesitated, his gaze dipping to the table. "I have seen the results of the marriage alliance between Tarenhiel and Escarland. For that reason, I would like a marriage alliance between Tarenhiel and Kostaria."

Essie breathed her own spit into her lungs and held her breath, trying not to cough. That was...unexpected.

Weylind made a choking sound, bracing himself against the table. "I beg your pardon. There is no way I am marrying one of my sisters to a troll. It was bad enough marrying my brother to a human."

Essie swatted Weylind's arm and raised her eyebrows at him. "Excuse me?"

Weylind huffed, some of his anger disappearing when he glanced at her. "That marriage alliance worked out far better than expected, and I am thankful my brother is happy." His jaw tightened and he gestured at Prince Rharreth. "But this...this is unacceptable."

Prince Rharreth's face remained impassive. "I would suggest a marriage alliance between Escarland and Kostaria instead, but they have no more princesses and I have no sisters. Besides, Escarland will be content with trade, and it is the enmity between Tarenhiel and Kostaria that will cause continued tensions without a marriage alliance to keep the peace."

"That is a good point." Averett dragged the words out.

"No." Weylind shook his head so hard his hair slapped Essie's face. "Absolutely not."

"Your sister Melantha is a traitor to Tarenhiel." Prince Rharreth's tone remained flat. "I am assuming you will not order her execution. That means your only option is to banish her. Unless you intend to pardon her, but that would be a gross injustice caused by preferential treatment for your sibling."

Was that noise Weylind's teeth grinding? Or maybe his knuckles cracking? Essie kept her smile plastered in place. Prince Rharreth had been doing a good job of keeping it professional up to this point, but he apparently couldn't resist that dig.

Averett leaned over and whispered in Essie's ear, "It's rather satisfying to watch Weylind squirm when it's *his* sister."

Essie nudged Averett with her elbow. He needed to remember to be regal.

"Even if you banish her, where would she go? Escarland won't take her, and she will be in danger wandering by herself through other kingdoms." Prince Rharreth waved to Averett, though he went on before Averett could say anything. "But, in a marriage alliance with me, I would ensure her safety here in Kostaria. She could restore her honor by sacrificing for her kingdom. You could decree marriage to me to be her punishment. It would allow her to return and visit Tarenhiel, something she could not do if she were banished. Besides, I am no longer a second son. I am offering to put your sister—an elf—on the throne of Kostaria."

Weylind opened his mouth. Closed it. Glared, though Essie wasn't sure if his anger was because he didn't want to marry Melantha to a troll or because that troll happened to be right.

Essie rested a hand on Weylind's arm. "Ask Melantha. See what she says. She might surprise you."

Weylind pointed at Prince Rharreth. "I am *not* marrying my sister to a troll who tortured Farrendel."

A valid point. Essie had been trying not to think about how Prince Rharreth had been the one to capture Farrendel in the first place. But, she forced herself to remain calm and think rationally. "I...don't think Prince Rharreth tortured Farrendel. He's still alive, after all."

Weylind's brow scrunched and, for the first time, he studied Prince Rharreth as if really seeing him.

Prince Rharreth rested a hand on his injured shoulder. "I didn't torture him, but I did stand by and let it happen, which is hardly better. But it seems your brother has far more honor than I have given him credit for these past fifteen years. He gave me only what I gave him."

For the first time, Essie noticed the burned ends of Prince Rharreth's sleeves and the reddened skin around his wrists. Burned skin that matched the marks around Farrendel's wrists.

But Farrendel hadn't killed Prince Rharreth. Considering how far gone Farrendel had been, Essie was surprised to find some part of him had still been thinking. Perhaps not rationally. But thinking, at least.

Weylind closed his eyes, his spine sagging. "I will consider the marriage alliance. That is the only promise I am willing to make now. I will, however, speak with Melantha to ensure she is willing." He opened his eyes, his gaze sharpening. "And I will speak with Farrendel and gain his perspective on you and the marriage alliance."

Prince Rharreth nodded, probably realizing that was the best concession he was likely to get. "Very well. As long as the possibility of a marriage alliance is written into the treaty, I am willing to leave the final choice in Princess Melantha's hands."

Essie wasn't sure how she felt about the marriage alliance. A part of her thought that if Melantha had been willing to betray her kingdom and her own brother for the trolls, then the trolls were welcome to her, and good riddance. It would serve her right to be used as a bargaining chip in a marriage alliance.

And yet, Essie knew just how hard a marriage alliance could be, and hers had been an exceptionally fortunate one. Not every marriage alliance turned out as well as hers and Farrendel's.

Most of that was due to the fact that both she and

Farrendel were the kind of people willing to put in the effort and sacrifice needed to make a marriage like theirs work.

But was Melantha that kind of person? Essie seriously doubted it. Granted, she didn't know Melantha that well. Melantha had done her best to avoid Essie, and Essie's strongest memory of her was of Melantha's sneering expression as she disavowed Farrendel.

If Melantha hadn't managed to figure out how to love her own brother in the past hundred years, how was she possibly going to find even a shred of happiness in an arranged marriage?

Did Essie even care if Melantha found happiness? She should hope that Melantha had changed through this experience, as Farrendel had seemed to believe. After seeing the state Melantha had been in, Essie should be forgiving enough to think that Melantha had suffered enough already.

Essie had some sympathy for Melantha. There was far more hatred between the trolls and elves than had ever existed between the elves and humans. A marriage alliance would not be easy.

But Essie struggled to fully pity her. Not after what she had done to Farrendel. Melantha had deeply hurt someone Essie loved. That was hard to forgive.

Not to mention, it would make this troll prince her brother-in-law. Talk about awkward family reunions.

From there, the meeting worked its way into the nitty-gritty of the treaty. Weylind worked in a clause that had Averett agreeing to station Escarlish troops along the border for the next year while Averett, in return, gained additional trade and the agreement that a few elven warriors would be sent to train with the Escarlish army to better integrate the use of magic and weaponry.

Finally, Master Wendee, Sindrel, and their assistants put the treaty together into an official format and made copies. All of the monarchs read the treaty over, making sure all the wording was satisfactory.

Essie tried not to squirm. All she wanted to do was return to Farrendel, but this moment was important. If he couldn't witness the ending of the war he'd fought for so long, then she would do it for him.

At last, Master Wendee and Sindrel laid out three copies of the treaty on the table.

Averett pulled out a pen, the carved wooden one that Essie had gifted him. "Unless any of you have magnificent speeches about peace between our kingdoms that you intended to give at this moment, let's sign this treaty."

Essie stifled a snort. Avie didn't want to keep any of them any longer than he had to after they had spent hours discussing this treaty, and he was basically daring any of the other kings to drag this out.

When neither Prince Rharreth nor Weylind said anything, Averett smiled. "Very well. Here's to a new era of peace and prosperity between our kingdoms." With a flourish, Averett signed each of the three copies, then handed the pen to Weylind.

Weylind straightened his shoulders and faced Prince Rharreth. "I have hope that this war is finished." He signed all three treaties and held out the pen to Prince Rharreth.

Prince Rharreth took the pen. He studied it a moment, as if unsure it would be fitting to sign a treaty with an elven-made pen. But, he swiveled the three copies and signed them.

Essie resisted the urge to sag in her seat. The treaty was

signed. The war was officially over. Farrendel could finally know peace.

Would this peace last? Or was this just a temporary lull before the fighting broke out again?

And, would Melantha agree to the marriage alliance proposed in this treaty? Would Prince Rharreth hold to the terms of peace if she didn't?

CHAPTER
TWENTY-NINE

F arrendel woke to a deep, dull pain. At least it was no longer sharp. And the bedding beneath him was softer than stone, though it still pressed onto the bruises on his shoulder blades and back.

He tried to shift, but that sent a deeper wave of pain through his chest.

"Rest easy." Weylind's voice came from beside him.

Farrendel drew on what little strength he had to peel his eyes open, resulting in a blur of orange lamplight and shadows. He had to blink several times to bring the tent into focus.

Weylind sat in the chair next to him with a human lantern on the table, filling the tent with a golden glow. He set aside a sheaf of papers. "How are you feeling?"

"I am fine." Farrendel drew in a deep breath, and it stabbed through his chest. He was not fine. He could still sense troll magic and stone inside him, fighting against the elf magic attempting to heal him. The numbness of the human medicine had worn off, leaving him torn and seared. "Where is Essie?"

Weylind pointed and leaned to the side, giving Farrendel a view of the space by the stove. Essie lay on a bedroll on the floor, sleeping deeply enough that she was making light snoring sounds that she insisted were just heavy breathing.

"She never faltered. She was a tap root for us. I do not know what we would have done without her." Weylind's voice was low, even as he swung his gaze from Essie back to Farrendel. Something like a smile twitched the corner of Weylind's mouth. "You may say that you told me so. Your Elspetha already did."

"Of course she did." The red of her hair blurred as Farrendel tried to keep his eyes focused, but it was hard with the headache building at his temples. He shifted again, and another stab of pain shot through his chest. His hands shook at his sides. "What time is it?"

"It is the middle of the night." Weylind's gaze studied him. "I believe I should fetch the healer. You look like you are in pain."

"I am fine." Farrendel had to speak between gritted teeth. The pain surged deeper.

"You are certainly not fine." Weylind pushed to his feet. "I will return momentarily." He strode from the tent.

For a moment, Farrendel lay still, concentrated on breathing, and listened to the sound of Essie's snoring competing with the crackle of the fire in the stove. He was not sure how he had managed to miss such an annoying sound, but it now reminded him of home. Of waking up to her still snoring loudly in her mound of blankets in their room in Ellonahshinel. Or of the blue room in Buckmore Cottage with her giving him a sleepy look as he swung back through the window.

Home. In his own bed. Pain free. And clean. How he wanted to be clean.

After a few more minutes, Weylind returned, followed by the same elf healer and human surgeon who had tended Farrendel before. Not that Farrendel remembered much of that except pain, then numbness, and Essie.

Dark circles splotched underneath the surgeon's eyes, and lines furrowed the elf healer's forehead. Had they slept at all since tending Farrendel? Or had they been healing the wounded all this time?

The healer stepped forward and rested a hand on Farrendel's shoulder.

Farrendel sucked in a breath as the warm healing magic clashed against the cold inside him, resulting in a burning pain.

The healer grimaced and drew his hand away. "Too much troll magic inside him yet."

"Understood." The surgeon rested a leather bag on the table, pulled out a needle and a vial.

Farrendel swung his gaze to the ceiling. He remembered enough of receiving a shot of that morphine before. The numbness had been welcome, but knowing someone was inserting something beneath his skin yet again was not.

The surgeon tapped his now filled needle with a finger. "Nylian, his arm?"

The healer peeled back the blankets from Farrendel's arm, turned it so that the inside of his elbow faced up, and swabbed it with a dab of some cold liquid.

Farrendel braced himself. Weylind's hand rested on his

shoulder, pinning him down. Something pricked the inside of his elbow, then a cold sensation pushed into him.

Weylind sank onto the chair once again, his hand leaving Farrendel's shoulder. "Thank you for coming, Nylian, Maxwell, and delaying your rest."

The surgeon nodded. "We were needed."

The elf healer gave a nod as well, and both of them left the tent.

The numbness spread up Farrendel's arm to his shoulder, easing the pain as it went. He sank deeper into the blankets. "Thank you, shashon. This is better."

"I know you need sleep, but there is something I wished to discuss." Weylind rested his elbows on his knees, staring at his hands.

By that posture, it must be serious. Farrendel blinked and forced himself to focus on Weylind. "I will stay awake."

"It is Melantha." Weylind rubbed at a palm with his thumb. "Prince Rharreth has asked for a marriage alliance as part of the treaty, and he requested to marry Melantha."

Another marriage alliance. His people had gone from never agreeing to such things to being bombarded with them from every side.

Not that Farrendel would ever regret marrying Essie. Marrying her was the best thing to happen to him, even if he had not known it at the time.

But Melantha…and Prince Rharreth? Farrendel could not picture it.

"Before I agree, I need to know what part Prince Rharreth played in your torture. He claims he did not actively torture you the way his brother did. I am not sure I believe him." Weylind's shoulders hunched, his head hanging as if from the weight of this decision.

"He..." Farrendel was not sure what he thought of Prince Rharreth. Yes, he let Melantha make Farrendel more comfortable. But he had still allowed the torture to continue. "He is utterly loyal to Kostaria. But he is more honorable than his brother."

"That is not high praise." Weylind grimaced and shook his head. "A rock would be more honorable than King Charvod was."

"I do not think he will hurt Melantha." Farrendel did not wish to remember anything of those days of agony, especially the last three days where the torture had been unrelenting without food, water, or a shred of mercy.

But Prince Rharreth had tried to convince his brother to punish him instead of Melantha. Hopefully, that meant he had enough honor that he would not harm her. At least, not physically.

Still, Farrendel was not sure it would be a marriage he would wish for his sister, even Melantha.

"That is a comfort." Weylind's words came out on a heavy sigh. His head hung, as if the weight on his shoulders remained heavy. "I also need to know what you wish for justice. You were the one she hurt the most when she betrayed Tarenhiel. If you do not believe marriage to the soon-to-be troll king is sufficient punishment, I will consider other options."

Did Weylind think Farrendel wanted Melantha harmed? After everything, she was still his sister.

How did he feel about Melantha? She had betrayed him. But then, she had helped him. Now, there was just a tangled ache where once they had been siblings.

After this moment, would Farrendel's family be whole ever again? Or would they always be scattered across the kingdoms, split by pain?

No, Farrendel had no wish for this pain to linger. Whatever he had to do, he would do it, if it meant that the ache that began over a hundred years ago when the elf queen was killed did not continue to tear his family apart.

It was becoming harder to keep his eyes open. "No, I do not wish her punished. All I want for her is mercy."

Weylind's hand rested on Farrendel's shoulder for a moment. "I should have expected nothing less from you. You love too easily, but it is your strength."

Farrendel was not sure what Weylind meant by that. How was loving too easily a strength instead of a weakness as he had believed? But he was too tired to puzzle it out.

Weylind picked up the stack of papers he had been studying. "I have the treaty here, if you should wish to read it."

Farrendel lifted his hand, noticed how much his fingers were trembling, and dropped his arm back to the blankets. With the way his eyes were swimming in and out of focus, he would not be able to read it anyway. "I will read it later."

Weylind set it aside, and Farrendel let his eyes finally fall closed. A part of him could not take it in. This war had started before he had been born. And he had been fighting it from the moment he was old enough. Before he was old enough, to be honest. After over a hundred years, would it end with a few pieces of paper and three signatures?

Could this really be the end? It seemed far too good to be true.

Farrendel was hollowed out, empty. The thought of having to fight yet another war threatened to break another piece inside him. Yet, he did not dare reach for Essie's optimism either.

A cold breeze brushed his face. Footsteps scuffed across the tent. "How is he?"

Averett's voice. Farrendel managed to turn his head, but he could not force his eyes to open. The numbing sensation of the human medicine was lulling him back into sleep.

Weylind's hand on Farrendel's shoulder was replaced with Averett's heavier one. Averett squeezed his shoulder, then the chair creaked as Averett claimed the seat.

Farrendel normally would not like being so crowded while he slept. But, right then, knowing that his brothers—all of his brothers—were watching over him, made him feel safe. After two weeks in that dungeon, it was a feeling he had not been sure he would have again.

CHAPTER THIRTY

Melantha woke inside an empty shelter grown of branches and roots, its inside lit only by a single magical light near the ceiling. Her feet no longer ached. Her healing must have finished while she had been asleep.

How long had she been unconscious? Last thing she remembered doing was pouring all of her magic that she could grasp into Farrendel. She had exhausted herself. Between that and her body's weakness, she had passed out.

Melantha pushed to her feet. Yet, the moment she moved, something tugged against her ankle.

She lifted the ragged ends of her dress and peered at her feet.

A root snaked from the floor and wrapped around her ankle.

She was still a prisoner, this time of her own people. Melantha sank to the floor, hugging her knees to her chest. After all the time captured by the trolls, hanging her hopes for rescue, she had forgotten that she was still a traitor in

Tarenhiel. The rescue had never been for her. Only for Farrendel.

She had not even gained the redemption she had sought. She had broken her own feet, yet, in the end, that annoying human princess had been the one to rescue him.

Melantha groaned and rested her forehead on her knees. Her dislike of Princess Elspeth no longer had anything to do with her being a human. Well, not only that. It was mostly because she was too perky, too perfect, too sugary sweet. It was enough to make an elf's teeth rot out just from spending too much time with her.

In short, Princess Elspeth was everything Melantha had never managed to be. Content, even in difficult circumstances. Compassionate and kind to everyone she met. Happy, instead of simmering with anger. It was infuriating.

Footsteps crunched, and her brother's voice sounded outside. Several other voices answered him.

Guards. Her own brother was keeping her under guard.

Then again, she deserved it. She had been a traitor to her kingdom and betrayed her own brother to torture and death.

Was Farrendel all right? What if Melantha's magic had not been enough to save him?

If Farrendel had died...would Weylind consider execution a fitting punishment, even for his own sister?

The canvas was pushed aside, and Weylind ducked through the opening, giving her a brief glimpse of the deep darkness of night. Was it the middle of the night? After being down in the dungeon for so long without the sun, her hours were mixed up.

He straightened, letting the canvas fall into place behind him, before he looked at her. His brown eyes were as cold as the ice of this kingdom.

Almost, Melantha wanted to be back in that dungeon. There, she could pretend that her family would still love her once they were rescued and things were as simple as surviving.

She forced herself not to quail beneath Weylind's gaze. "How is Farrendel? Is he all right?"

Weylind's jaw tightened, and for a long moment, it seemed he would not answer.

Melantha's stomach clenched. No. Surely Farrendel had not died. He was too strong for that, and he had wanted to return to his human princess far too much to die when rescue was so close.

"He is resting." Weylind's jaw worked, as if that much was more than he had wanted to tell her. As if he did not believe she deserved to know.

Melantha let out a long breath. This had been her goal. Return Farrendel to their family.

Yet, why did it all feel so hollow?

"How could you do this, Melantha? Betray Tarenhiel. Betray Farrendel." Weylind paced, his hands clasped behind his back, his face drawn.

"It was wrong. I am sorry." She did not have any defense for her actions. It was not as if she had not meant for this to happen. She had. She merely had not meant to get caught in it herself or have to witness Farrendel's torture. "But I helped him. Has he told you that? I kept him alive. Convinced Prince Rharreth to let him have a blanket. Healed him enough that he could use his magic. I broke my own feet to escape my cell and fought six trolls to stop them from killing him."

Weylind whirled on her, eyes still hard. "And did you do that for his sake? Or for yours?"

"What?" Melantha reeled back, gaping at her brother. "I..."

Had she truly done all of that for Farrendel? Or had she done it because of what she could get out of it? Earning redemption and forgiveness. Proving that she had changed.

But if those were her motives, had she changed? Or was she still manipulating Farrendel to try to get what she wanted?

Perhaps she was still selfish enough to try to earn redemption by helping him. But that had not been her only reason. She had genuinely wanted to make sure Farrendel lived. Maybe she was not as saccharinely good as Princess Elspeth who did things purely unselfishly, but she had managed to be a mix of selfish and unselfish. It was good enough, right? As much as could be expected?

But Weylind's gaze had gone from hard to such a depth of pained disappointment, Melantha had to look away. She and Weylind had always been close. They had done everything together when they were growing up. Then they had weathered all of their family's storms as adults.

But all that lay shattered between them, thanks to what she had done.

"I helped him for his sake and for mine." She stared at her hands in her lap. "Please, Weylind, can I see him?"

She needed to see for herself that he was all right. None of the healers knew how to work alongside troll magic the way she did after all the practice she had. She could still help him.

More than that, she needed to know how she stood with Farrendel. They had forged something of a new bond in that dungeon cell, but would it last now that they were rescued? He had needed her because she was the only one there. But now that he had the entire family caring for him, would he still be as forgiving toward her?

Weylind faced her, back rigid. "No, you are not allowed anywhere near him. I will protect Farrendel from you. If he ever wants to see you again, it will be up to him, not you."

She flinched, hunching under the pain. After her betrayal, what else had she expected? Even if Farrendel forgave her, that did not mean he had to restore the brother-sister relationship. She had given up all rights to that relationship the moment she had tried to use the trolls to murder him.

"I understand." Melantha swallowed and stared at the floor by Weylind's feet. If Weylind was this angry, what was he planning to do to her? She was a traitor. By elven law, he could order her execution in the forsaken wood.

Surely Weylind would not order that for her.

Yet, his only other option for punishment would be banishment. Where would she go? Escarland would not take her. The other human kingdoms were not accepting of elves. Perhaps there was another elven kingdom at the far distant end of the continent that would take her?

Perhaps Weylind would pardon her. Maybe give her a lesser punishment? Did she dare hope for such a thing?

She hugged her knees tighter to her chest. "What happens to me now?"

Weylind heaved a long sigh. "I do not know. You are a traitor to Tarenhiel and plotted the murder of a member of the royal family. Even a supposed change of heart cannot change the fact that, in the eyes of the law, you must be punished. I cannot turn a blind eye to your crimes nor can I sweep such egregious acts away with a pardon."

Something in her chest crumpled. No pardon. That

meant, this ordeal was far from over. If anything, it was just beginning.

"But...you are still my sister." Weylind's face twisted, his dark eyes filled with pain. "I will not have you executed. I could not bear it, nor would Farrendel wish it."

Of course, he would not. He was far too good for that. He and his human princess were alike, in that way. Melantha stared at Weylind's boots. "I will be banished, then."

Banished. Never to see her family again. Pain seared Melantha's chest, her breath seizing with an intense longing for the deep forest of Tarenhiel, her room in Ellonahshinel, her family sitting around the dining table. All the simple, wonderful beauty of home.

A home that was no longer hers. That would never be hers again.

In trying to return her life to what it had been before her mother died, she had lost the life she currently had. She should have been more thankful for the things and people she had. Instead, she had lost everything.

"You have a choice. Banishment or..." Weylind halted his pacing to face her. "Prince Rharreth of the trolls has asked for a marriage alliance as part of the new peace treaty."

And, obviously, Weylind was not going to marry Jalissa to the troll prince. No, if anyone was sacrificed to a marriage alliance with the trolls, it would be the sister who had made herself an expendable outcast.

"A marriage alliance would make our treaty with the trolls stronger. I am not sure the treaty will hold for long without something more binding than a piece of paper behind it." Weylind's voice took on its official, emotionless tone. "There would be benefits to you, as well. You would be a queen. I would declare that your marriage to Prince

Rharreth was your punishment. It would be essentially banishment and would satisfy those who would argue I am granting you preferential treatment. Yet, you would not technically be banished. You could still visit Tarenhiel on a limited basis in an official capacity."

But not as family. Perhaps only when Farrendel was elsewhere, visiting his new Escarlish family.

Or, worse, when he was present and everyone could coldly shun her as punishment for what she had done.

Would she deserve anything else? After all, cold shunning was exactly what she had been doing to that human princess.

"But I understand if banishment would still be preferable. I have talked with Farrendel about Prince Rharreth, but Farrendel was too tired to say much besides that he believes the troll prince is honorable." Weylind's back and tone had gone stiff once again.

"He was..." How to describe Prince Rharreth's actions? "He started out cold, but not cruel. He merely followed orders. But he eventually softened, allowing me to help Farrendel. He was even punished for it, once King Charvod discovered what he had done."

And Prince Rharreth had pushed her to be a better, more honorable person. His coldness toward her at the start had been fueled by his own disgust at her betrayal of her kingdom and her own brother.

In her torn dress, the marks on her back were probably visible. Of all the ironies. She had once scorned Farrendel for being scarred and imperfect. And yet, now she was also scarred, and would be for the rest of her life.

"I see." Weylind's shoulders relaxed, as if he had been worried about marrying her to a cruel troll. Or, maybe he was more worried about making a peace treaty with a cruel troll than about her.

Prince Rharreth was not cruel. Not the way his brother had been.

But did she wish to marry him?

No, not really. She did not want to marry any troll. Nor did she want to stay here in this dark, ice and stone kingdom for the rest of her life. Her breathing quickened, the cold and darkness already pressing against her. She would suffocate here. Slowly wither and die like a plant robbed of the sun.

But she would help her kingdom. By helping Farrendel, she had done her best to redeem herself for betraying him. Maybe with this, she could redeem the wrong she had done in betraying her kingdom by instead sacrificing herself for it.

There were those among the elven court who would believe that she had continued to choose the trolls over her own people.

But her family would know the truth, would they not?

Besides, she would never marry an elf now, not after what she had done, much less marry an elf she could love. Why should she not marry a troll? One loveless marriage was just as good or just as bad as another. She might as well save her kingdom while she was at it.

It was either marriage or banishment. And, if she was going to be banished to a foreign kingdom, she might as well be its queen rather than a penniless, homeless, friendless foreigner.

Melantha straightened her back. "Very well. I agree to the marriage alliance."

Weylind's eyebrows shot up. "You can take some time to think about it."

"It is what is best for Tarenhiel." Melantha raised her

chin. "If you were willing to sacrifice Farrendel for peace with Escarland, then why not sacrifice me for peace with Kostaria?"

"You are still my sister, Melantha. I have no wish to see you hurt, even after everything you have done." Weylind scrubbed a hand over his face.

She had put him in a hard position. Having to choose between justice for one sibling and mercy for another. Between what was best for his sister and best for his kingdom.

"I know. And, I am sorry." There was not much else she could say, even if those three words seemed so small compared to the magnitude of what she had done.

Weylind nodded and turned toward the door. "I will ask one of the guards to send in a tray and will convey your acceptance of the marriage alliance to Prince Rharreth."

Without a backward glance in her direction, he left.

Melantha held herself cold and regal until after an elf warrior delivered a tray of food. He stuck the plate inside without looking at her.

Then, and only then, did she allow herself to break. She curled into a ball on the blanket left for her, pressed her face into the crook of her arms to muffle the sound, and sobbed.

After all she had endured, she remained a prisoner. There was no more hope. She was never going home again.

THIRTY-ONE

F arrendel lay on the operating table in the hospital tent once again, the wood warming against his back and a leather pillow providing scant padding for his head. He stared at the canvas ceiling, fighting the urge to sit up and lash out.

This was not torture. He was not pinned down. He was not helpless.

Yet, something about being laid out on the table made his skin crawl.

Focus on something else. Anything else.

He was finally clean, mostly. He had been strong enough to sponge himself off with a cloth and hot water earlier and wash his hair, not that it was too difficult with it cut so short. He had even managed to pull on clean trousers, though he had nearly passed out doing so.

Those trousers were now rolled to his knees, waiting for the healers to remove the last of the stone lacing his ankles and legs. He was still missing a shirt, also waiting for this surgery to be over.

Essie's hand smoothed his hair, drawing his gaze to her as she stood by the table near his head. She gave him a smile. "It will be over soon. Then you won't be in any more pain."

Farrendel nodded and forced himself to draw in a deep breath. Pain lanced through his chest from each place where stone still lay buried inside his body. His wrists throbbed. Agony stabbed through his ankles. The stone wrapped around his collarbone pounded pain into his temples.

A human surgeon, the elf healer, and various nurses bustled around, laying out supplies. Both Weylind and Averett stood off to the side, eyeing Prince Rharreth in the other far corner.

Farrendel's breathing hitched, and he clenched his fists. It took all of his willpower to lie there, knowing Prince Rharreth was about to use his magic on him again. Supposedly to remove the rest of the stone, but would the troll prince do so? He had helped before, but what if he did not this time?

If Farrendel reached through the heart bond, he could feel a faint crackle of his magic, even with the stone still inside him. If Prince Rharreth tried anything, Farrendel would be ready.

The human surgeon cleared his throat. "I did not suggest it last time because he was too weak, but we can use ether to numb his senses this time."

Farrendel shook his head, his nose and throat burning with the memory of the human ether the trolls had used to keep him senseless on the trip to Gror Grar. "No."

The elf healer shook his head as well. "With the troll using his magic, Laesornysh needs to be conscious to keep his magic in control. It would be dangerous if he lashed out while unconscious."

"I have an ether that won't make him unconscious. It will just dull his senses and the pain." The surgeon gestured to a nurse, and she presented him with a glass bottle.

"No." Farrendel put as much strength into that word as he could. No more human chemicals. He would rather feel the pain.

Essie's fingers trailed from his hair to his shoulder as she sighed. "You heard him. Sorry, no ether."

The elf healer's jaw tightened, dark circles still smudged beneath his eyes. "My magic should be enough to dull his pain."

That did not give Farrendel confidence. The elf healer looked like he could still use more rest after all the expenditure of magic he must have done after the battle. Would he have enough magic for this surgery?

As much as Farrendel hated lying there, he had no wish to put this off any longer. It had been three days since his rescue, and he would not regain any more strength until the stone was removed.

"All right." The human surgeon picked up a scalpel and turned to Prince Rharreth. "Ready?"

Essie's hand moved to Farrendel's forehead, her touch soft and warm. Still, Farrendel knew that she would hold him down if he tried to lift his head. She turned her shoulders to put her back to the troll prince, elf healer, and surgeon. "Focus on me, Farrendel."

He met her gaze and tried not to tense as soothing elf magic flooded into him. He felt the pressure of the scalpel against his collarbone, even if he did not feel the pain.

Icy magic surrounded Prince Rharreth's fingers a moment before pain surged through Farrendel's bones.

The elf healer cried out and stumbled back. Prince

Rharreth cut off his magic, but not before the full force of it dug into Farrendel's collarbone. Farrendel could not help a moan.

Weylind was at Farrendel's side in an instant, glaring at Prince Rharreth.

The elf healer hunched over his hand. "I am sorry, Daresheni. After all the healing I have done, I am not strong enough. I doubt any of us are. We cannot rest properly with all this stone around us."

In other words, Farrendel would either have to bear the brunt of the troll magic or he would have to wait longer for the rest of the stone to be removed.

Unless...He gripped Weylind's arm and waited until Weylind met his gaze. He kept his voice and gaze firm. "Fetch Melantha."

"No. I will not allow her anywhere near you." Weylind's jaw hardened, his eyes flinty.

How had Essie ever managed to get their brothers to work together if Weylind had turned this stubborn over every little thing? Farrendel tightened his grip on Weylind's arm. He had to see Melantha again and reassure himself that she was all right. This was finally his opportunity to persuade Weylind to stop being her guard dog and let her see him. "Fetch her. She will help."

After what she had healed him from in the trolls' dungeon, assisting him now would be a simple matter.

"I will send for her." Averett stepped from the tent so quickly he probably missed the glare Weylind sent after him.

"Are you sure about this, Farrendel?" Essie stared down at him, a wrinkle between her eyebrows.

Everyone, including Essie, expected him to hate

Melantha. Perhaps it was understandable since their last memory of Melantha was of her betrayal.

And, yes, her betrayal still hurt worse than the stone embedded in him. Everything was so strained. Painful. If he could erase his memory of her betrayal, he would.

But Farrendel had seen the sincerity of her change of heart. She had expended every last ounce of her strength and magic to make sure he survived until rescue. She had taken physical punishment because she had helped him. They had spent long hours in that dungeon, talking as they had not talked in years.

More than anything, he just wanted his sister back. The one he knew he could count on to plan his last-minute wedding and stand by his side willing to defend him. The sister he remembered running to as a boy, and she had always been there for him. He had not had a mother, but he had his older sister Melantha.

Until suddenly, he did not.

He had lost the relationship he had once had with Melantha. But did the pain have to remain? Could he fix things?

Right now, his jumbled feelings did not matter. If he was to make his family whole, then it would be up to him to take the first step. None of the others would extend a hand to Melantha until Farrendel did it first.

Averett pushed aside the tent flap, followed closely by Melantha.

She looked better than when Farrendel had last seen her. Her black hair was glossy and clean. Her dark green dress, too short around her ankles, was clean and not torn.

But the weary lines remained on her face, her eyes still pained and somewhat wild.

As soon as she stepped inside, her gaze focused on Farrendel. She pushed past the others and rushed to his side. "Farrendel. Are you truly all right?"

Surely the depth to her voice and her eyes was too sincere to be faked. They had been through too much together in the past two weeks for him to believe anything else.

Perhaps he could not forget what she had done, nor could things go back to the way they had been.

But he could forgive.

He reached a hand to her and gripped Melantha's shoulder. "Isciena."

Melantha stilled, her eyes filling. A single tear traced its way down her cheek. Tentatively, she reached out and gripped his shoulder. "Shashon."

Brother. The word settled deep inside him, dulling some of the pain.

Standing next to the table, both Essie and Weylind remained stiff, their bodies positioned as if they intended to step forward and shield Farrendel from Melantha if necessary.

But Prince Rharreth studied Melantha with dark blue eyes before he nodded. "My lady. I assume King Averett apprised you of the situation on the way here. If we can proceed?"

A green glow surrounded Melantha's hand where it still rested on Farrendel's shoulder. Soothing healing magic flooded into him, sweeping away every last hint of pain.

Farrendel relaxed against the table, breathing easier than he had in days. There in the dungeon, he had taken for granted the strength of Melantha's healing magic. Magic ran deep and strong in their family. It would be a mistake to dismiss Weylind's strength in plant growing magic or Melantha's skill in healing just because their magic was not as flashy as Farrendel's.

This time, when the human surgeon sliced with his scalpel and Prince Rharreth drew the stone free, Farrendel could not feel it beyond a light pressure.

"Melantha?" Farrendel turned his head toward her.

Melantha glanced at him, though green magic continued to coat her fingers.

The others turned to him as well, and Weylind especially glared, as if he thought Farrendel should not be talking to Melantha, even though she was still their sister.

Farrendel gestured to himself as best as he could without moving his arm. "This is your battle, isciena. Here, you are a warrior."

This time, Melantha did freeze, her gaze locking on him. A twitch to her mouth might have been a smile. "Linshi, shashon."

Weylind's gaze swung from Melantha to Farrendel, as if he was trying to puzzle out their conversation.

Farrendel did not have the energy to explain. Melantha could tell Weylind, if she was so inclined.

Essie's fingers trailed through Farrendel's short hair, and Farrendel closed his eyes, concentrating on that sensation rather than that of the surgery. With each bit of stone removed, he could breathe easier, as if the stone had been a weight pressing on his lungs.

Finally, the surgeon worked his way to Farrendel's wrists, and Farrendel opened his eyes for that, watching as Prince Rharreth and the human surgeon removed the broken sections of stone that had been lodged in Farrendel's wrists for two weeks, ever since those human traitors clapped the stone manacles around his wrists.

He was free. No more stone. No more pain. He had spent two weeks clinging to the hope of this day, and he took a moment to savor it now that it arrived.

Melantha rested her hand on his wrist, and the last lingering ache disappeared. A warm flood of healing magic surged through him, filling him from the depth of his chest to his fingertips and toes.

When Melantha withdrew her hand, she straightened, something of the controlled sister that he remembered returning to her bearing. "That is the last of the stone."

Farrendel pushed onto his elbows, then swung his feet off the table and tried to push himself upright. His head spun, unused to sitting upright after so long lying down. When he swayed, Essie wrapped an arm around his shoulders and helped him the rest of the way upright. Even when he steadied, she kept her arm around his shoulders.

As much as he did not like being an invalid, he did not pull away from her.

Weylind strode forward, arms crossed. "Then I will escort Melantha back to her shelter."

Melantha shot a glance to Farrendel, her eyes pleading.

Farrendel was not ready to see her escorted away either. He had not talked with her since their rescue, and he could not see her married tomorrow without speaking with her. Nor could he leave Kostaria until he settled things between them. "Wait. I wish to speak with her."

Weylind turned, face set. "You do not have to, Farrendel."

"I still wish to speak with her." Farrendel tried to make his voice strong.

"Then I will stay." Weylind crossed his arms, standing between Farrendel and Melantha.

"No." Farrendel did not need Weylind hovering.

Essie squeezed Farrendel's hand, her gaze searching his face. "Do you want me to stay? Or would you rather talk with her alone?"

A part of him wanted Essie to remain there, ready to save the conversation if it stuttered. But if she remained, then Weylind would continue to hover. And Melantha might not speak freely before either of them.

"Alone. But please do not go far." He hated that those last words sounded pleading. He hated being weak.

"All right." Essie kissed his cheek. With a glance at Melantha, Essie herded all the nurses, healer, surgeon, Averett, Prince Rharreth, and Weylind from the curtained off room in the hospital tent.

Farrendel gripped the edge of the surgical table, willing himself to remain strong and steady. "Thank you for coming to heal me."

"It was the least I could do. I owe you so much more." Melantha stared at the ground, her arms wrapped over her stomach. Farrendel could not remember seeing Melantha so uncertain before. She always held her head high, confidently navigating royal life in Estyra. He had envied her for that ease and confidence. Her shoulders hunched. "I am so sorry. For everything. If I could go back, I would do so many things differently. I wish…"

She trailed off, but Farrendel could hear the unfinished wish. It was the same wish aching inside his chest.

Farrendel shifted. The table lacked a back to lean against, his ribs still sore as Melantha's magic worked to heal the deep wounds. "I might have ended up here even without your betrayal. Thanfardil would have arranged for my kidnapping either way."

"It would have been more difficult without my help." Melantha's arms tightened over her stomach. "I was so foolish to let him manipulate my anger and resentment like he did. I should never have done it. I never...I am so sorry."

"I know." Thanks to the past two weeks, he did know that. "I am thankful you were here. I would not have survived without you, though I am sorry for what you had to endure."

Melantha nodded, giving him a brief glimpse of the drawn, haunted look on her face.

It was a look he knew all too well. He felt that same shattered emptiness. And, while he would be going home, she would be stuck here for the rest of her life, unable to leave the darkness of this place behind.

Yes, she would be queen. But that meant she would have far less freedom than Farrendel and Essie had to move between kingdoms and visit family.

For her sacrifice, Farrendel would be forever grateful. Melantha's marriage to the soon-to-be troll king could establish a lasting peace. Farrendel might never have to fight and kill again, thanks to Melantha.

"If you need anything, do not hesitate to ask. You are not alone." Farrendel could not imagine going into a marriage alliance without the overprotective support of his family. They had hovered—annoyingly, suffocatingly—when he had first married Essie. But they had cared.

"Am I not?" She shook her head, pain in her voice. "This might as well be banishment."

Strangely, after everything, he did not want that for her. Now that he knew the depth of her pain and anger, all he wanted for her was to find the peace and happiness she had not managed to find in Estyra. "I hope you find the freedom in your marriage that I have in mine."

Melantha glanced at the curtain. "Is that what you found with your human princess? Freedom?"

"Yes." He did not hesitate. With her magic still lending strength to his muscles, Farrendel reached out and gripped her shoulders. "If you need help, I will come. Even if no one else will."

"Linshi, shashon." Melantha reached out and gripped his shoulders. Her eyes studied him. "You have not yet told her how difficult the next months will be, have you?"

Farrendel dropped his gaze to his bare toes. No, he had not. How could he explain what it had been like the last time? The blur of weariness and healers and Weylind badgering him into going through the motions of living. Eating without really tasting. Dressing without caring what he wore. Sleeping because he did not care enough to move to do anything else.

Right now, the relief of rescue staved off the nightmares. But, they would return, and when they did...he was so tired of fighting his own mind. Weary of the constant battle.

Essie had seen the cracks in him when they were in Escarland and some of the careful balance he maintained tipped out of his control.

Control had been ripped out of his grasp again. If he spiraled like he had before...this time, Essie would bear the brunt of the burden, a burden he had no wish to place on her shoulders.

When he returned to Tarenhiel, he would have to try. Harder than he had last time. Even if he did not feel strong enough. He had picked up the pieces of his life once. Surely he could do it again.

Melantha must have seen his answer in his eyes, even if he did not say it. She squeezed his shoulders before stepping back. "Then I make the same promise. If you need anything, I will come."

Farrendel nodded, her words a soothing balm. Perhaps, their relationship could never go back to what it was. But, maybe, it could be better.

THIRTY-TWO

Melantha strode from the healers' tent with her head high, her back straighter than it had been in weeks.

Farrendel had forgiven her. Somehow, incredibly, he had reached out to heal what she had destroyed. After the past two weeks, it was the brother she had tried to murder who understood her best.

As soon as Melantha stepped outside, Princess Elspeth hurried forward, brushing past her as if intent on returning to Farrendel without saying a word to Melantha.

Weeks ago, Melantha would have been content to coldly walk by, but Farrendel was not the only one she had hurt. "Princess Elspetha, please wait a moment."

Princess Elspeth turned, though her body still leaned in the direction of the tent as if her need to return to Farrendel was a physical pull. A canvas bag was slung over her shoulder. "Yes?"

Melantha refused to feel the sting of the clipped tone. It was the least she deserved. With a deep breath, she met

Princess Elspeth's gaze. "I am sorry for the distress my actions caused you."

And for plotting to murder Princess Elspeth along with Farrendel, though Melantha did not mention that.

Princess Elspeth's eyes remained cool, her expression neutral. "Thank you for apologizing."

With that, she swept into the tent, not waiting for any response from Melantha.

Not that Melantha had planned to say anything more. It was not as if she wished to ask the human princess for advice on navigating a marriage of alliance or anything. Melantha might be disgraced, but she still had some pride.

With her head high, Melantha faced her family. Jalissa talked with the human king and princes. When Melantha's gaze turned to her, Jalissa's face hardened, and she turned her back.

Melantha refused to feel the stab of pain. She was getting married tomorrow, and, most likely, she would not have her sister at her side. This was the last day their family would be together for a long time, and they were not even speaking to each other.

A few feet away, Weylind stood with his arms crossed, two elf warriors at his back, waiting to take her back to her prison. He would call it a shelter, but the root shackle said otherwise.

Yet Prince Rharreth also waited, off to the side. Was he waiting to speak with her?

Melantha turned in his direction, walking swiftly so that Weylind would not have a chance to intercept her. She halted in front of the troll prince, facing him with all the dignity she could muster. "Did you wish to speak with me?"

Prince Rharreth's dark blue eyes searched her face. "You agreed to marry me."

It was said as a statement, but the underlying question hung in the air between them.

"Of course I did. I know it is hard to believe, but I still love my kingdom." Melantha forced herself not to back down from the intense scrutiny of his gaze. Perhaps only this could earn her redemption in the eyes of the rest of her family. "I hope your word and honor proves to be more true than your brother's."

Prince Rharreth's mouth tilted down, though he did not refute her insinuation that his brother had possessed no honor. "I have promised peace with Tarenhiel, and I keep my word."

"I will hold you to that. If you break your word, I am not above breaking my healer's oath to kill you, even if it kills me in the process. I would consider it a worthy sacrifice for my kingdom." Melantha clenched her fists. Farrendel had called her a warrior, back there in the hospital tent. If only that was what she was.

"That will not be necessary." Prince Rharreth reached, as if to touch her, but he drew his hand back before he so much as brushed a lock of her hair. "I know what my brother did to you. But I promise you that you have nothing to fear from me."

Melantha raised her eyebrows. Did Prince Rharreth mean that? Yet, he had taken a whipping for her, his back probably still sore since he would not have been able to heal himself as Melantha had. Even though he had not succeeded in sparing her all of his brother's punishment, he had done his best.

It gave Melantha reason to hope, even though she had thought herself beyond such self-delusions.

But, for a moment, she let herself believe that her marriage to this troll tomorrow would not be utter misery. Perhaps she would never find the happiness that Farrendel had with his human princess, but maybe Melantha could find the freedom she craved.

If she found a way to cool the simmering, consuming anger gnawing through her chest, she might even be content.

WHEN ESSIE STEPPED through the canvas door, she found Farrendel still sitting on the surgical table, staring at his hands. He glanced up, his silver-blue eyes dull and listless. He held up his arms, showing her the insides of his wrists. "More scars."

Fresh, red scars marked where his wrists had been impaled. First by the manacles, then by whatever bindings the trolls had used when hauling him across Tarenhiel and Kostaria, and finally from the stone pinning him to the floor of that dungeon cell.

Essie set down her canvas bag beside the table and gently grasped Farrendel's hands, running her thumbs over the scars on his wrists. "You know the scars don't bother me. Nor does the length of your hair. I love *you*, Farrendel."

He gave a tiny nod, though the spark didn't return to his eyes.

Being fully dressed would help. Essie knelt, dug in the sack, and pulled out the folded shirt and tunic she had hauled with her from Tarenhiel.

She placed the shirt and tunic in his hands. "I thought you might want these."

He ran his fingers over the light green tunic, the same one she had borrowed and worn the day they married. At last, a hint of a smile cracked his mouth, a flicker of light returning to his eyes. "This always reminds me of you."

"And here I was wearing it all over Ellonahshinel because it reminded me of you." Essie forced herself to grin, her tone light, as she dug in the sack and pulled out his stockings and boots.

The comment earned her only a twitch of a smile from Farrendel, a smile that was replaced with a grimace as he eased his shirt over his head.

Even with Melantha's magic, it would take a few days for the healing to be complete and the soreness to fade. Nor would the magic replace the weight and strength he'd lost during the two weeks of immobility and little food.

It hurt, seeing him like this, and Essie wasn't sure what he wanted from her. Did he want her to be cheery? To pretend everything was normal? To be quiet and subdued? It was hard to know, and Farrendel wasn't the type to tell her what he wanted, especially right now. He probably didn't even know.

The tunic hung on him almost as much as it had hung on her when she wore it. The shoulders drooped and the fabric billowed around his middle. Instead of hiding how gaunt he'd become, it accentuated the hollowed-out look.

Essie had to bite her lip to keep her smile from trembling. He would heal, eventually. Rescue, it seemed, was a process.

She knelt on the floor. "Do you need help with your stockings and boots?"

"No. I can do it myself." Farrendel claimed his stockings from her, swaying from the movement.

Essie bit her lip, forcing herself to stay still and silent as he struggled to pull on first one stocking, then the other. He'd had so much of his dignity stolen from him. It made him more determined to do everything himself. But it still hurt to just sit there and watch him struggle. "All right. But there is a difference between accepting help from a loved one and having an indignity forced on you. I know they probably don't feel that different right now, but I am here, all right?"

He didn't look at her as he worked on his second stocking, his breathing coming hard, as if that small action taxed his strength. When he straightened, he braced himself against the table, as if he was struggling not to pass out.

Essie held up his boots. "Right now, it's just the two of us. No one else will see if you ask for help. It might be better to save your strength for walking out of here when everyone will be watching. If you want to reclaim a bit of your pride, I think that would be the time for it."

He stared at the boots for a moment before his gaze dropped to his feet. When he spoke, his tone was weary. Defeated. "Could you? Please?"

"Of course." Essie plastered the smile back on her face as she worked the first boot onto his foot. "Besides, you'll eventually be able to return the favor. Someday, I'll be pregnant and won't be able to see my feet, and I'll be asking you to put on my shoes for me."

When she glanced up after tying the bootlaces, the tips of his ears were a hint pink. Ah, yes. There was her awkward elf.

She smirked and returned her attention to his second

boot. "Yes. Hugely pregnant. With our sixth child. Or maybe seventh."

"Seven." Farrendel gaped down at her as if she had just suggested he dye his hair magenta.

"You're right. Five would be more realistic." Essie tied the laces of Farrendel's boot and stood. Though he was still gaunt and the tunic baggy, the boots did help him look more normal. Essie stepped closer and traced one of his tapered ears. "I hope our children have your pointed ears."

The tip of the ear she was tracing turned even more pink as Farrendel ducked his head. After a moment, though, he lifted his gaze back to hers, reached out, and ran his fingers over her braid, pulling it over her shoulder. "And your hair."

"Please. Don't inflict my red hair on our hypothetical children." Essie linked her hands behind his neck. Hopefully he hadn't noticed how greasy her hair was. It was in a braid because bathing hadn't been a priority while they had fought and shivered their way across Kostaria.

"Why not? If you can dream of seven children, I can dream of red hair." The hint of a smile on his face grew wider. "It is pretty. And it is a beacon on a battlefield."

"Ah. Now I understand your fascination with my red hair." Here she was picturing tiny little half-elf babies, and he was thinking about a full-grown elf warrior. Though, it didn't take too much effort to imagine a warrior with red hair tossing in a breeze and Farrendel's type of magic sizzling around him. Or her.

Farrendel just smiled back and let go of her braid to wrap an arm around her waist, pulling her closer. "Someday."

Essie leaned her forehead against his. "Yes. Someday."

As much as it stirred something in her to imagine their

children, he was not ready yet. He was barely holding himself together right now. It would take him time even to get back to where they were before the trolls had captured him.

"Essie?" Farrendel cradled her face, tipping her chin so that she was looking at him. "I know it may not always seem like it, but I do want our someday. I chose this. I will fight for it."

Before she had a chance to reply, he kissed her. Not a peck. Not a frantic kiss on the middle of the battlefield surrounded by his blazing magic. But a real kiss that promised his heart, his soul, their someday.

She dug her fingers into his short hair and kissed him back with all the emotion she'd had building up inside her from the moment she'd left him behind while she escaped. She'd missed him so desperately. She'd missed his shy smile. The way he'd get up early and swing through windows and loved hot chocolate even more than she did.

She trailed her fingers down his neck and traced his collarbone, feeling the length of one of his new scars.

Farrendel made a sound in the back of his throat and yanked away from her, his hands coming up between them as if to protect himself from a blow. His breathing had grown ragged again, a wild light in his gaze before he squeezed his eyes shut.

Essie froze, not daring to move or even speak while he gathered himself. How long would it take before he stopped flinching as if he expected her touch to hurt?

After a moment, Farrendel lowered his hands. "I am sorry. I just…I need time."

"I know." Essie kissed his forehead before she stepped back. "I have one more thing for you."

She bent and pulled his sheathed swords from the canvas sack. "I brought these for you."

He took the swords, running his fingers over the sheaths and hilts. Instead of buckling them on, he hugged the swords to his chest as if they were a favorite, childhood blanket.

Essie held out a hand to him. "Are you ready to face the others?"

Farrendel nodded and pushed off the table with his free hand. As soon as his feet touched the ground, his knees buckled. He managed to catch himself with his grip on the table, but Essie still hurried to prop herself under his arm.

His jaw set, Farrendel shakily strode from the healers' tent. Essie suspected he was leaning on her as little as possible, though she still stayed at his side in case he stumbled.

Outside, their siblings crowded around them. Weylind took Essie's place helping Farrendel walk while Averett hovered on Farrendel's other side, though Farrendel was too busy gripping his emotional support swords to reach out for more help walking.

By the time they reached the tent only a few yards from the hospital tent, sweat beaded on Farrendel's forehead, and he gasped in panting breaths. He sank onto the cot, one hand braced on the cot's side bar, shoulders hunched.

Averett pulled the end table from the corner, positioning it as if it were a dining room table while Julien arranged the chair and folding stools around it.

Circling around the table, Essie sat on the end of the cot, shoving aside the pillow. Perhaps she should have taken one of the seats, but she would rather sit close to Farrendel. Even if he was too busy trying to stay upright to even notice her.

Edmund and Julien mumbled something about fetching

food while Weylind and Jalissa grew the table into a large, round table. After a moment, Jalissa also left to help Edmund and Julien.

Farrendel swiveled, easing his feet onto the cot and curling tight to fit in the space left, his sheathed swords gripped to his chest. Bracing himself on an elbow, he pointed at the pillow she had dumped on the floor. "Could you hand me that?"

Essie reached down for the pillow, then halted, a slow smile crossing her face. She patted her lap. "Use me as your pillow. You'll be able to stretch out more."

Well, that was the excuse she was going to give. She'd always heard the whole head-on-lap thing was romantic. Time to test it out.

Farrendel glanced from her, to Weylind and Averett talking quietly across the table, and back to her, raising an eyebrow. This probably crossed all sorts of elven etiquette boundaries. Farrendel wasn't big on cuddling when others were around. She normally wasn't the type to show affection to this level in public either, but after coming so close to losing him, she didn't care.

He apparently didn't care what the others thought either. Or he had realized that once he was lying down and the others were sitting, he would be hidden by the table. With a shrug, he curled on his side, resting his head on her thigh. It took a little shifting before both of them found a spot that was comfortable.

She ran her fingers through the short strands of his hair. Shorn as it was, the haircut really was awful. Long enough to fall into his eyes in one section, short to his scalp in other places. "You're just going to have to sit up again in a few minutes. Julien, Edmund, and Jalissa will be here with lunch shortly."

"I will eat later." Farrendel had his eyes closed, his muscles relaxing.

"Are you sure? You need to eat." Essie linked her fingers through his where his hand lay on the cot.

"Not hungry now." Farrendel squeezed her fingers. "Besides, I am too comfortable to move."

"I guess that's a good reason." She rested her free hand on his hair, tracing the tip of his ear with her thumb.

Carrying a tray, Jalissa swept into the tent, her expression still as hard as it had been when she had refused to acknowledge Melantha. Her gaze swept over the tent, passed Essie and Farrendel, then snapped back to them. Her eyes softened, and she raised an eyebrow.

Julien and Edmund entered on her heels, also carrying trays. They glanced in Essie's direction and paused.

Essie grinned. If they didn't like it, they would just have to deal with it. Or tease her relentlessly.

Instead, Edmund smirked and brandished his tray before taking a seat. "Lunch is served."

"Apparently the cooks saved a side of roast beef for a victory feast." Julien set his tray next to Edmund's and also claimed a seat.

Jalissa slid into the last seat—the only chair—and straightened her skirts. "The cooks also made fresh bread."

Fresh bread. They hadn't had fresh bread in the past week. Everyone was too busy fighting and moving camp every day to take the time to bake. Essie would have lunged across the table for it, but she couldn't with Farrendel's head in her lap. "Averett, can you pass me some of that bread?"

Averett broke a chunk off the end of the loaf, passed it to Jalissa, who handed it to Essie.

After letting go of Farrendel's hand, she broke the chunk of bread in half. She held half down to Farrendel. "Here. You can nibble on bread while lying down."

He cracked one eye open and gave her a mock glare. "You got crumbs on me."

"Sorry." She brushed the breadcrumbs from the side of his face and the tapered end of his ear.

He took the bread from her. "Try not to drop food on me."

"Um..." She was not exactly neat when she ate. As Farrendel well knew. "I will do my best."

"That is not reassuring." He took a bite of his bread, chewing slowly as if savoring it. "This is...much nicer than anything I have had in weeks."

Essie couldn't think of anything to say to that. Here she had been thankful to have fresh bread after only a week. It had been two weeks since he'd been captured, and whatever he'd been fed in that dungeon was probably far worse than camp rations.

She settled for patting his shoulder. "If you decide you're hungry, I'll pass you some roast beef once you finish the bread."

"Maybe."

She took that to mean he was doubting that he would be hungry, not that he was doubting she would give him more food.

Jalissa set a filled plate in front of her, and Essie winced. She was probably making everyone else feel terribly awkward, what with Farrendel using her as a pillow and them totally ignoring everyone else while they talked.

She'd told herself she didn't care, but she remembered how annoyingly mushy Averett and Paige had been when they were first courting. Not that they weren't still mushy with each other occasionally, but romance seemed to be tempered with practicality after a while. Back then, Essie hadn't thought she would end up just as annoyingly mushy.

"Thank you for dishing out food for me." Essie smiled at Jalissa and glanced around the table. Thankfully, her brothers and Weylind were eating their roast beef and studiously pretending they didn't see Essie and Farrendel being cuddly.

Essie dug into her roast beef, holding the plate near her mouth. It wasn't the proper, etiquette-approved way to eat, but it did prevent her from drooling meat juice from the roast beef onto Farrendel's face.

Once she had eaten several bites, enough to stop her stomach from growling loudly next to Farrendel's ear, she glanced at her brothers, focusing especially on Edmund. "You aren't going to tease me about this?" She pointed down at Farrendel.

"It's tempting. But you're expecting it now." Edmund's expression remained far too casual as he stuffed another bite of meat in his mouth.

"So you're not teasing me because that's the more unexpected option?"

"Exactly," he said around the bite of meat he was chewing.

"We like to keep you on your toes." Julien waved his fork at her. "Even if all that lovey-dovey stuff is making us nauseous."

And, there it was. Essie resisted the urge to dignify that comment with an eyeroll.

Averett glanced at Essie, shook his head, and turned to Weylind. He struck up a conversation on ideas for withdrawing the armies from Kostaria, and soon Julien and Edmund were drawn into the discussion.

With the others busy talking, Essie turned to Jalissa, not sure how to ask this question. "Are you going to help Melantha get ready for the wedding tomorrow?"

Jalissa's expression stiffened, her gaze dropping to Farrendel. "I have no wish to speak with her. Not after what she did."

Essie understood that. She was finding it hard to be charitable toward Melantha. But Farrendel seemed inclined to be forgiving, and Essie would respect that choice and support him.

Farrendel shifted, as if he was trying to glance at Jalissa. He wouldn't be able to see much with the table in the way. "Jalissa, isciena, do not shun her on my account. Please."

"She tried to have you killed." Jalissa stabbed her roast beef.

"Yes." Farrendel curled tighter, hugging his swords to his chest, his gaze swiveling back to the bread he still held. He'd only taken two bites from it. "But, in the end, she saved me with her magic several times when she could have let me die, if that had truly been her desire. I know what it is like to be shunned by elven society, something I have endured because I know my family will stand with me. Now she will be shunned, and I would not wish for her to have to face that alone."

"But..." Jalissa shook her head, her fingers clenching on her fork. Across the table, Weylind was staring at his plate, obviously listening to the conversation, but not offering his opinion.

"She's sacrificing herself for the good of Tarenhiel by marrying a troll." Essie knew firsthand how bewildering that could be, though she could not imagine being in Melantha's shoes.

Because Essie had known almost nothing about Farrendel, she had been able to go into the marriage innocently confident things would work.

Melantha, on the other hand, was marrying a troll who'd had a hand in keeping her captive for the past two weeks. Not a good basis for a marriage, even without the depth of enmity that existed between elves and trolls. From what Essie had heard, Prince Rharreth had tried to ease her captivity where he could, but that still wouldn't erase the fact that the first two weeks he and Melantha had known each other had been while she was locked in his dungeon.

"Because she has no choice." Jalissa jabbed her roast beef over and over until Essie was tempted to take the fork from her to spare the food the mangling.

"Just because she doesn't have many good choices, doesn't mean she has no choice. She could have chosen banishment. Or pushed harder for a pardon. Instead, she's picking the option that is best for Tarenhiel." Essie broke off a bite-sized piece of roast beef and held it out to Farrendel.

He stared at the roast beef, sighed, then juggled his swords so that he could hold them and what was left of his bread in one hand and take the bite of roast beef. A bite he turned into two bites. But at least he wasn't protesting that eating with his fingers was unsanitary.

"I suppose." Jalissa's posture didn't change, but the set of her shoulders relaxed a fraction.

Essie slipped Farrendel another piece of roast beef. She felt a little bit like she was feeding a dog scraps beneath the table, but it seemed the only way she could convince Farrendel to eat something. "She is still your sister."

"And this is her wedding." Jalissa sighed, her stiff posture crumbling. "This is not how we imagined it would be."

Probably not. Essie's wedding hadn't been like she had imagined while growing up either. But, she wouldn't go back and change anything. She'd ended up married to exactly the right elf, and she hadn't spent months fretting over the planning.

Essie glanced around the table again. How long would it be before their families would be together like this again? Tomorrow after the wedding, Jalissa, Essie, and Farrendel would leave for Tarenhiel. Edmund, Julien, Averett, and Weylind would take longer to return as they would remain with the armies as they withdrew.

And, after that? Things would go back to normal. Averett would return to Escarland. Essie would remain in Tarenhiel with Farrendel. Jalissa would probably go to Escarland to take up her position as ambassador. Edmund and Julien might remain in Tarenhiel for a while, in case the trolls broke the peace.

And Melantha would stay in Kostaria. Essie wouldn't miss her that much, but she ached for Farrendel. She now knew what it was like to have family scattered across kingdoms. His would be even more scattered than hers. Those family dinners in Ellonahshinel wouldn't be the same.

Averett pushed his plate aside. "I would like to go over security for the wedding tomorrow one last time."

"Yes." Weylind nodded, then glanced at Farrendel. "We should allow Farrendel to rest."

Averett, Julien, and Edmund gathered the dishes while

Weylind used his magic to somehow ungrow the table so that it returned to a small end table.

Jalissa glanced at Essie, met her gaze, and nodded. Then she swept from the tent.

Essie hoped she'd done the right thing in counseling Jalissa to speak with Melantha. Healing took time, and reconciliation might not be possible. But, Essie would hate for Farrendel's siblings to boycott this wedding, only to regret it later, if healing and reconciliation with Melantha did happen.

After all, Jalissa had once told her that what elves regretted, they regretted for centuries. That would be a long time to regret not attending a sister's wedding.

Farrendel nudged Essie and held up what was left of the chunk of bread she had given him. "I am not going to finish this."

She hadn't even given him that big of a piece. And he'd had three chunks of roast beef. It was far too little. He should be eating more.

But, she wasn't going to argue. At least he had obliged her by eating as much as he had.

"All right." Essie quickly dropped the leftover bread on a plate before Edmund whisked it away.

As the others left, leaving her and Farrendel alone, Essie eased Farrendel's head from her lap and knelt next to the cot. She brushed a strand of hair from his face. "Do you wish me to leave as well so you can rest?"

He gave a tiny shake of his head, his silver-blue eyes flicking to her. "Please stay."

"All right." Essie leaned forward and kissed his cheek. "I missed you so much."

"And I missed you." Farrendel's hand moved to brush

the back of his fingers against her cheek. Before she pulled back, Farrendel's hand cupped the back of her head as he kissed her.

As much as she wanted the kiss to linger, she pulled back after a moment and patted his shoulder. "You're supposed to be resting."

"This is better." He gave her that tiny, mischievous smile she loved so much.

Her feet and legs were starting to tingle from being crouched next to the cot, so she straightened. After the lack of sleep she'd had for the past few days—weeks, really—she wouldn't mind a nap as well. Her bedroll was still pushed to one corner of the tent, but they had a few hours before anyone else came back to check if they needed anything, and she wasn't ready to be done cuddling yet.

As Farrendel was still hugging his swords tight enough that Essie didn't dare attempt to pry those away from him, she circled the cot. "Scooch."

"This cot is still not intended for two people." Farrendel's voice held a trace of a laugh.

"But you're lying on your side this time. There's a whole six inches of space. Plenty of room." She eased onto the cot behind him. Actually, six inches wasn't that much room. Her hip was balanced on the bar again.

Farrendel's back was stiff. Actually, all of him was rigid.

That's when she realized what she'd done. She was at his back, and, after what he'd just endured, he might not feel safe with someone at his back where he was vulnerable.

"Is this all right?" Essie carefully rested a palm against Farrendel's back.

He sucked in a breath, as if her touch hurt, and flinched away from her.

She quickly withdrew her hand, though it was hard not to touch him when she was balanced precariously on the edge of a far-too-small cot. "I'm sorry. I can get off and nap on my own bedroll."

"No. Stay. If you wish." With a shuddering breath, Farrendel's muscles relaxed. "It took me a moment to remember it was you."

That was not comforting. She wasn't sure she wanted to know what his first thought had been. Probably something about torture and trolls.

She shifted, trying to find a more comfortable way to lie on the bar of the cot without tipping herself off or bumping into Farrendel.

Huffing out a sound that almost sounded like a laugh, Farrendel wiggled forward, giving her more space.

That was better. She carefully tucked herself against Farrendel. When he didn't flinch, she wrapped an arm around him. Through his shirt, she could feel his jutting ribs. She rested her forehead against his back. Even his spine was sharp. "See. I told you. Plenty of room."

"Yes." Farrendel clasped her hand, and her fingers brushed the hilts of his swords that he must be still gripping with his other hand.

Tomorrow, they would witness Melantha's wedding and start the journey for Tarenhiel. Perhaps everything wouldn't return to just the way it had been, but, with time, they would get there.

It had taken two weeks. A battle across an icy kingdom. But she had Farrendel back. Right then, that was all that mattered.

FREE BOOK!

Thanks so much for reading *Death Wind*! I hope Essie's and Farrendel's story touched your heart and brought a smile, even if this was a darker installment in the series than the first two. If you loved the book, please consider leaving a review on Amazon or Goodreads. Reviews help your fellow readers find books that they will love.

A larger, downloadable map and a downloadable list of characters and elvish are available on the Extras page of my website.

If you ever find typos in my books, feel free to message me on social media or send me an email through the Contact Me page of my website.

If you want to learn about all my upcoming releases, get great book recommendations, and see a behind-the-scenes glimpse into the writing process, follow my blog at www.-taragrayce.com.

Did you know that if you sign up for my newsletter, you'll receive lots of free goodies? You will receive the free novella *Steal a Swordmaiden's Heart*, which is set in the same world as *Stolen Midsummer Bride* and *Bluebeard and the Outlaw*! This novella is a prequel to *Stolen Midsummer Bride*, and tells the story of how King Theseus of the Court of Knowledge won the hand of Hippolyta, Queen of the Swordmaidens.

You will also receive the free novellas *The Wild Fae Primrose* (prequel to *Forest of Scarlet*) and *Torn Curtains*, a fantasy Regency Beauty and the Beast retelling.

Sign up for my newsletter now

DON'T MISS THE NEXT ADVENTURE

Troll Queen

Essie has her elf back...but his mind is still stuck in that dungeon.

The war is over. A peace treaty has been signed. But Farrendel and Essie still have a battle ahead of them. Will Farrendel be able to build a new life with Essie now that he no longer has a war to fight?

Melantha has ruined her life and the lives of all those around her. Now that she finds herself far from home and married to a troll who was once her enemy and captor, can she figure out what love and honor truly mean before it is too late for all of them?

Not everyone in Kostaria is happy with peace or with their new elven queen. If Rharreth and Melantha cannot find a way to bring peace to their troubled kingdom, war threatens not only their happily ever after, but Essie and Farrendel's as well.

The epic adventure and slowburn romances of the Elven Alliance series continue in this clean, romantic fantasy perfect for fans of K.M. Shea and Kenley Davidson.

Find the book on Amazon Today!

IN THE MOOD FOR FAE FANTASY ROMANCE?

STOLEN MIDSUMMER BRIDE

Steal a bride. Save the library. Try not to die.

Basil, a rather scholarly fae, works as an assistant librarian at the Great Library of the Court of Knowledge. Lonely and unwilling to join the yearly Midsummer Revel to find a mate, Basil takes the advice of his talking horse companion and decides to steal a human bride instead.

But Basil never expected to find a human girl waiting for him, wanting to be snatched. Nor had he expected a girl like Meg, an illiterate farm girl who has no use for books.

With the barrier with the Realm of Monsters wearing thin and the chaos of Midsummer Night about to descend, will this unlikely pair put aside their differences long enough to save the Great Library from destruction? And maybe find a spark of love along the way?

From Tara Grayce, author of the bestselling *Elven Alliance* series, comes a new no spice fae fantasy romance inspired by Shakespeare's *A Midsummer Night's Dream* and perfect for fans of K.M. Shea and Sylvia Mercedes!

Find the book on Amazon today!

Also by Tara Grayce

ELVEN ALLIANCE

Fierce Heart

War Bound

Death Wind

Troll Queen

Pretense

Shield Band

Elf Prince

Heart Bond

Elf King

COURT OF MIDSUMMER MAYHEM

Stolen Midsummer Bride

Forest of Scarlet

Night of Secrets

A VILLAIN'S EVER AFTER

Bluebeard and the Outlaw

PRINCESS BY NIGHT

Lost in Averell

ACKNOWLEDGMENTS

Thank you to everyone who made this release possible! To my writer friends, especially Molly, Morgan, Sarah, Savannah, Sierra, and the entire Spinster Aunt gang for being so encouraging and helpful. A special thanks to H.S.J. Williams for the lovely, motivating fan art and inspiring chats about tortured elves. To my dad for pitching in to help find the last-minute typos and giving suggestions that made the book better. To my mom for always being ready to smother me with a hug. To my brothers for being good sports. To my sisters-in-law Alyssa and Abby for adoring Essie and Farrendel. To my friends Bri, Paula, and Jill for always being excited about my books no matter what I write. To my proofreaders Tom, Mindy, Heather, and Deborah, thanks so much for helping to eradicate the typos as much as humanly possible. But thanks most of all to Jesus.

Printed in the USA
CPSIA information can be obtained
at www.ICGtesting.com
CBHW061057020524
7904CB00012B/94